THE
BLOOD
OF THE
COVENANT

Also by Brent Monahan

DeathBite (with Michael Maryk)
Satan's Serenade
The Uprising
The Book of Common Dread

THE BLOOD OF THE COVENANT

A Novel of the Vampiric

BRENT MONAHAN

St. Martin's Press ❧ New York

THE BLOOD OF THE COVENANT. Copyright © 1995 by Brent Monahan. All rights reserved. Printed in the United States of America. No part of this book may be used or reproduced in any manner whatsoever without written permission except in the case of brief quotations embodied in critical articles or reviews. For information, address St. Martin's Press, 175 Fifth Avenue, New York, N.Y. 10010.

Production Editor: David Stanford Burr

Library of Congress Cataloging-in-Publication Data

Monahan, Brent.
    The blood of the covenant / Brent Monahan.
        p.   cm.
    ISBN 0-312-13436-3
    I. Title.
PS3563.O5158B56   1995
813'.54—dc20   95-31031
                                        CIP

First edition: October 1995

10 9 8 7 6 5 4 3 2 1

For S. Michael Schnessel, who still lives

THE
BLOOD
OF THE
COVENANT

CHAPTER ONE

December 25

Remember too those angels who were not content to maintain the dominion assigned to them, but abandoned their proper dwelling place; God is holding them bound in darkness with everlasting chains, for judgment on the great day.

—Letter of Jude: 6

Father Dante Ferro yanked shut the door of the Bibliotheca Anathemata and jiggled the knob several times to be sure it was locked. Before he picked up the large leather portfolio he had leaned against the subterranean wall, he blew on his fingertips. The deepest chambers of the Vatican were cool even in the summer, and this was December . . . the day of the Lord's birth, to be exact. No mere cold, however, had ever chilled Father Ferro as had the information inside the portfolio. He shoved the keys inside the folds of his cassock, picked up the portfolio and started briskly for the hand-operated elevator halfway down the corridor.

On this Christmas Day morning, the halls of the Apostolic Palace were largely deserted, of staff and clergy alike. Father Ferro saw no one on the palace's top floor until he turned the corner and was confronted by two members of the Swiss Guard standing at attention in front of the massive doorway to the papal apartments. Lifting his portfolio in front of him as if it were a huge calling card, Father Ferro announced himself. The guard to his right opened one of the doors, and Ferro entered slowly, giving himself time to drink in what he expected would be a unique experience.

Seated behind a massive baroque desk at the far end of the cavernous rococo study, the shepherd to millions of faithful looked puny. Dante observed privately that grand architecture was proper in churches, where it glorified God, but in living spaces it only diminished the men who created it. The Pontiff's vestments gleamed in the hard winter light pouring through the windows. He had not changed clothes after offering Christmas morning Mass and the traditional address for world peace, suggesting to Father Ferro that his urgently worded petition was being taken seriously. Alongside the Pope stood his secretary, Monsignor Squillante, the man Father Ferro had contacted about the documents inside the portfolio.

"Come, Father," the monsignor bade, curling his fingers inward several times to quicken Dante's entrance.

As the priest hastened forward, *il Papa* rose and stretched forth his right hand. Father Ferro kissed the ring with ceremonious respect, even as he boldly returned the Pope's assessing stare.

"You haven't lost your policeman's bearing, Father Ferro," the Pontiff observed in barely accented, well-formed Italian.

Father Ferro released the hand and drew himself erect. He was not surprised that the Holy Father had been briefed about his personal life, especially in light of his, Ferro's, almost frantic plea for an audience. "I suppose not, Your Holiness. I was a policeman much longer than I've been a priest."

"And how is it that you came to unearth these documents that lay so long forgotten in the vaults below us?"

"I sought them out," Dante answered. "As curator of ancient writings for the Holy See it's my obligation to stay knowledgeable about outside sources . . . by reading journal publications and by communicating with other scholars. I first read in the *Journal of Written Antiquities* about the appearance of the Scrolls of Ahriman . . . in Princeton of all places."

"Where?" Monsignor Squillante asked.

"Princeton, New Jersey. A town halfway between New York City and Philadelphia. And then I had a conversation about them with Professor Mustafa Elmasri."

"Another excellent scholar of Akkadian," the monsignor hurriedly informed the Pope, using knowledge picked up from Father Ferro's petition for audience.

3

Dante smiled to himself. The Holy Father's right-hand man was his patent ally. "Elmasri reminded me that Alexander the Sixth had the translation of these lost scrolls banned and all copies confiscated and destroyed. That was in 1503. Of course, the Bibliotheca Anathemata is filled with such things, so I began searching."

"And you were obviously successful," the Pope said, his gaze fixed on the burden in Father Ferro's hands.

Dante obligingly placed the portfolio on the desk and zipped it open. The musty odor of centuries-old paper escaped into the study. "To a certain degree. Here is the decree banning the translation. This is one of the books. And here is a fragment of a scroll in Greek, translating the end of the second Ahriman scroll. What happened to the rest, the good Lord only knows."

"And this fragment has caused you fear?" the Pope said quickly, clearly wanting Father Ferro to get to the point.

Dante was not cowed; what he had to say was too important for him to be hurried by even the chief Prince of the Church. "I am a religious man, but not to the point of mysticism or fanaticism," he asserted. "And I will always have one foot firmly planted in the secular world. I mean, I am slow to believe in matters of the metaphysical." He pushed the ancient book toward the Holy Father. "Please read this translation. The things it states are truly miraculous, especially considering the era in which the original scrolls were written. But what has chilled my heart is that this Greek fragment goes beyond what Aldus printed in his translation. In minuscule notation, the Greek scribe writes that the very end of the second Ahriman scroll contained a warning. He faithfully reproduced the Akkadian that survived, but because either the elements or creatures ate away the outermost vellum in many places, the scribe was unable to decipher the warning. Or perhaps unwilling."

"But not so with you, Father Ferro," the Pope said evenly.

"No, Your Holiness. I have gleaned that the warning is preceded by seven predictions. Once all the predictions have come to pass, a disaster will befall mankind such as the world has never known."

Dante kept his hand pressed against the book, so that neither the

4

Pontiff nor his secretary could see that it trembled. "If I have filled in the missing segments correctly, six of the predictions have already been fulfilled. I believe that disaster is imminent."

Alice Niederjohn stood at one of the mansion's side windows and watched the two young people she hardly knew loading a white Mazda sedan in the bright Christmas Day sunlight. One was her own daughter, Frederika Vanderveen. The other, Simon Penn, was responsible for uniting Alice and Frederika after a separation of eighteen years. Alice had made the psychically taxing drive up from Philadelphia only to find that hardly more than an hour could be spared for reconciliation, reminiscence, and catching up. Her daughter had to hurry away, to pursue the possibility of a spectacular job offer, she said. Flying off to Europe with this likable and bright young man who claimed to be just a friend but who clearly hoped to be much more. Leaving Alice alone, inside the house she had fled eighteen years before. She observed with satisfaction that Frederika and Simon worked smoothly together, as they transferred a black gym bag from the car's passenger compartment to the trunk, followed it with a pair of sizable metal cylinders, finally loading their few suitcases, all with fluid, synchronous motions.

Alice remained at the window a full minute after the car had backed out of the driveway and disappeared down the Princeton street. She did not want to turn, to face the mansion alone. Despite its silence it seemed sentient, as if insensate wood, marble, and plaster had been infused with the spirit of her dead ex-husband. If one could feel from the grave, he no doubt still hated her for fleeing from his suffocating dominance, for embarrassing him before a world that, until then, had known only his triumphs. Finally, Alice summoned the courage to turn and gaze around the room. There had been a number of things she had regretted leaving behind. She struggled to recall them all. Some of them were old sheet music and books. And then there was a box filled with loose family snapshots, dating back to the turn of the century. She opened several built-in cabinets, searching.

The front door knocker banged twice. Alice opened the door.

5

Standing on the porch was a big-boned woman with wiry blond hair poking out from under a Russian-style fur hat. It was difficult to judge her age, as much of her face was covered by enormous sunglasses. In her gloved hands she held a large gift basket of fruit.

"Good morning," the woman said pleasantly. "Is this the residence of Miss Frederika Vanderveen?"

"Yes, it is."

"This is for her. Is she home?"

"No. You just missed her."

"Oh. Too bad. She'll be back later then?"

"As a matter of fact, she won't for some time," Alice said. "She and her boyfriend are flying to England."

The woman's mouth turned down in disappointment. "Oh dear! I'm sure the person who ordered these won't want them left here. Do you . . . do you mind if I use the phone and call the shop?"

"No, of course not. Come in." As the woman walked inside, Alice was struck by a thought. "Your shop is open on Christmas Day?"

The woman smiled. "We never close."

As Alice shut the door, she was sure she smelled the odor of suntan lotion. The woman set the fruit basket down on the foyer table.

"The telephone?"

Alice blinked in thought. "I don't live here. I mean, it's been some time since I . . . There used to be one in the kitchen. Down that hallway at the rear of the house."

The woman glanced down the corridor, then back at Alice. "Did she say exactly *where* in England they were going?" When Alice seemed startled by the question, the woman hurriedly added, "I was thinking the person who sent this might want a similar order wired over there."

"No. She didn't say." Alice heard her own voice grow small. Suddenly, letting the delivery lady inside the house didn't seem like the smartest idea. True enough, she looked too old to be dangerous, but her long-toothed smile was just a trifle too forced. And she continued to stand at the inner end of the foyer regarding Alice from behind the dark sunglasses, making no effort to get to the telephone.

The door knocker sounded again. Alice turned with relief to answer it. Standing on the porch were two uniformed police officers, one tall and fat, the other short and skinny. A patrol car was parked at the curb, directly in front of Alice's automobile.

"Good morning, ma'am," Tall and Fat said, even before the door was fully open. "We're looking for a Mr. Simon Penn."

"Is something wrong?" Alice asked, feeling instantly foolish. Why else would two patrolmen be at the door?

"I'm afraid so," Tall and Fat answered, as Short and Skinny made an abrupt turn and headed toward the driveway. "He may be in danger. Is he here?"

"No, he's not. He left with my daughter only a few minutes ago."

"Left for where?"

"Danger from whom?"

Fat and Tall blew a plume of warm exhalation onto his fingertips. "Do you mind if I come inside, ma'am?"

Alice stepped to the side of the doorway. "Why not? Half the town seems to want in."

"Excuse me?" the officer said, entering the house.

Alice turned and found the foyer and the hallway deserted. "There's a woman in the back making a telephone call. She's here delivering a gift for my daughter." Alice nodded at the fruit basket as she closed the door. "Danger from whom?" she repeated.

"Some man assaulted a young woman in town last night, apparently just to find out where Mr. Penn was living."

"Then my daughter's in danger also, because she's with him."

"And where is that?"

"They're on their way to England. They left . . ." Alice paused because the policeman suddenly seemed to stop listening. His attention instead fixed on the fruit basket. He pivoted it around a full circle, peering through the red cellophane wrapping. Then he made a quick move to the front door, throwing it open.

"Where's the delivery van?" Fat and Tall asked, more to himself

7

than to Alice. Only the patrol car and Alice's sedan stood in the street.

"You know your back door's open?" Short and Skinny asked Alice, coming down the hallway from the kitchen.

"You see anyone else back there?" Fat and Tall asked his partner.

"Nope."

"A woman making a phone call?"

"A woman? Nope. Just some footprints in the snow . . . like someone ran away fast."

Fat and Tall turned and gave Alice a grave look. "Strange. There's no identification on that basket. I never seen a gift delivery business didn't stick its name somewhere."

"And she was strange herself. For one thing, she wore sunglasses and suntan lotion," Alice offered.

"Let's close both doors and talk through this real slow," Fat and Tall suggested.

"Bless you, Jesus. The greatest Jew who ever lived," Murray Diamond thought to himself as the short line moved steadily toward the United Airlines ticketing counter. Last night, all the twice-a-year Christians dragging themselves guiltily to Christmas Eve Mass had left the Atlantic City casinos half empty. Murray had come away from the empty blackjack table with twelve hundred dollars in winnings. And this morning, the Christian fathers slept late in their beds after midnight battles with assembly instructions, the mothers slaved at ranges preparing the ritual family feast, and the kids sat in front of the fir trees engaged in orgies of present unwrapping, making Newark Airport as deserted as Times Square on New Year's morning.

The bigoted Protestants and Catholics could laugh all they wanted about how Jews gathered around the cash registers this time of year and sang "What a Friend We Have in Jesus." That was just how Murray felt. He owned a chain of stores that unapologetically ripped off the success of the Nature Company. His chain was called

"Natural Things," after a song Barbra Streisand had recorded back in his youth.

It had been a good holiday season, for more reasons than store profits. Murray had recently met Linda, the quintessential "pink-nippled, freckle-faced Goyische punim," as Lenny Bruce had put it. Both he and Linda had recently slogged their ways through bitter divorces, and neither was in a hurry to get serious with anybody. Pretty, stacked, thirty-six (ten years Murray's junior), but with a child's capacity for wonder, Linda was just what Murray needed. She showed zero interest in gambling but had loyally feigned enthusiasm for Murray's obsession even before he had begun winning. When this morning she had seen a TV ad for Disney World and confided that she regretted never having been there, Murray had hustled them into a taxi and headed straight for Newark Airport. She deserved it.

"Jeez, look at that girl," Linda remarked, drawing Murray from his reverie. "I wonder what's the matter?"

Murray turned. The "girl" made Linda look like a Marine Corps drill sergeant. She held a wad of pink tissues in one hand; her mouth contorted downward in anguish; her other hand had just removed sunglasses, revealing large eyes, red and wet from crying; hanks of her thick, blond hair stood out in disarray. But it wasn't hard for Murray to imagine what she looked like on a normal day. This was a woman who smiled back at you from the cover of *Vogue* or *Cosmopolitan* while you were waiting to pay for your Ring-Dings at the 7-Eleven. The young man comforting her was nice-looking but no way in her class. He held her hand and spoke softly to her, in between stealing anxious looks around the terminal. This was something other than a lovers' spat. Murray looked away as the young man's eyes shifted in his direction. Murray hated witnessing such emotional scenes, only because he could never learn what caused them. Sometimes the fact of not knowing would bug him for days.

"Could be anything," Murray answered Linda, then rubbed his

hands together to warm them from the chill of the cold terminal air. "They say it's an emotional time of year."

Linda dipped her head. "The guy's coming our way."

Murray turned. The lucky fellow was indeed headed straight toward them. With the beautiful girlfriend's image blocked from view, Murray concentrated on the man. He looked to be in his late twenties, sandy-haired, fairly tall and probably lanky under the overcoat. His pleasant features telegraphed intelligence.

"Excuse me," the fellow said as he closed the final few feet between himself and Murray. "Would you two happen to be flying to Orlando?"

"We would," Murray answered.

The fellow jerked his head around just enough to indicate the beautiful woman. "We've got a problem. I'm Simon Penn, and that's my wife, Frederika. We're supposed to be on the next flight to Florida for our honeymoon, but my wife's mother just died of a heart attack." His face hardened in anger. "Some stupid agent just delivered the news. Blurted it straight out."

"Ah, jeez, the poor thing," Linda commiserated.

"She had cancer, but she was supposed to be all right until we got back," the man said, then blew out his exasperation in a forceful sigh. "I guess the cancer was too much for her heart."

"That's tough luck, buddy," Murray said, seeing the opportunity coming. "And now you're stuck with tickets?"

"Yes. And you haven't bought yours yet."

Murray pushed his hand into his coat pocket, feeling for his wallet. "No, I haven't. Linda, honey, would you shove our bags outta line? Let's step over here, fella. Are they first class?"

The man followed Murray a few steps away from all other ears. "No. Economy."

"Oh, that's too bad. We always travel first class," Murray lied. "Which flight?"

"The next one. This would guarantee you seats."

"That's not a problem today. I also have these frequent flier discounts, from all my traveling, see?" Murray said, embellishing the lie. "How much did you pay?" The fellow told him. "I'd like to help you, but then again, they aren't what my girlfriend wants. How about knocking off a hundred?" It wasn't like real *handeling,* but then again this wasn't like real business.

"Sure, whatever."

Murray took out his wallet. "Lemme see the tickets first. You two look like the genuine article, but some real lowlifes pull scams like this, y'know?"

"I understand," the fellow said, handing over the ticket folders.

Murray scrutinized them. Round trip. Open-ended. "If you're married, how come her ticket says Frederika *Vanderveen?*"

"Oh, we originally got them just for a vacation. We were planning to marry next June, but then her mother was diagnosed, and we had a hurry-up ceremony last month for her benefit."

"Gotcha. Can I see some identification?"

Simon Penn obligingly produced several proofs of his identity, including a Princeton University library card with his photograph on it.

"Okay, fine." Murray took out the cash he had won at the roulette wheel and began counting it. Then the young fellow's gorgeous, long-legged companion caught his attention. She was watching the transaction, and when Murray's eyes met hers, she gave him a forlorn yet devastating grateful smile. Murray's heart melted.

"Look, here's the full price," Murray said, dropping another hundred onto the pile in the young man's hand. "A wedding present."

The young man touched Murray's shoulder. "Thanks very much. We really appreciate it."

"Yeah, Merry Christmas." The young man hurried back to his bride, and Murray stood watching them with a warm feeling as they carried off their luggage. And then he noted how little they were carrying. Besides her purse, the woman held only two things: a pair of cylindrical tubes made of black metal. Murray was sure the tickets were genuine. But the lack of luggage and those tubes would bug him for days.

* * *

11

It snowed on most of Romania that Christmas Day, including old St. Theodora's Cemetery on the outskirts of Schela. Virginal white blanketed all the graveyard's somber shades except for the heaven-pointing and disintegrating markers, mausoleums, and statues. No color existed above ground, not the sepia of a faded, glass-covered photograph, not the summer-sun-bleached pink of an artificial rose. St. Theodora's had not known a burial for seventy years; nor had it been tended in the past two decades. The necropolis was shunned, even in daylight. Because it lay in the shadow of the southern foothills of the Transylvanian Alps, the villagers of Schela were either too smart or too stupid (depending on one's point of view about the supernatural) to forswear their beliefs in evil habitations completely. Over the past twenty years, though sporadically, the local area had fallen victim to enough strange deaths and disappearances to arouse suspicions. And yet, the good twentieth-century folk of Schela had become too "scientific" to risk the ridicule of neighboring communities by opening graves and searching with mallets and wooden stakes in hand for undecomposed corpses. Instead, the burial ground was resolutely ignored, and the folk fervently wished that it would itself be buried beneath the briars, bushes, and deep needle sheddings of encroaching forest pine.

In the center of the silent cemetery stood a sizable mausoleum, fashioned of the local building stone. Its entrance was barred by a solid iron door. Carved into the stone above the door was the name KOZMA. Anyone brave enough to venture up to the door might have found that the old lock was free of rust and, in fact, protected from the elements by a coating of lubricant. Just behind the door, stone steps descended to a crypt, a square space some sixteen feet across. The crypt had been planned so that eighteen coffins could be accommodated, stacked three deep, six to each wall niche. Nine funerals had ended inside the crypt before its abandonment. Nine coffins occupied the space. Only eight rested in the niches. No fewer than thirty-three sets of remains littered the crypt. Most were little more than bones. Some still wore their flaccid skins beneath workaday clothing. One, a young woman who lay on the floor atop the bones of an eight-year-old boy, was not yet desiccated. The winter cold permeating the crypt had kept the insects and vermin away and softened the stench of decay.

Invisible in one corner of the inky-black crypt, five plastic storage crates and a metal steamer trunk sat like a latter-day pharaoh's treasure hoard. In another corner were stacked half a dozen large commercial bottles of spring water, several sponges, and towels. The ninth coffin rested on the stone floor, dead center in the crypt. On the floor to the right side of the coffin stood an oil lamp and a waterproof tube with paraffin-coated safety matches inside. Next to it lay an ancient stone hand, smashed from the wrist of a near-life-size statue. From within the hand issued a voice, metallic and husky with the smoke of brimstone.

"Radu. Radu Negru. Awake!"

A minute later, it repeated its words, this time more imperatively. Slowly, the coffin lid swung up and back, pushed by a naked arm. The arm was caked with damp soil, and the hand that belonged to it held the key to the mausoleum door. The other hand thrust up from the muck and groped for the coffin's edge. Two large, hollow tubes which had protruded from the soil erupted upward, driven by a man's face. He plucked the tubes from his nostrils and drew air in raggedly. He scraped the soil from his lips, then opened his mouth wide.

After a minute of filling his lungs, he pulled himself slowly into an upright position, to limit the soil's escape from the coffin. He groped for the container of matches and then for the lamp. When the lamp was lit, all the colors hidden in the darkness, colors long since vanished from the graveyard above, sprang to life. The hard greens of the plastic crates, the glinting brass of the lamp, the pale, translucent blue of the water within the bottles, the vivid yellow and orange of the flower-print dress on the woman lying atop the eight-year-old boy's bones, her skin a tallow tone. But dominant among the reborn colors was red. Red was the tube of matches; darker red the steamer trunk; black-red the blood dried upon the stones of the floor, of the walls, even of the ceiling. A desiccated lake of red.

He opened his eyes slowly, accustoming them gradually to the light. His irises glowed amber with life.

"I have not slept my full two months," the Vampire complained.

"No, you have not," the voice from the hand affirmed.

"How long?"

"Almost five weeks."

The Vampire shook dirt from his long hair. "What is your reason for waking me?"

"A task you promised to finish two-and-a-half thousand years ago is still unfulfilled," the voice said, shifting from Romanian to ancient Akkadian.

The Vampire rubbed his hands together, not to warm them but to remove dirt. There was nothing he could do immediately to bring warmth to his body. "I am in no mood for your Byzantine monologues! Say what you mean straight out."

"Another copy of the Scrolls of Ahriman has appeared."

The amber eyes blinked in astonishment. "How?"

" 'How' is not our concern. *Where* is. In the New World. We sent another to destroy them, but he has not succeeded."

"Did you send a novice?"

"Far from it. He served us for five hundred years. He was chosen because of his familiarity with America and his excellent command of English. But we found him to be a traitor."

"Not the first time that has happened," the Vampire remarked, relishing a rare opportunity to give back some of the sarcasm he was fed century after century.

Instead of answering the rebuke, the voice said, "The scrolls must be destroyed immediately. It is not by chance that they have surfaced after all these centuries. Mankind must not be forewarned."

The Vampire's mud-caked eyebrows furrowed. "You are adamant because the midnight hour approaches. The sixth prophecy has come to pass. Hasn't it?"

"Yes!" The word sibilated through the crypt with a ring of triumph.

14

The one who had been called Radu Negru stepped from the coffin without enthusiasm. "So . . . am I to kill the traitor? Am I to go to the New World?"

"First make yourself again like one of the living, and then you shall be told what is expected."

CHAPTER TWO

December 25

∽

Moses wrote down all the words of the Lord. Early in the morning

he built an altar at the foot of the mountain . . . and they sacrificed

bulls to the Lord as whole-offerings and shared-offerings. Moses

took half the blood and put it in basins, and the other half he flung

against the altar. Then he took the Book of the Covenant and read

it aloud for the people to hear. They said, "We shall obey, and do

all that the Lord has said." Moses then took the blood and flung it

over the people, saying, "This is the blood of the covenant which

the Lord has made with you on the terms of this book."

—Exodus 24:3–8

Half a holiday! That's all Ray Pental was going to get out of Christmas Day. Just enough time to watch all the beautifully wrapped presents ripped open with greedy abandon, to unwind the carpet fibers from around the electric train wheels, to assemble Barbie's motor home, to run to the WaWa convenience store for C batteries, and to return home to referee the first big fight of the day between Alison and Michelle, his nine- and seven-year-old daughters.

Ray had been a Princeton Township patrolman for five years and had received his formal promotion to detective just before Thanksgiving. With the change of jobs came a good salary hike and a few extra perks. The work was also supposedly easier and more interesting. "Interesting" was hardly the word, and "easier" was an outright laugh. Within days of accepting his detective shield all hell, as the saying goes, had broken loose in Princeton. An old widow who had lived in an apartment on Palmer Square for years suddenly vanished without a trace; a week later, a Princeton University guard apparently hanged himself in Firestone Library, kicking on a fire alarm as he was kicking off; just three days later, a professor and his wife had died when their home caught fire—ostensibly from smoking in bed; then a coed had almost been raped, and, the same night, an Egyptian graduate student had disappeared. Finally, two

18

days ago, a faculty member of the Princeton Theological Seminary had died when his house disintegrated in a gas explosion. Princeton had not seen this much accumulated mayhem in the previous five years. Practically from the day of his promotion, Ray had begun living at the police station. His marriage was degenerating quickly, especially after he put in only a guest appearance at a holiday party he had insisted to his wife that they owed their friends. He estimated he had clocked sixty-five hours of overtime in the past four weeks, and not even one of the missing persons had been located. The township had two veteran detectives—Andy Sutton and Harry Grimes. Consistent with the highly literate and demonstrably religious community, Sutton's nickname for the new member of the team was "Jonah."

When the phone rang at three minutes before noon, Ray had no doubt whatsoever that it was more bad news. Even worse, the call came once again from that most sacrosanct of institutions and largest employer in the town—Princeton University. The only good part about the call was that he was told to get his ass over to Firestone Library. Maybe at last some evidence had appeared to prove the guard's suspicious suicide was actually a murder. On the phone, Andy Sutton had warned him that he wouldn't believe what had happened, but he refused to play guessing games, especially since his wife, Karen, was boring a hole through his forehead with her stare.

Even though both he and Karen worked, Ray couldn't afford to live in Princeton proper. The drive from Hopewell to the library took twelve minutes, plus another two to get directed inside and up to the Rare Manuscripts Preparation room's rear entrance. Several university employees clustered in the hallway near the entrance, talking in low but agitated tones. Just beyond a pair of expensive wooden doors lay a metal gate, covered with heavy-gauge wire mesh. The gate stood ruined, its center gaping open as if a small bomb had been detonated. Bits of wire were strewn down the length of the twenty-foot corridor and into the flanking, fenced-in cages that held rare, old books. Ray noted that much of the wire had taken on a white discoloration. As he negotiated a path around the debris, trying to disturb nothing, he was struck by the incongruity of brutal, physical violence in such a refined, cerebral setting.

Mike Davis, a uniformed cop and Ray's best friend on the force, passed him coming from the other direction down the corridor. Davis was peeling the plastic seal off a roll of yellow cordon tape.

"What's happened here, Mike?" Ray asked.

Mike shook his head in answer. "You tell me. You're the detective."

The blood was harder to avoid than the wire. The trail began at the ruined gate and continued all the way to the corpse, which lay supine on the floor of the Rare Manuscripts Preparation room proper. The man had been good-looking, with Mediterranean features, probably a bit over forty. Ray guessed his standing height at five-ten. He had been a bit underweight, and what made him look even thinner was head-to-toe black clothing, like that worn by cat burglars. In stark contrast, his skin was so pale and smooth it looked like it was made of marble. Ray observed that his eyelids and mouth were closed. What made the scene seem more paradoxically peaceful was the funeral-home layout of the body, down to the large metal cross clutched in the corpse's hands, which were neatly folded across his chest. He lay in an enormous pool of blood, more than Ray believed one body could hold. At its limits, the blood had already dried to the color of eggplant, but closer in it had merely skinned over. A brushed-steel container which looked like a small coffin cast a shadow on the corpse. It and the rolling cart it rested on were smeared with blood. The apparent murder weapon, lying at the base of the "coffin," was a crude, wooden spear.

"Take a good look, Jonah, 'cause you're never gonna see anything this weird again in all your days." Andy Sutton stood at the opposite end of the corpse, filming the crime scene with a camcorder, making ultraslow pans. "The first fifteen minutes of this tape is my grandkids opening their presents. Gonna have to copy it off." Ray admired Andy's professional detachment, whether or not it was genuine. "The Polaroid's over on the desk," he told the junior detective. "Why don't you get it and start shooting?"

"Jesus Christ!" Ray exclaimed softly, as soon as he recovered his voice. He continued to stare at all the blood.

"Relax, Jonah," Andy said. "This is my effin' shift, so I own it. But I called you up for a few reasons. First, there's a typed letter inside this case that ties most of our shitcans together . . . if we can believe it."

"Shitcans" was cop slang for unsolvable suspicious deaths. Andy's words finally got Ray's full attention. For the first time, he noticed a uniformed cop conversing with a professorial-looking older gentleman and a university guard, as all three stared at him from the safe distance of the room's farthest corner.

"Second, you're back fresh from the academy. You can give me some pointers on state-of-the-art procedure. Come on, Pental, grab the effin' camera!"

Ray wracked his memory for something useful. Sutton's 20/20 vision, 20/20 thinking, and twenty years of experience defied help. "They told us not to put anything wet in plastic bags. The moisture builds up and can ruin evidence," Ray offered, taking the instant camera and using its viewfinder as a screen between himself and the stark reality of death.

"Do tell. I shoulda brought some of my grandkids' brown lunch bags. There's nothing small here worth collecting."

"What about a wallet?" Ray asked. "Keys?"

"Nope. No direct make," Andy answered, shutting off the camcorder and setting it down on a desk. "Yes, that is a bulletproof vest showing under his sweater. And yes, the murder weapon was made by somebody whittling down a broom handle. The shavings are over there." He smiled at Ray and snapped his fingers. "There's something I could put in a bag. And yes, all the metal lying in pieces over there was deep frozen, then kicked out. Near as I can figure, this guy used a liquid nitrogen tank to freeze open that gate. His killer was inside here and used the sharpened broom handle to spear him. Got him in a major artery, and he bled to death. We don't need the coroner's meat thermometer to tell me he's been dead most of the night. He's room temperature. Bizarre enough for you?"

21

"Plenty," Ray agreed, kneeling beside the body and shooting a picture of the wound area in the groin, where the torso met the leg.

"Too bad. I'm just getting started." Andy was pulling on plastic gloves. "Get the letter in this case, one cover shot, one close up." Once Ray took the pictures, Andy reached into the case, removed the typed sheet of paper and set it down on the desk. "Now read this: according to the writer, the guy on the floor . . . holding a cross, mind you . . . is a vampire. A couple-hundred-year-old vampire, no less."

Andy was notorious for his macabre sense of humor. When Ray's eyes jerked up to study the other detective's face he found no restrained laughter. Ray set his hands outside the edges of the paper, leaned into it and read. The letter contained four paragraphs. The first revealed that the corpse had used the name Vincent DeVilbiss and supplied the nearby address for a duplex DeVilbiss rented. It declared that he was a true vampire, given his supernatural powers by no less than satanic beings, whom he served. It exhorted the police to conduct an exhaustive chemical and physical autopsy to prove the last statement. The second paragraph described the vampire's quest for a pair of scrolls that had been housed inside the steel and Plexiglas "coffin" case. The Scrolls of Ahriman allegedly proved the existence of vampires, and the highly motivated DeVilbiss had killed both a library guard and the scrolls' translator in abortive attempts to steal them. The translator was Reverend Wilton Spencer, late of the Princeton Theological Seminary, killed at his home in a rigged gas-line explosion. The third paragraph declared that the scrolls had been removed for their own protection, since the dying DeVilbiss had affirmed that others of his kind existed and would continue the pursuit. The letter closed by promising that the scrolls' self-appointed guardian would soon be in contact.

Ray whistled atonally as he straightened up.

"Damnedest thing you've ever read, right?" Sutton said.

"Absolutely. It's not signed," Ray noted.

"It doesn't have to be. We know for sure who stole the scrolls . . . and probably who killed this . . . whatever he is." Andy

22

jerked his head in the direction of the room's far corner, where the university guard still stood. "The guy over there was on duty at the loading dock entrance this morning. It seems when the night shift guard went on patrol last night he found a bunch of lights busted throughout this part of the building. The place was closed early for Christmas Eve, so it could have been done anytime between closing, which was six, and midnight. He checked all the doors, including the wooden ones in front of the wrecked metal gate. Everything was locked up tight, so he figured it was a malicious prank. Nobody comes into the library until early this morning. Then it's two people, a young man and woman. They both work in the library, and they tell the guard they have to refill some airtight cases in the Rare Manuscripts Preparation section with inert gases. They're gone almost three quarters of an hour, and just when the guard is beginning to think something's not right, out they come, carrying a compressed gas tank and two metal cylinders. Cylinders just the right size for carrying off a pair of priceless scrolls, which are definitely gone."

"He doesn't question what's inside the cylinders?" Ray asked.

Andy shrugged. "Would you? They're both trusted employees."

"So . . . who are they?"

"The woman's name is Frederika Vanderveen. The guy . . . who is probably also the victim's killer . . . is a Simon Penn."

Ray felt the short hairs come to attention on the back of his neck. He had gotten a telephone call the night before from Simon Penn, ostensibly asking about technicalities of police work for a play he was writing. The scenario was something like: A young man is living with a young woman, but he is not her boyfriend. She is dating a no-good, who may have a criminal record, and she disappears. The young man thinks the no-good has kidnapped her. Some mention of hypnosis. Simon wanted to know if the police would help. Ray had been distracted during the brief conversation by his children fighting. He assured Simon the police would not get involved in a disappearance of less than twenty-four hours without a ransom call and suggested it would be better theater for the male friend to confront the no-good himself. As short and sweet a blow-off as Ray could manage. Which might very well have encouraged the carnage in front of him now.

"I know Simon Penn," Ray admitted.

Finally, Andy Sutton's unflappable countenance betrayed surprise. "No shit! How?"

"We've, uh, done theater together. Back when I had some free time."

Andy looked down at the corpse. "Theater, huh? Well, this ain't stage blood. You think he's capable of murder?"

"Murder, no. Self-defense, probably. I can't say. I really don't know him that well."

Sutton scratched the thinly follicled scalp above his ear. "Then you're lucky. I think *Mr. Penn thinks* he's in Act Three of *Dracula*. And so does Miss Vanderveen." He nodded in the direction of the professorial-looking man. "According to Dr. Gould, the head of this section, they had to work together to get the scroll case open. See the lock mechanisms on the opposite walls? Each has to have a key turned in it at the same time. As a curator, Penn had his own. If he can be believed, they got Reverend Spencer's key from the corpse. Then Penn typed the letter . . . with the old manual on his desk there. While he was composing, the woman probably loaded the scrolls into the cylinders. Fingerprints should provide some details."

"Have you investigated his claim that . . ."

"What, this guy being a vampire?" Sutton laughed. "The second I read the letter. Check this out." He plucked a pencil from his coat pocket and squatted stiffly next to the body. He probed the pencil under the corpse's upper lip and lifted. "Pretty nice set of canines, Detective?"

Ray bent closer. The hairs bristled again on the nape of his neck. "Jesus! They *are* longer than his other teeth!"

Andy scowled. "Come on! A little. Enough maybe to start a nut case believing he's a vampire . . . the nut case being either Simon Penn or the guy himself. And who's to say the guy wasn't pretty damned pale even before he ended up five quarts low." Sutton stood. "But ask yourself this, Detective: How many vampires have scars on their left cheeks? How many wear bulletproof vests? Aren't they supposed to turn to smoke to get through doors? And how many can be done in by one stab wound in the leg?"

Ray had lied to Sutton when he said he didn't know Simon Penn well. After dozens of rehearsals and performances with the man, plenty of time spent shooting the breeze in the wings while waiting to deliver their bit parts, Ray knew him better than several people he called close friends. In fact, a remark Simon had passed when they were both playing Roman sentries in Fry's *A Phoenix Too Frequent* had been chillingly, prophetically revelatory. Looking at the lance in his hand, Simon had bemoaned the death of what he called the true warrior, the fighter who had to look his deadly adversary in the eyes from the length of a sword or spear. The machine guns, airplanes, and mustard gases of World War I, Simon had affirmed, had left the battlefield to mere soldiers. He had said the words with such mingled disdain and longing that Ray was convinced (bizarre as it seemed to look at the librarian) that Simon would devote every fiber of his being if given the chance to become a Roland or Beowulf, the class of warrior who existed only in epic and myth. Ray looked at the corpse and the "coffin." Perhaps, inside his skull, Simon had been given his chance, on a battlefield where Good and Evil had to be spelled with capital letters. It was not difficult to see how all the recent murders and disappearances in Princeton could lead the normally levelheaded librarian beyond Detective Sutton's commonplace logic and modern society's rejection of the supernatural to the point where he accepted the unbelievable. Which was undoubtedly why he had felt the need to disguise his dilemma to Ray over the telephone. But Ray had missed his cues.

"I think you're gonna need some help answering all those questions," Ray told Sutton, bending closer to the corpse.

Dark and confining, the janitor's closet was like a womb. Solveig Persson sat on the closet floor, her knees drawn up tightly. The surrounding mops and brooms would have been invisible to any mortal, but although her amber eyes saw their shapes clearly, her mind was too preoccupied to register them. Her mind's eye fixed instead on the pleasant memory of the darkness under her childhood eiderdown comforter. It was a vivid recollection, even though it had been dredged up from a distance of one hundred and seventy years. She had grown up in Norway, in a small town called Hell, which in Norwegian meant "bright." By the time she was a teenager, she regarded the name as ironic; to her, the town had to be one of the most benighted, obscure dwelling places on the face of the earth. Growing up there in the early nineteenth century, she had felt trapped, silently panicked that she would never escape its mud-choked provinciality.

She had been right to worry. Too poor to escape to a new life, she had settled unhappily on a neighboring farm boy for a husband, a witless, callow youth who aged into an even duller but no less callow man. She had borne him a son and then a daughter, with hopes that they would fulfill her existence, bring her pride and companionship. Both were selfish tintypes of their father, unlovely, unloving, and unlovable. When they came of age, neither was able to attract spouses in a village with the meanest of marital standards. The prolonged winters were the worst part of her life, back when her name was Krista Knudsen. It was not the darkness; she had always loved the long nights of hard, black skies. The horror of winter was that there was no getting away from her family. One eventual stratagem she latched onto to ease her boredom was immersing herself in the ancient history and lore of the area, investigating every old Norse site, learning every legend. Close by her farm, an enormous rune stone protruded from the earth, relic of the dark, pre-Christian ages. She visited the stone every time she went out gathering wood, found herself running her fingers over the carvings, talking to the stone, pouring out her frustrations as if it were a wise friend.

And then one night the stone talked back to her. It whispered in a voice soft as the wind's that it understood. It suggested it could rescue her from the torment of existence at the dark edge of the world. It promised her not only an exciting life but one that never ended. Krista had been forty-three then. The rigors of Scandinavian weather and survival had a stranglehold on her youth. Permanently nut-brown from the endless summer sun, her skin was taking on the texture of a wrinkled leather bag. Muscle strains and sprains healed more slowly; a few teeth had disappeared. The only uncertainty now was the steepness of the inexorable slide into decadence. Nevertheless, she was not comforted by the overtures of the stone. Hearing a disembodied voice that spoke to her alone surely signaled the onset of madness, from too many years of white-night, black-day monotony. Forty-three years in rural Norway, she figured, were like ninety to the mind of someone living in a more temperate, more stimulating clime. She avoided the stone for weeks. When nothing else in her life suggested to her that her mind was failing, she returned to it. It spoke more persuasively than ever, promising proof of its power. She was instructed to use a sledgehammer and break off a spade-size wedge of the rune stone, a piece bearing a crudely carved human figure. Once she did that, it directed her to use the piece to dig beside a nearby stream. There, she found a hoard of ancient gold, intricately tooled into Celtic jewelry. Now, the spade-size shard spoke to her from her hand. She could have all the time in the world to spend this gold . . . if she would only kill her entire family.

Krista debated for a week. Daily visits to her secreted gold finally convinced her. One night, the caribou stew had a new ingredient. Although he had increased himself in no other way during his marriage, her husband had added pounds of protective fat. Alerted to the poisoning by his children's sudden agonies and noting that Krista had not touched her meal, he had staggered to the living room for his rifle. His wife had calmly bashed in his skull with the fireplace poker, then packed her most precious belongings while her children writhed into oblivion on the kitchen floor.

Krista almost failed to escape from Hell after the murders. The voice had not counseled her on swift, sure ways to flee across the world beyond her village. She later suspected that same voice had visited many people in many centuries and many lands and convinced them to murder, then silently reneged on promises, leaving its victims to be carted off to chopping blocks or insane asylums. Once she got herself to Sweden with her gold and her rune chunk, however, and changed her name to Solveig Persson, the voice kept its promise. The next best thing to eternal life was hers. It came about through the daily taking of a bitter-tasting golden powder (a precise quantity mysteriously delivered to her each month) and through the periodic drinking of human blood. Her senses became several factors more acute. Her strength trebled. Blows and wounds, although painful as ever, healed almost before her eyes, and the years slowed as if the sand in her life's hourglass had been replaced with damp salt. The only thing that clearly advanced her years was sunlight. She calculated that an hour of direct exposure on her arms, neck, and face were enough to age her a normal human's month. Across the span of one hundred and twenty years, she had come to look sixty. Although she kept to Sweden, Norway, Finland, and the British Isles between November and April and Argentina, Chile, the Union of South Africa, or Australia from June to September, she could never completely avoid the sun's rays. The voice inside the rune chunk made that impossible, by periodically demanding sudden trips for the purpose of murder. The levy for the golden powder came almost as regularly as its supply. She was the Devil's executioner, and she quickly realized that those to be killed (the number now exceeding a thousand) were invariably persons of quality, dedicated to bettering the condition of the human race. More diabolically, she was expected to help uncover such persons of promise and report on them for infernal evaluation and condemnation.

The bloodshed was increased by her personal need for the life-giving liquid. Like clockwork, ten days after having sucked to satiation, her body would begin to crave more human blood. If she ignored the urge, by the twelfth day every fiber of her nervous system would ache for blood, like a junkie deprived of heroin. By the fourteenth day her temperature would soar to a hundred and four and her fevered brain would begin to hallucinate. Twice (once by the misfortune of isolation on a small ocean steamer and once snowbound for two weeks) Solveig had been denied blood to this limit. The results had been excruciatingly identical. She knew that a fifteenth day of such deprivation would have compelled her to any foolhardiness, be it dashing naked into the midday July sun of a crowded Riviera beach to open the nearest person's carotid artery. Fortunately, quenching her thirst was usually a safe and easy task. She simply shadowed the haunts of human vermin, those who preferred to dwell in darkness. Pimps, whores, thieves, drunks, and addicts were shadows in the greater world anyway and were rarely missed. Because she could select these victims by opportunity, there was almost no chance of being caught. Those targets selected by the Dark Lords, however, could rarely serve her double purpose. They had invariably gathered the light of fame around themselves by the time Solveig learned about them. Not more than one or two a year could be found with their bodies drained of blood before alarms would be sounded everywhere she stalked. By requiring human blood to complete their powder's magic, the invisible powers diabolically ensured many more murders than they actually demanded.

For all the blood—both demanded and required—Solveig never complained, never suffered bouts of guilt. The voice had been clever; once she had murdered her own flesh and blood, taking the lives of strangers had become less traumatic. She had never lost her sense of right and wrong, but it made no difference to her. In order to live forever, she had selfishly rejected all beliefs in the sanctity of human life and substituted one Hell for another she preferred.

Solveig had returned twice to her birthplace. The first time, more than fifty years after murdering her family, a woman who had been only a child when she fled hunted up a photograph of the Knudsen family and accused Solveig of being the very same Krista Knudsen, claiming she had used witchcraft to maintain her age. Too many townsfolk clung to the old beliefs. Her second escape had been even narrower than the first. She did not dare return to the town again until 1972. By then it had become civilized and more or less part of the greater twentieth-century world. She left it carrying a postcard of the town square. On the back, in English, it read: "Greetings from Hell. Almost everyone here is Lutheran!"

After disposing of her family, Solveig, nee Krista, had never wanted another close relationship. She grew to love the night even more. Therefore, she never resented the major drawbacks of being a vampire. She migrated from season to season between extremes of latitude; she read; she attended plays and concerts. Over the last thirty years she watched many hours of television. Her desires had never been grand. But she did resent it whenever the voice from within her stone uprooted her without warning, as it had only six days before. It had ordered her across the Atlantic from Stockholm, demanding that she not even take the time to slake her returning bloodthirst. It had, moreover, forbidden her to kill for her own ends until it permitted. It directed her to Princeton, New Jersey, where her first order of business was the killing of a physics professor. This she had accomplished by putting herself in the path of his moving car and allowing herself to be thrown over the hood and roof and onto parking lot pavement. The man had been wary and difficult to overcome. She eventually arranged to have him drown in his car. This professor was supposed to have been the victim of another vampire. For one hundred and twenty years, Solveig had wondered if her pact with Perdition was unique. She had never had the courage to ask the voice. Now she knew there was at least one other of her kind. This one, who called himself Vincent DeVilbiss, had been caught breaking his infernal pact. He had had another obligation in Princeton—the destruction of a pair of ancient scrolls recently come into the university's possession. On Christmas Eve morning, Solveig had been instructed to sit and wait. If DeVilbiss returned to his rented house with the scrolls, she was to kill him and destroy the scrolls herself. If he did not return, it meant that someone human had terminated him and the theft of the scrolls fell to her. She had been told very little else, except to be assured that she would have no trouble killing DeVilbiss; the invulnerability element had been withheld from his latest delivery of powder. He would die as easily as any mortal.

Toward midnight on Christmas Eve, as church bells had tolled through the town with dignified joy, Solveig's stone spoke to her.

The voice, always before passionless in its humming monotone, had a furious edge. It ordered her to DeVilbiss's rented house, to shut off a broken water pipe, to clean up what she could of a fire that had raged in the basement and to expunge every clue to DeVilbiss's presence. Evil had clearly not had its way. After she had done all she could in the rented duplex, she was instructed to pose as a delivery person and gain access to a certain address on the chic side of the town. There, she would look for a Frederika Vanderveen, who owned the house, and a Simon Penn. If she found them she was to learn DeVilbiss's fate and if she could reach the scrolls through the young man and woman. Whether or not they helped her destroy the documents, they were not to survive. Solveig's first failure in the affair frightened her deeply. Perhaps there would soon be a third vampire in Princeton, sent to eliminate her. She was angry as well as frightened, because she had never been given such a complicated assignment and with so little background information. Ignorance was one kind of darkness Solveig did not enjoy.

"Have you found the man or woman?" the voice asked, vibrating out of the stone in her pocket.

Solveig started as she always did when the voice spoke unheralded. She caught her breath and said, "No. There was only an older woman at the house. She said that Frederika and her boyfriend . . . I assume that is Simon Penn . . ." The voice made no reply. ". . . that they had just left, to fly to England."

"What else did you learn from this woman?"

"Nothing. The police arrived only a minute behind me. I had to escape through the back of the house."

"Where are you now?"

"In a building across the street from the university library. You told me DeVilbiss was meeting Simon Penn in the library, to get the scrolls. Since Penn is still alive, and since DeVilbiss did not return to his house, he may still be inside the library. In fact, I am almost sure of it. There have been police cars parked near one of the entrances for a long time. I look out from darkness every few minutes. The last time I looked, an ambulance had pulled up as well." Solveig said a silent prayer that the voice would not order her across the street. The library was obviously closed for Christmas Day, and she would stand out as one of only a few curiosity seekers who lingered in the cold outside the building's gray, Gothic walls. Worse, the woman at the Vanderveen house had probably given the police her description.

"Resume your post now!" the voice commanded.

"But it is midday," Solveig complained. "I already have a terrible headache from need of blood, and the sun makes it much worse."

"Go!" The voice, even in command, never spoke loudly. Although the little word had no sibilant element, its sound was underlaid with a husky hissing, as if spoken by a huge snake.

Solveig left the janitor's closet and stumbled toward the hallway windows, cupping her hands around the sides of her sunglasses in a futile effort to lessen the pain of the bright sunlight. She stared across the street through narrowed eye slits.

"They are bringing out a body," Solveig reported in Swedish to the stone lying in the black recess of her coat pocket.

"Is it a man with dark hair?"

"I can't tell. It's covered by a white sheet."

"Is your car nearby?"

"Yes."

"Follow the ambulance. You must look upon the body's face."

Solveig turned from the window. Her legs felt wobbly. "I obey," she said. "But directly after I do this, give me leave to drink blood. I—"

"No! You will survive without it. You have exposed yourself enough in this town. Leave no more bodies behind if you value your continued existence. You will not kill again until you have left this country."

"Am I to follow the man and woman to England?" she asked, hurrying down a metal staircase.

"You will follow them," the voice acknowledged, "but it is not to England that they have gone."

Solveig lacked the courage to challenge the voice, but one matter had to be broached. "And what about the scrolls?"

"They will not be where expected either," the voice declared. "You face a formidable and forewarned foe."

Ray Pental forced himself to read the collected patrolmen's reports slowly. In comparison to all the other murders and the disappearances, this latest library killing was hemorrhaging information. It seemed that early this morning the township police received an urgent call from a woman living out in Long Island. Her daughter, Lynn Gellman, was supposed to have driven in for the holidays the night before. She had been calling her daughter's home every hour since midnight, with no response. She requested that a check be made on the house. The patrolman who investigated found the sliding glass door in the back of the townhouse unlocked. When he searched the upper floor, he found Lynn Gellman expertly tied to her bedroom chair, wearing only a bra and panties. She proved a tough number, wasting no time in hysterics. As soon as she had wrapped herself in a bathrobe she related in detail her encounter with a male intruder who could evidently see in near-total darkness, who was incredibly strong, and who had a single-minded obsession with learning where her former live-in boyfriend now resided. She had truthfully told the man all she knew: Simon Penn said he was staying with another member of the university staff. He had volunteered no name. The man then demanded to know Simon's closest friends. Lynn had remembered a few, but in her panic she forgot Richard Chen, a graduate student in physics.

The patrolman had alerted headquarters to get another cruiser over to Richard Chen's apartment. The graduate student seemed unsurprised that Simon Penn might be in grave danger. He had given the patrolman Frederika Vanderveen's address, on Hodge Road. Two more patrolmen—the last part of the force on duty Christmas morning—had visited the Vanderveen mansion and found only her mother. Simon and Frederika had left minutes before, headed, they said, for England. Among the things packed in the trunk of the young woman's car were two metal cylinders. Ray underlined that fact in red. A curious sidelight to the chain of events was the visit to the mansion by a woman pretending to be a delivery agent for a gift basket company. Her real motive had obviously been the location of Frederika Vanderveen and Simon Penn, and she had disappeared like smoke the minute the patrolmen arrived. Ray reread her description and underlined it, too. Then he returned to Gellman's statement that her unseen intruder could operate in near total darkness and was incredibly strong. He underlined that twice. It was the first mention in the case of legendary vampire traits.

"Come on, Jonah," Andy Sutton called over the divider that separated his cubicle from Ray's. "We can't hold this kid all day."

"Coming." Ray shoved the report into his top drawer and locked it.

The township was neither big enough nor bad enough to warrant a "sweat box" for interrogating people. Ray entered the municipal building's community meeting room holding a note pad. Inside were Andy Sutton, Harry Grimes, and the desk sergeant, who was monitoring a tape recorder in the center of the large conference table. On the side opposite the door a Eurasian male slumped in his chair. He was in his early twenties and wore his version of the Princeton grad student uniform: tennis sneakers, jeans, a plaid shirt under a grungy cable-knit sweater. His arms were folded defensively across his chest. In front of him on the desk, upside down, sat his eyeglasses.

"Richard Chen, this is Detective Ray Pental," Harry Grimes said. "He's responsible for a few unsolved cases that may tie in with this one."

"Detective."

"We'd like you to tell him everything you've told us," Grimes went on.

The grad student rolled his eyes and glanced at his watch. "Gimme a break. It's all on tape already. Let him listen—"

"Look, Mr. Chen," Sutton broke in, "the simple truth is folks often reveal more facts the second or third time they go over something. We could play hardball and remind you about the stolen nitrogen tank in the back of your pickup. We could hint that we could get the university to drop your fellowship or whatever you have, but let's all be on the same side. You've got a friend in trouble, right?"

"Right."

"Help him. Tell Detective Pental what you know."

Chen measured Ray with his eyes. When Ray offered him a smile, he unfolded his arms. "Simon had been living with a domineering bitch for quite a while."

"Lynn Gellman," Sutton said softly, for Ray's benefit.

"When he moved out on her, he needed a place to stay. He's a librarian over at Firestone, so he asked another librarian—Frederika Vanderveen—if he could rent a room at her place over on Hodge Road. She's a real looker . . . if you go for Dutch blond types. Simon had mentioned her to me months ago, but he really didn't know her. It was one of those 'worship from afar' things, y'know? He had it real bad for her, even though one of the few facts he did know was that she was weird."

"Weird in what way?" Ray asked.

"Well, for one thing, she only dated men a lot older than herself. And Simon said he spotted her digging dirt from in front of her father's grave one night. Evidently some fixation on aging or death. A few days after Simon had started living there, he and I had dinner together. He told me she was trying to contact her father . . . from the dead. She went to this guy who had just moved into town and who claimed to be a channeler. His name was Vincent DeVilbiss. Simon was afraid the guy was taking advantage of Frederika, so he went to DeVilbiss's place and confronted him."

At first blush, it sounded to Ray like a disturbed woman at the pinnacle of a love triangle. Plenty of murders resulted from that geometry. According to one of his lecturers at the police academy the right answer was almost always the simplest solution that included all the facts. The teacher called the theorem "Occam's razor." Who Occam was or what the idea had to do with a razor was never explained, but it made sense to Ray. The problem with the theory in this case was too many extra facts. How did ancient scrolls fit into a love triangle? Why did it end in a library after hours? And what was this insanity about a vampire?

"When was this confrontation?" Ray asked, remembering his advice to Simon over the phone the previous night.

"Three, maybe four days ago. Anyway, the guy wouldn't be frightened off or bought off. Once Simon had seen him, he couldn't get it out of his head that he knew him . . . from the TV news or the newspapers. He was sure he was some kind of criminal. Serial killer, maybe bigamist, he said. Then Reverend Spencer, the professor translating some scrolls in the place where Simon works, was killed at his house. Gas explosion . . . day before yesterday. When I finally reached Simon about it, he just says he's sure the death wasn't an accident, that he has to do some research at the library and that he'll meet me later. He comes by my apartment at about one o'clock and proceeds to tell me about a story he's just reread in the library . . . the thing he couldn't remember that had tipped him off about DeVilbiss. The book is the biography of a magician's club, and it's about a hundred years old. A dead ringer for DeVilbiss auditioned for membership in the club and took a real bullet in the chest."

"He auditioned under the name Vincent DeVilbiss?" Ray asked.

Chen shook his head, remembered the recorder and said, "No, but his description was right on, according to Simon."

The sergeant left the room, to check the front desk.

"And the guy in the book's description is how old?" Harry Grimes asked.

"About the same age as DeVilbiss looked. No aging, see? When the club members try to investigate how he did the bullet trick, he resists them. But one magician sees the wound healing up right before his eyes. The guy throws off several grown men, douses the theater lights and escapes in total darkness."

"And tell Detective Pental your reaction when Simon says all this to you," prompted Sutton.

"I said it had to be a look-alike that DeVilbiss had also read about and identified with. But Simon wasn't having any part of it. He had personally felt the strength of the man's grip. He went on about the guy sleeping during the day and avoiding the light. But the clincher was that Frederika had disappeared. Simon was sure DeVilbiss had her under some kind of hypnotic power. He had called the guy just before visiting me, and DeVilbiss all but admitted he had her. He was counting on using Simon's ability to get those ancient scrolls." Chen blinked in thought, then gave Sutton a sheepish look. "I *have* remembered something else: Simon left a translation of part of the scrolls with me. I'm supposed to mail copies to scholars around the world."

"We'll pick up the translation when I bring you home," Sutton said. "Please go on."

"Did he tell you why the scrolls were so important to DeVilbiss?" Ray broke in.

"He said they prove the existence of vampires."

Ray looked at Andy and Harry. They maintained enviable masks of imperturbability. When he looked back at the grad student, Chen shrugged. "What can I tell you? That's what he said. I've never seen the scrolls. But the guy translating them died a pretty gory death. And so have a bunch of other people."

"That still doesn't prove DeVilbiss was a vampire," Ray thought out loud. "Maybe he just had the delusion he was . . . undead."

"That's the same thing I said," Chen reaffirmed.

"Then why did you give Mr. Penn a way to kill the guy?" Andy asked.

Chen picked up his glasses and lowered the stems carefully over his ears. "I told you: all I did was give Simon a hypothetical means to kill a vampire . . . to kill anything made of complex molecules. You lower its temperature to near zero. Simon stole the cryo tank and equipment. He also stole my truck, but I'm not pressing charges."

"That's the least of his problems," Harry Grimes remarked.

"And yesterday afternoon was the last you saw Simon Penn or spoke with him," Sutton prompted.

"That's right. What I know about DeVilbiss's death and the missing scrolls came from you people. I didn't even know my pickup was gone, much less returned. Simon had a set of keys for it."

37

"Does he know about the delivery lady?" Ray asked his partners, tilting his head in the grad student's direction.

"No," Andy answered.

Ray reviewed the patrolman's report in his mind. "Have you ever seen, or did Simon ever mention, a woman about sixty to sixty-five years old? Tall, big-boned, blond-white hair, pale skin, lots of white teeth. Wears sunglasses and maybe suntan lotion?"

"In the winter?" asked Chen.

"Yes."

Chen shook his head, then looked directly at Ray. "But she sounds a little like a vampire, doesn't she?"

The Vampire (he always thought of himself in capital letters, whether as dir Vampir, der Vampyr, Nosferatu, Kian-si, Upir, Ekimmu, Wampira, Vrykolaka, or Kali) listened with wolflike ears, scanned with owl-like eyes across the town of Tirgu Jiu, seventeen kilometers south of the Schela cemetery. He had hoped against hope to find a baby in a basket at the front door of the orphanage, but his luck was not that good. Satisfied this corner of the town was deaf and dumb in a collective sleep, he stood on a pair of crates and boosted himself up to a lower roof, then used a sturdy drainpipe to climb to a second-story window set deeply into the orphanage's stone wall. A thin knife was all he needed to wedge between the window frames and raise the old latch. He slid inside the dormitory room and scanned its contents for nourishment.

Closest to the window slept a plump girl of perhaps six years. Her body no doubt held pints of rich, hot blood, but she was too bulky to wrestle through the little window—especially in the Vampire's weakened state. He settled on a thinner and younger girl, one he judged to be four years old. He removed the ether-soaked cloth from its plastic zip-lock bag and clapped it tightly over the girl's nose and mouth. She barely had time to wake from her dreams and fight her arms up to the cloth before she was unconscious again. The Vampire shoved her out the window, lowered her to the full extent of his arms and let her drop to the roof. He climbed outside, shut the window as best he could and reclaimed his prize.

If his Infernal Lord had not demanded immediate action, the Vampire would have driven into Bucharest. There, some ten thousand children and teenagers lived on and beneath the streets. Known as "throwaways," they were the legacies of the anti-abortion, anti–birth-control policies of the late dictator Nicolae Ceausescu. It was estimated that, throughout Romania, a third of a million children had been abandoned, kicked out of their homes or orphaned in the past twenty years. The Vampire would never leave Romania as base so long as life (and therefore blood) was so cheap. The orphanage in Tirgu Jiu was only marginally more dangerous a hunting ground. No one wanted the children. The luckiest ones were being exported to wealthy countries like the United States and Canada, where healthy, white children were still at a premium. The state employees would make a search and inform the police of a missing child but secretly breathe a sigh of relief that a bed was once again available.

The Vampire dumped the girl into his truck's passenger seat. If the police stopped him they could see that she was still alive. He would beg them to lead him to the nearest hospital, as she needed medical attention badly. Certainly, her two broken legs did. He clambered into the driver's seat, wrapped a muffler around his neck and pulled a pair of gloves on, all the while shivering like a wet dog. Despite several layers of clothing, he had not warmed much since climbing from the coffin. A sponge bath had made him even colder. From season to season, the crypt's temperature never varied more than a few degrees above or below 55. It was as near to ideal as the Vampire had found in this century. That notwithstanding, he resigned himself that if his Infernal Lord's timetable demanded any more bloodhunts nearby, discretion would force him to abandon his Garden of Eden for a generation.

Although he knew that he was not unique, the Vampire was confident that he was special among his kind. He cherished the conceit that now, in the twentieth century, he was the only one left of his heightened order. Ironically, his was of the order of vampire so famous in folklore and literature, even though it must have been the failure of others of this superior class that alerted the mortal world to what he was. Common vampires took an amber-colored powder every day, just as he did, to halt the aging process and to render them nearly invulnerable to harm. Common vampires drank blood at least once every two weeks, as he did, to prevent maddening headaches. But none of these creatures could hold aging perpetually at bay. This he had on the authority of his Infernal Lord. Every time any vampire was exposed to sunlight, he or she became older . . . and not by normal measures of time but rather like a videotape being fast-forwarded. The Infernal Lords had done this on purpose, to force vampires to conduct most of their activities at night, in the same blackness to which the dark angels had been confined since before man was created and in which they could still monitor to a limited degree the evil they instigated. But every vampire's subservient obligations made it impossible for him or her to avoid the sun from time to time, and if one lived for centuries, "from time to time" added up.

There existed, however, one means to reverse the sun's degenerative powers. The Vampire had earned this special knowledge early in his transformation, for he had proven himself a true enemy of the species of his birth through just a few brutal, remorseless acts. The secret beyond the secret of mere vampirism came out of the soil of a two-kilometer stretch along the banks of the Euphrates, in Iraq. If one lay enclosed within a moist mixture of this soil for at least seventy-two hours, the sun's privations were erased. The easiest means of keeping the soil moist was to contain it within a small space. Coffins provided perfect, ready-made containers, but they were illegal everywhere except in coffin factories, funeral homes, and cemeteries. Those easiest to appropriate lay inside crypts. Fear of the dead virtually ensured no man would enter an old crypt, much less peek inside a "narrow house" of the dead. The concept was so simple, so logical that several other undead had obviously evolved it. Unfortunately for the Vampire, they had been careless in some way—probably hunting too close to the cemeteries—and had been themselves hunted down and exterminated. This, the Vampire was convinced, led to man's scant but genuine knowledge of the undead and how to dispose of them. Some of the more favored class of vampire had been found in graveyard crypts, lying inside coffins filled with soil, which the vigilantes assumed was native earth. They were easily killed because they had to lie there for some three days for the soil to work and therefore became vulnerable from lack of blood and powder. Careless fools.

Plump snowflakes began tumbling out of the dying night, obscuring visibility on the road. The Vampire reached the edge of St. Theodora's Cemetery and hid his old truck behind a thick stand of brambles. He was too cold to waste time walking around the machine, so he grabbed the child by the hair and yanked her across the seat and out into the snow. Fingers still taloned into her hair, the Vampire dragged her through the white blanket toward the Kozma crypt, heedless of the trail they made. Halfway there, she became conscious. At first she mewled like a kitten. As she became aware of her pain and her surroundings, her feeble noises turned to moans, and then, at the crypt door, reached a crescendo in one long shriek. The Vampire struck her face with a powerful backhand, dazing her long enough to unlock the door and descend to the crypt with the frail body in his arms. After he deposited her near the steps, he realized that a string of her nasal mucus clung to the back of his hand. Grimacing with revulsion, he wiped it off on her thin dress and moved to the metal steamer trunk. He combed his long, sharp fingernails absentmindedly through his hair as he stared at the steamer's contents. Finally, he decided on a bar of Lindt chocolate. Behind him, the child was again making noises. He ignored her as he wolfed down half the bar in a few bites. He turned and watched with detachment as the girl discovered she could not stand on her legs. She struggled on her hands and elbows toward the steps. The Vampire had hoped she would look past the oil lamp's flame to the piles of corpses littering the stone floor. Invariably, that would shock a child into a trancelike state. By the time he had finished the chocolate bar, she had crawled up to the door and was banging her fist ineffectually against the cold metal. He drew in a ragged breath, growing angrier by the moment at the night he was being forced to endure. He rushed up the steps two at a time, swept the child into his arms and buried his canines in her neck.

The girl screamed once, then yelped a few times. Within a minute she had sunk back into unconsciousness, the nightmare of her brief life all but over. She was so light that the Vampire was able to move about the crypt and assemble his traveling kit while he drank. There was not much blood in the little body; her heart stopped beating in less than ten minutes. It was not enough to satisfy him, but it would have to do. At least he had stopped shivering; warmth as well as blood had flowed from her body into his. He withdrew his mouth from her neck and stared into the dull, dead eyes. More mucus hung pendant from her nostrils. He tossed her body onto the nearest pile and gave her no more thought.

The Vampire turned to address the ancient stone hand resting on the floor. After what the voice had said upon rousing him, he had no doubt it was still present in the stone, awaiting his return.

"For the first time in all these centuries, I decline to do your bidding," he assayed in a calm, conversational tone. He waited for several seconds. The voice refused him the satisfaction of a reaction. He turned his back on the hand and began assembling belongings. "It's suicide . . . a mission of forlorn hope. The scrolls were created precisely to warn men of my kind. Because knowledge and belief are two separate things, perhaps I might still have been able to surprise whoever knows their contents. But you also tell me you sent another of my kind to destroy the scrolls, and that he was a traitor. I am sure someone came to believe in vampires through him."

"He betrayed us by not killing those we ordered dead," the voice spoke at last. "He would not have risked his own existence by teaching others what he was. He died in the quest for the scrolls."

"You are sure of this?"

"Yes."

The Vampire laughed. "You have lied to man since the tree dropped its first apple. Do you also expect me to believe that the one who killed this traitor is *unwarned?*"

42

"No. He is warned. He is also resourceful and intelligent—for a mortal human. And he has an accomplice . . . a woman whom the traitor had captured and was holding, to trade for the scrolls. She, too, seems capable."

"And yet you expect me to accept this task," the Vampire said, without pausing from his packing.

"Yes."

"Why? Because I cannot exist without your powder? Perhaps two-and-a-half thousand years is long enough to live. I sleep more each century. What does continued life offer me?"

"It postpones the final price you must pay."

The Vampire snorted derision through his nostrils. "How many times have I rejected your threats of damnation? You have revealed too much that assures me there is no afterlife for man, either in a heaven or hell. Men are merely expendable pawns in the feud between you and God. When I die, you will be helpless to deny me the perfect eternity—oblivion."

"We are not interested in argument," the voice informed him. "We know you will destroy the scrolls without threats."

The Vampire straightened up. When he turned to the light, his mouth curved in a slight smile. "Oh? How?"

"You said it yourself: what has life offered you of late? You only consider death because you are bored. You hunger for a challenge. Now comes one only you can master." The sulfurous voice dropped to a whisper. "Success will reaffirm your claim as dominant creature on earth; failure will guarantee you the oblivion you profess to desire. You cannot lose."

"Oh, but I can. The sixth prediction of the scrolls has come to pass. Only one more remains. If I remember clearly, you may in fact be asking me to make the final prediction come true. Once that happens, the world will suddenly be overrun with creatures like me, and I will no longer be able to move with impunity among unbelievers. They will seek me out along with all the novices, as they did in their witch hunts five hundred years ago. I have dreaded this day since my second birth, and I see no profit in helping it dawn."

"But have I not just said this will make you a dominant creature on earth? If you succeed at this task, we will make you something even greater than you are: a demigod. You will no longer need to drink blood. The risk of your exposure will be cut in half. Your eyes will no longer glow amber. Again, the risk will decrease."

"Will I be able to move in sunlight without pain or aging?"

The infernal voice made a hideous imitation of a chuckle. "Ask rather to have wings. What is your answer, Radu Negru?"

The Vampire made a small bow of obeisance toward the stone. "Teach me all you know about this man and woman. But first tell me how much time I have to reach them and the scrolls."

"You have sufficient time," the voice answered. "It seems the man, the woman, *and* the scrolls are all moving in your direction."

Simon Penn reached the metal detector and X-ray machines for the ninth time and turned about to pace again the length of the terminal wing. The industrial carpeting, the neatly arranged billboards, the huge glass windows alternating with walls that held phone alcoves and bathroom doors matched that of a hundred other airports in North America. This one happened to be in Toronto. The monotony would have compelled Simon to turn his attention inward, except that he was already trapped inside his own skull, forced by barely subdued panic to review the horrible events of the past twenty-four hours.

Astonishing, Simon reflected, that a lifetime of ambivalent feelings toward God and the Devil, heaven and hell could be irrevocably resolved in the space of minutes. Not a mote of doubt remained concerning the metaphysical realm's existence. And yet, real as it was to him, he had no tangible proof to share with the still-doubting world. Evidently, unverifiability was something both Creator and Destroyer desired. The more time passed, the more convinced Simon was that DeVilbiss would not be proven a vampire. Even after witnessing DeVilbiss's powers and hearing the dying man affirm his unnaturalness, it had been difficult to believe fully in such a creature . . . much less one several hundred years old. But then Simon had raced to DeVilbiss's rented house to rescue

Frederika, who was handcuffed to a water pipe but even more securely held there by the ancient's hypnotic spell. Before he could descend to the basement to release her, Simon had been attacked by an animated Pierrot doll, out of which emerged in smoke and fire the very manifestation of satanic malevolence. Through the fortune of a broken water pipe and the resourcefulness of severing an electrical cable, Simon and Frederika had forced it back to hell, but they knew their pursuit had just begun. DeVilbiss had sworn vehemently, even as the last of his blood flowed across the floor of the Rare Manuscripts room, that he was an unwilling slave to "the landlords of hell." As soon as he realized his infernal masters had arranged for his death, DeVilbiss swung his allegiance back fully to mankind's side. He exhorted Simon to steal the scrolls, have them translated and published, so that the world would once again believe in the evil intent of the Dark Forces and the evil actions of their vampiric minions. On a selfish level, Simon knew the plan to be the only means to end the Devil's scorching pursuit. With his final breaths DeVilbiss had revealed the diaries he kept, to provide his opponent-turned-ally with hints for survival and proofs of infernally directed executions over the centuries. The latest diary had lain in DeVilbiss's rented car; the rest were secure in two Zurich banks.

It was the stuff of nightmares, and yet it was real. Simon resolved for both sanity's and survival's sake to accept the supernatural events that had assailed his senses with the same nonresisting equanimity as that of a baby beholding the two-dimensional miracle of television for the first time.

Simon's pacing brought him to the Gate 18 waiting area, where Frederika sat with her back to the dying sun. Beyond the plate glass windows, the plane that would wing them to Zurich rolled up to the boarding ramp, turbo fans whining. Frederika, busy erasing light pencil marks she had made in the margins of the black book on her lap, was oblivious to its arrival.

"It's almost dark," Simon observed, sotto voce, sitting beside her. "You look really conspicuous wearing those sunglasses."

"I don't care," Frederika answered, not looking up from the

book. "I've still got that headache, and the sunlight hurts my eyes."

"Did you take the Tylenol I got you?"

"Yes. It didn't help."

"It's that damned powder DeVilbiss was feeding you," Simon decided. "The devils who created it surely intended it to be addictive after a certain time. How many days were you on it?"

Frederika looked up from the diary. "He cured my cold on the sixteenth, with something in my tea. It was probably the same powder." Her head went down again.

Simon counted off the days on his fingers. "Ten days . . . followed by a cold-turkey stop. I'm worried. Maybe you should check yourself into an addiction clinic and let me go on without you."

"That's insane. One human against the Devil and his bloodsucking assassins? We'll be more than lucky if the two of us survive. I'll be okay."

Simon twisted around in his seat and grimaced at the setting sun. "I don't know. Let's at least say a prayer . . . ask for divine help in kicking it."

The dark glasses faced Simon straight on. "You mean literally?"

"Yes."

"Right here? Out loud?"

Despite his newfound, unshakable faith in the existence of the Almighty, Simon found himself embarrassed by Frederika's tone. "Yes," he replied, in a firm but soft voice.

Frederika returned her attention to the book. "God helps those who help themselves. You pray; I'll work on this."

Simon regarded the diary, the neat lines of printed letters, with no spaces between them to indicate individual words. Only the date above each entry and the abbreviation U.S.A. were readable. Frederika had been struggling to decipher the same page for two hours.

"You'll never get it without the key," Simon told her. "If I understood right, you need the headline to the lead story of that day, in the most important newspaper of the country he was visiting."

46

"I'm beginning to believe it. What was the biggest news item a week ago, Simon? Think!"

"I can't remember. I'll look up the *New York Times* in the main library as soon as we get to Zurich."

Frederika wet her forefinger and riffled peevishly through the diary. "The sonofabitch. I hope he's burning right now in the hell he served."

Simon offered no reply, absorbing her profile in silence.

Frederika's finger slowed. Without looking up, she said, in an unemotional voice, "Stop staring at me."

"I'm not staring," Simon answered, shifting his focus past her nose and down the length of the terminal.

"Yes, you are. I can feel it. Just like I felt it a hundred times back in the library. You're thinking now what you were thinking then: This is the woman with the terrible reputation. No real friends. The parade of passing men. The history of telling half truths. Right?"

Simon let the silent seconds pile up, expecting Frederika finally to be compelled to confront him with her eyes. She refused. "Right," he lied. Bad as her opinion was, it would only be worse if he admitted he had been staring in the library all those times, as now, out of pure physical beguilement.

"You're not the only one who's looked at me that way," Frederika went on. "I saw it in all the men I dated . . . especially after I went to bed with them. The word was out. They expected me not to be there the next day."

And inevitably true, Simon thought. He understood their motivation; they were trying to memorize her perfect face, a souvenir to keep the heart from beating completely hollow in the lonely nights ahead.

"You don't have to stare," Frederika assured him. "I'm not going anywhere without you." At last she turned her face toward him, peering over the frames of her sunglasses. Her eyes were no longer the deep blue he had marveled at when he first rented a room from her. They had mutated to an apple green—much closer to the hue of a vampire's amber irises. Frederika's face was no less exquisite because of the change, but the cause of it frightened him. Along with a greatly enhanced night vision, she now possessed strength far beyond that of any other twenty-four-year-old woman. Simon acknowledged that such powers were heady stuff, but he wondered why Frederika seemed to enjoy more than fear the gifts of the Devil's own powder, traces of which still clearly coursed through her veins. Simon had already been warned by one of her many jilted paramours of a steely coldness behind Frederika's ultrafeminine exterior. He had no way of knowing if the infernal powder also instilled evil attitudes in its partakers. He reflected grimly that he would be hard put to detect a change in the woman; in truth, he knew so little about her.

Simon had become initially attracted to Frederika Vanderveen for the shallowest of reasons: she was breathtakingly beautiful. A slightly more honorable attraction arose out of his desire to investigate mysteries surrounding her. One was her reputation as a "vamp" (he had only realized the irony of the epithet while pacing the terminal wing), seducing older, powerful men and quickly discarding them. The second was a secret Simon alone had uncovered: her obsessive relationship with her father, Professor Frederik Vanderveen. Her domineering, dominating namesake had been a vampire in his own right, a high-profile advisor to international agencies who fed the world's hungry, driven not so much by humanitarianism as by his ego's voracious appetite for public adulation. In the privacy of his home he was even less generous—particularly with his love—and expected unquestioned adoration and loyalty. To preserve what little her husband had not destroyed of her id, Frederika's mother had fled Princeton and vanished when her daughter was only six. Subsequently, the only child was allowed to believe her mother dead. Not many years later, when Frederika was away at boarding school, her father had suffered a fatal heart attack, leaving the child-woman to believe his lack of affection and her mother's abandonment stemmed from some unforgivable deficiency within her. Her need to understand her parents' rejection became so desperate that she had resorted to private, futile rites of necromancy and finally to the charlatan channeler,

DeVilbiss. The vampire had merely used her in his personal quest to steal the Ahriman scrolls from the fortresslike university library. By bribing his way into Frederika's home, Simon had been able to solve the two interrelated mysteries. He had at least partially exorcised Frederik Vanderveen's stern ghost by hunting down the mother and bringing her back to Princeton. Yet, in spite of all his investigations, Frederika remained a virtual stranger to him. What he had unraveled were puzzles surrounding the young woman. He was immensely grateful that Frederika had accepted as altruistic his motivations for snooping. But he had no illusions that, now aware of his fascination for her, such a person would willingly let him probe the dark depths of her fiercely private thoughts.

At least Simon knew the reason for Frederika's new obsession: she believed DeVilbiss's diary would answer why the vampire had fed her so much of his precious magic powder.

Simon gently removed the book from her lap, took the pencil from her hand, and closed the cover. "You're not doing your headache any good by attacking this. Close your eyes. I already know why he gave you the powder."

One eyebrow cocked appraisingly at him, Frederika was a dead ringer for Grace Kelly in *High Society*. "Really? Tell me."

"Bride of Frankenstein syndrome," Simon answered with a smile, trying to undercut the horror of their shared peril. Frederika's expression remained severely demanding, so he hurried to elaborate. "After several hundred years of searching, he finally found the perfect woman. He hypnotized you not only to help him get the scrolls but also because he wanted to get you helplessly addicted to the powder. Then, in order not to die, you'd have to become a vampire. That was the only way he could force you to understand him and buy into his . . . can the undead have a lifestyle?" Frederika still declined response. "With understanding would come love," he concluded.

"Are you serious?" Frederika asked.

"Totally."

"I was afraid of that. Talk about a little knowledge being a dangerous thing. What does DeVilbiss say to the Devil: 'Pardon me,

Scratch, I'm thinking of hitchin' up with this little gal here, and I was wondering if you could double my salary'? Why would the Devil give powder to a woman who would probably betray him?"

Seeing Simon's smile flicker out, Frederika offered one of her own, from her seemingly inexhaustible arsenal. She slipped her hand reassuringly into his. "It can't be as easy as that, Simon. We beat DeVilbiss because he wasn't nearly as clever as he thought; we beat the Devil by pure luck. Let's not become guilty of hubris ourselves. We have to get the real answers from them"—she held up the diary—"not educated guesses. Let's concentrate on gathering information . . . and avoiding the police." She closed her eyes behind her sunglasses and settled back into her seat, maintaining a tight hold on Simon's hand. "And on the rest of our plan. Can it beat the Devil?"

Simon tried to ignore the deep blue irises gone green. "If we stay focused and flexible, and pray to God for help."

"We throw the police off the trail by buying airline tickets to Florida," Frederika said, in a schoolmarm tone.

"Done," Simon replied, feeling the warmth between their palms radiating up the length of his arm.

"We take a shuttle up to Toronto."

"Carrying our decoy scroll cases in plain view. Done."

"We take a direct overnight flight to Zurich, collect whatever DeVilbiss has in those banks. We—"

"Copy a few centuries of headlines in the library," Simon broke in.

"Correct. Visit our bastard vampire's home for other ammunition, then contact Dr. Elmasri and fly on to Athens."

"And somehow convince him to return to Princeton, to finish translating the scrolls . . . all the while staying in sunlight as much as we can," Simon concluded. "A straightforward strategy. Tactics to develop as occasions demand." Frederika made no reply. She let go of his hand, but only to move it up to his face, to trail her fingers familiarly along his cheek. He was forced to cross one leg over the other from the power of the touch, at the same time hating the fact that he allowed such a small gesture to enthrall him completely. He

50

still knew so little of what went on in her head—not even for certain the degree to which her tortured mind had been healed by his actions. He was well aware that she had no close friends even before she had admitted it, so what kind of friend could she be to him? Most frightening of all was her artless talent and seemingly compulsive penchant for lying. He had been pleased by the acting job he had done at Newark Airport. But all his rehearsed speeches, his gestures and feigned emotions as the comforting husband had paled in comparison to Frederika's tears. And the devastating effect on their mark of her simple smile. Wasn't the problem of the fiery breath of Hades licking at his tail enough to deal with? Why couldn't he control his passion for this clearly dangerous near-stranger sitting next to him? And would it become even more difficult once her eyes were again deep blue?

Detective Pental slumped at his desk, chin propped on fists, staring through bloodshot eyes at the sheets of paper Simon Penn had allegedly given his friend Richard Chen. The sheets had already been authenticated by a staff member at Princeton Theological Seminary as the precisely formed handwriting of Reverend Willy Spencer, the translator of the notorious Scrolls of Ahriman. Ray had read the final passages half a dozen times, but he forced himself to restudy the words, hoping to understand how the very intelligent Simon Penn came to believe in the fantastic:

> These instrumentalities of evil may no longer walk the earth, as they did when they were beings of the light. The blessed air is to them as the sea is to man; if they enter it for any time they may perish. The air protects man as the ocean protects fish, an ever-present refuge. Nevertheless, the legion of darkness are an enemy of vastly superior intelligence, who will devise methods of harvesting despite the hazard.
>
> Their most diabolical method is to turn man against his own kind. This they do by finding those who do not fear God, offering such ones unending life in exchange

for doing their bidding. To help these venal creatures in their tasks, they change them into something more powerful and vicious than their kind, as a shark is to a sturgeon. For their own sake, they cause these supermen to drink the blood of their own kind to survive, and to move in the same darkness to which they themselves are confined. Such servants of evil are known by their pale skin and the amber hue of their eyes.

Ray glanced wearily at the late hour on his desk clock, then at the portrait photograph of his wife and daughters. Even if the scrolls had been correctly translated, it didn't mean they told the truth, he thought. They were supposed to be two-and-a-half thousand years old. That was the time men believed in Baal and Ptah. Back then, vampires lived side by side with giants and fire-breathing dragons.

To become a detective, Ray had completed two semesters of evening criminology courses at Jersey City State, followed by the past summer at the police academy. They had prepared him well for burglaries, extortion, rape, murder, blackmail, counterfeiting, arson, bunko, and frauds. But not one minute had been spent surveying the supernatural.

Ray wheeled around in his seat and stared through the slats of the Venetian blinds at the darkling, dying hours of Christmas Day. He had never fully lost his childhood fear of the dark, which he thought stupid, since nothing—not even anything totally natural—had ever attacked him out of its inky cloak. Then again, the *Trentonian* had recently run a full-page cover headline: LOCAL MAN DEAD IN COLORADO VAMPIRE KILLING. It was not the *New York Times,* but neither was it a grocery store tabloid. He rolled down his shirtsleeves and rebuttoned his cuffs. What was it Hamlet had said to Horatio about more things in heaven and hell than we know of in our philosophies?

"Ray!"

The detective looked up the hallway. His boss, police chief Francis Littlefield, was striding in his direction. As always, the chief wore the jacket of his three-piece suit. His shoes were just as spit-

and-polish bright as they had been that morning. In keeping with the nature of Princeton, Francis (never Frank) was more politician than policeman. Law and order had as much do to with intellectual acts as physical ones in this high-priced burg. A fat salary had lured him away from upscale Madison, which was the only New Jersey town that gave more parking tickets than Princeton (the police's principal activity).

Littlefield clutched a well-stuffed manila folder in one hand. In the other he held a lit cigarette. Smoking was forbidden in the building. He controlled his habit until after all the other Township Hall offices (Mayor's, Violations Bureau, Health Department, Civil Rights, Tax, Engineering and Sewer) were closed. Ordinarily at this hour, he could be found at either the Nassau or Peacock Inn, hoisting bourbons. Ray knew what was holding him inside Township Hall on Christmas Day evening: the airlines had finally tracked down two passengers, now en route to Orlando, Florida, holding tickets in the names Simon Penn and Frederika Vanderveen.

"Glad you're still here," Littlefield said, vocal cords ragged from decades of smoking. "I know how much OT you've been putting in. You deserve tomorrow off, but I need you to take an A.M. tour over at the hospital."

Annoyance at Littlefield's words dissolved rapidly into curiosity. "Something to do with our vampire?" Ray asked.

Chief Littlefield's cigarette hand thrust out. "I don't want to hear that word . . . not even in the station!"

The mistake had left Ray's mouth before he could catch it. He and every other officer in the station that afternoon had been given a scathing lecture by Littlefield, immediately after a call came in from the *Trenton Times* asking about the vampire just killed on the Princeton campus. Someone among the eight people who had been inside the Rare Manuscripts section that morning and had read or heard about the "vampire note" was busy peddling information to the media. Every once in a while, the inevitable date rape happened on campus. Everyone in the township police knew it. And yet, invariably, the official report was never filed. If it had been, a yearly national study on campus sex crimes would have contained Princeton University's venerable name. It was simply not to the benefit of students to sully the name of the institution from which they were working so hard to graduate. P.U. had sweated to amass one of the top five endowments in the nation. It was also by far the town's largest employer. No one wanted its reputation marred, especially by something as circuslike as a scroll-stealing vampire. Even before the leak to the media, Littlefield had received admonishing calls from the university's president. If the story wasn't desensationalized soon with "hard facts," it meant his job come next election. The chief promised to personally crucify any officer caught talking about the case outside the station, to the media or otherwise. The alarm in Littlefield's eyes spoke eloquently of his fears: the *National Enquirer, Hard Copy,* Paul Harvey. Now Ray felt obliged to help two people involved in this case: Simon Penn, whom he had blown off on the telephone, and Francis Littlefield, whom he owed for his recent promotion. The problem was that one wanted him to believe in the supernatural and the other wanted him to disprove it.

"Sorry," Ray said, then shut his mouth.

"Kick that can over here," Littlefield commanded, of Ray's wastebasket. Once it was in range, he used it as an enormous ashtray. "It's that goddamned old lady who came to the Vanderveen house with the fruit basket. She showed up at the hospital."

"When?"

"About fifteen minutes ago. Some orderly finds the lock to the morgue broken. It's pitch black inside, so he reaches in and flicks on the light. The old woman comes charging at him like a bat out of hell. He says he tried to stop her but she knocked him aside like he was made of feathers; I think he was so spooked by the dark, the morgue, and her flight that he just fell backward before she even touched him."

"Is he an old guy?" Ray asked.

The chief looked annoyed by the question. "No. Mike Davis said he played defensive tackle at Trenton State a few years ago. But he still could have lost his balance."

For the first time in his life, Ray Pental felt his skin crawl. "Was his ID positive?"

"Identical." The chief tossed the butt of his cigarette into the basket, drowning it in a Styrofoam cup half filled with coffee. "All the slab drawers were shut. The orderly thinks she didn't have time to find DeVilbiss."

"So she may be back."

"Right. We need to know what she wants with him, and especially if she knew him when he was alive. You know, have her swear he was a nut case with superhuman delusions. We've got to sweep this vampire nonsense aside no later than tomorrow, Ray." Littlefield squinted at his detective. "What's the matter? You look worried."

Ray cleared his throat. "Maybe I should be. Doesn't it scare you that she's searching for someone in a pitch-black room?"

"Scare me? No. Maybe she had a penlight. I'm sure there's a simple answer."

"Occam's razor."

"What?"

Evidently, his chief had not had the same criminology instructor. "Nothing. Has the coroner done any special tests, like the note suggested?"

Littlefield plunked the folder down on the top edge of Ray's cubicle divider. "The coroner hasn't done anything yet. But what exactly should he do: saw off the corpse's leg bone and count the rings? Anything over a hundred and he's supernatural?"

Ray shrugged. "Maybe look for different-type blood platelets. I don't know. There must be parts of the body that record age."

"I hope so," Littlefield said. "I want quick, incontrovertible proof that the guy is as human as you or me." A telephone rang near the front of the station. "Maybe that's Florida calling." The chief left the cubicle in a hurry. Ray noted the perfect taper of his razor-cut hairline. He made a mental note to ask Littlefield in less tense times where he had his hair cut. Ray was sure it cost a small fortune, but maybe he'd treat himself once or twice a year.

55

Ray glanced again at his clock. He shoved his papers in the top drawer of his desk and locked up. As he was pulling his jacket on, he spotted Littlefield's forgotten manila folder on top of the cubicle divider. He grabbed it, resisted the temptation to peek inside, and headed toward the chief's office. Littlefield was just hanging up his phone. A fresh cigarette protruded from tightly pursed lips like the barrel of a gun.

"Fuck!" Littlefield greeted Ray. "That was Orlando. Airport police picked up 'Mr. Simon Penn and Miss Frederika Vanderveen' as they got off the plane." A single bead of sweat had appeared on his forehead.

"What's wrong?" Pental said obligingly.

" 'Simon Penn' turned out to be some schmuck named Murray Diamond. He'd bought the tickets for himself and his girlfriend in Newark Airport around noon, from a man and woman who fit our fugitives to a T. Our librarians bought themselves the hours their ticket holders were up in the plane and got cash for tickets they put on Penn's Visa card. More cash to run with, on a day the banks are closed."

"Tough luck," Ray offered tersely. He could have mentioned how he was not at all surprised. He could have amplified Littlefield's opinion on how smart Simon Penn was, that the quiet, seemingly ineffectual librarian had a nature resourceful enough to make him more elusive than Dillinger. But that would have led to a discussion on how a person that smart could kill someone else and be totally convinced that someone was a vampire.

Ray said nothing.

CHAPTER THREE

December 26

✧

If evil need not be and should not be, if things have somehow gone

wrong and evil has intruded itself into a world which could have

been free of it, who or what is responsible? It cannot be man,

because so much of the evil in the world is beyond all human

contriving, and so the roots of evil are found in superhuman

agencies—God . . . , the Devil, evil spirits, the dead, creatures of

the underworld and the night.

—Richard Cavendish, *The Powers of Evil*

cVᎣ

When Father Ferro was summoned for his follow-up meeting concerning the scrolls, the place designated was an inner, subterranean chamber of the palace, one well hidden from the outside world. Dante wondered as he strode toward Vatican City if the meeting place was symbolic, if the intent was once again to suppress the scrolls, as in the days of Pope Alexander VI.

This morning after Christmas, Father Ferro walked with no burdens in his hands, and he was thankful. As he left the Piazza del Risorgimento and entered the Vatican walls, he elevated his arms from his sides and rolled them in small circles. His deltoid and trapezius muscles ached from a strenuous early morning workout. He had traded the badge for the chalice, the secular world for the sacred, but there was no way he would give up his alternate morning rituals of running and pumping iron.

Dante Ferro had been born into a family of policemen. The family lineage traced back to mercenary soldiers of the fourteenth century, called *condottieri* by the Italians. In the sixteenth and seventeenth centuries, his relatives were tamed into house guards for some of the more affluent Florentine families . . . including the Medici. This branch of Dante's clan was German. Every once in a while, marriage to northern Italian stock would reveal through offspring their dormant blond-haired, blue-eyed genes. Not so with

Dante. He possessed the chocolate-brown eyes, curly, near-black hair, and olive complexion so common among the Italian. His cheeks were still full and round at fifty-eight, contradicting the age suggested by his gray-salted hair. The wrinkles of age and humor around his eyes were softened by an unnaturally long set of lashes. As a child, Dante's mother and aunts had constantly embarrassed him by swearing to various female saints that he had a face any woman would kill to own. The same comments had outraged his father, who had made machismo a way of life. Dante's two older brothers were cut whole from their father's cloth. They both, for example, played the uniquely Florentine sport Calcio Storico. It was a brutal five-hundred-year-old game, with elements of soccer, rugby, and football but mostly of street brawling. The leather ball provided little more than a focus of attack, and anything short of murder was fair. Dante detested the game. But he played it for the family's sake and played it well, gaining two broken ribs and losing one molar during the years he participated. Dante also became a policeman. His father and brothers were too good to him, too loving, and too afraid for his masculinity to disappoint. He had seen the fear in their eyes every time he listened to opera, every time they found him reading the classics, every time he admitted he had spent a Saturday afternoon taking in the art treasures of the Uffizi Gallery or the Palazzo Pitti. Or worse, the Accademia, the repository of the towering David and the other marble masterpieces of "that fucking faggot Michelangelo." Dante only knew for certain that he was exactly what his family feared when he became a teenager. Even after he accepted his nature, he did nothing about it, so deeply had his father and brothers inculcated their homophobia in him.

Dante learned to sublimate his sexual desires into pursuits of perfection. The first was of a physical nature, training his body into a form even the great Michelangelo would have been proud to copy. The second was mental, using his keen mind and sensitive ear to master several foreign languages, both modern and ancient. His conquest of Latin, ancient Greek, and Akkadian was a private matter. Handling English and French like a native became his passport out of the ranks of common police work and into the guarding of foreign dignitaries. Diplomatic work also necessitated his relocation to Rome, out from under his family's vigilance. Safe at a distance, he no longer had to date women to quell their fears; inventing affairs was sufficient. On holiday get-togethers, they joked with him as the "perpetual playboy," always too loudly, always trading exaggerated winks among themselves. Times became more liberal, but it was clear that none of the Ferros wanted that liberalization to touch Dante.

The morally ambiguous world of international diplomacy, with its ever-shifting rules and alliances, appalled Dante and brought him closer to God. Every time he returned home from his job, there was the old dome of St. Peter's out his front window, as it had stood for centuries. He found himself attending Mass more and more frequently, the unchanged rituals and the immutable laws behind them providing a wellspring of comfort. One winter night, staring at the dome, he startled himself by entertaining his first serious thought about the priesthood. His father had died of cirrhosis of the liver on Dante's forty-fourth birthday. It took less than nine years for his older brother, Paolo, to loyally duplicate Papa's alcoholic suicide. Franco, the remaining brother, was shot dead by a cuck-olded husband a year later. Given such abundant cause, Mama Ferro succumbed shortly afterward to that pandemic disease among Mediterranean females: worry. Dante became the patriarch of the Ferros, with no one left to embarrass. He had served enough years to earn an early police pension, allowing him the luxury of training for the priesthood. Thus, he avoided the temptations of his latent desires: the only emotion stronger than his fear of disappointing his family was his loathing for priests (hetero- or homosexual) who betrayed their sacred vow of chastity.

Dante was disappointed to find no Swiss Guards outside the chamber doors. It signaled that the Pontiff would not be part of the meeting. The right door stood open a crack. Dante knocked lightly. A male voice called him inside. He stepped into the room's warm, indirect lighting and found himself gazing across a large, oval conference table, fashioned of the finest rosewood. He had not been given the roster for the meeting, but he anticipated awesome Church power. He was not disappointed. Monsignor Squillante, the cardinal Secretariate of State, was seated directly across from the doors and under a Burgundian wood carving of Christ on the Cross. In front of him, fanned across the table, were all the documents Dante had presented the previous morning. To Squillante's right and left sat men Father Ferro dealt with on a semiregular basis. Cardinals Chelli and Del Gesu were the heads of the Apostolic Chancery and the Datary, respectively. The Apostolic Chancery had been created in the fourth century, to preserve all the Holy See's letters and records. The Datary arose in the eleventh century, out of a necessity to authenticate documents. Both Chelli and Del Gesu had been gone from Rome when Father Ferro had made his startling find, forcing him to bypass them and approach Squillante directly, for time's sake. Tough as Ferro had been as a policeman, his stomach churned at the prospect of facing the combined ire of these proud, territorial cardinals. Both men were septuagenarians. Chelli looked like he was made of papyrus; Del Gesu's shrunken head was dominated by rheumy, old eyes, a prodigious proboscis, and elephantine ears. But the Church was not the street; power here had nothing to do with physical vigor or beauty.

The monsignor made perfunctory reintroductions. Father Ferro was invited to sit. He took a chair on the door side of the room, across from Squillante. Del Gesu was the first to speak. He prefaced his words with the briefest of smiles, one Dante could not be certain was genuine. "Who would have guessed such a great emergency could arise from our cellars, eh?"

Father Ferro looked Del Gesu directly in the eyes. "It seemed to be quite urgent, considering—"

"You were right in bringing this to our immediate attention, Father," Monsignor Squillante assured him. "Thank you for your concerns. We have reviewed all the materials. We have also made discreet consultations with a few trusted scholars outside of our walls. There is no question in our minds that these old scrolls which have resurfaced in America are genuine."

Ferro relaxed minutely.

"But," Squillante continued, "precisely because they are some 2,600 years old, we believe their warning of a worldwide vampire plague is no longer valid."

"But how can you think that?" Dante demanded, the sudden tensing of all his muscles pulling him up and forward in his seat. "You accept the scrolls' age, and you must realize that six of the seven predictions have already come true. Do you doubt my translating?"

Squillante looked to Del Gesu for a reply.

A pair of half glasses hung on a gold chain around Cardinal Del Gesu's scrawny neck. He fitted them delicately onto the bridge of his nose, then consulted Dante's notes on the table. "Not at all. And we are satisfied that you have filled in the gaps correctly. The first prediction clearly refers to man's conquest of the skies with wings. The second . . . man's ability to create 'pillars of deadly fire in the sky' . . . is the harnessing of atomic fission."

"Followed by man discovering 'the invisible spiral ladder' of DNA," Dante added forcefully. "Each prediction involving man's scientific advances, each event occurring in the proper sequence, each in this century, with an almost geometric shortening of the time span between successive occurrences. How can you dismiss these scrolls because of their age when they are speaking of this very era?"

Cardinal Chelli chuckled and looked to his left for support. "Their miraculous prescience still does not guarantee that the dire warning at the end will come to pass."

"Why not?" Father Ferro demanded, barely controlling his anger.

"The answer hangs behind me," Chelli replied, referring to the Burgundian cross. "That wooden shape represents more than ancient art. By one tree the Devil conquered us; by another he was conquered forever. We believe the words of the Bible are literal truth. Not just some of the words but all of them. Therefore, as it tells us, at one time there were abundant demons and witches upon the earth. And, we have no doubt, vampires as well. So many nations' folklores contain vampire stories that they must have existed.

But all that ended with Christ's sacrifice. The Cross of Calvary transformed the world, rewrote the mystic rules, and undoubtedly rendered the elaborate warning of the scrolls useless."

"Exactly," Squillante picked up. "Directly after Adam's temptation Satan was banished from earth, to eternal darkness. And yet he found surrogates to torment and tempt man. Witches, demons, and vampires. And then God gave us the Resurrection, and the Devil's last hold on earth slipped away. All but our collective memory of these creatures vanished. Since then, salvation has become purely a matter of each man's direct relationship with the Creator."

Dante stared at the self-satisfied tribunate for a moment. "But what if the plague of the scrolls' warning isn't caused by the Devil?"

Three easy smiles disappeared as one. "How can that be?" Del Gesu asked.

Father Ferro eased back into his seat. "Do you think it's chance that every prediction in the scrolls refers to an accomplishment of mankind? Could the predictions not as easily have used natural milestones . . . the great Japanese earthquake of 1948 or the meteors that just crashed into Jupiter?" Dante paused for a reply.

"Finish making your point," Squillante said. His face, among the three, showed the most foreboding.

"If, after Christ's sacrifice on the Cross, salvation has become purely a matter of each man's relationship with God, perhaps his damnation is a matter of his direct relationship with Satan. Perhaps the Devil no longer can force undying monsters upon us, but we are now advanced enough to buy the secret from him. At the price of our souls."

"Can you be more specific, Father?" Monsignor Squillante asked.

"Frankly, no. I am just thinking . . . and worrying . . . out loud. I believe that those ancient scrolls did not surface at this precise time by chance. I fear that if the warning were no longer valid, they would not have appeared."

The two cardinals looked at the monsignor, who looked again at the priest. "Will you excuse us for a minute, Father?"

Dante nodded and took himself from the room, closing the door solidly behind him. The requested minute expanded to five. Then Monsignor Squillante opened the door and gestured for Dante to retake his seat.

As he slowly circled the long table, Squillante said to Dante, "When Niccolò and Maffeo Polo became among the first western-ers to visit the Far East, they impressed Kublai Khan so much with their religion that he requested they return home and bring him one hundred missionaries, to spread the word among his people. When the brothers petitioned Gregory the Tenth for such men, the Pope saw fit to send the 'heathens' only two Dominicans, who soon lost heart and turned back. Kublai Khan was then emperor over China, Tibet, Mongolia, India, and Burma. That was in the year of our Lord 1271. Perhaps a billion more souls would have been Christian had Gregory not virtually ignored our Lord's Great Commission." Squillante took his seat. "The three of us are not eager to commit a similar sin of omission."

Despite the monsignor's comforting words, this time Dante did not let down his guard. "Then the Church will involve itself in the publicizing of the scrolls?" he hoped aloud.

"Yes. We want them to come to light," the Secretariate an-swered. "We can only guess why Alexander the Sixth had their translation banned . . . possibly simply because it said the earth circles the sun. And even if the predicted vampire plague never occurs . . ." Squillante paused; his eyes rolled heavenward, and his right hand traced the sign of the Cross across his face and chest. ". . . it seems to us that these miraculous writings can only help to plead the truth of God's existence."

"As well as the Devil's," Del Gesu added archly.

"Nothing wrong in that," Chelli said, in his cracked, small voice.

"There remains, however, one large problem," Squillante went on. "One that your talents are uniquely suited for, Father Ferro."

"Translation," Dante replied, with assurance.

"Perhaps that, too, in time. Actually, we were thinking of police work. Only minutes before you arrived, we received word that the scrolls were stolen. The translator, a Presbyterian pastor named

64

Spencer, was killed a few days past. Yesterday, another man was found dead, inside the library where the scrolls were kept. They have vanished, apparently stolen by two of the library's employees."

"Terrible," Father Ferro responded, truly rattled.

"Almost as if the Devil were still at work," Del Gesu said, raising one hoary eyebrow at Chelli.

"Terrible indeed," Squillante said. "Apparently, others put as much stock in these rolls of parchment as you do, Father Ferro. In your work as a diplomatic bodyguard, did you ever hear of the *Serafini Segreti?*"

"I can't say that I have, Your Reverence," Dante answered carefully. He, along with all the high-ups in the Roman police force, had heard vague rumors of the Vatican's quasi-army. It reputedly did the dirty, political jobs that the Christian world's most powerful religion could not. Dante hoped that this did not include such things as the arming of IRA provos or the extermination of Central American Communists.

Monsignor Squillante turned his toothy, yellow smile to the cardinals flanking him. "You see? Perhaps the seraphim are more secret than you believed." Father Ferro reflected that this "keeper of secrets" truly embodied the original meaning of "secretary." Squillante refocused on the librarian priest. "The Church occasionally has need of special secular services. Finding stolen scrolls, for example. Fortunately, there are good Catholics in almost every country and every walk of life who are willing to serve in this way."

"I see," Dante replied.

"Understand, however, that you will deal alone with outsiders, offering only yourself and your past talents on the Church's behalf. Is this acceptable to you, Father?"

"Yes, Your Reverence."

"You do have the right to refuse."

"I wish to see this through to the end." If the scrolls' testament brought just a handful of lapsed Catholics back into the fold, as he suspected they would, it was well worth the effort to Dante.

The monsignor gently pushed the old documents across the

table toward Dante. "Good. Then do your best. Go home and pack a suitcase with street clothes; arrangements will be made for you to fly to America this morning." Squillante glanced at Del Gesu, who was stifling a yawn. "Perhaps the Devil *is* behind this after all, Mario. Father Ferro will no doubt keep us informed."

Simon told himself that it was a matter of subjective fears, but the Customs line seemed to be crawling forward. He looked at the line to his right, and its queue of airline passengers didn't seem to be faring any better. He had thought that Swiss customs officers would be more efficient. Was it Bertrand Russell, he tried to recall, who had defined the difference between heaven and hell? In heaven, the English were the policemen, the Germans the mechanics, the French the cooks, the Italians the lovers, and the Swiss the administrators; in hell, the English were the cooks, the Germans the police, the French the administrators, the Italians the mechanics, and the Swiss the lovers.

What made Simon so nervous was that the Zurich airport wasn't that crowded. The officers just seemed to be taking their methodical time, scrutinizing everything coming in. It seemed ironic to Simon, given the country's reputation for accepting the money of every world scoundrel without question. He turned back to Frederika, to give her a look of assurance. She peered over the tops of her sunglasses to return his smile. She clutched DeVilbiss's diary in her right hand; one of the empty metal cylinders hung from her elbow; the other hand held her suitcase and purse, and she slid her train case forward with her foot whenever she moved. As they had approached the line, without explaining her reason, Frederika had gestured for Simon to go first.

At last, Simon's turn came. He fished into his coat pocket for his passport.

"Anything to declare?" the customs person asked in English, noting the passport's U.S. eagle insignia.

"No, nothing," Simon answered. He placed his declaration form on the counter.

The officer flipped open the passport, glanced at the expiration date and the photo, then typed Simon's name and passport number into his computer. No alarms flashed out of the machine. Handing the passport back, the official said, "What's in the tube?"

"It's empty," Simon replied. He unscrewed the top and offered a peek. Gesturing to Frederika and her identical container, he added, "We like to collect posters, and they get bent up unless we protect them this way."

The officer nodded his understanding. He waved his hand. "Thank you. Next!"

All Frederika had to do was flash her smile and ask the officer for suggestions on the best places to dine in Zurich. The man barely maintained enough presence of mind to record her name and passport number. She could have carried several sticks of dynamite in with her.

Once they had walked a distance from Customs, Simon remarked, "Who says you can't get along on just good looks?"

"You certainly can't," Frederika countered. "And why didn't you try sweating a little harder?"

Simon could see that she was squinting behind the sunglasses. The tone of her remarks matched his level of badinage, but her expression seemed grim. "We were lucky, but they still got our names," she said. "So will any hotel concierge. I figure another twelve hours' grace, max, before Interpol puts out an all points bulletin on us."

"But you have a plan," Simon came back.

Frederika nodded, maintaining her long-legged stride across the terminal. "Inside DeVilbiss's Swiss passport, I found a card for a photography shop. On Stadelhoferstrasse. I think we can find new identities there."

They had found more than enough Swiss francs in DeVilbiss's black bag to pay for the ride from the airport into town. The photography store was open, the ground-floor business of a very old commercial building. The shop was an incongruous mixture of sleek, whistle-bright and technologically advanced equipment sold among creaking, unpolished wood floors, dusty display cases, and flickering fluorescent lights. The solitary man behind the counter was shifty-eyed and ferret-faced, giving Simon instant hope that this was the place to purchase illegal documents. To their increased fortune, there were no other customers in the place.

"Darf ich Ihnen helfen?" the man asked.

"Ich hoffe," Frederika said, without losing a beat. *"Wir sind Amerikaner."*

"Ach, so!" the man exclaimed. "I speak English, if you wish."

"You speak German?" Frederika asked Simon.

"Only a *Bissel.*"

Frederika again faced the salesman. "English it is." She checked that no one was coming through the front door, then removed DeVilbiss's Swiss, Italian, and British passports and spread them across the counter. The man regarded them with no question in his eyes. Frederika opened the Swiss passport, where the shop's business card lay, and pointed to DeVilbiss's photograph. "This man is a good friend of ours. He tells us he's also a friend of yours."

Now the man put on an exaggerated look of perplexity. "I . . . don't seem to remember him. His name is DeVilbiss?"

"He has several names," Frederika replied. "We want other names as well."

Simon drew his hand from his coat pocket. He held the equivalent of a hundred dollars in Swiss francs. "This should help your memory."

The man accepted the money. "I remember his face now. I took that picture. I can take passport pictures for you also. But I cannot help you to find other names."

"Who can?" Frederika asked. Her hand suddenly held a hundred-dollar bill. The man reached out for it, but she pulled it back.

"You are police," the man decided.

"Exactly the opposite," Frederika answered. "Who *can?"* she repeated.

The unnamed man assessed the couple. "In what canton is the city of New Orleans?"

"We have states, not cantons," Frederika said, "and the answer is Louisiana." She offered the bill.

The man accepted it. "I will take your photos." He pushed a pad and pen toward Simon. "Write who you wish to be, your addresses and so forth." As Simon wrote, he added, "You will need to be at the passenger train storage yard at ten o'clock tonight. There is a building with a big red sign painted on its side above the tracks. A man will meet you there. I do not know his name. I only call a telephone number and leave photos in a post box."

"How much does he charge?" Frederika asked.

The man shrugged. "I do not know. It is not my business." He sidled out from behind the display cases. "This way." He pointed toward an opening masked by filthy black curtains. "I will take your pictures in there." He accepted the pad from Simon and studied it. "Congratulations on your recent marriage, Mr. and Mrs. Mitman. Did Mr. DeVilbiss come to your wedding?"

"No," Frederika answered, sweeping up the three passports in a single motion and returning them to her coat pocket. "It was a daytime affair."

The Vampire's mood was black. His Infernal Lord had stated that he had sufficient time to reach the couple who had stolen the scrolls. By that, the voice had meant "just enough time." The Vampire had to tear through the night, across the treacherously icy and mountainous countrysides of Romania and Hungary, to reach the railroad hub of Budapest. Dawn prevented him from driving farther. His intent was to take a train to Vienna and thence across Austria into Switzerland, not the most direct rail route but the quickest one. He had hoped the holiday time of year would keep people at home with their families, but it was obvious that once the Iron Curtain had fallen, every Hungarian with spare cash was heading to Innsbruck or St. Moritz.

The train was packed. Only one compartment among those of the nonsmoking cars had empty seats. The reason was clear: a very large and violent-looking man was puffing furiously on a cigar. Its vile smell seeped through the compartment's closed door into the aisle. No one dared to enter and challenge the man. The Vampire opened the door and slid in his two suitcases. The smoker, who was about thirty years old and looked like a heavyweight prize fighter who had lost more bouts than he won, greeted the Vampire with a glare of hostility several degrees beyond unwelcome.

The Vampire pointed to a prominent sign on the compartment wall. "This is a nonsmoking car," he observed, in Hungarian.

The occupant, in turn, pointed to the window with his cigar. "The window's down. I only lit this when the train stopped. I'll put it out when it starts again." The open window had lowered the compartment's temperature to the point where the man's breath was whitely visible.

The Vampire held the brute's fierce stare, unblinking, until the smoker looked away, out into the dawn light. The battle apparently won, the Vampire looked to the luggage racks. His mood turned a deeper shade of black when he saw that the lone occupant had placed his luggage on the opposite side of the compartment, as yet another offensive gesture to deny space to others. The Vampire put himself directly in front of the man and hoisted his suitcases up. Between these he shoved his umbrella, making sure to place the handle on the window side.

The Vampire sat, staring at the other man through his black sunglasses, muffler against his lower lip, gloved hands gripping opposite sleeves. The train lurched forward. The brute continued to smoke.

"The train is moving," the Vampire pointed out.

"Just a couple more puffs."

The Vampire decided that the magic number was ten. He counted slowly, to give the smoker a chance. The man was, after all, clearly a troublemaker . . . the sort his Infernal Lords wanted on the earth. But beyond a certain point—the count of ten to be exact—his rudeness would cross the line into intolerability. The cigar went out the window on eleven. Just one beat extra, but too late. The Vampire let their accelerating speed push the smoke out of the compartment for a few seconds, then lifted the window back into place. A minute later, the conductor entered the compartment and asked for the Vampire's ticket. His nostrils flared at the noxious odor lingering in the compartment but, looking from one angry face to the other, he retreated without a lecture.

The sun had broken over the city's lower rooftops. The Vampire returned to the window and grabbed the shade.

"Wait a minute," the brute said. "I want to look outside. I can't smoke; you can't have darkness."

The Vampire smiled at the man. "Enjoy the view. Look all you can." He sat down on his padded bench, put his head against the compartment's outer wall and spread the morning newspaper across his face and chest.

The first name ever given to the Vampire was Bakum. His place of birth was in the east of present-day Uzbekistan, the religion of his people polytheistic, and the social structure divided into three castes. At the top of the structure were the chiefs and priests, followed by warriors, and finally husbandmen and cattle breeders. Bakum belonged to the lowest caste, but his father's herds were large and, as firstborn male, he stood to inherit them all. For his caste, his family's status and wealth were great, and nothing mattered as much to him as his pride. Bakum had two older sisters and one brother, a year his junior. The brother's name was Vatra.

Bakum was known throughout the region for his keen mind, but his brother's fame at discourse grew even faster. Their father died soon after Bakum's eighteenth birthday, and the heir's first edict was to banish Vatra from the clan. Vatra had picked up the rudiments of cuneiform writing from a wise man who had no children. The ruler of the region was Hystaspes, and his need for recorders of court proceedings was great. Vatra was welcomed into the royal house as a scribe. Already at court was a man recently arrived from Median, named Zarathustra. By the force of his intellect he had gained great favor with Hystaspes. Zarathustra's secular suggestions had resulted in a system of irrigation ditches and a bumper harvest of crops that had swelled the king's granaries. His sacred philosophies had begun to convert the court and several of the priests to the worship of a single God, whom he called Ahura Mazda. Vatra embraced Zarathustra's thinking and quickly grew in favor with the king. Within several months he was a priest . . . and two castes higher than his brother. The year was 586 B.C.

At the end of that year, Vatra began to have dreams of direct visitations by an angel from the Ahura Mazda. Wisdom far beyond man's state of advancement was revealed to him, as proof that the dreams came from a superior being. The point of the visitations, however, was a dire warning. The One True God was pleased by Vatra's piety and devotion and had chosen him to warn the earth of the Devil's ways. Thousands of years before, God's favorite angel had rebelled, leading legions of angelic followers in a disastrous war against their Creator. Lucifer, the bringer of light, was cast into eternal darkness. No longer were he and his followers allowed to roam the earth. Man was free to determine his fate, through his own acts of good and evil. But the malevolent angel now known as Satan saw a way to continue his influence on earth: he would offer unending life to those men willing to work evil on his behalf. The symbolic sealing of their servitude was the periodic need to drink the blood of their former brethren. At a particular time in the future (that time pinpointed through seven specific events), such creatures could multiply with great speed, threatening the very existence of mankind. Through Vatra, the dream angel declared, God would rebalance the scales. The young priest was instructed to write down all he had dreamed, not on clay tablets (as was the fashion of the region) but on the hides of sacredly sacrificed calves. He was warned to speak to no man of this until the scrolls were completed.

The fame of Vatra increased throughout the region until hardly a day passed without Bakum hearing praise for his brother. Bakum had never been a believer, but now he visited the shrine of the increasingly maligned god Mitra and spoke out loud a deal: if Mitra would strike Vatra dead, Bakum would throw his family's influence and wealth against Zarathustra and the new upstart god Ahura Mazda.

To Bakum's astonishment, the stone god spoke. It had a small voice, like wind disturbing a zither. It thanked Bakum for his devotion and offered a much more exciting proposition: if he killed his own brother and destroyed the scrolls Vatra was secretly writing, Bakum would be granted unending life. He would walk among men no longer as an equal but as a superior being, invulnerable to aging or injury. Bakum did not debate long. He sent a slave to the court of Hystaspes with a message for his brother. He wished, he said, to know more about this god of all, the Ahura Mazda. If Vatra would forgive his brother's former jealousies and return to teach his clan, a sacrifice of twenty cattle would return with Vatra to Hystaspes's court.

Vatra rushed to his death. To be sure the supernatural being within the statue would not renege on its promise, Bakum took his brother to Mitra's temple, ostensibly so that they could destroy the idol together. Vatra's courage was great; only when he had half the skin of his back flayed off and was threatened with the loss of his eyes did he reveal the hiding place of his scrolls. The voice from the statue ordered Bakum to slit Vatra's throat and drink the blood. Bakum hurried to obey, eager to silence his brother's cries for mercy. To his amazement, the voice then ordered Bakum to take the bronze hammer and chisel he had brought as a ruse and actually attack the statue, breaking off its right hand. This he was to keep with him night and day, so that the supernatural being might never lose track of him.

Bakum journeyed immediately to the caves where the scrolls were hidden. When they were burned, the voice counseled Bakum not to return to his clan. There would be no question who had killed the young priest. It promised, however, that Bakum would have riches and fame beyond the imaginings of any mere herdsman. Near the cave, Bakum found the first supply of the golden powder that extended and elevated life.

The voice's promise was fulfilled as soon as Bakum reached the Babylonian farmlands of Akkad. Here, the agriculture that Zarathustra preached to Hystaspes's herdsmen had been established for centuries. The Babylonians' chief male god, who made his home in the temple of Nippur, was Enlil, the Lord Wind, who separated the wheat from the chaff. A crucial element of Enlil's myth was his dying each spring, just as the prevailing wind failed, to be resurrected each fall by the goddess Inanna. At the suggestion of the voice, the vampire-novitiate entered Nippur. Bakum strode into

73

the temple on the god's holy night of death, was challenged as a stranger by two guards, used his unnatural strength to rip their arms off and, before he could himself be dismembered, declared himself the incarnation of Enlil. From his belt he withdrew a gleaming dagger. He invited the chief priest to stab him in the chest and promptly laid himself upon the altar, waiting. The boldness of his actions so frightened the priest that the king himself stepped forward and sank the dagger deep. Bakum cried out and let his head and arms hang limp, feeling his blood flow freely across his chest and onto the stone altar. From the bag that hung from his belt, the voice within Mitra's hand warned all to leave the temple and not return until the following night. The exalted gathering trampled each other in their haste to flee.

The next night, Bakum resurrected as Enlil in their dumbstruck presence. Using the temple as his home, he was worshiped, fed, and pampered, and every ten days he was offered a sacrificial virgin female, whom he first ravished, then drained of blood. He controlled the city of Nippur for two hundred years, living with no fear of his subjects, going so far as to consume his bitter amber powder, mixed with fermented honey and water, before their eyes. They called the mixture ambrosia, and the spreading word of it crept into the mythology of neighboring lands as the nectar of the gods, until in ancient Greek it came to mean "not mortal."

Partly from his natural bloodlust, partly out of boredom, and partly because kings have always justified their need by waging war, Bakum periodically ordered the farmers into battle with their neighbors. He led them on nighttime forays where he would demonstrate his supernatural powers and invulnerabilities, slaughtering to his heart's content and drinking blood to the contentment of his stomach. When the city was conquered by vastly superior forces, he left by night without looking back.

In 1290, the Vampire appeared in his fifty-ninth guise, as a voivode, or prince, of Fagaras. He rode with his followers out of southern Transylvania and built a fortress at Cimpulung, moving later to Curtea de Arges. Using the name Radu the Black, he established the first Walachian state and, from this, the country of Romania. His method of settlement was extermination of the tribes in his path. Already nineteen hundred years old and wearied of normal pleasures of the flesh, he determined to establish an unbeatable record for the number of murders that could be credited to one man. Compelled to commit evil in order to receive his monthly ration of powder, he elected to pursue evil as an art form, to exhaust the methods by which death could be accomplished. He came to realize that his confinement largely to nocturnal hours was a great impediment to his goals. He devised slaughter by proxy, seeking out the type of men who would later be called psychopaths, training them, giving them the benefits of all the evil methods he had acquired, killing their opponents until they had become strong enough on their own, and always encouraging them to greater evils. His prize pupil was the Walachian prince, Vlad IV. After five years of the Vampire's diligent tutelage, Vlad gained the epithet "Tepes," or the Impaler. According to the Vampire's careful count, no fewer than fifty-three thousand men, mostly Turks, met their end atop the wooden stakes of the man who would later be called Dracula.

By the beginning of the twentieth century, the invention of mustard gas, bacteriological warfare, and ultimately the atomic bomb proved to the Vampire that the slow but steady elimination of good men, by himself and other vampires, had had a telling effect on human history. The more wonders the surviving leaders created, the less they were inclined to give the original Creator any credit. With each declaration that God was dead, so also died conscience and compassion. In spite of so many labor-saving inventions and so much capacity to produce comfort for every human, the most powerful of the Vampire's former species ignored the potential and invested intellect and resources instead on the subjugation of their own people and the racial cleansings of others. The Vampire lost all heart when, in just half a decade, Adolf Hitler became responsible for the spilling of more innocent blood than his own superhuman efforts had claimed in twenty-five hundred years.

The simple truth was that there was a limit to the evil a vampire could cause; for a truly dedicated human, the boundaries for evil were apparently limitless. The Vampire took to his crypts for increasingly longer periods, rising only to eat, drink and bloodsuck . . . and to look with dread to the time when he would become merely one among a legion of his kind.

The train swayed, the wheels clacked along rails with rhythmic regularity, daring passengers to remain awake. Any normal person who had driven through the night would have been lulled to sleep long before. But the Vampire had slept for five weeks, so his body was fully rested. His mind puzzled every imaginable permutation of the general plan his Infernal Lord had approved.

The compartment was drafty and cold. Eastern European railroad cars never achieved warmth in the winter, and the opening of the window had guaranteed chill temperatures. The Vampire tolerated the cold of the crypt; otherwise, he detested it. He lifted the newspaper just high enough to glance at his watch. He consulted his railroad timetable. The Hungarian trains did not run with the punctuality of those of the German and Austrian systems, but they were not far behind. All things being equal, they would be pulling into Gyor within a few minutes. From there, he could take another rail line into Neustadt and avoid entering Vienna. Although this new route was the hypotenuse of a triangle formed of the three cities and should have sped his progress, the timetables simply did not work to his favor. Nevertheless, the Vampire determined to sacrifice the extra hour and the exposure to harmful midmorning sunlight. His count, after all, had reached eleven.

Buildings flashed past the compartment window with greater and greater frequency. The Vampire laid his newspaper on the seat without folding it. He stood slowly and moved up against the brute's knees, reaching for his top suitcase.

"I thought the conductor said you were traveling to Vienna," the brute remarked, reaching into his pocket for another cigar.

"Change of plans," the Vampire answered, placing the suitcase near the door. He pulled down the shades that isolated the compartment from the car's aisle.

"I hope you're not leaving on my account."

"I am, true enough."

"Sorry. Thanks for closing the curtains. Now that you're leaving, I suddenly want all of them down." The man laughed coarsely at his own joke.

The Vampire moved again to the luggage rack. "Glad to oblige." He brought the umbrella down, keeping it parallel with the floor, until it was aligned with the man's ear. With unhuman quickness, he took the umbrella shaft in his left hand and, with his right, gave the handle a hard, clockwise turn. From out of the ferrule sprang a four-inch blade, like that of an ice pick. Before the man could react, the Vampire had shoved it into his ear, until the finishing cap wedged against flesh. The man's eyes popped open; the cigar fell from his hand. An expulsion of fetid air escaped his lungs. The Vampire swung the umbrella handle in a small circle, whipping the brain matter apart. He caught the man as he slumped forward, dead, and shoved him back into the bench cushions. He withdrew the umbrella and pressed the blade against the floor, hiding it once again within the shaft. Continuing his blurred ballet, he reached across the compartment for the opened newspaper and laid it across the corpse, adjusting the hands around its edges to keep it in place.

The Vampire took his handkerchief from his trousers pocket and wiped away the blood that had oozed out of the punctured ear. Some of the red liquid clung to the man's rough pores. The Vampire had no desire to snack on such vermin. He spat on the dead man's ear and neck and scoured the flesh roughly. His intent was to cause the persons who found the body to believe death had come by heart attack. By the time an autopsy revealed the truth, he would probably be back in Romania. He hummed with satisfaction as he surveyed his work, adjusting the newspaper so that it seemed to be sheltering a sleeping man. As he retrieved the cigar from the floor, he felt the train begin to slow.

"We're going to the cafeteria; you want a fresh cup of coffee?" Dr. Loery asked Ray Pental, as he emerged from the morgue.

"No thanks, Bill."

Ray's gaze lingered on the Princeton Medical Center's chief of pathology and his assistant as they walked down the hall, arguing heatedly about the New Jersey Devils. He glanced at the empty cup on the floor beside his chair and confirmed that it had been smart to decline Dr. Loery's offer. Since reading the front-page headline of the morning's *Trenton Times,* the coffee already in his stomach had turned to acid. VAMPIRE KILLED IN PRINCETON U. LIBRARY it trumpeted in huge type. The story was accurate right down to the fact that the "vampire corpse" had been taken to the medical center. Back at the station, Francis Littlefield was no doubt beating the walls gray with the newspaper and pacing the soles off his expensive Italian shoes, desperate to learn the informer's identity.

When he had gotten his own cup of coffee, seeing doctors lounging in the cafeteria had seemed strange to Ray. The doctors he visited in offices never took rests. A five-minute break probably cost them fifty dollars. Ray had to rethink his attitude toward hospital physicians, especially the pathologist. Autopsies, after all, weren't like other examinations. The patient didn't care how long you took, what the diagnosis was, or what it cost. Truth be known, Ray's current assignment was the strange job. What was a stakeout but professional lounging? Stupidest of all, he was staking out a morgue on the very remote chance an old lady who was caught snooping once would return in broad daylight.

A custodian rounded the turn in the hall, pushing a wheeled bucket with a large wooden handle. He lifted a sopping mop out of the bucket and began swabbing the floor. The odor of powerful antiseptic rolled aggressively down the corridor. Ray hated the smell. He looked around for a place to retreat, but none offered a view of the morgue door. Bracing himself, Ray entered the pathology lab.

Lying on the autopsy table was the corpse of an old woman, opened from shoulder to shoulder and sternum to pubis with one great Y cut. The illumination pouring down from the enormous overhead lights brought every gruesome detail into stark clarity. Up on one side hung the hook and counterbalance system used to haul literally dead weight onto the table. Equally high, on the opposite side, was the microphone the pathologist dictated into as he performed his dissections. Atop a cart next to the table stood two ba-sins, each resting on a scale. Inside one basin lay the woman's liver, spleen, adrenals, and kidneys, repacked within a clear plastic bag; in the other sat her brain. The table was situated so that Ray's first view of the corpse was from crown to feet, so that he looked into the dim cavity where her brain had been and then to the inverted cap of her frontal scalp, pulled down over her face. The part of the cranium that had been sawn off sat on the table alongside her left ear. A stainless steel power saw lay next to her right ear. Whatever had been highly fluid had seeped down the table drain, but, among all the chrome and steel, blood red remained the dominant color. The acid in Ray's stomach crept up to his esophagus. He averted his eyes and hurried past the cadaver drawers, searching for a place where he could sit and close his eyes. He was all too aware that inside one of the drawers lay the corpse of the man tentatively identified as Vincent DeVilbiss. Dr. Loery had been given permis-sion to explore only so far as to confirm that death had been caused by massive bleeding from a severed femoral artery. The case was so unusual and there had been so little evidence of the man's identity that no one wanted to take the responsibility yet for performing a complete autopsy.

Ray considered as he passed the drawers that national publicity about this mysterious dead man might be good in a way; maybe someone would come forward soon with the real lowdown on him. With any luck, he'd turn out to be a psycho with Bela Lugosi delusions. Whatever would shove all the supernatural speculation back into the closet was fine with Detective Pental. Now that this Halloween door was open and Ray forced to peek inside, he was having trouble dismissing it by pure reason. And that was beginning to piss him off.

Ray found a semienclosed area at the back of the morgue, where gurneys were stored. He hopped up on one of them, wanting to get off his shaky feet. Two items dug into his right buttock. The first was his .38 special Smith & Wesson revolver inside a fanny holster. The other was the taser clipped to his belt. At the academy, all the detective candidates had been subjected to the taser's shock, to make them respectful of the punishment they would be dealing out if they used the weapon. The voltage, if liberally applied, was more than enough to stun even a vampire. Or so Ray hoped.

Ray had barely situated himself on the gurney when he heard the morgue door open. He unclipped the taser and listened intently. He did not register the now familiar voices of the pathologist and his assistant. Instead, as he most feared, the noises were those of cadaver drawers being opened, one by one, slabs being rolled out and back, and drawers resealed. Ray timed his drop to the floor to coincide with the closing of a drawer. He waited until the next drawer was opened before peering around the divider.

A woman was folding back the white cloth from a pale face. The woman, however, was the exact opposite of the one Ray anticipated seeing. She was rather short, bespectacled, dark-haired and dark-skinned, and only about thirty. Heavy gold bracelets and ornate rings diminished the professional image of a lab coat over a flower-print dress and a clipboard in one hand.

Ray padded forward as noiselessly as possible, but the woman's senses were alert. Gasping her surprise, she swung sharply in Ray's direction and let the sheet drop.

"Police," Ray said, keeping the taser raised. "Who are you?"

The woman's dark complexion drained of blood. Her eyelids batted up and down several times behind her wire-rimmed glasses. "I . . . I'm Dorena Durazo. I'm looking for someone who died yesterday."

Ray took another step forward. "What's the person's name?"

"Ellen Turner." The woman regained her composure with unusual speed. Her jaw set for a moment. Then she added, "I'm a biochemist with Bristol Myers–Squibb. This hospital is a beta test site for some of our new drugs. Mrs. Turner was a patient here . . . part of a control group. I need to take tissue and blood samples."

"Okay, Ms. Durazo—"

"Dr. Durazo."

Ray moved to the open drawer. "Sorry, Doctor." He lifted the sheet. The waxen face beneath it belonged to Vincent DeVilbiss. "Do you have identification on you?"

"Of course." The woman handed Ray her clipboard. She dug into her Coach handbag and produced a matching wallet. The driver's license confirmed her identity; a laminated card granted her access to the medical center. Yet another card proved that she was an employee of Bristol Myers–Squibb and the Ph.D. variety of doctor.

"Where's Bill Loery?" Dr. Durazo asked. The question put Ray at greater ease. The nameplate outside the door gave Dr. Loery's first name as Heywood. Only those who knew him would be aware of his nickname.

"He's taking a coffee break," Ray said, handing the wallet back. "Why don't we wait—"

The rest of the sentence was unnecessary. Bill Loery, who made a good double for a clean-shaven Santa Claus, came through the door finishing a sugared doughnut. White powder clung to his upper lip, forming a thin mustache. He came to an abrupt halt, surprised by the presence of two live bodies.

"Hi, Bill!" Dr. Durazo said. She strode forward with her hand extended. "Dorena Durazo, from Squibb."

Confusion was mixed into Dr. Loery's smile. "Right. Hello."

Before the pathologist finished his greeting, the biochemist said, "I'm looking for an Ellen Turner. She was on our latest anticoagulant and died yesterday."

"Ellen Turner?" Loery shook his head. "Wait a moment." He ambled over to a functioning computer and typed in several commands, followed by the name of the patient.

While Dr. Loery investigated, Ray asked the woman, "You specialize in blood chemistry?"

"Yes." Dr. Durazo fairly grinned her answer at the detective, growing more at ease by the moment.

Dr. Loery's wild, white eyebrows knit momentarily as he stared at the computer screen. "Hmmph! Here she is, but she's alive. Room 414."

"Ah jeez!" Durazo exclaimed. "And those stupid bastards have me hunting down here like a ghoul. Sorry." She began backing out of the room. "Wait'll I get my hands on them!" She exited into the corridor and moved away with haste, leaving the door to swing back hard.

"What did she want?" Loery asked Ray, rolling DeVilbiss back into cold storage and closing the drawer.

"Blood and tissue samples, she said. How well do you know her, Bill?"

Loery shook his head. "Not very. She's been down here a couple of times. But the researchers don't ordinarily come to the hospital. We know by the charts what they need. They have a kid come and pick the samples up whenever one of their patients dies."

"She was looking at our mystery man when I found her," Ray revealed.

The old pathologist laughed. "She was sitting in the cafeteria. Got up the moment we walked in. You know, that business about us having a dead vampire was on the local radio as well as in the newspaper. She looked pretty darned embarrassed. Maybe she was just curious."

"Could be," Ray agreed.

"Well, she won't be the last one," Loery said. "I hope we can get him out of here pretty soon."

"Speaking of getting out," Ray answered, as the pathologist's assistant came through the door, "I'd better get back into the hallway." He decided a bad smell was better than the macabre sights. He glanced at his watch as he went through the doorway. One and a half more hours and he was off duty. Maybe there was still time to salvage Christmas and his marriage.

Der Weisse Turm looked nothing like a white tower. An ordinary coffee shop in the middle of a block near the Zurich train station, it had captured Simon's attention because it reminded him of the place in Philadelphia where he had first met Frederika's mother. At least the wall and floor tiles gleamed white, promising hospitallike sanitary conditions and setting off the storage cases of cold cuts, salads, and baked goods. Aside from a few service counters, the place was crowded with small white tables and matching iron chairs.

82

Simon glanced at his watch. Seven-thirty. Frederika was half an hour late. He was in a mild panic and itched to do something, anything rather than sit impotently. But this was their appointed meeting place; they had made no contingency plans. After leaving the photo shop that morning they had agreed to split up, for the dual purpose of eluding anyone looking for them as a couple and to double the number of tasks they could perform.

As the waiter passed the table, he gave Simon a sympathetic wink, sharing the pain of a fellow male who seemed in the process of being stood up. On the way back, the waiter asked if Simon wanted his coffee cup refilled. Simon nodded.

A woman walked briskly along the sidewalk, on the other side of the shop window. Simon noted her long flame-red hair and white coat and refocused on a handmade decoding wheel next to his empty coffee cup.

"Sorry I'm late," Frederika's voice sounded moments later, from directly in front of the table.

Simon looked up and found himself staring again at the red-headed woman. The lipstick shade, the earrings, and the coat Simon had also never seen before. She held large shopping bags in both hands. He looked sharply to his left to hide his anger from her, but it was a futile act.

"I really am sorry," Frederika insisted, "and I can explain." She set down her burdens and pulled out the chair opposite Simon. "Believe it or not, I found a place to sleep, and the next thing I knew it was quarter after seven."

Just the suggestion of sleep made Simon yawn, relaxing his taut jaw. "You didn't take a chance—"

"No, not in a hotel. A storage area next to the changing rooms in one of the department stores. They had this pile of black draperies lying in a corner. Maybe from a window display. I buried myself in them and conked out."

"I'm glad they didn't find you and call Security," Simon remarked, still smarting. "You don't look rested." Her color was more pallid than ever. Brown circles and pinch marks detracted from her still-green eyes. She was perspiring lightly. He assumed it was from rushing to their rendezvous.

"I don't doubt it. My dreams were nightmares, of that thing in the basement. Never mind my health; do I look like a different person?"

"Yes. Except that you had blond hair and subtle lipstick when your picture was taken."

"So, I'll wear the wig whenever we don't use our passports." Frederika asked if Simon had eaten yet. Nothing since lunch, he said, except for his fifth and sixth coffees of the day. Despite all the caffeine, his eyelids were half closed. In the past three days, by his calculation, he had shorted his body some fourteen hours of sleep. "I'm now sharing your headache," Simon said.

Frederika shook her head. "I don't think so. If anything, I borrowed more from someone else. But we'll be all right . . . as soon as we get those passports and some sleep."

"Hang on. The powder's effect has to wear off soon," Simon encouraged, gently stroking Frederika's hand. She made no reply.

After having their photographs taken, Simon and Frederika had stowed their belongings in large lockers at the train station and then set off in different directions. Frederika's objective was to stay out of the sunlight, shopping for items they had not packed. Simon bore the brunt of the tasks. His first order of business was to visit the Crédit Banque de la Suisse and the Amalgamated Eurobanque as soon as they opened. Both stood on Bahnhofstrasse, a mile-long stretch that had once been a muddy ditch where frogs bred and which was now the most expensive real estate in the world. He had transferred the chain holding DeVilbiss's safe deposit keys from around his neck to his pocket; he had practiced the dead vampire's signature; he had memorized the box numbers. All he needed to complete the transactions was that mental attitude theater people called moxie. He dredged up his Stanislavsky training and "became" Vincent DeVilbiss, confidently marching up to each clerk, declaring that he needed to get into his safe deposit box and had very little time. Neither bank agent questioned his identity. Left alone in a small room with the first box, he found two diaries (with starting dates of 1774 and 1811), almost $18,000 in Swiss francs and what Simon estimated must have been half a million dollars worth of old diamond rings, necklaces, bracelets, and brooches. He wondered, as he dumped the box's contents into a large brown paper sack, whether the diaries would mention which victims had supplied DeVilbiss with this trove. At the second bank he found two more diaries, dated from 1853 and 1919. Considering how long the man had lived and what deeds he had done, the books seemed too thin. He also found more money, in various foreign currencies (some of it dating back to issues from the turn of the century). Most importantly, he found two handmade alphabet wheels, which were sure to facilitate the process of decoding the diaries. Simon took the paper sack to a third bank on the street and bought himself his own safe deposit box, in his real name. He left behind all but the wheels, $5,000 worth of the francs, several of the rings, and the oldest book. He reasoned that the diary Frederika had would contain information on enough recent killings to convince the police of DeVilbiss's murderous nature, and the oldest diary was most likely to ruminate on the nature and weaknesses of the powers that had given him unending life.

Upon reflection, rewarding his morning successes with a big lunch had not been a smart idea. Simon had felt bubble-brained almost immediately, and the diversion of blood to his stomach nearly had him nodding off in the booth. It was only with Herculean resolve that he dragged himself to Zurich's main public library, where he researched newspaper headlines to match the entry locations and dates in the oldest and newest of DeVilbiss's diaries. As the afternoon wore on, he turned his attention to the decrypting of the earliest entries in the 1774 diary, copying out the first seven pages. The first city of record was Florence. Simon had scant knowledge of Italian and could only guess at cognates from Latin. The evenly spaced letters further confounded translation. The one fact he was able to glean was sufficient to suspend his yawning: by 1774, DeVilbiss had already lived some three hundred and ten years.

Finally, the tedious decrypting became too much for Simon's

exhausted brain. He quit the library to explore Zurich on foot, trying not to become panic-stricken by the vivid memory of the very real monster from hell who, less than forty-eight hours before, had tried to exterminate him. He knew that only the most wary attention to survival would do. He kept to lighted areas of the city as the December night came early. He turned often and studied those behind him; he avoided crowds. And now, he was as safe as he could make himself, sitting in a brightly lit restaurant with the woman he so loved and feared.

Simon's waiter returned to the table with menus, winking again at his male customer, but this time with the approval of a silent confrere. Simon ordered a salad niçoise, and Frederika chose one built around grilled chicken. As soon as the waiter headed toward the kitchen, Simon dug into his coat pocket.

"Would you hold out your hand, please?" he asked. "No, your left one."

Frederika obliged. The ring Simon produced held a one-carat diamond of old-fashioned cut, sitting high in its setting. When he slipped it onto Frederika's fourth finger, it fit precisely. Before she could comment, he said, "We're supposed to be married."

"Yes, I know, Mr. Mitman," Frederika replied, turning the ring in the light, "but you should have gotten me a wedding band as well."

"I did." Simon placed three bands of different widths on the table. "They're all real. Part of DeVilbiss's ill-gotten gains. Don't be shocked if you find dried blood on them."

"Where's yours?" Frederika asked.

Simon stuck his hand into his trouser pocket and brought out a simple band between thumb and forefinger. "I hope you approve."

Frederika took Simon's ring and worked it down his fourth finger. "I do. For richer, for poorer. In sickness and in health. Forsaking all others. Till death do us part." She recited the vow looking straight into Simon's eyes, her expression calm and earnest. His weary mind, already reeling with emotion, tingled when she tested her three bands, selected one, and offered it and her ring finger to him. He was not being mocked; of that much Simon was sure.

Beyond that, with such a woman, he could not tell what she intended. He placed the ring on her finger and waited to see what else she would do or say.

"Did you buy a newspaper?" Frederika asked.

"What? A newspaper. No. You think we'd be international news?"

"Not us. The missing scrolls."

Simon nodded. He suddenly remembered Frederika's admonition in the Toronto airport and stopped staring at her.

"What about calling Professor Elmasri?" she asked.

Simon winced. "Damn! I forgot. Ordinarily, I have no trouble keeping things like that in my head."

"I understand. We're both exhausted."

"I should have made a list."

"It's okay. We'll call first thing tomorrow. I should have done it, when I consulted the telephone directory."

"For what?"

"Our old friend, DeVilbiss. He's in there. An address in the town of Zug."

"That's great!"

"I thought so. It's close by. As soon as we get our passports and some rest, we'll see what a vampire's home looks like." Frederika held up her rings again. "So, tell me about the rest of your day, Mr. Mitman."

Simon and Frederika shared almond cakes and sipped coffee slowly, willing the clock to wind around to ten P.M. There was nothing more they could do until they had new identities. At nine-twenty, a policeman strolled into the shop, apparently on duty. He stared in Simon's direction for a moment, and the librarian returned the look until the officer turned away.

"Let's get to the train yard," Simon suggested.

"It's still early," Frederika noted.

"I know, but I need to move."

Simon watched Frederika count various colors and sizes of paper money onto the check that had lain so long on their table. He silently supported the simple logic of making each denomination different to the eye and the touch and wondered if the United States was the only country foolish enough to make all its bills in one color and size.

Frederika stood and gestured for Simon to lead the way out. The policeman did not follow. They walked into the train station at a distance from one another, each stowing into a locker the things they had picked up during the day. They continued through the mammoth terminal like strangers with coincidentally similar goals, and exited out the building's back end toward the tracks.

Simon stood guard, then followed, as Frederika ducked under a chain and sign that forbade access to the yard. The train storage yard was not far, but it represented a markedly different section of town from the bright, quiet, and expensive Bahnhofstrasse area. Soot permeated everything, including the remains of a day-old snowfall. The far end of the yard was ill lit, made more dangerous by the movement of the huge cars. Frederika held her hands hard against her ears, to soften the sudden noises of steam expulsions, groaning axles, and shifting switches.

The couple navigated through the maze of concatenated cars by using the "building with the big red sign painted on its side" as polar star. The sign was the faded remnant of a Coca-Cola advertisement that had been painted on the bricks decades before. Instead of looking refreshed, the badly flaking figure of the drinker appeared to be some long-dead creature, drawing new life from a familiar-shaped bottle.

A brakeman shambled into view, forcing Frederika and Simon to conceal themselves. A few minutes later, he rode a long string of passenger cars out of the yard. The train's progress left one track empty. From the gloom on the opposite side of the newly opened space emerged a man in a long black coat, wearing a black fedora. He looked to Simon like a character from *The Third Man*. In his left hand he clutched an envelope big enough to hold passports.

"That must be him," Frederika said. "Let's go."

Simon tried to restrain her, but she had already rushed beyond his reach.

"*Guten Abend, mein Herr,*" Frederika said in a calm voice. "*Haben Sie etwas für Uns?*"

"Practice your German somewhere else, Mrs. Mitman," the man replied, with a British accent. "I speak perfect English." His gliding gait carried him into a pool of overhead light. He kicked up little explosions of snow with each step. His face was more Gallic than German, the overall shape thin, the nose large, the hair shiny and black in the sparse light, as if brilliantined. His eyes were deepset, and out of the twin caves his pupils shone like freshly broken coal. His smile did nothing to soften his underworld appearance.

Frederika pulled her genuine passport from her coat pocket. "Let me see your work, please."

The man looked to Simon, as if silently questioning why the male of the pair allowed the woman to play the dominant role. Simon gestured for him to follow Frederika's directive. The forger drew one of the passports from the envelope, thumbed it open, and extended it over the track that separated them.

"It's excellent work. Primo," the man assured.

"Looks pretty good to me," Frederika conceded.

"Worth every penny, as you say."

Simon stepped forward, laboring to pull from his trouser pocket the thick wad of paper money he carried. Frederika had paid for their dinner; this was the first time he had exposed the bills since he had wrapped all $5,000 of the safe deposit notes around the francs he already had. He realized with dismay that there was no way to conceal the wad from the forger. The man could see clearly that Simon held a small fortune in his hands.

"How many pennies would that be?" Simon asked.

The man stuck his ungloved right hand into his coat pocket. "Why, Simple Simon, all you've got." His hand came back out, wrapped around a .22-caliber pistol. The end of its barrel was fitted with what looked like a silencer. He took one step backward, so that Frederika and Simon could be covered simultaneously.

Frederika darted an angry glance at Simon, then refocused on the forger. "A thousand dollars each. That's more than reasonable,"

89

she said, holding out her hand for the envelope.

"Why is it reasonable if you have so much more than that?" the man wanted to know.

"Because we've got to live on what we have there for some time. We can't exactly wire home for more money."

The man shrugged. "You're a beautiful woman. Sell your charms." He pointed the pistol at Simon's heart. "Put all the money down, on the top of that rail!"

Stepping smoothly forward with no hesitation, Frederika took an angling path over the track toward the man's left-hand side, arm still extended. "Fifteen hundred each. That's our final offer."

"Final offer, my ass!"

Frederika rushed forward. The man swung the pistol at her chest and fired, point-blank. The bullet exited the barrel with a weak, spitting noise, but Frederika's considerable momentum instantaneously reversed as it hit her. She fell backward hard and lay unmoving on the ground, right arm extended, left heel balanced precariously on the cold steel rail. A small black hole showed obscenely just to the right side of the zipper slide of her new white coat.

"No!" Simon yelled, and rushed with mad fury toward the forger.

The man swung the weapon back and aimed the muzzle between Simon's eyes, halting him in midcharge.

"Fools," the man exclaimed, spit flying from his teeth with the force of his anger. "If you hadn't shown me all that money, I would have settled for a thousand each. Or if she had let you give me the money I'd have walked away. Instead, she made me kill her. And now I have to kill you both."

"My God!" Simon gasped, looking wide-eyed past the man's left shoulder, first toward ground level, then slowly raising his line of sight.

The forger grinned evilly. "Oh *ja*, right. I'm not falling for—"

What remained of the sentence was driven from the man's lungs by the impact of Frederika's tackle. She and the man tumbled onto the railroad track as one, the man fighting to soften his fall with his left hand while swinging the gun around to find his attacker's face. Frederika glared at him with raptorial concentration as she grabbed his arm and bent it relentlessly upward. Before Simon could recover from his shock and spring to her aid, the weapon discharged with another muffled explosion.

The forger's eyes went wide. He coughed weakly. The pistol fell from his grip as his hands clawed for his throat. Between his fingertips, thin streams of blood spurted.

Frederika retrieved the gun and threw it in Simon's direction. He caught it automatically. Without pause, she plucked the envelope off the ground, then rose slowly to her knees, groaning.

"Don't move," Simon ordered. "I'll get help."

"I don't need help," Frederika countered in a grim tone. She planted one foot on the track, then straightened herself into a near-upright position. The red wig sat askew on her head.

"But didn't you stop taking . . . ?" The truth filled Simon's mind and then, immediately, his face.

"No," Frederika answered. She coughed deeply, put her hands on her knees, and spat a thick pink froth onto the snow. "Hide the gun in your pocket and go stand guard while I drag him out of the light."

"No, you go—"

"Do what I say, dammit!" Frederika commanded. "I can't spit up blood in the open. I'll be fine in a few minutes. Go ahead, that way!"

Simon gave a last glance at the forger. The man's eyes bulged from their sockets. His hands were still wrapped around his neck. He sounded like he was gargling. Simon trotted down the tracks toward the station. When he turned around a few moments later, he saw the forger's horizontal legs disappearing behind a darkened passenger car, his heels carving parallel lines in the snow.

Simon stared at the thick roll of money still clutched in his hand. He shoved it deeply into his trouser pocket. His vision began to swim, so he squatted beside a relay box and wrapped one arm around it to steady himself.

For the past two days, fears had been scratching at Simon's conscious mind for attention, but he had refused to give them heed. Frederika had openly loathed the vampire who called himself DeVilbiss and the evil entities that controlled him. It was unthinkable that, of her own free will, she would continue to take the infernal powder DeVilbiss had force-fed her. But that was exactly what she had done. That was why her irises had not returned to their normal blue color. Yet that was not all a vampire took. She suffered from the terrible headaches because the powder was not enough. The scrolls stated it clearly: the Dark Forces had tied the gift of unending life to the taking of human blood.

Simon started back in the direction in which he had seen Frederika dragging the wounded forger. He retraced his path at a trot, until he came to the darkened passenger car. He braked his advance and set one foot carefully in front of the other, avoiding even the softest crunch of snow and ballast. He inched around another car and stopped.

Frederika knelt over the body of the forger. Her hands pinioned his arms firmly to the ground, and her mouth was fixed to the wound in his neck. The man's body jittered like a wind-up toy gone crazy. Blood no longer reached his brain, which was telegraphing frantic warnings to every muscle to do something about it. The faint sound of slurping came to Simon's ears.

Frederika's head came up. She turned to face Simon, her lips and chin smeared with the dark liquid. Her pupils caught the stanchion light and glowed a hellish amber.

Simon swung around the car and retreated toward the station. His throat began to trickle with sweet, protective saliva. He lost the battle with his gorge seconds later. Rising from hands and knees, Simon spat and snorted the last of his supper onto the ground. He kicked snow over the vomit, all the while watching for Frederika's reappearance. She was evidently intent on draining the man dry. He made his way back to the switch relay box, cleaned himself as best he could and took up his guard.

Frederika appeared three minutes later, tightrope walking along one steel rail with unhuman assurance. The red wig had been straightened. Perhaps by using snow, she had managed to get the blood off her mouth.

"You have to go into the station and get my old coat," she instructed Simon, still at a distance.

"Is he dead?"

"Yes. I put his neck on the rail. Hopefully, they'll run him over before they find him and think they killed a derelict." Now up close, Frederika read Simon's face. "What?"

"You didn't have to rush him."

"What do you mean? He was going to kill you."

"No, he wasn't. He just wanted the money."

"Don't be naive. That's not true," Frederika said, calmly.

"The truth is . . ." The truth was that she had provoked him into shooting her, as an excuse to kill him and drink his blood. The truth was that Simon had yoked himself to a woman who was keeping powers that only the Devil doled out.

"I'm waiting," Frederika said. "What's the truth?"

"I'll get your coat," Simon said, but made no move toward the station.

"If it's anyone's fault," Frederika accused, "it's yours. If you hadn't flashed all our money, the man would still be alive."

"You're right," Simon replied. "But I told you: I'm dead tired."

"And, because of that, almost dead."

Simon kept his eyes on Frederika. "There's blood on your hands."

"You haven't asked how I am!" Frederika pointed out, loud enough to create an echo among the motionless cars.

"You're fine," Simon said, turning his back on her. "You're a goddamned vampire."

Simon walked into the station and fetched the old coat. Frederika stood waiting not far into the shadows of the yard. She already had the white coat off and dangling from her right hand. In her left were her passport and the two phony ones. All the while she tugged on her old coat her eyes never left Simon's.

"Let's not say another word until we're in a hotel room," she told him. "We both need time to calm down."

"I agree," Simon said. "No use being at each other's throats."

As Simon had expected, Frederika betrayed no response to his words. She walked into the station with not the slightest indication of having been shot point-blank in the chest. In silence they collected all their belongings from the lockers, used the rest rooms to change into their most presentable clothing, rendezvoused and walked side by side out to Bahnhofstrasse. Despite the winter darkness, Frederika had once again donned her sunglasses. Simon wanted to kick himself for the way he had allowed his powers of observation to be blinded by his passion for the woman.

"Before I went to Der Weisse Turm, I walked through a couple of hotels," Simon said. "I vote we stay at the Savoy Baur en Ville. They probably won't expect us to spring for a four-star establishment."

"They'll check them all if they think we're here," Frederika replied, eyes fixed forward. "But I'm all for luxury, especially if our days are numbered."

Simon likewise kept his face forward as they walked. At least she had referred to numbered days in the plural. Frederika had stuffed her ruined coat into a plastic shopping bag. She shoved the bag into a refuse can a block from the Savoy, then gestured for Simon to lead the way.

The hotel was palatial, its facade a beautifully preserved relic from a gilded age gone by. Fresh flowers festooned the high-ceilinged grand foyer, which had been turned smartly contemporary with warm woods and beige, textured wall hangings. Simon approached the check-in counter without Frederika.

"You have a reservation for Mitman . . . a double," he assured the uniformed clerk.

The clerk held up his forefinger. *"Momentmal, bitte."* He disappeared from view. Simon pivoted with a slow, casual motion, taking in the entire foyer. He saw that Frederika had positioned herself near one of the doors, able to flee at the first sign of trouble. She clutched both metal cylinders fast against her chest.

In a few moments, a pretty young woman replaced the male

clerk. "May I help you?" she asked in English.

Simon repeated his ruse, handing over the forged passports. The woman checked the computer and, unruffled, inquired when the reservations had been made. Simon supplied a date. The clerk smiled easily, more than capable of dealing with the apparent dilemma. "We have a room for you on the fifth floor, Mr. Mitman. How would you like to pay for it?"

Simon withdrew his roll of bills. "Cash." Finally, the woman seemed nonplused. "We're leaving Switzerland tomorrow and want to get rid of our francs," he confided. "How much for the night?" The woman told him, and he peeled off the correct amount. She recorded information from the phony passports and returned them. The rest of the formalities were textbook, down to the obsequious bellhop who conducted them to their room.

While Simon handed the bellhop a tip, Frederika moved to the window to take in the view. Simon counted to ten, opened the door to be sure the hallway was empty, then locked and bolted them inside the room. When he turned, Frederika had removed her coat and was resting her bottom on the ledge over the air-conditioning system, arms folded across her chest. The bellhop had turned on one bedside lamp, which provided the room's only illumination. Frederika's shadow, immense and black, clung to the wall on her right.

"I never said I'd stopped taking the powder," Frederika declared. "You kept telling me I should and assumed I agreed."

Leaning back against the door for support, Simon felt like a hollow lead soldier. "Do me the courtesy of removing your sunglasses, so I can see you." Frederika took off the titian wig as well. "What I assumed was that you were smart enough to stop without my badgering. How much do you take each day?"

"One teaspoonful."

"That jar we took out of DeVilbiss's car was large, but the powder can't last you more than, what, another month? What then?"

Frederika sighed. "By that time we'd better have people believing in those scrolls. Unless we can turn the ones hunting us into the *hunted* real soon, we'll be dead within that month . . . powder or

95

not. You think I wanted to continue taking that wretched stuff? I only did it to keep us safe. We're up against vampires, Simon. The undead! How can we hope to fight hell without stealing some of its fire?"

Simon's shoulders sank inside his coat, which was held in place by the pressure of the door. "You're a big girl. I have no control over you. You do what you want."

Frederika came off the ledge. "What I want is for you to start taking the powder, too."

"What?"

"Listen to me! Granted, you were very tired, and that's why you pulled out the money before you thought about it. But tonight's not the last time we'll be tired. Or confused. I wasn't one hundred percent sure the powder would protect me from a bullet, but I had to save you. I don't want to be forced to go through that kind of pain again."

"That's crazy," Simon countered. "You didn't have to rush him. You heard him say all he wanted was the money."

Frederika whipped around and paced to the far corner of the room. "Bullshit! If that were the case, he'd have carried a switch-blade, not a gun with a silencer."

"I don't agree. And I'd told you there was plenty more money in DeVilbiss's deposit boxes. You could at least have seen if he went for the money."

"And have him shoot you dead without warning?" Frederika shook her head. "No. There's enough powder to last both of us for another two weeks."

"And what do I do when my headaches and sweats begin?" Simon asked. "Look for another criminal to pounce on, or just forget the hypocrisy and open some little old lady's throat?" Simon noted that Frederika's irises had changed from apple green to amber. No doubt, the forger's blood had provided the final, critical element to turn Frederika into a full-fledged vampire. He watched her lids bat up and down rapidly and a film of water cover her corneas. Her injury looked so genuine. But, then again, so had it at Newark Airport.

"You stink, Simon," Frederika said in a small voice. "He shot himself. The blood was squirting all over the snow."

"So why not lap it up, right?"

"Yes, exactly! Why not? I knew it was what I needed. But I would never have drunk *innocent* blood. I did what I had to, dammit. This concerns more than me. More, even, than you and me. Thousands of lives are at stake here." Frederika wiped her wet eyes with the back of her hand. She moved slowly toward Simon. "You can be protected by the powder for almost two weeks before the need for blood sets in. By that time, we'll have accomplished what we set out to do. You'll never have to drink blood . . . and if God is merciful, I won't have to again."

Simon straightened up and folded his arms across his chest. "How do you know that once you begin taking the powder you can just quit? How do you know that stopping cold won't kill you?"

"I . . . don't believe it works that way."

Simon turned on the overhead light and watched Frederika squint with discomfort. "But you're not sure. You have no perspective. Just as you can't judge objectively what the powder's doing to your mind."

"My mind is fine."

"Is it? That powder was concocted to enslave people. Who knows what subtle ingredients are in it, things that suppress the conscience? I say it made you bold enough to overcome your reasonable doubt that that bullet might kill you. I say it drove you to force him to shoot himself, so you had an excuse to drink his blood."

Frederika lifted her hands feebly. "I say no; you say yes. What now?"

"I don't take the powder . . . and neither do you. We thank God it got us through this crisis, but from now on we'll have to survive on natural gifts. Agreed?"

Frederika's lips parted for a quick reply, then pursed. She regarded Simon for several seconds. "You said several times that you can't think straight. Neither can I. Let me sleep on it."

"Only until morning," Simon said. In the moments she had paused to frame her reply, he had formulated a plan. He would force himself to rise the next morning before she did. He would dress silently and take the jar of amber powder to his bank deposit box, for which only he knew the code numbers. He would force Frederika to abandon the powder, but if she became gravely ill at least he would have it still, either to wean her off it slowly or else to help some clinic learn how to cleanse it from her system.

Frederika glided toward Simon, holding him in place with a hypnotic stare. Wearing a sheer white evening dress, pale except for blood-red lipstick, trailing her ever-growing shadow, she was the Central Casting image of a modern-day vampire.

"So, are we back to being buddies?" she asked.

"We're more," Simon answered. "We're blood buddies. Now each of us has killed to save the other."

Frederika's chin lowered several degrees, so that she used her eyebrows like gunsights. "True. Then you won't object to helping me here. Pull down my zipper, please."

Frederika turned slowly, presenting her back to Simon. He tugged the zipper down as far as it would go. A week before, he had weathered her attempt at seducing him in the bedroom she rented him. The confidence gained from that episode, coupled with his lingering distrust of her, made even her flawless beauty no match.

Frederika shrugged out of the dress, letting it slide to the carpet. She stood in a bra and slip. "I can't see. What does the exit wound look like?"

Simon studied her narrow porcelain back. Between her shoulder blades he made out an area of flesh, slightly proud and the size of a quarter, where the unbroken skin blushed bright pink.

"Damn, that's amazing. It looks almost healed. I have to check the gun tomorrow. Looks like . . ." Despite his resolve, his blood was pounding in his heart and his groin. ". . . like the bastard used hollow-point bullets. They blossom on impact, you know."

"My lung still burns if I take a big breath," Frederika confided. "It hurt like hell when I was hit."

Simon fought the desire to touch her. With the magic powder as

98

the stakes on the table, there was no way he would cede her the upper hand. "I'll bet. I wouldn't know what to do for it even if we had medicine. Sorry."

"That's okay." Frederika turned and faced Simon. Her bra was tight enough to shape her breasts into twin spheres. She looked down and ran her forefinger between the cups. "This side's completely healed. I'll be okay. Maybe a bath would help. Can I go first?"

Simon pushed open the bathroom door. "Be my guest. I'd drown if I took one. I'm just gonna . . . crash on one of those beds right now."

"That's fine." Frederika glanced at the rings on her left hand. She went up on tiptoes and kissed Simon firmly. "Till death do us part, my husband." She entered the bathroom and turned on the light. Without closing the door, she bent to the tub fixtures.

Simon squeezed his eyes shut and pivoted away from the ultra-erotic image, taking one blind step into the room. He scudded in slow motion toward the bed, clawing off his suit jacket and tie as he went. Suddenly, he felt as if a petcock had been opened in his heel and all the energy of his being were draining out. Beyond the equivalent of one full night's rest that he had shorted his body, he had in the past three days weathered the death of a friend, the discovery and then defeating of a vampire, near annihilation at the claws of a demon from hell, and witnessing the murder of a forger. And now he was sharing a hotel room with another full-blooded vampire. The revelation of Frederika's nature had overtaxed the limits of his strength. He could no longer deal with her, on any level, tonight. He stank of sweat, but he wouldn't be able to stay up long enough to bathe. Nothing mattered except the oblivion of sleep.

The phone rang while Karen Pental was tucking her younger daughter in bed. Ray stood in the living room studying the television listings (late night was the only time that he had any say about program selection). He flung down the guide and strode into the kitchen, certain it was yet another politely veiled demand that he pick up his detective shield and climb into his car. As he lifted the handset from the cradle he stole a glance at the clock over the sink. It was 9:25 P.M. Might as well forget his plans for the well-earned, much-delayed vacation day tomorrow; he'd be too much of a zombie to skate with the kids on Carnegie Lake. By the time he woke up it would probably be the middle of the afternoon. Karen was going to kill him.

"Hello," Ray said, in a low, defensive tone.

"Ray, this is Father Driscoll. Sorry ta—"

"Father! How are you?"

"Touch of the sniffles ta be truthful, but I'll live. I'm sorry ta be callin' ya so late in the evenin'," Father Driscoll apologized, his County Tipperary accent still evident after a twenty-year absence from Ireland.

Ray shifted the phone to his other ear, so he could lean against the wall. "That's okay. What can I do for you?"

There wasn't much Ray wouldn't do for the man. Joseph Aloysius Driscoll had been his parish priest since Ray was an altar boy. A wise, patient, kindhearted man, Father Driscoll presented a shining example of what a life devoted to God and His work could accomplish. His influence on Ray had been so great that, for a time, the young man had seriously contemplated joining the priesthood.

Father Driscoll cleared his throat, a habit he was given to when nervous. "Ah, I know you'll find this hard ta believe, but there's a car parked in front of your house, with a representative from the Pope sittin' in it."

Ray glanced through the kitchen at the dining room window. The curtains were drawn, blocking the view to the street. "I believe it if you say so, Father."

"The representative's name is Father Dante Ferro. He's on a very special and secret assignment, and he contacted me to learn who might be of help to him in Princeton. I told him you were a detective there . . . and a good Catholic."

Ray laughed lightly at Driscoll's strange words. "I can't say one has anything to do with the other."

"But they do . . . leastways in this case. I know the hour is late,

100

but he hoped ta catch you before you went ta sleep."

"I'm on vacation tomorrow, so I'll be up late."

"Ah, good. Will you do me a personal favor and speak with the man, Raymond?"

"Of course, Father."

"Thanks. Farewell." With no more explanation, Father Driscoll rang off.

Ray moved to the window and pulled back the curtain. A linty, light snow was falling. Through it, past the picket fence that edged the property, a black limousine sat in the street, white smoke puffing from its tailpipe. He made out the figure of a man behind the wheel, but the windows in the back of the limousine were opaque.

"Ray?" Karen called down softly from the top of the stairs.

"Yeah?"

"Who was that?"

"Father Driscoll. He needs someone to run an errand for him."

"Now?"

Ray moved toward the hall closet. "Just to pick up a few things from the drugstore before it closes. He's got a cold, and Mrs. Finnegan's off for the holidays. I'll be back in half an hour . . . forty minutes tops."

"If you're not back in an hour, I want an annulment."

"I'll tell Father Driscoll." Ray shrugged into his parka and slipped out the front door. Karen had disappeared from the top of the stairs, no doubt gone to bed to read the Dick Francis novel he had bought her for Christmas.

As Ray neared the gate, the limousine's rear door opened, invitingly. Ray ducked his head inside. The man sitting alone in the back seat was small and well proportioned, looking to be in his fifties. He wore a full-length camel's hair overcoat, completely unbuttoned, so that Ray could see he was wearing a rep tie rather than a priest's collar. He didn't wear the expression of a priest either. His attitude was more worldly, Ray judged, noting one leg crossed casually over the other and his right arm extended along the length of the seat back.

"Get in, Detective Pental, please," the man invited.

"My wife thinks I'm taking the car on an errand."

"Then we shall wait for you around the corner."

Ray nodded and eased the door closed. The limousine moved off silently, the crunch of the snow under its tires louder than the purr of the engine.

Ray climbed into his car and drove around the corner, to where the limousine waited. He opened the black door again and climbed inside. Sitting, he saw the car phone, from which the priest had undoubtedly cued Father Driscoll to make his call. As he turned toward the priest, he found himself staring at a face that was an odd mixture of cherub and politician.

"Good evening, Mr. Pental," the man said, suggesting his nationality by the Italian purity of his vowels and the softness of his consonants. "So sorry to bother you at this hour, but the reason for my visit is a matter of great urgency. I shall probably be back in Europe by morning." The man thrust out his hand. "I am Dante Ferro. Father Ferro now. But, until a few years ago, I was a policeman like you."

Surprised as he was by the man's last words, Ray was even more stunned by his grip. This small, middle-aged man evidently still did upper-body workouts. "Interesting."

Ferro redirected his attention to the bar beyond his knees. "Would you care for a drink or coffee?"

"How about espresso?"

Ferro laughed. "Sorry. This is not an Italian limousine."

"Then coffee will do." As Ferro had pointedly avoided mentioning Father Driscoll, Ray said, "Since you're in such a rush, why don't you tell me straight out why you're here?"

"I can do that in two words: the scrolls."

Ray absorbed another shock. "The scrolls stolen from the Princeton University library?"

The priest offered Ray a pure white porcelain mug and poured coffee out of a pewter-colored carafe. "The same. The Scrolls of Ahriman. The Church believes they are genuine. The Holy Father himself has reviewed this situation, and he wants them found, authenticated, and translated."

"We've alerted all the national and international law networks," Ray answered. "I think the Church'll have to be patient about any help it can—"

"No, it can't wait," Ferro countered. "The Church must become involved in finding these scrolls. We already know much about their contents. They contain grave warnings for mankind and a timetable for when a global disaster will begin."

"What kind of timetable?"

"Accurate prophecies of scientific advancements. Seven in all. The sixth one has just taken place . . . interestingly, at the same university from which the scrolls were stolen. At the Plasma Physics Campus, they have just attained what they call the 'break-even' state in fusion energy. The first six discoveries have occurred with increasing frequency. I calculate that the seventh prophecy will happen within a few months. And then the disaster begins . . . unless the world is warned by these scrolls."

"What do you mean by disaster?" Ray asked, raising the mug to his lips.

The priest returned the carafe to the bar with ceremonial slowness. When he turned back to Ray, the studied warmth had disappeared from his face. "I promise to tell you after you have answered my questions."

"Might this disaster have anything to do with vampires?" Ray fished.

Ferro blinked several times in rapid succession. "Why do you ask that?"

Ray sensed a more profound blackness slipping around the limousine. The insanity inside the library was pursuing him from halfway around the world. "The scrolls were apparently stolen by a librarian named Simon Penn. He left us a corpse and a long note. It declared that the dead man had wanted to destroy the scrolls, and that he had been a vampire. Evidently, the Loyal Opposition is as interested in the scrolls as the Church is."

"Quite possibly." Ferro's eyes narrowed. "Did you hope I would laugh at your last words?"

"Frankly, yes."

Ferro shook his head.

The limousine was well heated, but a shiver rippled down Ray's spine. "So, the warning does have something to do with vampires?"

"Yes. A plague of them. Are you still willing to speak with me?"

"I've been ordered to keep a tight lid on this case, but I could approach my chief on your behalf and see if he'll—"

"No." The priest punctuated his interruption with an emphatic wave of the hand. "I could have done that myself. Actually, I believe I can learn much more through you, Mr. Pental. First of all, any murder blamed on vampirism is certain to gather a carnival atmosphere around it. That is clearly one reason why you have been instructed not to talk of this business. Your chief will tell me nothing. Secondly, under the best of circumstances police agencies rarely share everything with each other, much less with a religious organization. I know from experience. But we are not just any religious organization. We have the ability to solve problems with swiftness and . . . what is the phrase in English?"

"Without due process of law?" Ray suggested.

The priest's eyebrows went up. "That is not the phrase I was looking for, but it will do." Father Ferro leaned back against his door and squinted at Ray, as if attempting to peer into his soul. He made a little purring noise in his throat before he said, "If I had not been a cop for more than thirty years, I would not have the right to say this. I consider myself a true cop and a true Catholic. But I also know with whom my ultimate allegiance must be placed." He reached into his coat pocket and withdrew a small Bible. Its gold cloth marker had been fixed between two pages, and Ferro opened to the place. He smiled at Ray. "This phrase will not escape me." He looked down. " 'Render therefore unto Caesar the things that are Caesar's, and to God the things that are God's.' The scrolls came from God and belong to God."

Ferro set the open Bible conspicuously atop the bar. "There are things in these scrolls which must be revealed for the good of mankind. The Holy Father and his cardinals agree. The time has come for any true Catholic who is involved to respond . . . without reservation." He reached inside his suit jacket and withdrew a small spiral notepad and a mechanical pencil. "Tell me about Simon Penn."

The priest had promised to be gone from Princeton within hours. Francis Littlefield would see that nothing or less than nothing happened to prove the occurrences in Princeton had any metaphysical link. The only chance Ray seemed to have to help Simon prove the contentions of his letter was to enlighten this emissary from Rome. Ray talked. As a professional investigator, he knew the questions Ferro would ask and offered them without prompting. When he had exhausted his knowledge of Simon Penn, the evidence Penn had left behind, and what Penn had told his friend Richard Chen, the priest gave a nod of thanks and turned to a clean page of the notepad.

"Now, about the accomplice . . . Miss Vanderveen. Is she Roman Catholic?"

"No. If anything, the opposite."

Ferro looked up. "And what would that be?"

Ray shrugged. "A pagan? A worshiper of the Dark Side?"

"What makes you say that?"

"From the things Mr. Penn told Richard Chen. Penn got involved with her in the first place because he spied her digging dirt from her father's grave late one night. Then he caught her using it for a ritual to raise the dead—her father, to be specific. She went to DeVilbiss because he claimed to be a channeler with the dead. She's apparently obsessed with death and the next world."

"Interesting," Ferro muttered. Ray noted that he was translating into Italian as he scribbled.

"She has a reputation for being weird from many circles. Has almost no friends. Dates much older men, but never for long. Keeps largely to herself. Secretive."

"Any record of arrest?"

"No. She's clean as far as we could tell."

"And you believe she's gone off with Mr. Penn."

"Yes. Along with the scrolls. To Europe."

"We believe the same." Ferro closed his notebook.

Ray glanced at his watch. "I've got to be getting home. Now that I gave you all that, what're the chances of me being kept informed?"

Father Ferro held out his hand for Ray's empty coffee cup. "I believe the chances are good. Much as I hate to think about it, Mr. Pental, I fear a great battle is about to be waged. The faithful will need very much to stay in touch."

CHAPTER FOUR

December 27

◦◯◦

Love seeketh not itself to please,

Nor for itself hath any care,

But for another gives its ease,

And builds a heaven in hell's despair.

—William Blake, *The Clod and the Pebble*

❍❍❍

Simon entered the cave alone, a torch in his left hand, a spear in his right. A rivulet of water ran through the center of the cave, toward its mouth. The water was a rusty red. Simon looked back. Beyond the small opening, sunlight flooded a meadow filled with poppies in bloom. Simon picked his way forward, following the twisting passage in its downward course. He paused. The water ran counter to the pull of gravity.

Simon looked down. He saw that the breastplate covering his chest was made of plastic, an adult-size version of the armor he had received for his seventh birthday. The scabbard dangling from his left hip was also plastic, as was the hilt of the sheathed sword. He slapped his spear against a stalagmite and listened for the echo of metal. It answered with a dull thwack. What had been an iron lance moments before was now only a broom handle, whittled to a point. Simon turned to find the light of the outside world. It had vanished.

From the cavern ahead issued a low hissing, growing more intense by the second. Simon searched the passage for its best defensive position. He backed into a tiny alcove and rammed his torch into a fissure in the wall. He raised his spear and waited.

The angry hissing intensified, and now the passageway filled with a sewer stench. The foul odors assailing Simon's nostrils were

unmistakably of decaying life. And then it was before him, a reptilian creature out of Greek mythology. It had three heads on long necks. The first face bore a resemblance to Vincent DeVilbiss, its eyes glowing bright amber; the second had the forger's large beak and shining black pupils; the third face was nearly identical to the creature from hell, with pupils like a cat's, burning red. All three opened their mouths together. Three sets of fangs loomed before him. They bellowed as one. A blast of foul air flung Simon backward into the alcove. The torch went out.

Simon sat up, drenched in sweat, blind in the blackness. For a moment, he existed simultaneously in nightmare and reality. Then he registered the mattress beneath him. He twisted around and lunged for the place where he remembered the bedside lamp had stood. He found it and stabbed at the switch.

Blessed light flooded the room. Simon turned from its glare and looked at the other bed. It was empty. Never slept in. His eyes roamed the room, searching for information. The alarm clock displayed 2:02 in red, liquid-crystal numbers. His suitcase lay propped against the wall where he had left it, unopened. His coat and trousers were neatly folded across Frederika's bed. He had not set them there. He recalled vaguely that he had stepped out of the heap of his pants as his last act before burrowing under the bedclothes.

Simon threw back the covers and set his feet on the floor. His heart still beat against his ribs like a blacksmith's hammer on an anvil. He went to the door and turned on the overhead light. Without needing to illuminate the bathroom, he could see that it contained no toiletries, nothing of Frederika's but the pooled-water and towel-crumpled evidence of her bath. He retraced his path and threw open the armoire doors. The space was empty of all but hangers.

Both metal cylinders were missing. Simon checked for good measure under the beds. No other place remained in the room where such large items could be concealed.

"Dammit!" Simon swore, repeating the word until his breath ran out. He snatched up his trousers and sat on the edge of Frederika's bed, intending to thrust his legs into them. His hands

109

felt the distinctive change of weight. He dug into the pockets. His keys were still there, but the Swiss army knife attached to them was gone. So was all his spare change and the thick wad of money. He finished tugging on his trousers. His passports and wallet sat on her night table, but the wallet, too, had been cleaned out. She had not left him one franc.

Both diaries were gone as well. Simon picked up his parka. The outer pockets had been turned out and the forger's gun was gone, but the large, zippered pouch hidden under the winter lining still contained the seven pages of translation and the decoding wheel Simon had secreted there.

Simon put down the parka and closed his eyes. Why had she fled? What was she up to? He could think of only two fundamental motivations: either she considered him a liability and had determined to continue their plan alone, or else she had been turned to evil by the powder and the blood and was in the process of seeking out the Devil, to exchange the scrolls for the promise of immortality.

Thanks to international dealings in his library work, Simon knew the telephone code to reach the United States. He punched in a long string of numbers and waited. By the third ring he realized that the six-hour time difference made it only a few minutes past eight P.M. in Princeton.

"Hi. I'm not in right now," Richard Chen's electronic voice said. "You know what to do." The machine beeped.

"Rich, it's Simon. I need the biggest favor ever. I'm sure you know by now that I killed DeVilbiss and stole the scrolls. It was self-defense; he *was* a vampire. I'm fine but out of the country. Here's the favor: tomorrow, as soon as the library opens, I need you to get into Room B9F without anybody seeing you. Open up the grille over the air duct on the wall directly across from the door. Inside, you'll find a long metal container. It's got the scrolls inside. They're not safe there. You've got to move them to someplace else where they won't be found, but don't risk taking them out of the building. I know how much I'm asking, but it's incredibly important . . . and it's got to be done the minute the library opens. You'll need a Phillips head screwdriver to open the grille. You'll also need something to jimmy the door. I know you'll figure it out. B9F. I'll call tomorrow, to find out how you did. Thanks, buddy."

After he hung up, Simon moved to the window and looked out on Zurich, as if expecting to spot Frederika in distant flight. What he saw instead was a pair of police cars pulling up to the curb directly below him. Four officers left the vehicles and entered the hotel. Simon threw on his shirt and jacket, scudded into his shoes and grabbed his parka, suitcase, and the bagful of items he had gathered on the previous day's shopping. He consulted the building plan on the back of the door and exited the room at a trot. The hotel was deathly quiet.

As he passed through the doorway to the fire stairwell, Simon heard the elevator opening. He pushed hard against the door to speed its closing, then leaned against it. Several moments later, he heard knocking from the end of the hall where his room lay. It was a polite sound, like that produced by a maid wanting to clean the room. But maids did not come knocking at two A.M. He descended the staircase swiftly and silently, entered the hallway to the floor below, walked to the service elevator and called for it. The button panel inside indicated that two levels existed below the lobby. Simon punched A and waited. With each passing floor he expected the machine to stop and stern-looking men in uniforms to be standing just beyond the doors, but the seemingly interminable trip ended without incident. He threaded through A-level's dimly lit passageways toward the rear of the hotel and thence up a back stair into an alley filled with packed refuse. He realized he would be conspicuous enough exiting the alley in the middle of the night; lugging a suitcase and shopping bag exceeded prudence. From the bag he took a woolen ski cap and leather gloves and put them on. He shoved his remaining belongings behind a pile of flattened cardboard crates that leaned against the hotel wall, then straightened up, contemplating his next actions.

Somewhere else in the city a siren wailed. Simon was just one of many emergencies. He started walking. It was damned cold, and he lacked even the change to be able to loiter in a warm shop over a cup of coffee. But at least he still had the key to his safe deposit box. The game had been altered, but he was a participant. And more motivated than ever to play it to the end.

Two days after Christmas, the main branch of the Zurich public library was not high on the general public's agenda. Simon sat alone at one of the central reading room's long tables, scanning the *International New York Times* for news of the scrolls' theft. He was finding nothing. The same had been true of the *Washington Post*. A document more important than the Rosetta Stone, the Magna Carta, and all the Dead Sea Scrolls put together was missing, and it didn't even make Page Six. But Simon was not completely surprised; the reason the minions of hell were in such hot pursuit of the scrolls was precisely because their dread contents were all but unknown to the world. He was the lone warrior whose quest it was to get their message onto every Page One on the planet.

Simon checked the clock on the wall. The hour approached noon, which he had already guessed from his growling stomach. He refolded the newspaper, revealing a scrap of paper beneath it, on which he had printed Vincent DeVilbiss's telephone number and address. He had also jotted several numbers on the other side of the paper. He had spent a considerable part of his late morning trying to track down Dr. Mustafa Elmasri. The man who answered the phone in the University of Athens's Department of Classical Languages had spoken no English. With diligence and urgent persuasion, Simon had finally located a person in the university's central administration office who both spoke English and was willing to divulge the professor's home telephone number. When Simon dialed, no one answered.

A man sat down directly across from Simon. He smiled broadly as Simon studied his handsome, middle-aged face. The man wore a full-length camel's hair overcoat, unbuttoned to reveal a university-striped silk tie and an expensive wool suit. He set an equally expensive briefcase down on the table.

"Good morning," the man said, in mildly accented English.

112

Simon nodded his reply, wondering if he really looked so patently Anglo-Saxon.

"Doing some research?" the man persisted, folding his arms casually across his chest.

"No. Just reading the papers," Simon replied carefully.

"You won't find anything about the scrolls, Mr. Penn," the man declared, still smiling. "I have checked already."

Simon glanced around the room.

"I brought no one with me. I am not the police. I'm a friend. Dante Ferro." He extended his hand across the table. "With greetings from Mr. Ray Pental."

Simon's hand came out with the wariness of a wild animal accepting food from a human. "You're not a cop?" Simon asked, thoroughly bewildered.

"Well, I used to be. I'm a priest now. I work in the Vatican." Ferro laughed at Simon's dumbfounded expression. "Yes, I'm sure it's difficult for you to believe, but it's true."

"How . . . how did you find me?"

"I simply put myself into your shoes. I know that the Zurich police got a tip of your location last night . . . don't worry how. The tip was telephoned in by a woman. Was it Miss Vanderveen?"

Simon stared speechless at Ferro.

"Don't be shocked. There are ways for a mere mortal to get such information," Ferro assured, as if reading Simon's mind. He lifted his chin and pointed to a fresh shaving nick, just above a patch of razor burn. "You see? I am no vampire. The woman expected you to be sleeping in that hotel room. Who else but Miss Vanderveen could know that?"

Simon nodded.

"I congratulate you on your latest escape from the police. Once I received that information, I knew you would be too clever to try to check into another hotel or to try to leave the city by any means of public transportation. The police have also alerted the taxi companies and even have patrols on the major highways, picking up all hitchhikers who fit your description. I said to myself, 'Where would you go, Dante, if you were an intelligent librarian and had time to kill until the search grows cool?' "

"If you know so much, do you also know where Frederika is?" Ferro shook his head. "May I make a suggestion? If I have reasoned where you are, perhaps the police will also. You seem to be in much need of sleep and a meal. There is nothing I can do about the sleep, but I would be pleased to buy you lunch, Mr. Penn."

"Where?"

"The Kronenhalle. The food is delicious, it is public, but it is not a place where policemen eat."

"Agreed."

"Excellent! Let us be on our way."

The priest had parked his rented car in the Zähringerplatz. In the time it took to leave the library and cross the crowded street, Simon had ample opportunity to pose several trivial questions about the workings of the Vatican and about his friend Ray Pental, things that only a person with intimate knowledge could answer. Father Ferro replied precisely and without reserve, through a smile that indicated he understood Simon's purpose. Unlocking the car door, Ferro said, "You have my oath as both a priest and a former officer of the law that I will not deliver you to the police."

"Thank you. Where is the Kronenhalle?"

Ferro pointed. "Just two blocks down and to the left. At the bottom of Ramistrasse. Would you prefer to walk?"

"Yes," Simon said, from the opposite side of the car, scanning the area for escape routes, "but I'd like you to drive there. I hid my belongings under some cardboard crates in the alley behind the Savoy Hotel."

"I know it. On Poststrasse."

"I can't go back there, especially if somebody's found my stuff. Would you do me a favor and pick them up, then meet me at the restaurant?"

"Certainly." Father Ferro got into the car and pulled into the congested traffic.

Simon watched the car disappear around a corner. The stranger

114

had passed his final test, allowing him to walk away from their encounter. He was probably who he claimed to be, but Simon would never let down his guard completely. Thirty-six hours earlier, Frederika had cautioned him to trust no one, with the implicit exemption of herself. She who had given him the warning had ironically provided the ultimate lesson.

Looking at the cathedral-like spires of the venerable Zentralbibliothek, Simon felt homesick for his quiet, sequestered life inside Princeton University's Firestone Library. Whether he won or lost this battle with the Devil, he knew his life would never again enjoy that degree of calm. He turned from the sight and headed south at a leisurely pace, drinking in the beautiful city. Through his voluminous, voracious reading, he knew that Zurich had been a major birthplace of twentieth-century arts and letters. Here, James Joyce had worked on *Ulysses,* the Dadaists had founded the Cabaret Voltaire, and a host of other artists fleeing the madness of World War I had developed their arts and crafts. But Zurich was no haven for Simon Penn. He knew absolutely that supernatural madness was converging on him. He would have to escape Zurich before nightfall. Perhaps the cop-turned-priest would provide the means.

The Kronenhalle was a pleasant surprise, an informal museum of twentieth-century paintings. Along its walls, Simon found original works by Miro, Chagall, Picasso, and Klee. Self-consciously, he cinched up the knot in his tie. Father Ferro entered the restaurant a minute later and assured Simon that his belongings were safe in the trunk of the car. The maître d' recognized Ferro and engaged the priest in French, in a short but spirited conversation. He led Dante and Simon to a corner table and concluded his dialogue while Simon admired the first-class room.

"Did you live in Zurich at one time?" Simon asked, when he and Father Ferro were seated.

Ferro lifted his menu. "No, but I escorted certain prominent Italian citizens up here from time to time. Some worked in international finance; others were politicians. All of them had expense accounts. There is never any question about luxury when it is someone else's money."

"I do have money," Simon assured, speaking of the $8,000 in Swiss francs he had removed from the bank in the morning and which he had distributed among his pockets and into his shoes. He would never again display a wad of cash.

The priest waggled a forefinger. "You are my guest, Mr. Penn. My banker has more money than God."

Simon laughed at the witticism and at the Italian's amazing knowledge of the subtleties of American English. He was liking the man more by the minute. They engaged in small talk about the restaurant and its history until the sommelier and waiter arrived to take their orders.

An awkward silence occurred as soon as the waiter had left. "Clearly, we each have much to explain to the other," Ferro said. "Why don't I start?"

"Please."

As he half filled Simon's wine glass with a good year of Piesporter Goldtröpfchen, Ferro trundled out the facts he had gathered, about all the major players in the Princeton Advent drama and the sequence of events as he understood them. Simon corrected him and filled in the gaps as briefly as possible. Then the priest explained why the Vatican was so intent on having the scrolls recovered and translated.

"So, you see," Ferro concluded, "there is a definite urgency about all this. Because of the frequency with which the first six prophecies have been fulfilled, I believe it is only a matter of months . . . perhaps weeks . . . before the final prophecy comes to pass."

"A world filled with vampires," Simon echoed. Despite the warmth of the restaurant, he felt suddenly cold. "But the scrolls don't say exactly how it will happen?"

"Unfortunately, no."

At that moment, the main course arrived. Famished, Simon resisted the temptation to wolf down his delicious medallions of veal. Across the table, Father Ferro cut apart his rosemary-scented roast chicken with a surgeon's delicacy. Simon wondered if the man had possessed such a fastidious nature when he was a cop.

116

"And now it is your turn," Ferro prompted, before slipping a small piece of chicken between his lips. "I am most intrigued by your bold flight from Princeton."

"Before I begin," Simon replied, "tell me again about this woman who visited Frederika's house just after we left."

Ferro recounted precisely Ray Pental's description of Solveig Persson. "All who serve Satan are clearly not among the undead," he concluded. "The woman was out in the full daylight."

"No, she's probably a vampire," Simon responded. "The legends are wrong about that detail. In fact, DeVilbiss came into my library in the middle of the day. But, like the old woman, he was quite bundled up. And he also wore sunglasses. Light definitely disturbs them."

"Start from the point where you leave Miss Vanderveen's mansion," the priest prompted.

Simon related in detail the flight across New Jersey, up to Canada, and thence to Zurich, to the point where he and Frederika went to the train station. He paused, not wanting to go on.

"It is difficult to speak of from this point?" Father Ferro sympathized.

Simon pictured the priest on the opposite side of a confessional. "Yes." In spite of Frederika's actions he felt as if he were betraying her, even if he told the story objectively. Yet, he had to voice his pain and confusion to a sympathetic ear. He advanced, step by step, through the misfortune with the forger, Frederika's explanation in the hotel room, and what he awoke to discover. The only events he omitted were Frederika's drinking of the dying man's blood and her provocative request that Simon examine her exit wound.

"She turned me in to protect me," Simon argued. "When I refused to take the powder, she felt she couldn't protect me anymore. And the only way she could prevent me from following her was to have me arrested. At least then I'd be safe."

"She did this purely out of concern for you," Ferro said, reaching for a toothpick.

"Yes," Simon answered firmly.

"How can you be so certain?"

"How? The way she held my hand. The looks we exchanged. Things she said."

"But she's an accomplished liar," the former cop countered, leaning back in his chair with the insouciant look of a dispassionate Devil's advocate. "Everyone interviewed by the police has attested to that. According to Detective Pental, you and Miss Vanderveen put on a real show in Newark Airport. The man you sold your tickets to is supposedly a very streetwise fellow. You have had theatrical experience, yet the man told the police it was Miss Vanderveen's tears that convinced him. Mr. Pental thinks it was also her great beauty. Is it not possible that your nearness to this beauty has blinded you as well, that you accepted what she wanted you to see?"

Simon was silent for several seconds, but his emphatic answer was "No."

Ferro finished using the toothpick, snapped it in two and laid it on his plate. He nodded slowly at Simon's fierce eyes. "All right. But you can't deny that Miss Vanderveen is not a normal person."

"What do you mean?"

"The word Detective Pental used was 'weird.' I mean that several centuries ago she would have been burned as a witch."

Simon scowled. "Now you're being melodramatic."

"Isn't visiting this DeVilbiss character for channeling with the dead weird? What about digging dirt from her own father's grave?"

"How—"

"Or using it inside a chalk pentagram to raise his soul? Isn't 'weird,' in fact, the word you used to describe Miss Vanderveen to your graduate student friend?"

"You found Richard Chen?" Simon said softly, even more in awe of the Vatican's emissary.

"No. I heard this secondhand, from Detective Pental. Your friend was interviewed by the police."

"How the hell did they link him to me?"

Ferro shrugged.

"Goddamn! Sorry, Father." Simon pushed his chair back from

118

the table. "Please excuse me. I've got to make a telephone call."

"Certainly."

The word did not go unnoticed by Simon. It was the same expression of unquestioning acceptance the priest had used when Simon had sent him off alone in the car. The man seemed surprised by nothing Simon did, as if he were pulling marionette strings Simon could neither see nor feel.

Father Ferro pointed the way to the public phone. Simon glanced at his watch as he walked. Quarter after one. Quarter after seven Princeton time. He dialed, got an operator, and placed a reverse-charge call to Richard Chen. The familiar voice that answered had no trace of sleep in it. The instant the operator was off, Simon said, "Did you get my message?"

"Yes," Chen answered, "and so did the police. They have this line tapped. I'm probably gonna be arrested for obstructing justice here."

"What happened?"

"They dragged me out of bed at one A.M. and took me over to the library. There were about twenty people there ahead of us."

"And?"

"They unlocked Room B9F and asked me to do what you had said."

"Don't keep pausing, Richard; come on!" Simon commanded.

"There was a black metal cylinder inside the duct, just like you said. And it had ancient scrolls in it. But they were the wrong scrolls."

"What?"

"After your boss examined them, he said they'd been in the case along with the Ahriman scrolls, but these were in Aramaic. Not the right ones. Don't ask me anything else, Simon; I'm totally confused. Are you all right?"

"I'm not hurt, and I'm still free, if that's what you mean," Simon managed.

"Well, you won't be free for much longer if you stay on this line. Whatever the hell you're up to, good luck."

119

Simon suddenly felt like he was going to piss his pants. "Richard! Don't hang up! Two questions: Do they at least believe DeVilbiss was a vampire?"

"I don't think so."

"Shit. And did you mail that stuff?"

"No. The police took it."

Simon slapped the wall in frustrated anger. "Okay, okay. Thanks for everything." He raised his voice. "Whoever's listening: anything Richard's done I tricked him into. Lay off him; he's totally innocent."

"Thanks, Simon," Richard's subdued voice said.

Simon hung up and visited the men's room. The ache in his bladder was mostly psychological, the same discomfort he experienced just before an opening night theatrical performance. Looking in the mirror as he washed his hands, he asked himself if such an intelligent-looking man could have been so completely blinded by Frederika's beauty and mysterious nature. He could not answer.

Father Ferro sat cross-armed and cross-legged, looking quite at ease when Simon returned to the table. Several franc notes lay on top of the bill.

"I already knew what you learned," Ferro reported, as Simon lowered himself heavily onto his chair, "but I also knew you had to hear it from your friend. There was a premature bulletin sent out early this morning that the scrolls had been located, followed by a correction. Now are you ready to reassess your relationship with Miss Vanderveen?"

Simon's memory swept back to the Customs line at the Zurich airport, to Frederika's insistence that he go through first, and to the guard's beguiled disregard of her metal tube once he had seen that Simon's was empty.

"She has the scrolls," Simon said, as much to himself as to the priest.

"How could she have fooled you? Weren't you in the room with her?"

"Yes, but I was busy typing a letter for the police."

"Three metal containers were missing from the room," Ferro

stated. "You thought two were empty, but she fooled you. You hid other scrolls inside the library."

Simon nodded.

"How long were you on the telephone?"

"Maybe a minute."

Ferro stood. "Let us be gone. When I was a cop, you couldn't trace an international call in so short a time, but technology improves every day." He gestured for Simon to precede him. "Before Miss Vanderveen was hypnotized and held captive by DeVilbiss, how many hours had you spent alone with her?"

Calculation was no effort; Simon remembered each occasion clearly. "About fifteen."

"Not even a full day of hours," the priest pointed out, as they exited the restaurant together.

"It was very concentrated," Simon defended. "You can get to know a person quite well in a short time if you're working on it."

"Not if the person is secretive. But even if you did know her personality then, she could have been greatly changed by that powder she was given. Perhaps no one knows the creature Frederika Vanderveen has become." Ferro indicated his car, a silver BMW. "It would be most instructive to learn from the woman herself. What was to be the next step of your plan?"

Simon dug into his coat pocket. "To visit DeVilbiss's den . . . to gather proof that he was a vampire and that supernatural forces controlled him. Frederika found an address and telephone number yesterday. I've got it here. In a town called Zug."

"Not far away. Perhaps we can catch her."

"She'll be there," Simon said, swinging into the passenger seat. "No matter what you think, she's still on our side."

Ferro fired up the engine. "She'll go there anyway. If she wishes to live forever, a single jar of powder is not enough. She needs to deliver the scrolls as payment to join this unholy club."

Simon shook his head as the car surged into traffic. If politics bred strange bedfellows, then vampire hunting was even worse. Necessity had teamed him up with a priest who apparently categorized people as either good or evil. The concept of a good vampire

121

was beyond Father Ferro. Simon admitted to himself that, had that vampire not been Frederika Vanderveen, he would have readily agreed. The fact of the switched scrolls was also damning. He hoped that she had carried them secretly with her for the same reason she concealed taking the infernal powder: his disapproval. Before they had entered the library together, to move the scrolls and to create the letter about DeVilbiss, Frederika had suggested that they take them to Europe. Her idea allowed their translation to continue the moment Professor Elmasri was enlisted to their cause. Simon had thought that the possibility of their capture by servants of Satan was too great to risk carrying the scrolls, and he had vetoed her plan. He thought about sharing his thoughts with the priest but held back, not wanting to mention Elmasri, their ultimate objective. He determined to hold his tongue as much as possible, to let events rather than speculation determine which of them was right.

"It is one matter if the Devil seeks you," Ferro went on. "Another if you seek the Devil. She will go to DeVilbiss's den, as you call it, because she knows no other place where Satan can be reached."

"She might have other clues," Simon said, after a moment's reflection. "From the diaries."

"Ah, yes," the priest exclaimed, steering skillfully through downtown traffic. "Another gift she stole for the Devil, to prevent the world from believing."

"Not necessarily," Simon countered, unable to hold to his resolve. "I think she took the oldest diary because it was written in Italian. She speaks the language; I don't."

"But the oldest diary will tell her how DeVilbiss first contacted the Devil."

"If it does, we'll know it, too." Simon reached into the lining of his coat. "I have a copy of the first seven pages, already decoded." As he held them up for Ferro to glance at, he yawned openly.

"Excellent. They may be of great use. Why don't you put your seat back now and catch some sleep, Mr. Penn?"

"Call me Simon," Simon invited, welcoming the suggestion.

"Our mutual cause should take us beyond formality."

"I agree," Dante said, glancing at Simon and smiling.

Ray swung his head left and right, searching for a telltale mailbox on The Great Road. Houses on the southern edge of Princeton were well separated and invisible, even in the dead of winter, behind dense, gray-brown curtains of trees. It wasn't the mansion enclave of West Princeton (where million-dollar piles of brick and marble shouldered each other), but the acreage of most properties made it a pricy neighborhood nonetheless. Far richer than Ray could afford. And information he had dug up said that Dorena Durazo was the sole resident on her four acres. Blood research evidently paid more than Ray imagined. Unless Dorena was up to her old tricks again.

Ray had been mulling over the business of the scrolls and the alleged vampire ever since meeting with Father Ferro the night before. The priest had clearly believed in the possibility of vampires. He also firmly believed in the authenticity of the Scrolls of Ahriman, and that they were a direct testament from God. As far as Ray was concerned, the jury was still out on whether or not vampires existed, but there was no question that those scrolls had been resting in Firestone Library. Or that several people wanted them badly. And now there was the added mystery of how they were not where Simon Penn had told his friend they would be. If it wasn't a big act on Simon's part, that meant that the woman he had fled with was acting as a free agent. But for whom? Veteran Detective Sutton had predicted it would get more bizarre. Clearly an understatement.

Ray's focus on the case had only sharpened as the morning wore on. Subfreezing temperatures had descended over Princeton on Christmas Eve and persisted, so that much of Carnegie Lake had become solid enough for skating. Ray had seen the ice-drilling tests posted on the police station bulletin board the day before and, when he got home, had announced that he would take his daughters skating first thing in the morning. The inevitable household

123

delays piled upon one another, until "first thing" got them to lake-
side at a quarter to ten. Lateness was no problem on such a large
body of water. Even though only a fraction of its surface was cordoned for skating, a thousand could have slipped, slid, spiraled, and
even snapped the whip without getting in each other's way. And
yet, of course, the cordoned area was never enough for some . . .
especially since the new-fallen snow had to be swept aside. Two
foolhardy sixteen-year-old boys had barrel-jumped the yellow-
flagged ropes to reach the already smooth expanses of windswept
ice near the canal spillway area. The lead teenager had promptly
plummeted through a thin patch where the water flowed quickly.
The depth there was over his head, but he found himself standing
in frigid water only up to his knees. Under him was the wobbling
roof of a car. By the time Ray and his girls had arrived, most of the
skaters had abandoned their sport to watch the teenager being rescued and the car being dredged out. Ray noted with relief that the
vehicle had gone down on the West Windsor Township side of the
lake . . . someone else's jurisdiction. His relief sank when, an hour
later, a diver and a tow truck pulled it out of the water and he saw
the car's make and license number. He and the rest of the force had
been keeping an eye out for this black Honda Accord for almost a
week. It belonged to Martin McCarthy, who was not just another
missing Princeton professor but the working associate of Dr. Dieter
Gerstadt, who had died in the suspicious home fire.

Ray had shepherded his girls safely to shore, pulled off all the
skates and poured hot cocoa for both of them before jogging
around to the canal tow path where the West Windsor cops were
giving the dripping car the on-site inspection. He flashed his badge
and was allowed close enough to confirm that the body of a man lay
propped against the steering wheel. The case would not remain just
West Windsor's. Ray backed away, before this shitcan was hung
around his neck.

Ray would work on the case, all right, work his ass off, in fact,
but he would do it his way. Which meant with a mind much more
open to the unbelievable than Grimes or Sutton would ever allow.
The two physics professor partners, according to Simon Penn's

note, had been as much targets and victims of Vincent DeVilbiss as those who stood between the vampire and the ancient scrolls. But for what reason? In all the horror fiction Ray had read, there were only two kinds of victims vampires pursued: people to suck vital fluid out of and people to ejaculate vital fluid into. And "pursued" was hardly the proper verb; people just chanced in the way and were inevitably "chosen" by proximity. The dead professors proved the literature wrong. Which suggested that the classic vampire image was also wrong. Which allowed that a more reasonable type of long-lived, blood-drinking creature might indeed exist. A sidebar in yesterday's *Trenton Times* vampire article contained some interesting facts on vampire lore and beliefs. The first was that one in seven Americans was convinced some form of such creatures existed. No one was more surprised than Ray himself when, staring at the waterlogged Honda, he found himself inching one mental foot over the line, onto the side of those thirty-seven million supposedly credulous souls.

Back at home, Ray had made much to Karen of the fact that the car was found on West Windsor turf. Not his responsibility. Nothing to threaten his well-earned day off. He changed to clothing he only wore in the house and made a show of putting on the slippers he got for Christmas. When Karen and the girls pulled out of the driveway, to take in a matinee showing of the latest Disney movie, Ray was already half changed to outdoor wear, his badge shoved into his back pocket.

At the station, Ray had been so absorbed in his thoughts that he never heard Grimes baiting him about workaholics getting just what they deserved. For lack of any other hook, he had latched on to one lead: Dr. Dorena Durazo. Long before Ray had allowed the possibility of the earthbound supernatural, he had learned to trust the intangible, insupportable intuition of his sixth sense. Now his deepest instinct told him this woman had definitely entered the morgue looking for DeVilbiss. She had not questioned with her eyes, much less her mouth, what a cop was doing standing guard over a few drawers filled with stiffs. She had waited for the pathologist and his assistant to go on break before entering the room. And she was a blood chemist, looking for a bloodsucker. If she didn't merit investigation, Ray told himself, he should be back on the beat.

Internet was proving a godsend for police work. Without getting up once from his desk, Ray accessed the New Jersey DMV and downloaded a full page of data on Dr. Durazo, including her present address and the driver's license she had previously held. Prior to moving to New Jersey, she had lived in Dallas. With the aid of a resource notebook, Ray gained access to the Texas DMV database and found Durazo's last known address there. The residence turned out to be a dormitory. Two phone calls revealed it as the housing unit for the Texas Woman's University School of Nursing but a sublet grad student residence as well for the University of Texas Southwestern Medical Center. Another call confirmed that Dorena Durazo had received her Ph.D. with honors from UTSMC in the cell regulation graduate program, specializing in hematology.

One final electronic outreach, followed by a phone call, confirmed Ray's intuition. Dorena Durazo had been arrested for the extracurricular lab activity of creating hallucinogenic drugs and for selling them on the nearby campus of the University of Dallas. Caught red-handed, she had thrown herself on the mercy of the court. Her excuse was the impossibility of support from her family due to the racial prejudices that condemned her Mexican parents to menial jobs. Although she had a prior arrest for shoplifting she had not been convicted, and the legal system made this inadmissible as having no bearing on the current case. The sympathetic judge allowed her to pay off her debt to society with community service. Her record was sealed, but Ray had by pure chance linked up with the frustrated narcotics cop who collared her. The guy was particularly irked that the judge had ignored the fact that Durazo was at the time being paid $14,000 in fellowships, above free tuition toward her degree. He had wished Ray well in "nailing her ass."

In college, Ray had lost his senior-year roommate and best friend to LSD, when Phil Sloane had attempted flight out their fifth-story dorm window. Over the years, between personal losses and job-related body bag cleanups, Ray had developed a high degree of intolerance to drugs and the people whose lives revolved around them. Lowest on his list were the over-the-counter and prescription abusers, whose destructive forces rarely reached beyond themselves and their immediate families. Then came the abusers of that time-honored and socially acceptable drug, alcohol, who did the majority of its killing in bars and on the highways. Way above, an entire factor higher on Ray's hate list, were the hard-drug purveyors and users. The feeding of their costly addictions fostered brutal, premeditated crimes, before and during use. The entire fabric of society was being torn apart by these twentieth-century laboratory-designed examples of "better living through chemistry," making the job of law enforcement much more dangerous in the process. If Ms. Durazo had reverted to her grad school extracurricular habits, Ray would do more than nail her ass.

Dorena Durazo's mailbox displayed only the road number, but it was sufficient. Ray drove past the driveway. He had already weighed how far he was willing to go to get answers. He stopped his car near a bridge at the road's low point, parked on the shoulder and jogged back. He waited until The Great Road was free of traffic and opened the mailbox. Several bills and what looked like a late Christmas card all had Durazo's name on them and no one else's. Ray returned the mail, shut the box and started up the drive at a brisk pace.

The house looked like one of the summer bungalows that blight the New Jersey shoreline, thrown up by weekend carpenters. One of its nonfunctional shutters was missing; Dutch blue showed here and there through the clapboards' battleship gray top coat. Either the woman cared nothing for material possessions or else had bought the place purely for the value of the land. Ray bet on the latter. He walked straight up to the front door and knocked, expecting no answer. The property had no garage, and no car sat in the rutted driveway. Ray knocked again without reply. He walked around the back cautiously, but not for fear of discovery. The sun had melted the morning's light snowfall, so that it flowed over a treacherous layer of ice that already overlay deeper snows long since solidified. What passed for a lawn only directly after mowings

127

ascended unevenly to a dense woods. Aluminum clothes poles, connected by sagging lines of gray cord, bowed stiffly toward each other like Japanese politicians. On a stake stood a rotten, miniature version of Durazo's house which no self-respecting crow would inhabit.

The back of the bungalow had a pair of doors, one sliding glass and the other of steel. The second led down to the cellar. Ray tested the sliding door with his right hand while his left dug into his pocket for a thin-bladed screwdriver. Ray had developed his law-man's ethics by way of lifelong Hollywood infusion; he believed devoutly that justice should always triumph. Although he would never have admitted it to his fellow officers, he accepted that situations occasionally arose where good cops were justified in bending the rules, to offset the bad guys' advantages. In this case, for example, if Dr. Durazo entered the medical center's morgue illegally to get information, his conscience was clear in turning the table on her. If she was innocent, she'd have lost nothing more than a few Btu's of heat when Ray went in and out the door. Ray also accepted that his personal sense of justice counted for nothing if he were caught; his job and pension would be history.

The sliding door was as cheaply constructed as the rest of the house. It had so much free play in its upper runner that Ray lifted the latch over the locking plate with no trouble. He entered into an informal dining area and closed the door behind him slowly, listening for the rapid clicking of claws on wood or linoleum. Still holding on to the door, he stamped his feet several times, but no four-footed guardian stirred. He locked himself in.

Ray searched the kitchen, living room, and two bedrooms with professional thoroughness, leaving no fingerprints and no signs of his explorations. His hopes of finding correspondence with DeVilbiss were in vain. Ray knew the man had come to Princeton very recently, apparently (as indicated by his rented car) from Seattle. Durazo had lived in the area for three years. Ray's best guess was that DeVilbiss had acted as one of Durazo's drug suppliers, via ships docking in Seattle from the Far East. But there was no evidence of drugs in the house either. With each passing minute, Ray's gut feelings became less certain. Perhaps, after all, Durazo was only a horror-obsessed hematologist hoping to find the proof of vampirism in a corpse's blood.

Beyond the bathroom door, Ray found the house's nominal guardian. The second-largest cat he had ever seen (after the twenty-five-pound Ragdoll Karen had owned as a teenager) stood alert in the bathtub, with all its tabby fur standing on end. It looked like the former heavyweight champion of the neighborhood, sporting one milky eye and a ragged half ear. But all its teeth were still in place, and it displayed them to the back molars, hissing from deep within its throat like a steam safety valve, to make the message of the fangs and fur totally unambiguous. It did not, however, show any inclination to defend its home, so Ray quickly returned the door to its near-closed position, hoping that would be enough to satisfy the beast.

One last door remained unopened. It had a deadbolt on the side exposed to the kitchen. Ray turned back the bolt and swung the door in. Beyond it lay a set of stairs, descending into cellar gloom. Up from the darkness wafted a pungent, farmyard smell. Ray found a light switch. He flipped it on and went down cautiously.

The entire space of the small cellar had been turned into a chemical laboratory. It was as neat as the upstairs was untidy. Ray saw neither skeletons nor skulls, no sparking Tesla coils or frothing beakers, yet he felt distinctly apprehensive. No matter how clean and tidy, this was a scientific laboratory in a bungalow basement. The stuff of *Frankenstein,* Vincent Price, *Re-Animator.* Ray suppressed the feeling, concentrating on the workbench directly in front of the bottom step. On it was a computer and several notebooks. To the far left sat a small television set, connected to a VHS machine. In front of the set lay a pile of videotapes inside their boxes, identically labeled. The spine of each tape read TALES FROM THE CRYPT. Ray's apprehension redoubled.

Ray flipped through the notebooks. They were filled with scientific shorthand, lines of symbols he only vaguely remembered from high school chemistry class. Above the notebooks and computer, a wall cabinet was bolted to the cinder-block wall. Its door was padlocked, but the hinges were merely screwed in. Ray patted the screwdriver in his pocket. Before tackling the job, he had to find the source of the barnyard stink that was roiling his already nervous stomach. He walked around the far side of the stairs.

On another table sat four cages. Three of them held rats. Not the small, white, antiseptic laboratory variety they raised by the thousands in Bar Harbor, Maine, but the huge, dark gray, mangy, razor-toothed kind Ray had last seen down in Trenton, scurrying in and out of the giant culverts that emptied into the Delaware River. Sewer rats. All three were horribly dead, the fur torn from their throats and red flesh exposed to the bone and cartilage. All four cages had been violently deformed, wire bars bent aside enough that Ray could have passed his hand sideways into them . . . except that the thought would never have entered his mind. The fourth cage lay empty. No dead rat. No flecks of blood, as in the other tortured enclosures.

Ray grimaced at the sight. Dorena Durazo was not going to be happy. The furry beast upstairs had evidently figured a way into the cellar other than through the bolted door. Ray took a step backward. Or maybe not. Maybe it had been something wilder. Like a rabid raccoon. It had to be something really big and furiously powerful, to bend those wires as it had. And surely the rats must have been frantically biting at it as it worked. Ray grimaced again, so that his eyes were nearly shut. He turned warily, not wanting to be ambushed by whatever had wreaked the carnage. The cellar was nerve-rackingly silent.

Keeping his back to the central steps, Ray sidled toward the workbench with the locked cabinet above. He pulled out the screwdriver and lifted it toward the hinges.

From behind the computer appeared the fourth rat, with not the slightest sign of injury. Catching the overhead light, its little eyes shone amber. It glowered at Ray, showing no fear. Ray yelped at the sight and retreated a step, instinctively swinging the blade of the screwdriver between himself and the vermin. It did not so much as flinch at his outcry.

"Shoo! Scat!" Ray shouted at the creature. It angled its head up at him, as if taking his measure. Big and ugly as it was, it was only a rat. Ray swallowed his fear and revulsion and reconsidered his position. He wanted badly to get into the padlocked cabinet, and this rodent was not going to stop him. He cried out again, brandishing the screwdriver, waving his other hand and stepping forward with a heavy, menacing tread.

The rat leaped straight at him. Ray sidestepped and caught it with the blade of the screwdriver. For an instant, he felt its weight impaled on the tool, and then its momentum pushed it off and onto the floor. It scuttled under one of the glassware-filled tables. Ray looked at his screwdriver. The point was smeared with blood. He considered pursuing and killing the rat so that he could feel safe, but he found nothing adequately long and lethal. He abandoned the idea and fitted the screwdriver into the first hinge screw and began turning blindly, his stare fixed on the dark place where the rat had vanished.

Just as the first screw was nearly out of its hole, Ray caught the faint, crunching sounds of approaching car wheels. Cursing under his breath, he retightened the screw with frantic energy, then bounded up the steps two at a time. The door was locked. He had forgotten to latch back the deadbolt before he descended. Only one means of escape remained: the cellar door.

Ray hurried down the steps. Directly above him, he heard the front door being opened. A sudden impulse made him grab one of the identically labeled videotapes from the counter top. He crossed to the cellar door and groped into the dim shadows for the latch.

A hurtling mass struck Ray low in the right leg. Nerves already piano-wire tight, he kicked back automatically and sent his attacker flying. With it went a piece of Ray's trouser leg, held firmly in sharp rodent teeth. The rat righted itself and scurried off once again into the darkness beneath the tables, moving as if the screwdriver wound caused it no pain at all. Above, the radio came on loudly. Ray wasted no time in using the noise to mask the opening of the door. He inched it steadily upward with his back, keeping his attention fixed on the floor. Daylight poured mercifully around the door's edges. On the wall beside the door was a light switch. Ray tried it and uttered a silent prayer of thanks as the far side of the cellar plunged back into darkness. Ray crawled outside and lowered the door into place. There was nothing he could do about locking it. Dorena Durazo might very well discover that the house had been entered; that mattered little to the detective, so long as he made a clean getaway.

Ray peeked up from his prone position on the ground, at the sliding glass door some ten feet distant. He could see no one inside. Angling away from the large expanse of glass, he slid backward on the water-coated ice toward the driveway. Once he reached the house's corner, he stood and bolted toward the safety of the woods, flinging water off his clothes this way and that. He maintained a precarious balance until he was almost to the border of the woods, then went down on his back in a muscle-wrenching fall that had him seeing double for several seconds. He expected at any moment to hear the sliding glass door being pulled back and a woman's voice commanding him to stop, but only faint radio music reverberated from the house. He regained his feet and limped into the cover of the woods, circling wide as he headed downhill to his car, clutching the videotape as the only trophy of his risky actions, glancing at his watch and wondering how in hell he was going to beat the family home when he wasn't even sure he would be able to drive.

Simon awoke to Dante speaking softly in Italian. When he turned his head from the hard cushion of the car door, he saw that the priest was speaking into a cellular phone that he had taken from the center console. Dante shot Simon a smile and finished his conversation.

Putting down the phone, Dante said, "I had to let certain people know we have arrived."

"What people?"

Dante laughed. "Even I don't know who they are, but I'm assured they are devout Catholics."

Simon straightened up in the seat. He saw that they were coming into a town. "Is this Zug?"

"Yes."

"How far have we traveled?"

"About thirty kilometers."

The cramps in some of his muscles told Simon something was wrong. He consulted his watch. "Three-fifty! I've been asleep almost three hours, and we only covered eighteen miles?"

"I had to stop at my hotel," Dante answered. "And there were other telephone calls to make . . . also a few special purchases. You were in *sonno profondo,* as we say in Rome. In a dead sleep, I think is your expression. I felt it was safe enough to leave you parked on the street."

"And if you were wrong, you would have found me in a real dead sleep," Simon remarked, wanting the priest to know that he found the decision ill considered.

"Here we are in beautiful Zug," Dante announced, ignoring the rebuke. "We will be staying at the Parkhotel. Four stars. Since I know you fled from the Savoy, I thought you might object to anything with less extravagance." He grinned at his own sense of humor.

From where Simon sat, Zug looked anything but beautiful. Beyond his window flashed rows of featureless factories and warehouses. The mountains ahead to his left side, however, were impressive. Rough meadow growths and dense stands of conifers segmented cascading expanses of snow.

Dante pulled off the main road, briefly climbed one lane and turned left onto another, labeled Industriestrasse. The Parkhotel was grand relative to the size of the town. Dante parked in a large lot across the street.

"Tonight, will you need anything from your shopping bag?" Dante asked.

"Probably not."

Dante popped the trunk lid remotely. "Good. Then I will be able to carry your suitcase and mine. I have already reserved a room under my name. I imagine you used the fake passports to rent the room at the Savoy?"

The thought of sharing a room did not please Simon, but he

133

realized there was no other choice. He had already sampled the BMW for sleeping accommodations. He nodded his head. "I'll wait out here."

"And then we can either go directly to DeVilbiss's home before darkness sets in or wait until morning, when I can assemble two or three other men to accompany us."

"If we wait, Frederika could beat us there." Simon fairly burned to find her again and learn from her lips her motivation for betraying him. More importantly, he had to discover what she had done with the scrolls. "She might clean the place out and leave us even less hope than we have now."

"She may already have done this, but we won't know until we get there," Dante said, swinging out of the car. "I'll get directions."

Simon waited until Dante had entered the hotel before leaving the BMW. He drew in a few fortifying breaths of cold air. The gentle decline of the land to the watery expanse of the Zugersee afforded an impressive view of the town and the country surrounding it. Below him to his left, he realized, lay the ancient part of Zug. One particularly handsome tower was topped by a sharp spire and had a steeply angled roof decorated in chevron patterns with blue and white tiles. Below the roof and a line of flower-boxed windows appeared to be a complex, astronomical clock. As he waited and paced, the sun inched perceptibly toward the peaks of the far western mountains. The frigid air held little of the moisture that, in summer, created atmospheric hazes; the view for miles down the lake offered a classic, picture-postcard clarity. Actually, it was better than a photograph, Simon reflected. The warm rays of the low sun peeking between lines of shot-gold clouds and sparkling on the surface of the cerulean lake, the crisply defined purple shadows in the deep folds of the bluish mountains turned the scene into a Maxfield Parrish landscape.

Simon heard the approach of feet, turned, and saw Father Ferro. "This is quite a view," he enthused.

Ferro nodded. "It makes one want to live forever." He marched around the car without admiring the scene and yanked open his door.

134

Simon was convinced the priest's remark was an oblique cut at Frederika, and it made him seethe. The engine came to life. Simon climbed inside and slammed his door.

"When you were a cop, did you ever shoot anyone?" Simon asked.

Ferro waited until he had left the parking lot before he replied. "When I was twenty-six, I shot a bank robber who pointed his gun at me."

"Did you kill him?"

"He pointed his gun at me," Ferro repeated, unruffled. "The hotel manager told me that the road listed in the telephone directory is actually in Oberwil. About two kilometers south. Watch for a building with red shutters, on the left side of the road. We don't want to lose any time."

The trip took less than five minutes, but Simon noted with alarm the darkening of the sky, particularly when the clouds hid the sun. They spotted the red shutters and turned left, immediately climbing steeply into a deep crevasse between towering mountains. The fir trees crowded in as if to reclaim the road for forest.

Imagining a host of bloodsuckers waiting at the end of the rough road, Simon automatically patted his parka pocket, then remembered that Frederika had taken the forger's pistol.

"I'll give you proof that Frederika left only to protect me: she took the forger's gun, so the police wouldn't blame me for that murder."

Dante shook his head slowly. "She took the gun for her own protection . . . from that event and for events to come. She will have to protect herself until she can make her deal with the Devil. You told me that DeVilbiss wore a bulletproof vest. She knows what you know . . . that vampires can be destroyed with less than a stake and a hammer. Killing from a distance, especially killing other vampires, is simpler than ripping out a throat with one's teeth, and guns with silencers are very difficult to obtain in Switzerland." He reached under his seat and withdrew a Walther P38 pistol with a silencer fitted over its nose. "This is one reason why I had to leave you for much time in the car. Do you know how to fire this?"

135

"I think so," Simon said, accepting the pistol.

"Be sure. It has a double action, which means you can carry it with a bullet in the chamber. In fact, it's ready to shoot now. If someone points a gun at *you,* can you kill him . . . or her?"

"Yes," Simon affirmed, in spite of the image Ferro had planted in his brain of Frederika brandishing the forger's pistol. "How many rounds does this gun hold?"

"How many bullets?"

"Yes."

"Eight. We have arrived." Ferro brought the BMW to a halt. The rest of the road was unplowed, although a set of rutted tire tracks continued up the hill through the ankle-high snow. "One of us should look around and the other stay in the car," Dante suggested. "Which would you like to be?"

"This is our plan . . . Frederika's and mine," Simon said. "You wouldn't have found this place if it wasn't for us. I go." He opened the door and willed his trembling legs to support him.

A breeze cascaded down the eastern cliff face into the steep little valley, stiff enough to make the pines whisper but not to disturb the snow on the ground. Simon trudged up the incline directly into the breeze, keeping to the tire ruts. At the bottom of the valley, direct sunlight was a memory. Simon pushed the hand that held the pistol into his coat pocket. The weapon's metal mass provided cold comfort.

Only two chalets stood along the final stretch of the road, dark and well distant from each other. The first had the name RATYCH displayed on a wooden sign which depended from the porch roof and swung uneasily in the breeze. The second, at the head of the road, was all but swallowed by shadow. The place could have received no direct sunlight until midafternoon, so deeply was it tucked into the crotch between the mountains and so overarched by conifers, dense to the point of blackness. It sat almost beyond shouting distance from the Ratych place, as remote as it could be while remaining accessible by car. The perfect lair for the modern vampire.

Simon paused at the Ratyches' driveway, debating whether or

not he should continue to the top of the road, so distant from the security of the car. As he searched for courage, the decision was made for him. A light went on inside the far chalet and, a moment later, out came the figure of a man. Or perhaps it was a boy. Whichever, it was not a person of great stature. The light from within the house silhouetted him and obscured his features, but Simon noted that he walked with a limp and that he held a broom. He started sweeping snow from the porch. As Simon's eyes adjusted to the distant darkness, he made out the boxy shape of a vehicle, parked toward the back of the chalet. The figure stopped sweeping and looked directly at him.

Simon turned abruptly and walked up to the door of the Ratych house, pointedly avoiding the return of the stranger's stare. He knocked, fully expecting no response. He peered through the picture window into the house. It was a small place, with few interior walls and an abundance of glass, not intended for heating in the winter but rather a summer residence. An open design for sun-worshiping city dwellers. In comparison, the chalet at the top was a fortress. Only a few windows pierced its walls, and those were quite narrow. DeVilbiss had chosen for privacy and darkness. His few neighbors were only around in the summer. But if that was indeed DeVilbiss's place, then who was tending it?

Simon peered up the hill again, as night seemed to descend like a theater curtain. The figure came off the porch in his direction, still holding the broom. Simon sprinted to the car, clambered inside and slammed the door.

"There's a man up there," Simon reported. "Could be more than one. Let's go back to the hotel, call up your friends, and come back at first light."

Dante steered the car into a K turn, reversing his direction. "First light may be too late. We have now warned whoever is there. Let us return to the town and collect the other men, then come back tonight." Halfway down the road, he reached for the cellular telephone and punched in a sequence of numbers.

Simon sighed softly at the prospect of Ferro's plan.

Dante set down the phone. "We're being followed."

Simon looked back. A set of bright headlight beams bounced down the hill in their direction. "Are you sure it's him? We've passed half a dozen houses. The car could have come from one of them."

"You think so? We shall see."

When Dante reached the main road he turned right, heading toward Zug. The headlights vanished for a time but reappeared, rounding the intersection with the red-shuttered building. "Zug is the central town in this area," Dante said. "This may still be a coincidence." He slowed the car to 40 kilometers per hour. The headlights barely closed the distance. "Can you see what type of car it is?"

"No," Simon answered. "I think the thing parked beside DeVilbiss's house was one of those big British wagons."

"Land Rover? Range Rover?"

"Yes. One of those. In a dark color."

Ferro eased further off the accelerator; the BMW slowed to 35. The vehicle behind began to gain.

"We'll be in the town's lights in a few seconds," Dante noted. "Then we shall see who it is."

Simon's throat burned and his stomach muscles ached with tension. He glanced back over his seat for the tenth time since they gained the main highway.

"It's a Rover, all right. Dark green or black."

"Whoever they are, they don't care about me," Dante said, again picking up the telephone handset. "I'm going to let you off where you can run for the hotel. Then I'm leading whoever this is to the police station. I will even telephone ahead to reserve them accommodations." He brought the speaker to his mouth. *"Geben Sie mir die Zug Polizei, bitte!"* He glanced at Simon. "I will go left at the Bundesplatz, then make three right turns. At the third corner, you will jump out of the car and run to the nearest building. Once the Rover passes, cross the street and go up the hill to the hotel. I'll go—"

Simon faintly heard a male voice speaking German from the telephone earpiece. The priest answered in staccato phrases as he skillfully steered around the plaza and into the first of his three right turns. Simon glanced back again. The dark Rover still followed, although it allowed two cars to separate it from the BMW. The second right loomed, then the third.

"Out!" Father Ferro shouted, tapping the brakes.

Simon leaped from the car and slammed the door behind him. The BMW catapulted away. Simon sprinted to the nearest alcove doorway and pressed himself into its meager shadows. The Rover went by. Simon noted only one human silhouette inside. Once it had passed and another car followed it, he dashed across the street. As he neared the opposite sidewalk, he heard brakes screeching and saw the Rover sluing into a wild U-turn. Simon ran north, until he reached a street with the unfamiliar name of Metallstrasse. He had lost his bearings. All he knew for certain was that the hotel lay one block up the hill, on a street parallel with the main road.

Simon continued onto Metallstrasse. As he neared the far corner of a brick building, he found himself approaching the open expanse of a large parking lot. Some six hundred feet catercorner across it, he made out what he prayed were the lights of the Parkhotel. He veered off the dark, deserted side street and slowed his pace to a trot. He was winded, more from fright than from running. Also, the potholes in the rutted alley were filled with treacherous pools of ice. The farther from the street he advanced, the higher rose the land to his left. He realized that beyond the nearest line of cars lay a cinder-block retainer wall. He was not in the parking lot but rather in a long alley that abutted the lot's lower end. He slowed again, to a brisk walk, and analyzed his surroundings. To his right lay the backs of a solid line of two-story buildings. To his left were cars and a wall now too high to vault. Behind him ran almost two hundred feet of alley and a street that might contain a dark Land Rover. Ahead another hundred feet, the wall of a building longer than its neighbors contained an overhead floodlight. In the welcome pool of light Simon could see the railing of what appeared to be a stairway up to the parking lot and the hotel. He hurried forward.

Coming closer to the overhead light, Simon realized there was a narrow space between the buildings, providing an accessway to the town's main street. He had run right past it in his haste and ignorance, compelling a long detour. He shook his head. Spilt milk; no way to reclaim the lost time. He counseled himself to remain calm and concentrate on his surroundings.

A figure appeared suddenly at the mouth of the smaller, perpendicular alley, head down and walking with purpose. The person wore a long woman's coat and a Russian-style fur hat. Simon vectored his forward momentum, throwing himself through a snowbank and against a large dumpster container, his heart pummeling the base of his throat.

Simon watched the woman hurry toward the stairs, her head still lowered, clutching a large purse before her. She came directly under the floodlight and slowed her tread, as if unsure of her location. She stopped, looking down the length of the alley. Simon felt the cloaking weight of the darkness where he stood and knew he was virtually invisible to any human eye. But the woman's gaze fixed precisely on him. She was tall. Big, not fat. In her early sixties. With blond-white hair. Just as Frederika's mother had described her to the police and Ray had passed along to Father Ferro. She started forward again, now only fifty feet from Simon. From behind the purse, she produced a thin knife.

Simon knew better than to run. He had experienced DeVilbiss's supernatural speed while matching wits against the vampire in the university library. This creature would be on him long before he could reach Metallstrasse. Instead, he held his ground and brought his hand halfway out of his pocket.

The woman came on. Forty feet. Thirty. Then she stopped, surprised by Simon's stand. But the confidence of a century and a half of butchering instantly renewed her composure.

"It is time for you to die, Simon Penn."

Even as Simon searched for a game reply, he knew his throat was too tight to speak. He had all he could do to draw the pistol from his pocket and aim it at the woman. His knees nearly failed him when she grinned in response. He blinked in anticipation as his finger tightened around the trigger. Flame licked from the weapon's muzzle; a muffled spurt of sound echoed through the

140

alley. The bullet struck the floodlit wall and ricocheted off, hissing as it rent the cold air. By the time Simon's eyelids winked open, the woman had somehow moved three feet to the right. He reaimed rapidly and squeezed off another shot. This time the bullet dug into brick with a spray of powder. Again, his target had miraculously dodged out of the way.

Simon realized he was telegraphing his actions, warning her when to dodge. His nimble mind adjusted without pause. He fired off five shots as fast as he could manage, in a random, wide spray.

The third bullet hit true, catching the vampire high in her left thigh, spattering blood across the snow. She yelped in agony, her knife hand thrusting out to a nearby car to keep her from falling.

Simon brought his free wrist under his gun hand to steady his aim. He leveled the sight directly between the woman's eyes and squeezed the trigger. The hammer made a hollow click. He was sure he had fired only seven shots. The woman, who had raised the hand holding her purse in an automatic gesture to ward off the impact, let it down slowly. Her face contorted into the most malevolent mask Simon had ever seen. He squeezed the trigger again; the hammer found no primer.

The woman pushed herself away from the car and came at Simon with more speed than any gravely wounded creature should possess. But it was not with supernatural speed. Given new hope, Simon spun around and dashed toward Metallstrasse. Before he had reached full stride one of his leather soles chanced on a patch of ice. He landed with all limbs windmilling the air, his skull striking the pavement hard. Through the numbing pain, he held tight to the urgency of rising and running again. Vision still swimming, he rolled over and brought himself onto hands and knees.

The woman towered over him, knife upraised.

"Now I shall kill you slowly," she told him. She tossed her purse onto a patch of snow and snatched the hair of his crown with such fury that his neck vertebrae crackled. His arms failed to obey his mind, and he watched helplessly as her knife hand moved inexorably toward his throat.

A guttural sound came from behind the woman. The instant

141

after her head jerked up and her neck extended in surprise, a sword blade sliced cleanly through flesh and bone and sent her head tumbling backward onto the pavement.

Simon's arms, finally reconnected to his brain, swung up in time to slow the timberlike collapse of the woman's torso. Her unguided hands flailed, the released knife sailing across the alley. Then her full weight came upon Simon, driving him back and down with such force that his knees winged out and his ankles and feet popped forward along the icy macadam. Blood erupted from the open carotid arteries in great gouts, catching Simon in the face and then spray-painting the snow beyond as the torso's momentum carried her chest into his face.

Every remaining drop of adrenaline released at once as Simon hurled off the dead weight, then rolled away in the opposite direction. For several moments, all he could manage was to lie with one cheek in dirty snow, sucking in air. Still within touching distance from him, the headless torso lay at last motionless.

And then, from beyond his feet, Simon heard the dull clang of something being dropped into the Dumpster. He rolled onto his back and looked for his savior. Nimbused within the security light stood the slight figure of a man, holding a thin, short sword in his right hand. He held in his other hand what looked like a long black wooden dowel. Abruptly, he was overcome by a coughing fit. He clapped his hand over his mouth, to muffle the rough noises. Then he bent his head as far away from his body as gravity would allow, squeezed his nose between thumb and forefinger and blew a stream of snot onto the ground. For good measure, he spit onto the same place. Simon's chest was still heaving with fright; his savior's movements seemed not in the least agitated but rather methodical.

Without saying a word, the little man pushed away from the Dumpster, set down his sword and dowel and walked up to the headless torso. Or rather limped. And Simon knew it was the person who had stood on DeVilbiss's porch. He took the woman's ankles in his hands, then looked down at Simon.

"Kennen Sie Deutsch?" he asked.

"Only *ein Bissel,*" Simon answered.

The man's mouth pursed in an expression of frustration. *"Ja, okay. Gif me please help?"*

"What . . . what are you doing?" Simon said, staggering to his feet.

"I put her in de . . ." He paused in thought, shook his head and pointed toward the Dumpster.

The crunching noise of shoes echoed, quickstep, from the narrow alleyway. Simon and his savior turned together, the little man angling as best he could without relinquishing his hold on the vampire's ankles.

Dante Ferro appeared in the light, holding a Walther P38, identical to the one he had given Simon. He looked first at Simon, then at the little man, then at the headless torso. The weapon relaxed downward.

"The woman who . . . was looking for me . . . at Frederika's house," Simon explained, his breathing still ragged. "She attacked me, and . . . this man came to my rescue."

"How could she know you would be here?" Dante asked, keeping his eye on the little man.

"I don't know."

"She iss a *Vampir,*" the man offered. "Dey haf come to Vincent's house, but . . . um, so wit you, dey see me and leave. She iss not alone. We must go. Can we put her in de . . . ?" Again, the word failed him, and he nodded at the Dumpster. "You do not want police, yes?"

"Is this the guy in the . . . Rover?" Simon asked Dante.

"Yes. I had a problem turning back in traffic, but I found his car and followed him up here."

"Well, he's right about the police," Simon said. "I had enough trouble explaining one vampire's death." Trying his best not to look at the decapitated body, he grabbed one of the ankles and dragged it in tandem to the garbage bin. Because he was so much bigger than the other man, the burden of heaving the body into the Dumpster fell mainly on him. Once they were done, he looked around for the head and realized it had been the source of the clanging sound he had heard a minute before. While he and the little man were busy, Dante had wrapped his fingers in his handkerchief and retrieved the purse.

"Do not take dat!" the man exclaimed, with clear agitation. "If we take any'ting and . . . stop by police, dey will know we haf kill her."

"I'll put it down when I've looked inside," Dante told him, unsnapping the clasp.

The man shook his head. "She iss a *Vampir*. A *evil Vampir*. Dat iss all you need to know von her."

Dante produced a small walkie-talkie from the purse. "I don't think so. This tells us you were right: she was working with someone else."

"You see?" the man said, reclaiming his sword but leaving the black dowel lying on the ground.

"Nothing else." Dante dropped the communicator into the purse and the purse into the Dumpster.

During the little disagreement, Simon had bent to the snow and scooped up a handful, using it to scour the blood from his face and hair. He watched the stranger moving as rapidly as his limp would allow, kicking snow over the patches of blood.

"I do not like this," Dante muttered, as he turned in a tight, vigilant circle.

"I lost the pistol," Simon told Dante. "Somewhere over—"

"I haf it," the little man said. He reached under the tail end of a parked car and came out with the weapon. He straightened up and held the Walther out, butt first, to Simon. Finally, Simon had reclaimed enough of his wits to look closely at the diminutive man. The most surprising thing about him was his age; he could not have been more than twenty-one. He had dark, thick hair and a dark complexion. The bone structure underlying the skin around his cheeks and brows was sharply angular, making him appear more Cossack than German. He had brown eyes and a hideous nose, hooked and wide of nostril. His lips were strongly bowed and thick, his eyebrows bushy and nearly grown together. From under the tousled hair on either side of his head, his ears stuck out like open car doors. Youth appeared to be one of his only assets.

"I am Wagner," he said, making the W sound like a V. "Wilhelm Wagner Essrag."

Simon reached for the proffered pistol.

Lightninglike, Wagner drew the blade of the sword across the outside of Simon's wrist. Simon yelped in pain and surprise. The young man whipped around and pointed Simon's pistol at Dante.

"Do not moof!"

"Don't shoot him, Father!" Simon called out. The pain was less than Simon had expected, so sharp was the sword's blade. "The gun is empty. And I think I know what he's doing."

"Put your arm in de light!" Wagner commanded Simon. "Still! Still!"

"He thinks this is a setup," Simon told Dante, while he turned his wound toward the floodlight. "He thinks we might be vampires."

"Maledizione!" the priest swore.

"Ja. Vampir," Wagner affirmed. "Because I am a friend von Vincent DeVilbiss."

Simon and Dante stared at each other in silence, each struggling to assimilate the implications of the little man's words.

Only a full half minute after he had cut Simon did Wagner relax. His shoulders slumped, as if all the fears that had filled him had flown off in a pack. He handed the pistol to Simon. "Excuse, please. Now I show you same." He exposed his left wrist and ran the sword across it like a bow over violin strings. Then he knelt and washed it in the snow. When he straightened up, his hands were nearly clean, but blood continued to flow from the self-inflicted cut.

"It is most wonderful to know that no one is a vampire, but we must go," Dante warned, picking up the vampire's knife. "Did either of you touch this?"

"No," Simon answered.

Dante tossed the knife into the Dumpster, then repocketed his handkerchief. "Let's go!"

Suddenly, Wagner's prodigious nose wrinkled up and his mouth opened, fighting a sneeze. Simon had dug into his pocket for a wad

145

of tissues and thrust half of them, just in time, into the man's hand. After the muffled sneeze, Wagner blew forcefully, wiped the blood from his wrist with the outside of the wad, then walked to the Dumpster and dropped the tissues in. After lowering the lid, he bent for the black dowel.

"Andiamo!" Dante called out impatiently. "The police are expecting me. I must get to the car and call them."

"We're coming," Simon said, pushing his pistol under his belt.

Limping along, Wagner aligned the little sword with the end of the black dowel and shoved it inside, creating a walking cane. He gave a counterclockwise twist to a gold ring at the top of the dowel, locking the two pieces together.

"You are called Wagner?" Simon asked.

"Ja. Not so de composer. I make no music. Like Faust's friend . . . you understand?"

"Yes," Simon answered, marveling privately at the dark parallel. "I'm Simon Penn, from the United States. That's Father Dante Ferro . . . a priest from Italy."

Wagner nodded. When he had finally caught up with Simon, he said, "Vincent is dead." Despite the certainty in his tone, his eyes searched Simon's, as if begging for contradiction.

"Yes. Vincent is dead."

Wagner flinched. "De evil *Vampir* hass killed him."

"Yes." There was no way Simon was about to tell Vincent's friend that he had been the vampire's executioner.

"Much *Blut* on your coat," Wagner observed. "I haf in de car a coat von Vincent. You wait."

Dante stopped beside Simon, and they both watched the young man limp briskly out of the alley and down the street to the dark green Land Rover.

"You told me the pistol had eight bullets," Simon said angrily to Dante. "It only had seven."

"It had eight," Dante asserted. "I loaded it myself. Give me the pistol!" Simon handed it over. Vincent exposed the breech and showed Simon the last bullet. "A misfire. But you're still alive.

146

Here." He pressed the bullet into Simon's palm. "I would keep it if I were you, as a good luck piece. Put it in your pocket." As Simon took his advice, the priest dug into his coat and came out with a handful of 9mm rounds. While he fed eight into the pistol's empty clip, he said, "So, DeVilbiss had a human friend. And this friend was not surprised by your appearance in Zug but rather prepared for it. Do you not find that incredibly strange?"

"Yes. He didn't even bother to ask my name. Stranger still that he'd be willing to kill to protect me. And that my presence signifies the vampire's permanent absence. Did you hear him ask about DeVilbiss's death?"

"I did," Dante said, handing over the pistol.

"Don't you have to call the police?"

"No. I didn't tell them who I was. I wanted to get us all out of that alley. Here he comes."

Wagner limped up the sidewalk and into the alley carrying a black, insulated nylon parka. While Simon traded coats he remarked to Father Ferro how, within twenty-four hours, both he and Frederika had had their coats covered in blood but, each time, immediate replacements had been handy, to protect them from the winter cold. Was it far-fetched, he wondered, to credit the coincidence to God's providence?

"Not if you recall that Jesus said, 'He who has two coats, let him share with him who has none,' " Dante replied.

"Where do you stay?" Wagner asked Simon.

"The Parkhotel. Just up the hill."

"You must leave," Wagner told him, after sniffling deeply and swiping the back of his hand under his nose. "Dey know you are in Zug now and will find you. We get your suitcases and go to Vincent's house."

"I don't know," Simon said, glancing at Dante.

Wagner touched Simon's shoulder with his forefinger. "I t'ink dey not come again, but if dey do, it gives a secret room dey will not find."

"I like the idea," Dante said. He turned to Wagner. "Why don't you go back to your friend's house and make sure it's safe? We'll pack our suitcases, check out of the hotel, and be there in half an hour."

Wagner held Dante's stare for a long moment, then nodded stiffly. The three men left the alleyway together and got into their separate vehicles. Dante waited until the Land Rover had pulled away before turning on the BMW's engine.

"Tell me exactly what happened to you after you jumped from the car," Dante said, reaching for the knot in his tie and tugging it down forcefully.

Simon described every detail, as well as his thoughts as each event occurred. "At least we're sure of one thing," he concluded. "Between cutting his own wrist and being a one-man influenza ward, Wagner's certainly not a vampire."

Dante threw his tie onto the back seat and undid his top shirt button. "One does not have to be a vampire to be evil."

"Which is one more reason that going to that house is crazy," Simon said.

"Not if it makes things happen."

"Like getting us killed?"

"That is a possibility. Perhaps I should go alone, and you stay behind. The room is paid for."

Simon folded his arms across his chest. "No way. Now that you know I don't have the scrolls, you want to get rid of me. But you can't, because I know where Frederika's going."

"And you won't tell me, eh? Even though I have rescued you from Zurich, fed you, and given you a gun."

"A gun that misfires," Simon countered, gesturing at the street. "I'll tell you, in time. Drive!"

Simon had thought he and the priest would merely collect their luggage and return to the car. Instead, Father Ferro sat on one of the beds and used the telephone several times, referring before each dial to a piece of paper he had in his wallet. He spoke in prestissimo Italian, incomprehensible to Simon. The moment he finished, he sprang from the bed as if it were aflame, grabbed his suitcase, and headed out of the hotel room, muttering in Italian. Only when they were back on the highway to Oberwil did he again speak English.

"Someone will clean up the mess in the alley before dawn. We will be on our own at DeVilbiss's house for about an hour. After that, two professional men will be parked down near the house with the red shutters."

Simon smirked. "What good does that do? How will they know we need help?"

"I am wired, as your police say. They are listening to every word right now."

Simon turned in his seat and looked out the back window. The road was deserted. "Are you really a priest, or are you a cop?"

"I told you: I was a cop; I am a priest."

"But these people listening to you are cops . . . old buddies?" Simon persisted.

"Think of them as guardian angels. Once we are inside DeVilbiss's house, be very careful of what you say. I may not be the only one who is using a microphone."

"I want you to be careful as well," Simon cautioned. "Our mad swordsman thinks evil vampires killed DeVilbiss. For God's sake, don't tell him it was me."

"Right."

Simon massaged his throbbing forehead. Evil from before the dawn of history was being fought with technology invented yesterday, and he was right in the middle of it. He felt less and less in control, swept along by events and players so wildly beyond his original plan that he felt in danger of drowning. He drew in several deep breaths and told himself he would be fine. He might have been the archetype of the meek academic librarian only days before, but he had evolved. Why shouldn't he feel positive? Even though DeVilbiss had faced him in the library without the powder's invulnerability coursing through his veins, the vampire had still possessed supernatural speed, strength, hearing, and sight, still had the advantage of five hundred years of murderous experience. Yet Simon had triumphed. A demon from hell itself had matched wits with Simon in DeVilbiss's rented house, but Simon had bested it. And this time, Simon had learned quickly enough against the vampire to get one bullet into her leg. Except for a hidden patch of ice, he would have outraced her to safety. Would Dante Ferro, for all his experience, have done as well? Maybe credit should be shared between self-willed metamorphosis and divine providence. He didn't care, so long as he survived and prevailed. Simon found himself staring at the fingers of his right hand, which he had been unconsciously flexing in and out. He remembered the feel of the broomstick handle he had fashioned into a spear on Christmas Eve, the weight of it, the feeling of triumph when he had used it to impale what he thought was an invincible foe. He clenched his fingers into a fist and found himself considerably calmer.

When they reached the place where Father Ferro had parked that afternoon, they found that the Land Rover had compacted enough snow to allow the BMW to drive all the way to the chalet. Approaching DeVilbiss's house, Simon saw that the front door stood halfway open. Father Ferro pulled into an open space beside the Land Rover, and both men unloaded their belongings and trudged onto the porch. From inside the chalet came throaty cries of rage. Dante set down his suitcase; his pistol was in his hand a moment later. He eased the door fully open with his shoe and peeked inside.

"Come in, come in!" Wagner's voice sounded. "I haf just get here before you, since I stop for groceries."

Dante entered, and Simon followed, guiding Dante's suitcase inside with his foot. The chalet looked ransacked.

"Dey did come back. Und dey haf got inside at last," Wagner growled. "Look! You see?"

"What did they take?" Dante asked.

Wagner spun around and around in his wild-eyed fury, inviting comparison in Simon's mind to a whirling dervish. "I do not know; I do not know."

"Did DeVilbiss keep things that proved he was a vampire?" Dante asked.

"No," Wagner replied. "Not'ing I haf see."

"Then nothing should be missing," Dante affirmed. "That's all they can want here."

"Keep looking, Wagner," Simon encouraged. "We'll check outside."

"*Ja,* okay."

The instant he had caught Father Ferro's eye, Simon jerked his head forcefully in the direction of the door. A long flashlight sat out on the porch. Simon picked it up and tried it. Its light shoved the night back powerfully. He stepped off the porch and headed down the hill directly toward the Ratych chalet. He heard the priest's shoes crunching through the hard snow behind him. It felt good to be in the lead. Every so often he swung the light in a broad arc, playing over the surface of the snow. Finally, he found what he was looking for. He stopped and squatted down.

"Woman's footprints . . . going and returning," Simon said. "One set."

"Your Miss Vanderveen has been here," Dante said.

"Look at the space between them on the way back," Simon pointed out. "She must have been flying."

"Like a bat," Dante said. "Wagner was right. A vampire did break into DeVilbiss's chalet."

"Goddammit!" Simon swore. This time he did not bother apologizing to the priest. "I'll bet she was inside that house when I went up to the door. She was waiting for Wagner to leave."

"Waiting also for the sun to set," Father Ferro injected. Two barbs, in quick succession. Simon had heard enough of them now to recognize a change in the priest's voice each time it happened. The sound made his fists ball up involuntarily.

Simon continued in the lead to the back of the dark house. They discovered a rear door, fashioned largely of glass. Simon tested the knob.

"Locked," said the priest. "Perhaps she broke in somewhere else."

Simon shone the light through the glass. "No. You see the wet marks on the carpet? She had a lock-picking kit I got from DeVilbiss's belongings. She must have used it, then locked the door when she left."

"How considerate. She cannot be far."

Simon turned and glowered at Ferro. "Say it a little louder. Maybe your professionals down by the red shutters didn't catch it."

Dante shook his head ruefully. "You want her to be caught as much as I do. Ultimately, this is not about Miss Vanderveen or her addiction to a certain powder. It is not about you or me. This is about a set of scrolls which must be translated and presented to the world within the next few weeks. Scrolls that are most likely in this woman's possession." He looked over his shoulder, up the hill to DeVilbiss's house. "I think we can go back now. We provided our deranged friend plenty of time to go through our suitcases, if he is also looking for the scrolls. I will sleep more soundly if the Dark Forces are convinced we are also only hunters. Please allow me to question him in my manner; I have been specially trained for such things." He started back up the hill, not bothering to see if Simon was following.

By the time Dante and Simon returned to DeVilbiss's home, Wagner had tidied up. The chalet was nothing like Simon imagined. It was decorated in an eclectic gathering of styles and periods, much of it modern and all tasteful. No ruined Carfax estate this. The place was not big, and the Bechstein grand piano dominated the modest living room. Places to sit were at a premium. Most of the room was devoted to music stands, shelves filled with sheet music and bound scores, a wall of stereo equipment, and hundreds of records, tapes, and compact discs. Recorded classical piano music reverberated from room to room.

Wagner led Dante and Simon on an unhurried inspection. Upstairs was a large loft, one side a book-filled study and the other Wagner's quarters. The first floor contained a guest bathroom, living room, small dining area, a standard kitchen, and a master bedroom with its own bath. Simon's and Dante's suitcases sat in front of the double bed.

152

"I am sorry you haf to sleep togeder," Wagner said, "but Vincent's bed is big."

"It doesn't bother me," Father Ferro said, smiling at Simon.

"Me neither," Simon said, although he had never become completely comfortable sharing a bed with anyone, male or female.

"Now I show you de secret room," Wagner said, entering the master bath. "De *Vampirs* haf not find it." Wagner opened the door to the shower stall, walked inside and pressed down hard on the soap dish. The entire wall of white tile swung inward. Behind it lay a tiny room. Simon realized that the secret chamber's far wall abutted the stairs. The configuration of the house was such that the room could exist without a stranger ever being aware of the missing space. Wagner switched on a light. The room was all but empty. As with the rest of the house, there were no sacrificial altars, no heaps of victim's bones, no capes, no coffin.

"It's as if the CIA swept in here and sanitized the place," Simon commented.

"But Wagner tells us nothing was removed," Dante replied. "We know so little about the true vampire; we must resist the temptation to fill in the voids with folk legends. There is definite information here: Vincent DeVilbiss clearly did not want to become a monster; he only wanted to live forever, to continue doing the things that make human life most enjoyable. To see his books and music is to understand that."

"But he *did* become—" Simon glanced at Wagner and modified his angry tone of voice. "He was willing to kill others to live forever."

"Only who de evil masters say to kill," Wagner defended. "He was much more good dan bad." The homely young man continued, in his halting English, to tell of his first meeting with DeVilbiss at a local concert, two years before. Wagner appreciated classical music but had no talent. Several weeks later, he and DeVilbiss chanced on each other at a second musical event and this time became friendly. Wagner described himself as a loner and credited DeVilbiss with being his first and only true friend. A few months into their friendship, a car ran a stop sign in Zug and broadsided Wagner's motorcycle, crushing his right leg and causing internal injuries that were almost certainly fatal. The hospital doctors described his swift recovery as a miracle, and Wagner let them think it. The truth was that Vincent DeVilbiss had learned about his accident and had hurried to the hospital, to administer a dose of a very special amber-colored solution. Wagner had been unconscious for the initial injection; the second dose DeVilbiss fed him orally. Both doses had come too late to restore his shattered leg bones totally. Later, after Wagner completed his recovery under his own powers, DeVilbiss hinted at his dark secret and its relationship to magic, amber-colored powder. Gradually, as Wagner earned the trust placed in him through loyal servitude, DeVilbiss revealed the price the demonic dolers of the powder exacted for their monthly deliveries. DeVilbiss insisted, however, that he paid far less than the Dark Forces of hell suspected, arranging time after time to spare the lives of innocent souls whose service to their fellow men made them anathema to the lords of the underworld.

"How interesting," Father Ferro said, in a soft voice.

"Dat is all to see," Wagner said. "I haf food for you."

On the way out of the shower, Simon examined the closed tile wall. The tolerance of its fit with the other walls was extraordinary. He would never have discovered its secret by himself and doubted that anyone else would. He tucked the realization away as one more fact tending to substantiate Wagner's close relationship with DeVilbiss.

In the kitchen, while the three men dined on cold Wiener schnitzel, French bread, Swiss cheese, thick slabs of ham, pretzels, and a bottle of Liebfraumilch, Wagner continued his tale. DeVilbiss had telephoned Wagner late on Christmas Eve, predicting that he might die and that if he did, someone might come who would help Wagner exact revenge. He had waited patiently for two days. This morning, long before the sun had cleared the mountains behind the chalet, he had his first visitor. The same woman he had just killed had knocked on the chalet door, ostensibly inquiring about houses for sale in the area. She had worn the typical avant-garde skiwear of the foreign tourist, and her story sounded plausible, but behind her designer sunglasses Wagner thought he caught a glimpse of amber eyes. Wagner had told her the chalet's owner had been away for many months and that he had been engaged as a house sitter, with no authority to speak about selling. Apparently satisfied with his response, the woman had returned to a red Audi sedan parked halfway down the road. She entered the passenger side, and the car drove off immediately. The woman had a partner. Despairing of another phone call from DeVilbiss, Wagner had looked outside every few minutes throughout the day for the promised avenger, which was how he had spotted Simon. He had had a premonition about Simon and had eventually decided to come down the road to parley. But Simon had fled. Wagner had hurried to the Land Rover and followed the BMW, electing to follow the "avenging angel" rather than the car from which Simon had jumped. When he had seen the woman standing over Simon, brandishing a knife, he had vented his outrage with one vicious swing of his sword.

"I wish vee had take her alive," Wagner said.

Ferro narrowed his eyes at Wagner and grinned. "That is the real reason why you invited us up here; you think we will be bait for another try."

Wagner shook his head, indicating he had not understood.

Dante dipped his head in Simon's direction. *"He and I* are worms for your fishing . . . trying to capture one."

Wagner laughed. "I haf kill one *Vampir.* You capture de rest." He rose from the dining table and headed toward the living room. "It grows cold. I make fire."

The music stopped. Wagner detoured, to change cassette tapes. "Vincent plays dis music," he shared, as a new selection began. He closed his eyes and swayed gently to the Chopin waltz. He seemed a pleasant enough fellow to Simon, solicitous, open, faithful. Watching him now, his behavior in the alley seemed impossible.

"The vampire woman you killed was in my home town, Princeton, when Vincent died," Simon told Wagner on impulse. "She tried to kill us there as well."

"Us? You und Father Ferro?"

Simon shot an embarrassed look at Dante, wishing he had held his tongue as the priest had counseled. "No, uh . . . a woman."

Wagner opened the screen of the large fireplace and began stacking logs and kindling. "Dis Frederika you spoke of?"

"Yes."

"Und she got *Blut* . . . blood on her coat so as you?"

"Yes, she did."

"When?"

"When the woman tried to kill us," Simon lied, wondering how tangled the priest would let the web get before he broke in. Father Ferro looked at him amused, one eyebrow cocked. "That woman vampire was the same one who murdered Vincent."

Wagner struck a match and set a fire starter log aflame. "But dis Frederika did not come to Europe wid you?"

"No."

"Vincent said he was in Princeton to get scrolls," Wagner said. "What is happened to dem?"

"They were taken from the library."

"By you?"

Dante abruptly came to the rescue. "Vincent is dead. The scrolls are no longer important."

Wagner opened the front closet, stooped for something bulky wrapped in plastic and carried it to the fire. "De scrolls haf not to do why you are here?"

"No. Vincent thought that other vampires would come here, to be sure he did not have proof of what he was," Dante said. He was a smooth liar, Simon noted, but not as good as Frederika. "We missed them. They know there is nothing here. You killed the only one we saw." He shrugged. "I think they will make sure we see no other vampires."

Wagner was silent. He pulled Simon's bloody coat from the plastic and laid it in front of the fireplace.

"Tell me more about Vincent's music," Dante invited, of Wagner. The little man obliged. Then they spoke of Zug and the local countryside. Because they discussed neutral subjects, the conversation (stilted as its grammar and vocabulary was) flowed for a time almost as freely as the wine. The light fireside chat had a *gemütlich*

156

air. But Simon did not feel *gemütlich*. Having just faced one monster, he felt as if he had brashly entered another's lair. Unlike Dante, he was not at all sure the Devil's minions would leave them alone.

Despite more assertions of intimacy with DeVilbiss, Wagner admitted that he had not been allowed beyond the chalet's kitchen and living room until the vampire left for Seattle. To his recollection, other than the dose DeVilbiss had given him in the hospital, he had never seen any amber powder. Nor had he seen DeVilbiss's animate Pierrot doll. Dante argued again that this was to be expected; if vampires did not live and behave virtually the same as humans, how could they hope to survive?

Hard as the men labored to buoy the conversation with talk of weather and winter, Andrew Lloyd Webber and Carl Maria von Weber, the magnet of their common interest invariably drew them back to vampirism. Dante was eventually compelled to explain his presence as a representative of the Roman Catholic Church. The complexity of his words exceeded Wagner's understanding. The conversation ground to a profound, embarrassed halt. After listening for several seconds to the sounds of the fire, Simon glanced at his watch. It was almost nine, and he excused himself for bed. Dante needed no prodding to follow behind him to the master bedroom. As they left the living room, Wagner opened the fire screen and fed the coat in.

As soon as he was inside the bedroom, the priest locked the door. He plucked a mechanical pencil from his pocket and scribbled a message on a small spiral notepad, asking Simon for the seven pages of decoding from DeVilbiss's oldest diary. On the back of the top sheet he wrote: *One of us must stay awake and armed. You sleep first. I will wake you when I am tired.*

So, Simon thought as he nodded at the message, Father Ferro was not as relaxed about the situation as he seemed. Simon was more than willing to postpone his watch; his body had been reminding him all evening of how many hours it was owed. He took his toilet kit to the bathroom, changed into pajamas, and readied himself for sleep. When he emerged, he found the priest changed to more casual clothing but nothing that indicated the man in-

157

tended to use the bed. Father Ferro drew a plush reading chair up beside the bathroom door, so the light from the fixture above the sink would fall over his right shoulder. From where he sat, his feet reached the lower corner of the bed. His pistol he had laid carefully on the floor within easy reach. He winked as Simon slipped under the eiderdown cover, but he made no sound.

Although Simon had hoped he would fall directly asleep, his mind was too agitated by fear, anger, perplexity, and foreboding. The whole time he had sat in front of the fire, he had fixated on Frederika, wondering about her motivations, what she had done with the scrolls, where she was at that moment. He worked hard at assuring himself that her actions were meant for his good and for the good of the world. In between, he fought to forget the images of the three violent deaths he had witnessed in the past four days. In the end, sheer exhaustion claimed him.

A noise woke Simon from his sleep. It was only a small sound, and perhaps its furtive quality was what had alarmed his subconscious. He sat bolt upright and clawed under his pillow for the pistol Father Ferro had given him. He saw in the indirect bathroom light that Ferro had vanished from the chair. A shadow crossed the light. Simon leveled his weapon at the bathroom door.

Dante emerged wearing a bathrobe, the sheets of paper in his hand. He blinked in surprise at seeing the black circle of the muzzle trained on him, then gestured for Simon to put the gun down. Reluctantly, Simon got out of the bed, tugged on DeVilbiss's ski parka, and exchanged places with the priest. A bookcase in the room contained leather-bound classics of Western literature, each in its original language. He selected *A Tale of Two Cities* before taking up sentry duty in the chair. As he opened to Chapter One, he wondered how Dickens would have characterized these times.

158

CHAPTER FIVE

December 28

∞

Player: We're more of the blood, love and rhetoric school. . . . I

can do you blood and love without the rhetoric, and I can do you

blood and rhetoric without the love, and I can do you all three

concurrent or consecutive, but I can't do you love and rhetoric

without the blood. Blood is compulsory—they're all blood,

you see.

—Tom Stoppard, *Rosenkrantz & Guildenstern Are Dead*

◦◦◦

S imon was shaken awake at five A.M. by a none too happy-
looking Father Ferro, who thumbed him out of the easy chair
and back into the bed. He awoke on his own at a few minutes past
eight and, since the priest seemed in no hurry to put down a hard-
back copy of *Il Gattopardo,* took his time in the bathroom readying
himself for the day. When Simon unlocked the bedroom door and
they emerged together, it was almost nine. The smell of strong
coffee greeted them. Wagner sat in the kitchen dressed in work
boots, bib coveralls, and a flannel shirt, watching a program on a
small-screen television. He had their places already set at the dining
table and grabbed the coffee pot as they entered.

"I take nothing with caffeine," Father Ferro told him. "Is there
any herbal tea?"

With all the uncertainties of the new day, Simon felt even more
jittery than he had the night before. He, too, opted for the tea, in
spite of the face of disappointment Wagner put on. Wagner had set
out traditional German breakfast fare: bread, fresh butter, and
honey. While they ate, he asked of their plans.

"We're not certain," Dante answered for them both.

"Well, I soon must go," Wagner said. "I haf work." Work, it
turned out, was embalming and doing cosmetic enhancement on
corpses, which explained much in Simon's mind about how the

160

little man could behead the vampire with such cold detachment. Wagner had a customer being delivered to a Zug funeral parlor at ten, so that the corpse might be presentable for viewing at six o'clock.

"You can stay so long as you like," Wagner invited. "I take my t'ings und go back to my apartment. I am done here."

"What will happen to this place?" Simon wondered.

"It will probably pass to the state," Dante said. "After all, it is not as if there are any brothers or sisters alive to claim his belongings."

"A shame to leave," Wagner said. "I take de tapes he made. You take all you want. Dis, for sample." He lifted a golden statue that sat dead center on the table. It stood five inches high and was the figure of a woman strumming a lute. The details of her tiny fingers were just short of miraculous, as was the beatific expression on her face. Dante accepted the statue and examined it closely.

"It is Saint Cecilia," Wagner revealed. "You know, de woman von Roma, who is holy for *die Musik.*"

"It looks like real gold," Dante said.

"*Ja.* Real. Is made by Benvenuto Cellini. Very . . . *teuer.*"

"Expensive," Dante translated.

Wagner shook his head. "No. I mean to Vincent."

"Dear to Vincent. Valuable?" Simon suggested.

Wagner pointed. "*Ja.* Exactly. He loved dis statue more dan all else in de chalet. He said it was . . . *sein Glückstück.*"

"I think it means his good-luck piece," Dante told Simon. He smiled at the statue. "I think I know why." Then, to Wagner, he asked, "If it was so dear to Vincent, why did he not take it with him to Seattle?"

"He say America have too many robbers. He was afraid he would loose it. He should have bring it." Father Ferro replaced the exquisite artwork in the center of the table, but Wagner pushed it back toward him. "If you not keep it, give to de church. To sell for de poor."

Dante looked at Simon, who nodded his agreement. The priest lifted the statue again. "I wonder if it really is Saint Cecilia. In paintings, she's usually depicted playing an organ."

161

"Probably is," Simon replied. "The lute in her hands is much more aesthetic."

Dante held the work so close to his face that his eyes half crossed focusing on it. "I'm sure he liked her because of his love of music, but I would wager he didn't know something else about her."

"What?" Simon said, blinking as a reflection from the gold struck his eye.

"We now know that vampires can definitely be killed by decapitation. According to the legend, when the Romans tried to burn Cecilia, the flames avoided her. A centurion finally killed her by chopping off her head."

Wagner's surprised expression seemed to indicate that he understood this English quite well.

"Even if it's not by Cellini, it must be worth thousands of dollars," Simon said, rising from the table. "Better to donate it to the Church than have it stolen and melted down for weight."

Wagner used his napkin to blow his nose, which no longer had a congested sound. Dante commented on how much better his cold seemed.

"I t'ink my body has killed all de *Bakterien* when de too much wine made dem drunk," Wagner speculated, contorting his homely face into a mock-somber expression. He clicked his fingers. "I haf a gift für Mr. Penn . . . my own gift." He went to the front door and snatched up his jackal-headed black cane. "I do not use dis never. Only haf I carry it because of de *Vampirs*. *You,* I t'ink, will need it yet." He handed the sword cane to Simon with a flourish. "Now I go."

The three men said their goodbyes. Simon and Dante followed Wagner out of the house and stood on the porch as the little man limped to his Land Rover. Dressed as Wagner was, Simon thought he looked more suitable for mucking out a barn than tending to a corpse. Wagner whipped the Rover around and set it plunging out of the firs' deep shadows into a day overcast by snow-pregnant clouds. His left hand thrust out of the window opening and waved vigorously.

162

"I think he lied," Dante said, as the vehicle bounced past the other chalet.

"About what?"

"About just taking the tapes of DeVilbiss's music. I didn't look in the loft closet last night, but I don't think what it held could have filled the back of that Rover. Look! You cannot even see him through the back windows. He was a true grave robber . . . and he did it quietly, as a grave robber would, while we were both in that bedroom sleeping."

Another subtle barb, this time directed at Simon's dereliction of guard duty. Simon felt himself start to shiver. "Let's get back inside and do our own packing."

"One moment," Dante said, grabbing Simon's arm. "Remember: no talking about anything sensitive in there."

"Yes, General." As Simon walked through the door, he twisted the gold ring around the cane's neck and exposed the blade.

"It is difficult to believe such a small sword could cut through a human neck with one strike," Dante remarked.

"Not really. Test it," Simon invited. "No, don't run your finger along the blade; across it. You can feel the sharpness just as well."

Dante touched the blade gingerly and grimaced. "Let me guess; you were a Boy Scout."

"Don't belittle it," Simon returned coolly. "My Scout training just saved you some blood. It's like a big razor, isn't it?"

"Let us pack and go," Ferro said in response, striding toward the master bedroom. Simon followed. He tried to be inconspicuous about stashing some of DeVilbiss's more ancient first editions in his suitcase, but Dante noticed the books and chuckled. The priest, on the other hand, did not seem at all guilty about grabbing the golden St. Cecilia off the dining table on the way out.

"Now I think we are free to talk," Dante allowed, stowing his suitcase in the BMW's trunk. "You promised to tell me the rest of your plan with Miss Vanderveen."

"After here, we were to go south to Lugano."

163

"Why?" The priest went down on his knees and peered under the gas tank, the statue still in his hand.

"What are you doing?" Simon asked.

"Looking for a bomb. That is how I would get rid of us if I were a vampire . . . although there wouldn't be much blood left to drink." He looked up at Simon. "You didn't mention it, but Miss Vanderveen *did* drink the forger's blood, didn't she?"

"I don't know," Simon answered. "I was standing guard."

Dante rose and walked to the front end of the car. "You know." He knelt and repeated his inspection. "They do not want us dead yet. Perhaps they have observed that we do not carry the scrolls. We are more valuable alive, to lead them to your beautiful vampiress. You *can* lead us to her, can't you, Mr. Penn?"

Simon opened his car door. "Remember, I invited you to call me Simon. All my friends do."

"Are we friends, Mr. Penn?"

"You have half that answer."

"And you the other half." Dante rubbed his free, snow-covered hand against his trouser leg. "Why Lugano, Simon?"

"Because she attended the American School there, from when she was twelve, I think, until she came back to the States for college. She thought there were still two or three people living in the area whom she could rely on to help get us across the border."

"Their names?"

"She didn't share them with me."

Father Ferro closed the trunk and walked around the car to the driver door. "The Italian border runs around three sides of Lugano. What is in Italy?"

Simon climbed into the car, compelling Dante to do the same. "First, you tell me why DeVilbiss considered the statue a good-luck piece."

Ferro adjusted the St. Cecilia statue on the center console where he had placed it, started the engine and backed slowly down the road. "Because the vampire was once a priest."

"What?"

"That is what he wrote in his diary, and I have no reason to

164

doubt it. He was born in Rome in 1464. St. Cecilia is a patron saint not only of his beloved music but also of Rome. But he was turned to evil when he lost his faith. He wrote that the Church itself was responsible for destroying it. Rodrigo Borgia was pope. *Capisce?*"

"And how could God care about men if he let such a person keep the Keys to the Kingdom," Simon answered.

"Exactly. There is another possibility why he favored the statue: it was through a saint's statue that the Devil first spoke to him. Ironic, eh? Enough to make him pin all his hopes on this life, I think. Of course, I have only those few pages you decoded, but Mr. DeVilbiss . . . his name was Innocente Farnese in those days . . . DeVilbiss seemed a very interesting man."

"He may have begun as a man, but he ended a monster," Simon judged.

"You would know," Dante granted. "Nevertheless, I wish I had known him. He is like my mirror image. I started my life in a violent job . . . killed a man, as you were so eager to learn. Then my faith grew. I turned to God and the Church. He started as a priest, lost his faith, and turned to a life of killing." He raised his graying eyebrows at Simon. "You wondered how coats were ready when you and Miss Vanderveen needed them, that perhaps it spoke of God's providence? I think it is not by chance that any of us have been cast in this passion play: you, I, DeVilbiss, and your beloved Frederika." They had reached the house with the red shutters and the main highway. "I ask again," Dante said as he brought the car to a stop at the intersection, "why did you want to reach Italy?"

"We didn't," Simon answered. "Our ultimate destination was Athens, to speak with—"

"Mustafa Elmasri," Dante said, finishing the sentence with confidence.

"Yes. Then he *is* the world's best Akkadian scholar."

"The best scholar *you* can reach. There are better, in Iraq, Iran, and Russia." Dante tapped his forehead several times. "Precisely what I would have done. You thought you would convince Elmasri to continue the translation of the scrolls."

"Right."

Dante drove onto the highway, turning right.

"Lugano's the other way," Simon told him. "You're heading north."

"I am," Dante answered. "I must leave this car in Zug. It is not a rental but belongs to someone in Zurich. We can go to Lugano by train. By the time we arrive, another car will be waiting for us." Before Simon could continue the conversation, the priest had snatched up the car phone, dialed, and begun to chatter in Italian. He finished his third phone call just as he was pulling into the train station parking lot. After he and Simon had emptied the BMW of their belongings, Dante stowed the golden St. Cecilia inside his luggage, hid the car keys above the sun visor, depressed the lock button, and shut his door securely.

The librarian and the priest carried their luggage into the Zug train station at quarter past ten. The next train heading south was a local, arriving in Zug at five minutes to eleven. A northbound train had just departed, and the station was all but deserted. Father Ferro purchased tickets while Simon scouted the area in vain for anyone seeming to act as a lookout. Outside, midday looked more like dusk, as the snow clouds scraped their pewter-colored bottoms over the nearby mountains. When he came back into the station, he found Ferro still standing at the ticket window. The station master reappeared and handed over a package the size of a thick paperback novel, wrapped in brown paper and secured by white twine, which Ferro stuck into a coat pocket. He ignored Simon, evidently preferring to bend the ear of the station master. Simon truthfully had listened to enough from the priest, so he bought the *New York Times* international edition, to search in vain for news of what the world knew of him and vampires.

Ten minutes before the train's scheduled arrival, the station began filling up. It was not a large structure, and a steady trickle of latecomers was enough to make the place seem crowded. Simon studied each face intently. He knew that, true to folklore, DeVilbiss had feared venturing into broad daylight. But he also knew that, unlike the legends, daring the sun was not an impossibility for the vampire. Perhaps only painful, blinding, or enervating. The masking snow clouds seemed to offer the servants of evil an open invitation to hunt by day, yet no traveler acted remotely uncomfortable. Simon was sure that hell had sounded worldwide alarms in its desperation to destroy him, Frederika, and the scrolls, so he continued his wary inspection of the crowd. He dismissed two young soldiers, three nuns, a grandmother having no luck controlling her two grandsons, and an obese man who could have been a long-lost twin of his Uncle Bob from Metuchen, New Jersey. Several lone men qualified, but they were so self-absorbed and seemed so taken aback by Simon's stare that he found it difficult to conceive of any of them as dangerous. No one in the crowd had amber irises.

Simon looked up from his newspaper when he heard the announcement for their train's arrival. He saw Father Ferro staring at a hunchbacked old man who had labored through the waiting room's door carrying a carpetbag. The man was trailed by the station porter, who had two large suitcases on his hand truck. The old man's skin was extremely sallow and splashed with liver spots. His nose looked like a rose-colored cauliflower. Simon recognized the condition, called acne rosacea. In his prime, the old man might conceivably have been as tall as Father Ferro, but it was difficult to judge from his stooped condition. He scudded past Simon and Dante without a glance at them, intent on getting to the train that had just pulled in. In his efforts, he puffed more than the locomotive outside.

Simon and Dante gathered their luggage and left the station. The train was three cars long. Noting the number of passengers sitting in the back cars, Dante angled toward the first. He paused for Simon.

Still scanning the surrounding area, Simon handed Dante his suitcase. "Get on and save me a seat. I want to be sure no one boards at the last second."

Father Ferro climbed onto the train. Simon waited until the platform lay empty and the locomotive made its first lurch. He hopped on and walked down the narrow aisle in the direction of the train's movement. The moment after he spotted the priest stowing their luggage inside an unoccupied compartment, he caught another image out the aisle window.

"Dante, come here! Quickly!" he called.

The priest pushed open the compartment door and stepped into the corridor. "What?"

Simon pointed. "Look back there! The Rover."

Receding from view was a dark green Land Rover sitting just off the road, beside an outdoor telephone booth and what seemed to be a small, vacant factory.

"There are no houses or apartments on that street," Simon noted, with tension in his voice, "and I certainly didn't see a funeral parlor."

"Did you see the license number?" Dante asked.

"No."

"It is probably not Wagner's. The back of that car was not filled with boxes and suitcases. There must be more than a thousand green Rovers in Switzerland." Dante turned from the accelerating panorama and faced Simon. "If he is not who he claimed to be, Wilhelm Wagner Essrag is still behind us now. Let us concentrate on what is ahead. I very much need the names of the people Miss Vanderveen planned to contact in Lugano." He paused for a second, his eyes holding Simon's. "Otherwise, getting them will be a long process. By that time, she may have slipped over the border."

Simon's head jerked back, finally understanding Ferro's words. "I'm not holding out on you. I told you; I don't know their names. *I'm* sharing what I know . . . but I don't think you're confiding in me. What will you do if you find Frederika?"

"What do you mean?"

"All you care about are the scrolls. Would you kill her to get them?"

Dante averted his eyes and shook his head at the landscape. "Don't be ridiculous. If I killed her and she had hidden the scrolls somewhere, then where would we be?"

Simon grabbed the priest's upper arm. "You're begging the issue. Promise me Frederika won't be hurt!"

Dante gave Simon's hand a withering glance, causing the young man to let go. "She's a vampire. What hurt can come to her?"

"You know that's not true. I've seen two vampires die already.

She didn't become one of her own free will, and the only reason she didn't stop taking the powder was to protect herself and me. As soon as the scrolls are safely with a translator, she'll stop."

Dante's eyes, lively and warm by nature, stared back still and cold. "That might have been her intent, but neither she nor you can know the power of such an infernal potion. She has taken this Devil's mixture for many days now. She may be completely changed to a creature of the night. From what I have learned of her, that will not be such a great change."

Simon's breath came with difficulty. It was only by a force of will that he resisted punching the priest in the face, despite knowing that the man was powerful and an expert at self-defense. "Enough, damn you! I understood your attitude toward her yesterday."

Dante cocked one eyebrow. "But do you understand your own attitude toward her? I think not . . . and that is why I keep reminding you what she was and what she has become. Looking in from the outside, I see clearly that you have been bewitched by this woman's beauty and mystery. Your friend Richard Chen has said the same thing; several people who worked with both of you in the library have reported it. Consider also that she is really little more than a stranger to you. Set your feelings aside, Simon, and realize that she is not longer the hunter but the hunted. She has made herself so."

Simon sighed deeply. "But she's not evil. Not an hour ago, you were willing to grant DeVilbiss a number of human qualities. This was a man who had voluntarily taken his first powder and who had taken it for five hundred years. I want you and your invisible army to keep that in mind when Frederika is finally found."

"Fair enough."

Simon fought to keep his eyes from welling with angry, frustrated tears. "From now on, let's agree to talk about her as little as possible . . . especially as a vampire. Our collaboration has been stressful enough as it is."

"I agree."

Simon leaned against the window. "Those telephone calls you

made . . . I assume you've sent people to Athens, in case she eludes us and reaches Professor Elmasri."

"Agents have been sent," Ferro confirmed, "but she will not find Elmasri, whether she eludes all of us or not."

"What do you mean?"

"Elmasri isn't in Athens. He has been in Florence for the past week, and will be for another. Do you remember last summer when the Mafia bombed the Square of the Uffizi, to try to blackmail the politicians into calling off their pursuit?"

"Sure. They threatened the big tourist trade."

"Exactly. The bomb did little damage to the Uffizi Gallery, but it caused a terrible fire in the city's ancient archives across the alley. Elmasri volunteered his time between semesters to help salvage information. He's also there because he has a lady friend . . . a *married* lady friend his wife doesn't know about."

"How do you know all this?" Simon asked, amazed.

"I tried to reach him in Athens last week, to talk about the scrolls. He answered by E-mail from Florence. I know about the woman because I am from Florence. My family is well informed, and none of them knows how to keep secrets . . . at least other people's secrets."

The obese man who looked like Uncle Bob from Metuchen left one of the compartments, heading toward the bathroom. Seeing him coming, Simon pushed open the door to their compartment and gestured for Dante to enter. When they were both seated, he said, "I have to tell you, Dante, I'm very frustrated. Let's say Frederika is still on our side. Even given that, all we've gotten out of this trip are a few diaries. And what proof are they? Authorities would say they were fiction, written on some old blank journal books found in an attic. I feel as if I've come three thousand hard miles for nothing."

Dante sat back in his seat, folded his arms, and shut his eyes. "Most journeys are frustrating when one is only halfway there. Be patient, Simon. Lines converge. Demons awaken." Without opening his eyes, he pointed in the general direction of Simon's suitcase, where Wagner's cane lay secure under two straps. "And the knight's sword is sharp indeed."

"Got everything?" Simon asked, as the train slowed for Lugano station.

Father Ferro yawned. His hands, filled with newspapers and belongings, were unavailable to conceal his wide-open mouth. Simon envied his ability to sleep on a train, especially given the circumstances. Then again, the priest was not the one being tracked by servants of hell.

"Sorry," Dante said. "Yes, I am together. Take your time getting off, so that we are last. If anyone follows then, we have reason to worry."

The train came smoothly to a halt. The first one off was the conductor, carrying two large suitcases. Behind him hobbled the old man and his carpetbag. From another car exploded the two young boys, gamely followed by their scolding grandmother. All five moved rapidly into the station, against the flow of a dozen people intent on boarding.

"That seems to be it," Simon said. "Let's go."

"Wait until the conductor returns," Dante counseled.

"I'll wait by the door." Simon picked up his luggage and headed for the exit, leaving Dante to do as he pleased. The priest followed right behind. The conductor reappeared from the station, mounted the first step of the last car, and blew his shrill whistle. As soon as he was on the platform, Simon put down his luggage and turned to scrutinize the three passenger cars. No one else emerged. The train glided down the track, clanking and hissing.

Simon consulted his watch and saw that it was a little past one o'clock. "What kind of car is waiting for us?" he asked Dante, who had dug into his wallet and found his scrap of paper filled with telephone numbers.

"An Alfa Romeo, but it is not waiting for *us*. I must see a contact who has worked many years at the American School. She should be able to tell me who were Miss Vanderveen's close friends. You are a wanted man, so I must visit her alone. In the meantime, while the sun is in the sky, have a little fun. This is a wonderful resort town. Room 216 will be unlocked for you at the Splendide Royal Hotel. You said you have money?"

"Yes."

"Take a taxi. Do not stop at the hotel's check-in counter. If you go out, watch for police. I will telephone you for supper, eh? *Addio.*" Dante's words were delivered with machine-gun rapidity. His impatience to be about his business was obvious.

"Thanks. You go with God also."

As he watched Father Ferro crossing the station hall with long strides, Simon feared a growing inessentialness in the battle between Good and Evil. He wondered if, as Frederika had done, the priest would eventually turn him in to the law authorities. But that would not happen until after Ferro had the scrolls secure. More likely he would just walk away, as he was doing now, and leave Simon to his own devices. Simon couldn't blame him; the Church was taking enough of a risk involving one of its priests with a wanted fugitive. Perhaps he had been wrong in assuming he was the major protagonist in what Dante had described as a passion play; perhaps Dante was God's chosen warrior, and Simon merely his facilitator. But "perhaps" wasn't good enough. Simon would push on, and only God or fate would inform him of his superfluity. He took a moment to orient himself, then headed for the muted sunlight beyond the station doors.

While Simon and Dante were saying their goodbyes, the little old man with the cabbage-rose nose was easing himself feebly into a taxi on the street side of the station. The driver, Rudi Mueller, slammed down the trunk lid, then skipped around the right rear fender to be sure the old bag of bones hadn't croaked from his wheezing efforts. He found the quivering figure sitting round-shouldered in the back seat, staring blankly ahead. Rudi slammed the door and strode around to his own seat. Christ, he thought, the guy's only about twenty years older than me. I hope I'm dead before then if I'm gonna be like that.

"You okay, mister?" Rudi asked into the rearview mirror as he buckled himself in.

"Okay." The old man's tongue darted out and back, out and back, as if he were trying to get a piece of cigar off his lips.

"Where to?"

The passenger's hand gestured vaguely to the left. "Up the hill. That way."

"Which street?"

"I forget," the small voice answered. "I'm visiting my niece. Visited her lots of times. Don't recall the street name, but I can show you."

Rudi rolled his eyes in annoyance as he switched on the ignition and the meter and put the taxi into gear. The old man's German sounded foreign. Even if the coot did remember his destination correctly, ten to one he had forgotten to convert his money to Swiss francs. Even if he hadn't, the old farts never tipped. He had been driving taxis for nearly thirty years, but this fare was definitely one for the memory books. Supper conversation at least.

"That way," the small voice repeated, accompanied by another vague gesture.

Street by excruciating street, with pull-overs to curbs, the honking of other vehicles' horns, angry gestures from impeded drivers, and even one U-turn, Rudi and his doddering fare made their way down through the old part of the city, across the Cassarate River, then up the lower slopes of Monte Bre, among densely nestled hillside residences. The pedestrians vanished; traffic mercifully thinned.

"That's the street!" the little voice exclaimed urgently in Rudi's ear. "Go back!"

Rudi stepped on the brake and looked over his shoulder. "That's not a street, old man," he said, unable to conceal his mounting annoyance. "That's an alley."

"Nevertheless, that's the way to my niece's house," the fare insisted.

Rudi sighed and threw the shift into reverse. Might as well humor the old boy. Maybe he was right. If he wasn't, Rudi would

173

summarily drive him back to the station, dump out the huge suit-cases and suggest that Methuselah call his niece to pick him up.

As soon as Rudi backed into the alley, he was forced to slow down. The thick, low clouds above had made the afternoon un-usually dark. But here, where a series of multistoried apartment buildings thrust up between the ground and the sun, the shadows were evening deep. The alley receded beyond the rear windshield into gloom. Rudi was relieved when the old man spoke again.

"Stop the car! This is the place."

Rudi glanced to his right. Another alley, wide enough only for foot traffic, branched off from the one where the taxi idled. This one was even darker.

"Nineteen francs," Rudi read from the meter. "Plus two for your luggage." The trunk wasn't opening until he saw the geezer's money.

"Certainly."

Twenty-five francs went into the driver's outstretched palm without demand for change. Exhaling a white plume of relief, Rudi stepped outside and popped the trunk open. By the time he had the big suitcases in his hands, the old man was out of the taxi and scudding into the side alley. Rudi hastened to catch him. He followed into the narrow, dark space.

The old man turned, an expression of surprise on his face. Here it comes, Rudi thought; this is the wrong place.

Instead the geezer dropped his carpetbag, as if it had become too much to carry, and said, "My gloves. I left them on the seat."

Rudi set down his burdens. "Relax, mister. I'll get them." He pivoted around and headed toward the taxi.

Rudi took three steps. Before his foot could touch the damp paving stone a fourth time, he was yanked backward with great force, spun, and driven violently into the alley wall. His nose crack-led loudly, and his front teeth popped into his throat. As he gagged, he was smashed again into the stuccoed cinder block. His uncon-scious bulk was allowed to collapse onto the stone walk.

The Vampire looked up and down the alley, assuring himself that he had chosen a private and seldom trammeled location for his

174

supper. He opened the near-empty carpetbag, then yanked off his coat and padded "hunch" and stuffed them inside. The wig fluttered into the bag, followed by fake eyebrows, latex mask, and hand coverings. He removed the paired caps from his four top front teeth, an appliance necessitated by the oversize proportions of his canine fangs. He stuck the caps carefully in his pants pocket. From the opposite pocket, he withdrew a small knife and, with the skill of ancient practice, punctured the driver's carotid artery, creating a stream large enough so that he would not be sucking all afternoon but not so large that he would choke on the effusion.

The Vampire sampled the blood. The dread tang that accompanied the offensive protein was absent; he could drink to this human's dregs without fear of the maddening itching arising from that one blood type. He was unaware of his moan of pleasure as he attached himself to the driver's throat. This was not some skinny little girl from a Romanian orphanage; this was a real feast, and one that could be enjoyed without gulping. No need to shadow his prey. Thanks to the statue now in the priest's possession, the Vampire had been informed early of their plans to travel by train to Lugano. By the time he had sated himself, his dread master might also have overheard whether or not the men would be linking up again with the woman.

The Vampire drank deeply from the open artery, knowing that he needed the strength of every drop. This hunt was unlike any he had experienced in his long life. His young opponents were forewarned, intelligent, and resourceful. They also had evidently enlisted the powers of the Roman Catholic Church. In addition, he had to be sure the Scrolls of Ahriman were destroyed before he could exterminate the lot of them. Most puzzling was the separation of Simon Penn and Frederika Vanderveen. From events and bits of conversation picked up, it seemed the two were operating independently. But then how could the woman's break-in at DeVilbiss's chalet be explained? Penn and the priest had done an excellent job of leading "Wagner" away from the house, and a woman had clearly been waiting down the hill for the opportunity. DeVilbiss's invaded chalet had borne the unmistakable smell of a woman . . . not a perfume or cologne but the woman's personal scent, generally undetectable to the normal human nose. Their coordinated actions mimicked a military offensive. If only the librarian and his putative priest friend had drunk the coffee "Wagner" had prepared for breakfast, he would now have no questions. The coffee had contained drugs not only to drain them of all energy but also of any will to resist interrogation. He would have gotten the location of both the woman and the scrolls from them within fifteen minutes after they had drunk the brew. Then he would have gorged himself like a tick on their blood. Without the help of the drugs there had been no way to fulfill his goals; they were two strong men, armed and wary, and he had regained less than half his supernatural strength.

The Vampire had arrived in Zug only a few hours before his adversaries. The infernal being who spoke from within his statue's hand had anticipated that the man and woman would come to DeVilbiss's chalet. But even a dolt could have guessed as much. After all, the voice had declared that all evidence of DeVilbiss's nature had been immolated in the United States. And his corpse provided few clues since, as the Vampire knew from experience, dead vampires looked hardly different from dead humans. What other choice did they have to prove the existence of vampires but to seek out this vampire's home? The voice's dictated plan was straightforward and, at least to the Vampire's way of thinking, highly rational: to get into DeVilbiss's chalet, expunge all proof of the man's vampiric servitude, move the secret room's bed, dresser, desk, and chair upstairs and pretend that it was a confidant's quarters, familiarize himself as much with the chalet as with the information on its owner that the voice had supplied and, finally, wait until the quarry came to him.

A female vampire had also been sent to Zug, as an unwitting sacrificial lamb. The Vampire had been kept abreast of her location, so that he could kill her in the act of trying to murder one or both of the pair, thus gaining their confidence as rescuer. The idea of keeping himself vulnerable, by only taking the smallest pinch of powder in the crypt and only drinking the pint or so of blood of the

176

child, had been the Vampire's own. It was a bold and risky gamble, but considering his Infernal Lord's warnings about the couple's wary natures, the Vampire felt it was required. And it had worked to perfection. Once he had cut his own wrist and shown it to the young man, every vestige of incredulousness disappeared. Even the goddamned head cold he had caught from the snot-nosed orphan had worked in his favor, for what supernatural creature could be plagued by such a minor infection? When the bastard who claimed to be a priest had insisted on going through the vampire's purse, he had truly worried about the discovery of the communicator. But they had not seen him drop its twin unit under the Land Rover when he used the excuse of fetching the young man a clean coat. More importantly, the trip for the coat had given him an opportunity almost immediately after cutting his wrist to swallow an oversize portion of the powder.

Once he learned from the voice that the men planned to head south by train, the Vampire knew another risk must be taken. Even as he painstakingly aged his looks sixty years inside a dark, abandoned factory building, he conceded he had no idea how many people would be occupying the train station. Professional as the wig, mask, clothing, hunch, and other details might be, they could not guarantee camouflage in broad daylight if the place were nearly empty and he could not maneuver behind bodies to prevent the men from coming right up alongside him. As it was, to minimize the danger he was forced to sit, until five minutes before the train was scheduled to arrive, in a taxi he had telephoned for, with the cursed sun pouring through the windows. A darkened train compartment was certainly preferable to waiting until dusk and driving to Lugano (the two kilometers to Zug alone had given him a blinding headache). But, more important, he had to stick close to the librarian. He had observed that Penn was not truly at ease with the mysterious Father Ferro. If Penn wanted to lose this man, he might have offered Lugano as his destination but jumped off the train somewhere else. Then the golden statue in the priest's possession would be worthless. The Vampire had sacrificed Penn his jackal-headed sword cane in the hopes that his Infernal Lord could inhabit

177

an image of animal anatomy as easily as a human's, but such (he had just learned after two thousand years of unanswered questioning) was not an infernal being's prerogative. During the train ride, the Vampire doddered several times to the bathroom, to learn from the infernal voice inside his stone hand if information had been dropped during the ride, but not a thing of value was said. Their strange silence was enough to unnerve even the Vampire. His Old Man, at least, had succeeded, and (unlike DeVilbiss or the Norwegian vampiress) he was still in the contest. Perhaps, the Vampire thought unhappily, before this business was done, the full range of his disguises would be tested.

The costume and character of Wilhelm Wagner Essrag had been entirely of the Vampire's devising. He had been inventing personae with increasingly more complex characters and looks ever since he became the Akkadian god Enlil. In those days, he could do little more than stain his skin with berry juice, paint his eyes with kohl and don regional costumes and wigs made from human hair. The bulk of his manifestations he created through language, accent, and bearing, drawing from his deep and ancient well of knowledge. Only in recent decades did his characters benefit from the invention of undetectable teeth caps, contact lenses, and that most wonderful of inventions, liquid latex. His favorite personae through the ages capitalized on his shortness and slight build. Several score of thugs who sought to prey on lone, veiled girls who strayed down Oriental bazaar alleyways or on solitary, wimpled nuns inadvertently locked out of their convents after Compline, found themselves the victims of a creature neither woman nor man.

The Vampire finished his drink by tossing a teaspoonful of the infernal powder into his mouth and washing it down with the feeble welling of blood which he knew invariably signified the victim's imminent death. He deposited his carpetbag in the taxi's front seat, then transferred his two suitcases to the rear. Satisfying himself that no one was watching, he first emptied the driver's pockets of money, then carried the corpse to the cab and tossed it in the trunk. The alley had been private enough, but what he really needed was total darkness, respite from the tenacious sunlight piercing the thick clouds. Despite the sun, he was feeling stronger by the minute. When he took his third full dose of powder tomorrow, he would be at maximum strength and invulnerability. All he needed was time.

Alison was playing with her Christmas toys; Karen was helping Michelle with her bath. It was the first opportunity Ray had to view the videotape he had taken from Dorena Durazo's house. Wincing from his lingering back pain, he bent low and inserted the tape into the VHS machine. The opening sequence for a Saturday morning cartoon flashed across the screen in bold primary colors. Just as the label on the tape read, it was the children's version of *Tales from the Crypt*. The opening story concerned two young girls being driven back from a postmidnight party by a chauffeur. The chauffeur turned out to be a vampire, intent on a late-night snack. The girls tricked him and locked him out of the limousine, but he eventually found his way in through the vent system, in the shape of smoke. Predictably, all it took was for one of the plucky females to lower the tinted-glass windows, and the rising sun dissolved the vampire into a charred heap of bones. The first set of commercials followed an "out-tro" by the ghoulish Crypt Keeper.

Ray stopped the tape and ejected it. He had seen enough. Much as he had prepared himself to find Dr. Durazo up to no good, the apparent truth was that the woman was simply a vampire nut. Her furtive visit to the Princeton Medical Center morgue had been provoked by screaming vampire headlines in the local newspaper and nothing more.

Durazo would not get another look. Vincent DeVilbiss's corpse had been transferred to Mercer Hospital, where the Trenton coroner's office had more extensive forensic expertise. But Ray expected no discoveries of a metaphysical nature. Dr. Loery had pronounced the corpse normal, and the Princeton pathologist had a crackerjack reputation. Occam's razor won out again; Simon Penn had been compelled to kill a man with Bela Lugosi delusions, a demented vampire wannabe fixated on priceless scrolls. Ray was happy for Chief Littlefield that Princeton was getting back to normal. As for the strange visit from the Italian priest, he too was obsessed by the idea of vampires. Ray decided that if Dante Ferro had lived in the fifteenth century, he would have been torturing and burning innocent people for suspected supernatural crimes. In both life and death, this character DeVilbiss had attracted other kooks from around the world. Ray decided to forget about Dorena Durazo and thank his lucky stars she hadn't caught him in her basement. He was done with her forever.

Until this moment, Ray had been frustrated that an earthshaking event was going on and he was standing impotently by on the sidelines. Now, convinced that the supernatural aspects were merely some weirdos' wishful fantasies, Ray would concentrate his effort instead on proving that his still-at-large friend had been justified in committing murder.

Father Ferro parked the borrowed Alfa Romeo on the Via Riva Paradiso and hurried into the Grand Hotel Eden. For a moment he considered going up to his room and changing out of his priestly garb. He checked his watch and saw that it was five minutes after eight. Too late.

The search for Frederika Vanderveen's adolescent schoolmates had proven more problematic and time-consuming than Dante had anticipated. According to his teacher-informant, the American girl had had only three close friends. Frederika had been fundamentally introverted and often, for stretches of time, noncommunicative. The friends, two girls and a boy, however, were absolutely devoted to her and followed any lead she was willing to give, enslaved by her beauty, her intelligence, the mystery and romance of her unconfided secrets, her penchant for questioning rules, and her artless ability to lie herself out of any situation. The boy, another American, left the school in his senior year when his father had been transferred back to Chicago. Dante was thankful that the two Swiss girls, now women, still lived in the Lugano area, and that both were Roman Catholic. One, Annaliese Antonelli, had married and had two children, which, Dante suspected, made her a less likely confederate in helping Frederika cross the border. The other, Marguerite Ochsenbein, was still single. She lacked confidence in herself, for several reasons: she was the only child of a high-strung mother, whose life purpose after Marguerite's birth was apparently frightening her daughter about the thousand and one ways a girl could do herself harm. Her father was a nouveau-riche, vociferously Catholic martinet, who saw no reason why either his wife or daughter should ever need to work for a living. Marguerite's mental and physical liberation had been one of Frederika's main causes in school, and Frederika had at least partially succeeded. Although Marguerite had so far allowed her father to scare away every man she had cared for, she at least had insisted on living in her own apartment (albeit half a mile from her parents' home) and working (a sinecure in one of her father's businesses). She fully credited her independence to her friend Frederika.

All this Dante had learned secondhand, from the woman's parish priest and confessor. The man had been tediously long-winded, but he had also been right; Marguerite still venerated her high school friend. When Dante later visited her, she had proudly shown him a large photograph of herself and Frederika, which she kept atop her television (the two tall, blond girls looking enough alike to be sisters). At least it proved, beyond Simon Penn's constant defensive arguments, the first evidence of a virtuous side to Frederika's personality.

To enlist Annaliese's and Marguerite's aid, Dante had invented a tale about Frederika being "in trouble" with the unnamed son of a famous Roman Catholic family. The story, he told each with a somber face, also involved lawbreaking, for which Frederika was being pursued. Frederika's young man and his family had enlisted the aid of "the highest authorities in the Church" to track Frederika down before she could be apprehended by the law. As with his visit to Ray Pental, Dante's visits to the women had been preceded by introductory calls from their priests. Neither woman seemed to doubt Dante's tale; both admitted that Frederika had been a rebel, constantly testing the thickness of authority's ice. However, when he danced around the subject of dabblings with the occult, both women emphatically denied that Frederika had ever indulged in such unchristian activities. Neither woman had yet heard from their former friend, and both agreed to contact Father Ferro if she called them or showed up at their door. The entire afternoon and early evening had been distasteful to Dante, but the Vanderveen woman had made herself the quarry in his quest to return the scrolls to safety.

As Dante entered the hotel's elegant L'Oasis restaurant, shrugging out of his cashmere overcoat, an elderly couple approached from the opposite direction. Together, they eyed the quality of his coat with disapproval. He had observed the look several times since donning the clerical collar: priests had no right wearing expensive clothing or dining in expensive restaurants.

"It's all right," he assured the couple, in Italian, as he handed over his coat to the check girl. "I'm independently wealthy." The girl did her best to conceal her laugh.

Simon Penn was already seated at one of the tables that looked out through huge picture windows on Lake Lugano and the mountain beyond. He had his menu propped open on the navy linen tablecloth and didn't look up until Dante was nearly upon him.

"Sorry to be late," Dante said, putting himself into one of the leather-upholstered chairs.

"That's okay," Simon answered. "Any luck?"

"Not yet." The less said between them about Frederika Vanderveen the better. "Anything interesting on the menu?" he asked, knowing full well that everything in this best among Lugano's restaurants was wonderful.

Simon duplicated Dante's order of truffled artichoke salad, saffron-accented clam chowder, and *petto di tacchino con morilles*. While they waited for the salad and during its consumption, Dante melted some of the chill between them by opening the subject of ancient literature. They found especial common ground in their mutual loves of St. Augustine's *Confessions,* Marcus Aurelius's *Meditations,* and—surprising to both—Thucydides' *History of the Peloponnesian Wars.* He found it refreshing to deal with the young antiquities librarian, so much more knowledgeable and enthusiastic than the pedantic, old priests who minded the Vatican's written treasures beside him, day after day. Getting on Penn's wrong side had never been his intention, but after learning Frederika Vanderveen's nature and recent actions, he had been compelled to try to open Penn's bewitched eyes. Few aspects of approaching old age were comforting to Dante, but the rage of hormones was definitely something he was glad to have behind him. Far better to be able to appreciate human beauty with the same detachment as he would admire a Botticelli painting.

Over dessert and decaf coffee, Dante learned that Simon, who had never before been to Europe, had allowed himself to play tourist for an afternoon, taking the funicular to the summit of Monte Salvatore, later enjoying the Thyssen-Bornemisza art collection. Dante's shared enthusiasm for the Swiss-Italian town, with its pastel-colored buildings climbing the hills along twisting *vias,* was clearly dissolving the young man's antagonism toward him. And then the telephone arrived at the table.

"Pronto," Dante said into the mouthpiece.

"This is the call you've been waiting for," an unfamiliar male voice said, in Italian. "Marguerite Ochsenbein. We're heading out right now and will be waiting for you at her building." Before Dante could reply, the man was gone, and a click signaled connection with the young woman he had left only three hours before.

"Padre Ferro?" Marguerite said, her voice soft and low-pitched. "Hello?"

"It is I, *signorina.* Is she there now?"

"Yes. She showed up at my door without calling, right after dark . . . less than half an hour after you left. She told me a different story—"

"She is very convincing with her imagination, as you yourself told me," Dante said. "Does she know you are speaking with someone?"

"No. She can't." Marguerite's voice was now a whisper, barely audible in the earpiece. "I'm calling from my bedroom. I waited until she went to take a shower."

"Good. Remain relaxed. I will be at your door in ten minutes." Dante hung up the phone, wanting the woman to do the same so that Frederika would not catch her calling. When he looked up, Simon was staring expectantly at him.

"You want to see Miss Vanderveen again?" Dante asked. "I can arrange it for you. Let's go."

Simon had already signaled the waiter for the check. Without looking at the total, Dante threw down several large-denomination bills and strode out of the dining area, heading for the coatroom.

"I want you to promise you're not going to hurt her," Simon badgered, behind him.

"We shall be as civilized as possible," Dante assured him.

"Because I've been thinking all day of what you said on the train," Simon continued, setting his chit on the coatroom counter. "You may be right about her being weird, but she has a great heart. She volunteers her time to teach adults to read. She donates her blood. She gardens, for god's sake. I know in my bones she wouldn't turn evil."

"Yes, all right," Dante said, hearing Simon's words through the noise of his own thoughts. "Put on your coat as we walk. We must hurry."

Marguerite Ochsenbein lived in a second-floor flat on Via San Lorenzo, just a few doors from the cathedral. In the short time it took to drive to the place, Dante instructed Simon on the course of the plan. Two men from the Vatican's invisible army would already be in place, watching the front and rear of the building. When Dante arrived, the man out front would join his partner, and Dante would ascend through the main entrance. Simon would wait outside on the street level as backup, in case Frederika bowled the priest over. Capturing Frederika was of secondary importance; the main objective was to wrest the scrolls from her. When Dante darted his eyes from the road, Simon returned his glance with a look of barely concealed panic. Despite having had the woman betray him and having watched her drink a dying man's blood, Simon Penn was clearly still in love with her.

Dante pulled into a vacant parking space near the cathedral. "All right. Let's go," he ordered. He waited until Simon had begun exiting the car before reaching under his seat and slipping the pistol, with its newly fitted laser sight, into his coat pocket. Then he, too, stepped into the cold night.

"Don't leave the street," Dante told Simon over his shoulder, as he moved toward a stocky man who stood guard in the shadows of a building a hundred feet to the north. As he walked, he unbuttoned his overcoat, showing his clerical collar. The man nodded several times and backed into an alley, disappearing from view.

Dante entered the building and climbed the old stairs to the second floor, acutely aware of the creaking of the wood under his feet. Coming to Marguerite's door, he slipped his right hand into his coat and around the pistol and knocked with his left. The door remained closed. Half a minute later Dante knocked again, with more force. The door opened.

Marguerite Ochsenbein ushered Dante into the apartment without a word. She nodded her head toward a hallway just beyond the living room and led the way. She stopped at the second door on the left, turned wide-eyed, and looked to the priest for direction.

Father Ferro gestured for Marguerite to call out.

"Frederika?"

No answer came from the other side of the door.

"Frederika, are you dressed?" Marguerite persisted. "I'd like to come in."

Still, the room beyond was silent.

Dante gestured for Marguerite to try the doorknob.

"It's locked," the woman reported, timidly.

"Stand aside!" Dante put his back against the opposite wall, raised his foot, and kicked out hard. With a splintering crash, the door burst open. Dante rushed into the bedroom. Except for an emptied suitcase on the bed, there was no trace of Frederika Vanderveen. Dante threw open the armoire, then peered under the high bed, muttering his frustration with each act. He realized the air near the floor was much colder than in the rest of the room. He stood up, walked to the window, and drew back the curtains. The window was opened a crack. Beyond it lay a fire escape.

"She left that way?" Marguerite said, incredulously, behind Ferro.

185

"Yes."

"How did she . . . how could she know I had called you?"

Dante pushed away from the window and strode past the confused woman. "Because she has ears like a bat."

Simon watched Father Ferro vanish into the building, then began to pace up and down the street. For half a minute, the magnificent view across Lake Lugano to the eastern mountains held his attention. Then he became too cold to enjoy any view. Increasing his stride and the length of the distance he paced out, he began flapping his arms across his chest, as he had seen others do in winter. The only warmth he felt was from embarrassment, when a couple of raggedy teenage boys walked past and gawked at him as if he were crazy. Turning at the end of his self-imposed track, he watched the teenagers walk southward. As they came even with the towering Renaissance facade of the cathedral one of them scooped up something from a corner of the stone steps. In the darkness, its shape looked to Simon like a small, dead mammal. The boy swung it up and onto his knit cap, and Simon realized it was a wig. As soon as the other teenager laughed, the boy tossed the wig onto the sidewalk. They ambled down the street, in search of better diversion.

Simon widened his course, walking down to the wig. He picked it up. The artificial curls were flame-red, the same shade and length as the wig Frederika had bought in Zurich. Simon turned a slow circle, concentrating on every shadow along the street. His movement brought him again to the church facade. Above him, the great rose window glowed from interior light. Simon climbed the steps and walked into the cathedral.

The grand church's interior was an ornate hodgepodge of ecclesiastical styles, gilded, marbled, and frescoed. Simon walked toward the altar, swinging his head warily from one side to the other, to peer beyond the winking votive candles into the dim alcoves and niches. Figures of saints abounded, in a multitude of sizes. For all its vastness, the cathedral was unoccupied. Or so he thought.

"Simon." Frederika's voice was faint. Its echo in the open space disguised its point of origin. "Over here."

Simon looked to his left. On the opposite side of an ornate metal screen stood a side altar. Within its shadows, Simon discerned Frederika's figure.

"Did you find the wig?" she asked, as Simon came quickly nearer.

"Yes. What—"

"It was all I could think of. Where's the priest?"

"Up the street, looking for you," Simon said, reaching the metalwork. "How do you know he's a priest?"

"My traitor friend Marguerite called him 'Father Ferro' on the phone. This powder you disapprove of so strongly gives me incredible hearing. Right through walls."

Simon tried to open the gate.

"It's locked," Frederika told him, coming forward. Her eyes glowed amber. She still looked beautiful, but disturbingly pale. "We're staying apart."

Simon slapped the iron with anger. "Why did you sell me out?"

"To protect you, of course. I wanted you in custody, where you'd be safe and couldn't follow me."

"That was you who broke into DeVilbiss's chalet last night, wasn't it?"

"Yes. I found absolutely nothing. The bad guys had gotten to it first. How did you hook up with this priest, and who was that little man in the house?" Frederika asked.

"You answer my questions first. Where are the scrolls?"

Frederika blinked in surprise. It was a look Simon doubted even she could feign. "How did you find out?"

"None of your business." Simon's eyes searched in vain for another direct means into the niche. On its back wall, a small door stood open, leading from someplace beyond the cathedral proper. "Where are they?"

"None of *your* business. Especially since you betrayed our pact and blabbed once already."

Simon shook the iron bars in his fury. "You accuse *me* of betrayal?"

One of Frederika's eyebrows arched. "They're perfectly safe.

That's all you need to know. Here." From her coat she pulled a familiar book. "A peace offering. DeVilbiss's latest diary. It's in English. I've had enough time to decode the entries from last September to a few days before his death. He documents the murders of five people in the Seattle area and five in Princeton . . . including the physics professor and the guard in the library. More than enough for you to prove self-defense." When she passed the diary through the bars, he saw with a thrill that the wedding ring was still on her hand. "Give me something in return; ditch the priest and go into hiding for a week," she said firmly. "Let me take the risks." With her eyes fixed on Simon's, she backed toward the door.

"With our original plan?" Simon asked.

"Why not?" Frederika returned to the gate. "Don't tell me you also told your priest friend about Athens."

"Elmasri's not in Athens. He's in Florence this week, working at the city archives."

Frederika's head tilted slightly as she assessed Simon's words and his face. "Where's he staying?"

"We don't know. He keeps it a secret. He's evidently a confirmed adulterer, and he's got a married girlfriend on the side in Florence. Look, come around to the front of the church. This priest is trustworthy, and we—" Simon found himself staring at a dot of bright red light that moved slowly down from Frederika's neck toward her heart.

"Run!" Simon shouted, shoving Frederika back from the bars, then pivoting wildly and throwing his body across the path of the red light.

Dante's form appeared from behind a thick column, pistol raised. He rushed toward the alcove. "Get out of the way!"

"No!" Simon shouted back. He turned to look behind him. Frederika had vanished. Suddenly, he was on the stone floor, knocked there by a violent shove.

"Are you crazy?" Dante yelled, yanking impotently at the metal gate.

"Me crazy? You were going to shoot her! After you promised!"

"I promised nothing," Dante said, stepping back from the metalwork to orient himself with the layout of the building. Pistol still in hand, he pivoted, to sprint toward the cathedral's main entrance. Simon's hand grasped his right ankle and pulled. Dante fell awkwardly, his pistol striking the floor with the sound of cracking glass as he was forced to protect himself.

"You sonofabitch!" Simon cursed through gritted teeth, clawing himself atop the older man. Acutely aware of Dante's athletic build, he wrapped his arms around the priest's torso with maniacal strength.

"Get off me!" Ferro commanded.

"Not until she's far away."

"That should be in a few more seconds," Dante said, letting himself go limp under the young man's weight. "Why do you think I pointed the pistol? I wanted to shoot her in the leg, to slow her. *You* were the one who told me DeVilbiss ran more than twice as fast as you. *You* said the vampire woman was slowed when you shot her in the leg. *You* said this one was shot in the chest and was barely bothered."

Simon rolled off the priest, came to his feet, and staggered back toward the screenwork. He picked up the diary with a trembling hand.

"What about reasoning with her? I had just told her she could trust you." He shook the book at Father Ferro, who had risen to his knees. "This is DeVilbiss's last diary. It's got proof of all his murdering. She stuck around here to help save my skin. You're dead wrong about her intentions. But you're right about her speed. She's gone . . . for good."

"For good?" Dante's mouth twisted into a bitter scowl as he picked up the weapon. The laser scope was bent and shattered. "The package I picked up at the Zug train station . . . it was this scope. If I had to shoot at her, I wanted to be sure it could not be fatal. If I misunderstand your beloved, so do you misunderstand me."

"I don't give a damn about you," Simon said, snatching his ski cap off the floor, then stalking straight toward the church entrance.

"Where are the scrolls?" Dante called after him.

"I don't know," Simon threw back. "You're in a church, priest. I suggest you pray for the answer."

CHAPTER SIX

December 29

Death's a great disguiser.

—Shakespeare, *Measure for Measure*

F ather Ferro was doing his twentieth push-up when the hotel telephone rang. The old voice on the other end sounded even more ancient filtered through five hundred kilometers of wire and amplifiers.

"Good morning, Your Eminence," Dante replied, even though it was a bad morning.

"Our agent heard a few minutes ago from Marguerite Ochsenbein. When she went out this morning to drive her car to work, she found it gone. It seems that Miss Vanderveen had enough time during her escape to steal a spare set of her friend's keys, as well as her passport."

Dante resisted the strong temptation to use the Lord's name in vain. This conversation was looking to be no better than the one Dante had had the previous night with Del Gesu. The cardinal's housekeeper had seen fit to awaken the old man so he could deplore at length the bad news from Lugano.

"I told you last night, Your Eminence," Dante said, with an even voice, "that this Vanderveen woman is smart as well as powerful. I cannot capture her with one or two men . . . men who cannot get into place until after their dinners and coffee."

"Then you have a problem, Father Ferro," Del Gesu replied, "because the Church cannot be caught actively involving itself

192

with fugitives. There is no way it will provide you with detectives or bodyguards. The *Serafini Segreti* is a volunteer army. It exists everywhere in the world, but it is small . . . even so close to Rome. If the only ones we can trust in the Lugano area are two workmen who require supper and coffee before they can help you, so be it."

Dante shook his head through the cardinal's long-winded retort. "But the fate of thousands, perhaps tens of thousands, may hang in the balance. If these scrolls are not found in time to prove the Devil's plan, a plague of vampires may blight the earth. Perhaps if I, as a private citizen, were to hire—"

"You are not a private citizen," Del Gesu said sharply. "Besides, we have been informed that the police know Simon Penn is somewhere in southeastern Switzerland. It is time to distance yourself from him and from the direct pursuit of the woman."

"There is no question of my maintaining distance, Your Eminence," Dante assured him. "The woman is certainly out of Switzerland by now, and if I know Mr. Penn as well as I think I do, he is planning to escape from me within the day."

"But you have said that is not possible," Del Gesu reminded him.

"Not so long as he keeps his lucky bullet on his person. You remember . . . the one that would not fire at the vampiress?"

"Yes. The one with the homing device in it."

Dante looked at the electronic paraphernalia sitting on the hotel room dresser. "He—or rather the bullet—has not moved from his hotel room since last night. Once he does move, however, I must know this time that the other men are able to move as well. I can do nothing without triangulation."

"We have had that assurance," Del Gesu said. "Of course, after last night, the woman should trust Mr. Penn less than she trusts you. I fear he has outlived his usefulness."

"I don't think so," Dante countered. "If anyone can find Miss Vanderveen it's her ardent lover." He picked up the telephone and took it as close to the window as the cord would allow. "This secret army that you are so proud of . . . whatever numbers you can muster should be sent to three places: the University of Athens, in case she works on the side of the angels and Mr. Penn has not informed her of Professor Elmasri's whereabouts; the Archive of the City of Florence, in case he has; and the Basilica of San Giovanni in Lateran if she seeks to deliver the scrolls to the devils."

"I understand about Athens or Florence," Del Gesu said, "but why would she come to Rome?"

"San Giovanni is where the one who called himself DeVilbiss was turned from the priesthood to vampirism," Dante answered. "Where the statue spoke to him about eternal life." Still, Del Gesu made no reply. "It's in those pages from the vampire's first diary that I faxed to you. She has the original diary in her possession. I think it is her only clue as to contacting the infernal."

"Mm," Del Gesu said at last. "I'll see that all three places are well watched. But we still have no real proof the woman carries the scrolls."

"No. Except that when she came racing out of the back of the Church of San Lorenzo, the weapon she used to knock over your 'seraph' was a long black metal tube."

Del Gesu cleared his throat noisily. "Very well, then. You continue to watch over the young man, as you have done so admirably. I think you have not lost your enthusiasm for shepherding important personages, Father Ferro. Truthfully . . . did you use all this technical equipment in your policeman's life, or are you at last taking the opportunity to play super-spy?"

"I used all of these tools, Your Eminence," Dante said patiently. "We used wireless radios every day. And we gave the politicians small transmitters to carry, in the event that they were kidnapped."

The cardinal made an inarticulate sound that could have signified disbelief or merely the fact that he was still listening. "Perhaps, now that you are a priest, you might rely as well on prayer."

"You are the second person to offer that suggestion," Dante said. "I will pray that His will be done on earth."

"Excellent. *Addio, padre,*" the old cleric said, and then the line went dead.

Dante looked out the window at the sun's rays bursting with unclouded effulgence over the eastern mountains. At least it would be a day to drive vampires into cellars. He returned the telephone to the night table. Sitting beside the lamp was the golden St. Cecilia, gleaming in the early morning light. Thinking of the bullet in Simon Penn's pocket, Dante picked up the statue and examined it minutely. He carefully peeled back the felt glued to its bottom. He hefted its weight. As far as he could tell, the antique statue was solid and had suffered no modification since its creation. It was nothing more than what it appeared to be: a saint playing a lute. He put the statue down and returned to his push-ups.

"It is almost nine o'clock," the metallic voice echoed in the room. "Time to rise," it coaxed in perfect German.

"Shut up!" the Vampire commanded, rolling out of the bed, his sudden move drawing the top sheet and blanket off the shoulders and back of the woman sleeping beside him. Nothing galvanized the Vampire more quickly than an inopportune appearance from his Infernal Lord. He could feel the blood pounding in his ears, so violent was the shock of the voice that yanked him from a deep sleep.

The woman came up on one elbow. "What's that, *Liebchen?*" she asked, her voice slurred from yet unmetabolized alcohol.

The Vampire rose from the bed and reached for his underwear. "The radio. I set it last night."

The woman rolled over and struggled to focus on the electric alarm clock sitting on the night stand near her.

"You talk to the radio? Hey, there's no radio with this clock. No radios in any of the rooms. I know. I been in plenty of 'em."

"It's my own personal radio," the Vampire said, moving around the bed with speed, snatching his trousers off the floor as he went. "I've got early business, and I'm sure you want to be on your way."

"No, I don't. I wanna sleep," the prostitute complained, collapsing back onto her pillow.

The Vampire reached into his back pocket, pulled out his wallet and withdrew a large-denomination note. He rolled the woman over, none too gently, and stuffed the money in one cup of her bra. "Time to go, *Fräulein,*" he said ironically. She had volunteered her

195

age as twenty-four. He guessed her to be thirty. Whatever her years, the woman was all but used up. She lay on her back like the dead, almost comatose again.

The Vampire whisked the covers completely from the woman's form. Despite the darkness of the shade- and curtain-drawn room, his amber eyes saw clearly the multiple black-and-blue marks he had inflicted. The volume of bourbon she had thrown down her throat between eleven and four was keeping her anesthetized; once the alcohol wore off she would feel like she had been knocked down by a streetcar. Visible damage barely told the story of her mistreatment. She would not be servicing johns with anything but her mouth for the next week.

She deserved it. She had smiled at him all night, never once betraying the loathing she undoubtedly felt over his small stature and enormous ugliness. The ones who showed their repugnance but who approached anyway he merely used as sexual garbage pails. Whores like this he was obliged to punish, to prove that sexual prowess had nothing to do with fairness of form. This pathetic bitch would remember him to her dying day as a real man . . . if not as something more. At least she had not put on a mask of impassivity. For that, she would have died horribly.

The Vampire's first memory was of his mother's face, studying him. She had stared with neither a smile nor a scowl, an impassive stare she employed until, by his fifth or sixth year, it was indelible in his mind. By that time, he was sure of the repugnance she hid behind her carefully constructed neutrality. He learned when he was ten that she had given him over to a wet nurse shortly after his birth. And she never spoke of his looks. That was the most telling proof of her loathing.

The irony behind his mother's attitude was that Bakum had inherited his coarsest, most unlovely features from her. She had been betrothed at three and later wed to Bakum's father purely to unite two cattle-rich families. She was tolerated by her husband in daylight, given his conjugal attentions irregularly. But his frequent fits of passion went to other women. The firstborn of their union became an innocent mirror, fanning the woman's rage at her own physical misfortunes, a constant, wailing reminder. The second son, Vatra, also inherited his father's heavy-boned angularities and his mother's large hooked nose and thick bowed lips, but all to a softer, subtler degree. Moreover, the shock of the parents' ill-favored genetic commingling could never compare to that of the firstborn's arrival. Bakum was the sole vessel into which his mother poured her anger and disappointments. Vatra suckled from his mother's own breasts.

Because he had used no subterfuge in slaying his own brother, Bakum dared not return to his tribe, even with the strength of a vampire. Thus, he was unable to kill his mother for her sins against him, unable to know for certain that he would have had the courage to shorten her miserable life. Thus, he redirected his hatred perpetually on the world around him, learning to his dismay that lakes of sacrificial blood were not enough to buy him peace. Thus, long before the supernatural voice spoke from the false god, evil had its talons deeply into him.

"Wait a minute," the prostitute said, as the Vampire shoved her arm roughly through the sleeve of her dress. "That voice was in German. The radio people here speak Italian."

"It's shortwave," the Vampire answered, shoving the woman around until he could reach the zipper at the back of her dress.

"Ach," the prostitute said, almost a sigh. She came to her feet like a marionette as the Vampire used his enormous strength. He kicked her high-heeled shoes into line beside one another, then hauled her up and lowered her into them. "Don' wanna go," the woman protested.

The Vampire propelled the woman toward the door. "Would you like it if I hit you a few times?"

"No."

"Then go back to whatever you call a home and forget you ever met me." The Vampire shoved the woman through the doorway, tossing her topcoat after her. She stumbled forward a few steps, then found her equilibrium, the uncanny sea legs of the hard-core drunk. She stared at the Vampire through one open eye, looked as if she was struggling to form a sentence, then waved her arm instead in dismissal. She turned the retrieving of her coat from the hallway carpet into a brief Chaplinesque episode, then lurched down the hall with all the dignity she could muster.

The Vampire closed the door. He walked across the room to the dresser and exposed the statue's hand, which he had concealed under clothing hours before. He knew well that the being which resided from time to time in the hand could not only speak from it and hear from it but also see from it. Could see, in fact, in absolute darkness . . . a feat beyond even the Vampire's visual capabilities. Unless the statue's view was obscured, as it had been all night. This was the reason for his Infernal Lord's ill-timed wake-up call; the demon had not been able to see the sleeping whore. The Vampire also knew from such incidents that the being maintained no constant watch over him via the stone hand. Otherwise, it would have been aware of his having picked up the whore in the bar and having screwed her within an inch of her life. Every few years, such poorly timed visitations compelled the Vampire to murder the unlucky witness. This bitch had come within a whisker of oblivion.

"You waste your strength on human garbage while the Scrolls of Ahriman remain undestroyed?" the voice chastised, in Akkadian.

The Vampire began searching for his second shoe. "I have plenty of strength . . . or will have, with one more dose of powder. You tell me where the scrolls are, and I will destroy them."

"They are apparently with this unpredictable Vanderveen woman, and she is again on the move." The voice repeated the dialogue Dante Ferro had just finished with Cardinal Del Gesu.

The Vampire held his tongue all the while the sulfurous voice whispered from the stone hand, but the moment it fell silent, he said, "It is quite ironic that the priest keeps track of Simon Penn with a secret homing device and unwittingly carries a little home for you. Too bad the young man doesn't have it, though."

"No. The priest will keep track of him, as he pursues the woman. It is better that the priest holds the statue, so that we know what the Church intends. Besides, the young man is alone; do you know for a fact that he holds private dialogues?"

The Vampire refused to contribute to his own mockery. Having found his shoe under the bed, he sat down directly across from the stone hand.

"What intrigues us," the voice continued, lapsing into its royal *we*, "is the priest's uncertainty of the woman's intent. He knows that she has learned about our gift of unending life. If she wishes to bargain for eternity, what better prize could she offer?"

"I am sure you will be waiting for her in Rome. At the same time, shall I find Elmasri and exterminate him?"

"No. DeVilbiss has already killed one prominent Akkadian scholar. While such people are not limitless, several more could nevertheless be found if you murdered Elmasri. It would only tend to prove that we do not want the scrolls translated. You continue to follow the priest, who follows the young man. Your most important task is to keep the scrolls out of the hands of the Roman Catholic Church. It possesses not only the means to have the scrolls translated but also the power to validate them by fiat and to demand the attention of the entire world's media when they do.

"Let us make completely unambiguous what we are about here," the voice went on. "Even though we knew for years that DeVilbiss was a traitor, we let him live until he had our powder analyzed and duplicated. He was compelled to bring doses he had hoarded to several biochemists before science had advanced to the stage where our gift could be approximated. Unknown to him, the last time we steered him to a venal woman scientist for help."

"A woman?" the Vampire said, smiling. "Was this one's name Eve also?"

"No. Pandora. Thanks to his public death and the saintly Simon Penn's insistence on proving DeVilbiss a vampire, this woman now knows for certain what power lies in the powder she duplicated. It will soon be as common on the black market as PCP or heroin." The voice laughed. The Vampire had only heard the noise once before, when his Infernal Lord had announced the coming of the Black Death to Europe. Human steel though he was and inured to any human outcry, the Vampire shuddered at the sound. "The

199

world will assume it is of man's invention . . . the latest monster of his science," it said, once it had composed itself. "Unless the scrolls are brought to light."

"I understand," the Vampire said. "If supernatural instigation can be proven, the world will turn to the Unnamed One as it has not done since the star shone over Bethlehem."

"We assumed you understood," the voice hissed. "Refrain from oblique allusions! Need I remind you that if the world *does* believe the scrolls, you are dead?"

The rising sun had found a narrow slit of an opening between the window jamb and the shade. The Vampire moved to bar the light. "I repeat: tell me where the scrolls are, and I will destroy them."

"We assume the woman works against us. If not Mustafa El-masri, she will eventually find some reputable Akkadian scholar. The instant she surfaces and we know absolutely that she carries the scrolls, you will be given the opportunity to prove yourself once more. When you succeed, you will be granted demigodhood. No more amber eyes. No more need to drink blood."

"But I shall still drink it," the Vampire affirmed, from the hotel room's reestablished gloom. "Otherwise, what excuse would I have when I continue to spill it?"

Having laid the day's purchases out neatly on the bed, Simon began the task of abandoning items from his suitcase. When he walked out of the hotel, whatever he took must all fit into his rucksack, his pockets, or his hands. He glanced at his new glow-in-the-dark watch, saw that it was quarter after four in the afternoon, and returned to his packing with the knowledge that he had little time to waste.

Fairly early in the morning, Dante Ferro had telephoned Simon's room. The priest's stated reasons were sharing that Frederika had not yet been found (although Marguerite Ochsenbein's car and passport had been, just over the border in Como) and announcing that he had arranged for a foolproof means to get Simon out of Switzerland, as soon as it was determined whether the woman had headed toward Athens or Florence. In the subtext of the priest's words Simon perceived an apology for the previous night. If no news emerged during the course of the day, Ferro offered to take Simon again to dinner. Once more, he adjured the librarian to watch for the police if he went out and to return to his room every hour or so to see if his phone light was blinking, so that he would not be left behind. To preempt the priest's predictable inquiry about what information he had given Frederika in the church, Simon volunteered that she had said nothing about her plans and, moreover, had stressed that Simon would in no way be part of them. He was perversely disappointed when the former cop accepted his words without further probing.

They ended the conversation agreeing to dinner at eight, again at L'Oasis. Simon had no intention of being there. Unless Ferro called with convincing evidence that Frederika had been spotted, he figured never to see the priest again.

As Simon had left his hotel room for his first shopping foray of the day, he reflected on the reason why Father Ferro stayed in another hotel. He decided it was because the man knew the police were closing in and he, as a representative of the Roman Catholic Church, could not be linked with a fugitive. If not that, it had to be because Simon had outlived his usefulness and could be left behind more easily. We'll see who's better at distancing himself, Simon thought, as he walked through the lobby. He wondered idly in whose name the room had been taken, but he steered wide of the check-in desk.

In his first trek through Lugano, Simon had picked up a torch-light and batteries, compass, heavy-duty wire cutters, a topographic map of the local region, hiking boots, and a Rambo-style knife for his belt. While he lunched on chicken cacciatore and linguine at a restaurant called Snack, he studied the map and verified that Lugano lay in the center of a twenty-five-mile-long peninsula bounded on three sides by Italy. Of all the ways for him to cross over—bus, train, car, or boat—the most unlikely was on foot. The terrain was rugged year-round, and hazardous when blanketed by snow. It was not a valid choice for any sane man and therefore, in

Simon's mind, the one most likely to succeed. As evening fell he would double back straight north, to the village of Vira. From a point a few miles southwest of there he planned to hike through forest, across the border and down to the Italian village of Tronzano. Hitchhiking the seventy miles south to Milan might take the rest of the night, but from that rail hub he could catch a train in a short time to Florence.

Simon began his afternoon foray by walking beyond the shopping district several blocks, to select a location integral to his escape plan. On the way back, halfway down the length of the pedestrian-only Via Nassa, Simon spotted Dante Ferro strolling half a block behind him. He pretended not to have noticed and loitered.

Within seconds, Dante came right up beside him, wondering out loud what Simon had purchased. To his relief, the ski mask and synthetic gloves in his bag were innocuous enough not to betray his plan. Dante reconfirmed their dinner date and moved on. Simon completed his list by purchasing a large rucksack on an aluminum frame, then hurried back to the hotel, dodging and weaving among tourists and townsfolk.

In spite of the shopping bustle, Lugano was a place of peace and order. Staring at the oncoming faces, Simon found it impossible to believe that many of these could become vampires and many more, victims. It was too absurd. Imagining as he might, he could envision no scenario that allowed such a supernatural calamity. And yet he held fast to the belief that the scrolls were genuine and that they had resurfaced for a reason beyond mere chance. Despite all impediments thrown up by logic, faith told him he must dog on toward Mustafa Elmasri, because Frederika had made herself the key, and she would undoubtedly find the scholar. Even if Father Ferro had counted him out of the struggle, he was still convinced in the cradle of his soul that he had a continued purpose. Simon Penn had become a fanatic.

At twenty-five minutes to five, Simon picked up the telephone and dialed directly to Richard Chen's apartment. In Princeton it was not yet eleven in the morning. As he suspected, Chen was out. So much the better, he thought, as he listened to Chen's machine play its uninspired offer to leave a message; he hoped the police were still tapping the phone, so that he would be exonerated all the more quickly. He knew the cheap machine accepted no more than a one-minute-long message, so he spoke quickly.

"Rich, it's Simon. DeVilbiss kept diaries in code. I've decoded the latest one. In it, he writes about killing Ray Wheeler and Professor Gerstadt. More important, the police can prove he was a killer by opening the storm sewers down by Carnegie Lake. In one drain there's the body of a man who DeVilbiss said was trying to rape a woman jogger. Just so they don't try to pin that on me, too, he writes about killing a woman named Tina Fromkin in November when he was in Seattle . . . some high-level women's rights activist. He stuck her body in the fallout shelter of a condemned government building scheduled for demolition. And, yes, I'm still playing tag with his friends. Pray for me. I hope to see you in the new year, pal."

Five minutes later, Simon stood in the lobby of the Splendide Royal Hotel making another phone call, this time in a public booth and to a local number. He called for a taxi, gave an address on the Via San Balestra, and asked that it wait for a few minutes if necessary. He hung up and moved swiftly to the hotel entrance, where he had the doorman hail him a cab. He gave the driver a different address than the one he had recited into the telephone and specified the route. The trip did not take long and near its end crossed the Via San Balestra, which ran east and west at right angles to the one-way street along which they traveled. When the cab pulled to the curb, Simon threw several franc notes onto the front seat, snatched up the rucksack and the sword cane and rushed out of the car. He walked southward with long strides, against the flow of traffic, watching for the borrowed Alfa Romeo or any other car that might suddenly pull to the curb. By the time any tailing vehicle made the several turns necessary to come back to where Simon was walking, he intended to be long gone.

The second taxi waited precisely where Simon had requested it. As the Via San Balestra only flowed westward, he ordered the driver to go quickly in the direction of a neighborhood named

Massagno. The man drove like a New York City cabbie, but for once Simon was glad to have a speed demon at the wheel. He studied the traffic behind, through the rear window. Already, the slopes of Monte Bre were purple in the falling night. Satisfied that they were not being followed, Simon altered his destination to the village of Vira. The driver shot his fare a questioning look in his rearview mirror, decided that no guile hid behind the young man's clear, wide-set eyes, and refocused his attention back on the road.

Simon consulted his luminescent watch. He could not believe he had only left the highway a hundred minutes earlier. He was cold to the bone, even beneath four layers of clothing. Bitter as the night was, the effort of his march had him sweating freely against his underwear. Air entered his lungs like fire and was expelled like smoke. His legs ached from hip to ankle, both from negotiating rough terrain that lay hidden under a frozen surface of snow and from plunging and plowing through the softer accumulation below. Never was the snow less than a foot deep; in some places he suddenly found himself wading through drifts up to his waist, turning even level progress into a trek.

Worst of all, Simon had not reached the barbed wire fence that separated Switzerland from Italy. Once he had cut his way through that, he still had another three miles or so overland to reach Tronzano, and he was fast running out of steam. The map indicated that the last half of the journey ran more ruggedly downhill. As it was, he was already fighting a constant decline to his right, as the land dropped toward Lake Maggiore. Several times he had found his progress blocked by a deadfall of trees, a line of impenetrable thickets, or a ravine too small to appear on his map but uncrossable nonetheless.

At least, Simon thought, he had had the presence of mind to pack a spare set of batteries. Snow clouds had blocked out the moon and stars, necessitating almost constant use of his powerful torchlight, which he was forced to shine low to the ground in order not to stand out in the night like the Statue of Liberty. Worst of all, flakes had begun to tumble out of the sky. They were tiny now, but

Simon knew they could be merely the point men for an army that would blind him and bring him to a halt. With ever greater conviction, he told himself that a train or bus ride using his phony passport would have been much less risky.

Simon paused to catch his breath. A clean, sappy smell of pine filled his nostrils. Behind him at some distance came the muffled sound of a twig snapping. It was not the first time Simon had heard such a noise. He twisted around and risked playing the focused halogen beam up through the trees, along the path he had pushed through the smooth, crystalline crust. It was probably some large animal following him. He knew that bears and wolves had been hunted to extermination decades ago, but a feral dog might do him more damage than some naturally wild creature.

With the beam still facing behind him, Simon backed downhill, only glancing at his advance and concentrating more of his attention on where he had been. His left hand fumbled through the thick glove to unsnap the leather strap that held the large knife within its sheath. He subdivided his attention again, laboring to see why the knife was not coming free.

The solid earth beneath the snow suddenly cascaded away. All Simon's muscles contracted at once. He felt himself sliding backward like a canoe over a waterfall. With a catlike contortion, he threw himself toward the uprushing ground but found no hold. Huge puffs of snow exploded from his clawing hands. Darkness swept in as the torchlight swung away to the limits of the nylon tether holding it to his belt. Walls closed in around him. His left thigh, then his left elbow, glanced off rock. He felt a hot rush of pain. Stiff vegetation slapped at his plummeting face.

Simon stopped with a jerk. He caught his breath, waited for his heart to drop down from his throat and for the shooting pain in his left side to subside. He realized that both his feet hung downward, touching nothing. He leaned forward slightly and followed the torchlight's beam. The great crack in the earth went down another fifteen feet or so beyond his boots before the walls came together in jagged, up-pointing angles. Simon craned his neck left and right. He had been saved from death by the sheer dimensions of his ruck-

205

sack. The outer bars of its aluminum frame had wedged between the granite walls. Just how securely it was anchored Simon could not tell without performing major acrobatics. He took several slow breaths and set to the business of saving himself.

The Vampire came up from his prone position in the snow and squatted on his haunches, pulling his cross-country skis carefully under him. They were more trouble than they were worth in the crenulated countryside . . . especially with the young man shining that damned lighthouse beacon in his direction every few minutes. And now the idiot had disappeared. Fallen, evidently.

Pulling himself upright by means of the evergreen branches beside him, the Vampire narrowed his amber eyes. The hapless librarian wasn't coming up under his own power. This presented a real dilemma. His purpose in trailing Simon Penn was to protect him from border patrols. Unless he could somehow determine that the bastard was unconscious, he couldn't help pull him out without revealing his identity. Even if he had taken the bothersome precaution of wearing a disguise, face to face the man was sure to recognize Wilhelm Wagner Essrag. He shoved his ski cap off his ears and listened intently for sounds of movement from the chasm. What he heard instead was the faint barking of dogs, coming from behind him.

The Vampire swore, turned his skis, and plunged his poles into the snow. Using his superhuman power, he worked his way obliquely up the slopes, following the general direction of Penn's telltale plunge through the forest. Coming to the crest of a small valley, he went into a tuck and began a schuss. Now he could discern two dogs barking, with increased urgency. His nose told him they were upwind. They had to have reacted to the sound of his approach, with ears even more acute than his. Still backtracking on Simon Penn's trail, he plunged downward through a mass of firs.

When he emerged, he found himself within two hundred feet of precisely the person he most hoped to avoid, the same person who had necessitated his presence at the border.

"Hans, Fritz, *ferma!*" the Swiss ski patrolman commanded twice, to restrain the dogs. He wore a waterproof white nylon shell over his clothing and ski cap. His belt and poles were white as well. The only dark items on his person were the butt of a revolver protruding from a white holster and an alien-looking, olive-drab contraption masking his eyes that could only be night-vision lenses. The dogs were full-grown German shepherds. From their size, the Vampire judged both to be male. They had stopped barking, but one growled through bared white fangs.

The ski patrolman was sure to wonder how the little man on the slope above him had maneuvered so skillfully in near-complete darkness. The Vampire had his response ready. It was yet another of his facile lies, sufficient to draw the officer closer. A white walkie-talkie was secured to the man's belt. The Vampire was betting the communicator would stay in place. He was, after all, neither in the company of a beautiful blond woman nor carrying any belongings.

The patrolman gave a series of sotto voce, one-word Italian commands to his canine companions. They responded by separating and moving up the slope on the oblique.

Keeping his infrared glasses fixed on the Vampire, the patrolman felt along his right hip until he found a nylon lanyard. He followed it to where it was attached to the butt of his revolver. As he unsnapped the holster, he called up the hill.

" 'ello," he said. "Oo are you?" His vowels had Italian purity.

"Was?" the Vampire called back.

"What are you doing 'ere?" the officer asked. The revolver was in his hand. He squatted down on his haunches and unsnapped his boots from the ski bindings.

"Leider, spreche ich kein . . . was ist das . . . englisch?" the Vampire said, doing his best to ignore the beasts working their way toward his flanks.

"Was tun Sie 'ier?" the officer said, straightening and immediately trudging up the hill. The Vampire replied, in German, that he was lost and following someone else's path in the snow as best he could. He then inquired who was asking. Immediately after the officer identified himself, he inquired how the unexpected skier

could see. The Vampire replied that he barely could; that he had made crude torches of dead fir branches and set them aflame with his cigarette lighter but that they cast little light and blew out easily. With each question and each answer, the officer walked closer. He was more wary than the Vampire would have expected, given the gun in his hand, his trained dogs and what the Vampire believed to be a convincing portrayal of a rather dimwitted tourist skier.

"Bitte, zeigen Sie mir etwas von Identifizierung," the patrolman demanded, holding out his free hand.

"Sicher," answered the Vampire, worming his fist into his parka, as if to drag out a wallet. He had purposely stopped at the crest of a rather sharp incline. He gave his buried hand a sharp jerk and pretended it caused him to lose his balance, sending him shooting down the hill directly toward the officer, free hand windmilling the air, his face a clownish mask of astonishment.

The patrolman tried to dodge out of the bumbling man's path, but a subtle dip of one hip turned the Vampire's skis, veering him again straight for the patrolman. The instant before impact, the Vampire's right fist thrust forward with immense speed, its force barely absorbed by the layers of nylon and wool, driving the officer's sternum into his heart.

Bone crackled; warm air whooshed from collapsing lungs. The officer's eyes were invisible beneath the night-vision lenses, but his mouth formed a near-perfect O as he fell backward. He managed to hold tight to his revolver as his body slammed hard into the snow. With a superhuman effort, he raised the weapon and pointed it at the Vampire's heart.

Between the dying and the undead there was no contest, no chance for justice to be served. The tip of one ski swung at the revolver with blurring velocity, whisking it aside before the trigger was jerked. The revolver was not of a large caliber. Its report was a sharp crack rather than a boom, but in the silent night and among the walls of barren rock, the noise echoed far.

The Vampire tumbled forward, snapping his boots from their bindings, rolling head over heels in the snow and coming up into a coiled squat. There was no question in his mind that, once the dogs saw their master attacked, they would be on him with a fury only one act could stop.

The first shepherd dog was upon the Vampire before he could regain his balance, knocking him flat with the momentum of its compact weight. Its fang-filled jaws yawned open, seeking its prey's throat. The Vampire reacted like a fast-forwarded video, grabbing the animal's lower jaw and snout and thrusting in two directions at once, breaking the hinges and severing vital parts of the dog's lower brain from its spine. The animal rolled over and away, thrashing in agony, making an unearthly belling noise as it did.

The second dog came from behind as the Vampire tried to stand, snapping with rage at the arm directly in its path. Despite having suffered hundreds of wounds over his lifetime, the undead's sense of pain never lessened nor became easier to ignore. The Vampire screamed as sturdy incisors ripped through his muscle and nerve and clamped around bone. He rose to his knees, then his feet, hauling the beast up with him, preferring the torture of the creature's dangling weight to its ability to whip its head back and forth on the ground. Its growl had the intensity of an open blast furnace; brown eyes stared unblinkingly into amber, oblivious to fear or the contemplation of its own mortality.

The Vampire cocked his free hand back, fingers curled into talons. Lightninglike he uncoiled, driving through the shepherd dog's belly and up the inner cavity, until he found the beating heart. The dog's growl changed to a sharp, guttural yip. The Vampire squeezed. The dog's jaws relaxed, then let go. It collapsed into the snow and lay still. The other dog and its master as well were corpses. The Vampire looked past the carnage to where Simon Penn's tracks disappeared among the firs. Momentarily forgotten, the massive heart steamed in his hand.

The cellular telephone rang inside the Alfa Romeo. Dante Ferro picked it up.

"Yes," Dante replied. "He's disappeared from my screen, too. I'm going out after him."

Dante left the car, which he had pulled as far off the road as possible. At the extreme of his vision, he could make out the border crossing between Switzerland and Italy, a gathering of yellow-white dots bisecting the highway.

Sitting in a car so close to the border was suspicious enough, but walking away from it into the forest was worse. And yet he had no choice. Simon had started cross-country more than a mile farther north, a prudent distance. But now, as he had come virtually to the border, something had happened to the good-luck bullet. If Simon had simply tossed it on the ground they would have noted a sudden lack of movement. This vanished signal was worse. Dante envisioned the young American falling off some sheer black cliff. He went to the trunk and took out a flashlight and a fifty-meter coil of nylon rope, hoping to God that whatever had befallen Penn would not require rappelling.

Dante trotted across the road and waded into the forest, heading directly eastward through a snowfall growing heavier by the minute. His plan was to move on a vector to the route Simon had walked, until he intersected the American's trail. The first several hundred meters were steep climbing, proving to Dante that no matter how fit he tried to keep himself, age was taking its toll. Just as his ascent flattened out, he thought he heard the faint barking of a dog above the wind. A few seconds later, he definitely heard the report of a gun, echoing off mountain walls. He had seen signs posted along the highway forbidding firearms and hunting in the forest; the gunshot was an ominous sound. He redoubled his efforts.

Within a few minutes, Dante had picked up the solitary track and followed it, his progress through the deep snow immediately eased. He again broke into a trot. Tumbling flakes cast a solid curtain at the limits of his flashlight's throw. Just as he began taking most of his breath through his mouth, his beam swept across the place where Simon had fallen. A bright beacon knifed up into the falling snowflakes from inside the earth, and he heard a familiar voice call for help.

"Simon!" Ferro called back.

"Dante? Don't come too close; it's slippery as hell."

"I won't. I have a rope. Will you be able to tie it around yourself?"

"Yes. I'm a little banged up, but I don't think anything's broken. I'm stuck halfway down. How did you find me?"

Dante unslung the rope from his shoulder and uncoiled it as he answered. "The bullet in your pocket, the one that wouldn't fire . . . it has a tiny radio transmitter."

"Then you damned well better save me," Simon said. "That vampire woman almost killed me because of your tiny transmitter. Misfire my ass!" He remembered the sharp echo from a few minutes before. "Did you fire your gun a while ago?"

Dante began tying the rope around a sturdy fir. "No, but I heard the gunfire."

"Do you know who it was?"

"Someone we don't want to see." Dante tested the half hitches he had tied and went down flat on his stomach. "The border patrol sometimes shoots guns to create avalanches."

"Can you get me up?"

"I believe so," Dante said, as he crawled carefully toward the chasm, anchoring himself with the rope. "But I will leave you to the patrol unless you tell me where Miss Vanderveen can be found."

"Get me out first, and I'll tell you," Simon bargained.

"On your word as a gentleman?"

"Yes . . . on my word."

"Very well. Shine the light on yourself." Dante stuck his face over the edge of the crevice and peered down. "Do not move! You are being held up by part of your backpack but mostly by the cane Wagner gave you. I will go back from the hole now, and then I'll send the rope down to you."

The rescue was accomplished without further mishap. As soon as he was on firm ground, Simon determined that his many layers of clothing had prevented any bones from being broken. The worst of his fall seemed to be torn jeans and bloody scrapes. While he examined himself, Dante took a close look at the sword cane.

"This thing must be made of ironwood or teak," Dante decided.

"You are not a small man. It is incredible that it could stop your fall without breaking."

Simon took the rucksack, with the cane still secure under its straps, and gingerly swung it onto his shoulders. "Just a bit more of God's providence," he replied.

"And now for your promise," Dante reminded him.

"I told her Elmasri's in Florence," Simon said. "My guess is that she got as far as Milan last night and had to stop because of daylight. She's probably in Florence right now. She'll get to him tomorrow somehow, and then you'll see that she's still on our side."

"I want to be there when that happens," Dante said, untying the rope from the tree. "The border is no more than five hundred meters that way. Do you think you can go on?"

"Absolutely."

"Good. And you have tools to cut through the wire?"

"I do."

Dante coiled the rope. "Let me see the bullet."

"Gone," Simon answered. "My pocket was ripped open. It's at the bottom of the crevice."

"Then you are truly on your own now. I will wait for you in Tronzano. Three hours only. If you do not show, I will telephone the border patrol that you need rescuing."

"Fair enough."

Dante shook off the snow that had accumulated on his face and clothing. "Let us both hurry. The weather is bad . . . and we do not know the reason for that gunshot."

"I don't want to know," Simon said, giving the chasm a wide berth. "See you in three hours or less."

Dante noted the young man's slightly limping gait, imagining how much the injuries must have hurt and the fact that Simon made nothing of them. His estimation of the American rose several notches. He turned his flashlight on Simon's old trail and followed it back toward the direction of Vira, head down and shoulders hunched up against the chill, southward wind.

★ ★ ★

The Vampire waited until a full minute had passed before rising from behind the stand of fir trees. If only the priest or the young American had mentioned exactly where this Elmasri person was in Florence, he would have killed both of them on the spot. Killed them and drunk a bellyful of their hot blood. Instead, he was forced to keep himself hidden under the fir branches like a timid fawn. In the bitter cold he so hated. He could not even follow the easier trail back toward his car in Vira, as the priest was doing. Not unless he wanted to stand impotently in the snow for another half-hour, until the old man was sure to be well ahead of him.

The Vampire laughed lightly, thinking of the mentioned bullet homing device, of the golden statue in the priest's car, and of the sword cane which had saved Simon Penn from death. It could have ended much worse tonight. Although the hunt continued, at least it seemed to be coming to an end. To Florence then, racing against the spin of the earth. Maybe he could rest awhile, away from daylight, until his Infernal Master told him exactly where to find the cursed Scrolls of Ahriman and all the foolish humans who sought to bring their message to light.

Ray Pental poured himself a second mug of coffee and glanced at his kitchen clock. Eight-twenty. He'd need the extra caffeine to make it through the midnight-to-eight tour of duty. First days back from vacation were bad enough, but catching the graveyard shift after a full morning and afternoon of family activities was sure to make the readjustment a bear. Promotion to detective had actually guaranteed him more midnight shifts, since he was the most junior of his team.

Ray ladled a heaping teaspoonful of sugar into his World's Greatest Dad mug and flipped open the morning's *Trenton Times*. What with the trip to Philadelphia to see the Wanamaker's Christmas light show and then over to Camden for the new New Jersey aquarium, this was the first chance he'd had to peruse it. His eyes scanned pages two and three. He noted with relief the absence of any vampire headlines. The undead was finally both dead and buried.

According to Detective Sutton, the Princeton police had suffered through a particularly bad murder about a decade before Ray joined the force. A young woman who worked as a telephone answering service operator had been found strangled on the Delaware and Raritan canal towpath (close by where Professor McCarthy's car had been dragged from Carnegie Lake). Many people were convinced they knew the murderer's identity, and, in a community as small as Princeton, the word spread. The *Princeton Packet* declared that the police had hard evidence against a suspect. It just wasn't so. The local newspaper headlines dragged on week after week, along with increasingly angry letters to the editor, denouncing the police's incompetence and demanding resignations. But, inevitably, other issues and headlines pushed the murder into the background, and everyone but those directly involved forgot. The murder was never solved, but no one ever lost his job over it.

The same situation prevailed in the vampire murders. Once Simon Penn's note was exposed, declaring DeVilbiss a vampire, there wasn't much farther to go . . . especially after the chief pathologist of the Princeton Medical Center said his preliminary autopsy revealed a perfectly normal corpse. Of course, Penn and Frederika Vanderveen eventually would be run to ground, and the whole thing would heat up again. But this time, the focus would be on two humans. For the time being, the circus had left town. Ray counted on a slow ease-back into his detective routine.

"Hey, Dad!" Ray's older daughter, Alison, called from the living room. "What movie is this from?"

"What?" Ray called back, not wanting to sacrifice his comfortable position at the kitchen table.

"It's some lady with rats in cages."

The words set the first alarm bell ringing in Ray's skull.

"What's happening?"

"She dropped one rat from a shiny box into a cage. It's throwing itself against the bars, and the rat in the next cage is going crazy. Is it a mechanical rat or a computer animation?"

The cerebral bell transformed into a five-alarm claxon blast. Ray pushed himself up from the chair on Alison's second sentence and dashed toward the living room on her third.

"Where's the remote control?" he asked Alison, trying not to sound as agitated as his movements might have suggested.

"Right there."

Ray picked up the control and stabbed the Off button.

"What're you doing, Dad? I want to see it!" Alison wailed.

"No," Ray answered firmly. "It's a very scary horror movie, and I don't want you having nightmares. Besides, it's close to your bedtime. Have you taken your bath?"

"No."

Using a well-practiced litany, Ray exposed one sin of omission after another, until Alison knew her continued protests were useless. Affixing her best scowl, she stomped toward the stairs. He knew his daughter well; she had retreated with a plan. She would be up by seven A.M. and in front of the television set, counting on having an hour and a half before he got home from work. He pictured the Rumpelstiltskin fit she'd throw when she realized he had removed the tape from the house.

Ray put the VHS machine in reverse and ran it back eighty numbers on the counter. He turned the television on and set the volume low. On the chair next to the remote control was the empty tape box with its *Tales from the Crypt* label. When he activated the tape machine he realized he had not wound back into the cartoon, but he let it run anyway.

Bespectacled, dark-haired, dark-eyed Dr. Dorena Durazo sat on a stool in her cellar, in front of a fixed camera. Just behind her on a work counter sat a clear Mason jar, filled with an amber-colored powder.

"Working from the same formula," she said into the camera, "I produced a second batch. The dosage given to the subjects was in direct proportion of their weight to that of a full-grown male. I had no idea of frequency of dosage, so I administered the powder orally, in a sterile water suspension. Twice a day to the first rat; once a day to the second. The first died of apoplectic seizures about

215

an hour after the second dose. You are about to see rat number two now. An hour ago, I nicked its tail in three places with a scalpel. Healing was nearly complete before I turned on this tape."

The scientist moved toward the camera until automatic focus was impossible and her shape had all but blackened the screen. When an image reappeared, the camera had been swiveled to face the counter that held the rat cages. Durazo came back into view, opening the top door of the narrow-gauge wire cage on the left and dumping the contents of a steel cylinder with small air holes into the cage. The occupant was a large sewer rat, identical to the ones Ray had experienced in Durazo's basement. The rat immediately threw itself against the near cage wall. The instant the scientist withdrew the cylinder from the door opening, it leaped up. The woman was prepared, and slammed the door down hard, snapping it in place. The rat hung from one of the bars by its teeth and kicked at the door with its hind legs. Durazo lowered a heavy metal plate over the cage's top, forcing the rat to let go. Then she disappeared toward the camera. A few seconds later, the view zoomed in and the focus sharpened. The rat seemed to be catching its breath.

"Look at the tail," Durazo's hollow voice directed. "You'll have to take my word for it that I cut it. The wounds are completely gone."

There was another rat in the picture, inside the cage joined immediately to the subject rat's cage. It was darting rapidly back and forth, its back humped up, its face never turned from its violent neighbor. It emitted shrill squeaks as it moved, and it was evident that it was not the only panicked rodent in the basement. The cellar reverberated with a racket like half a dozen sets of fingernails clawing along chalkboards.

Dorena Durazo gave no commentary as the first rat became galvanized again and launched itself in what seemed a self-destructive gesture against the bars that separated it from the other rat. When it rebounded, the camera revealed that its force had bent the wires slightly. It repeated the act, apparently no worse for the experience. The bars widened a bit more. On its third attack, the other rat leaped at its face and bit the attacker's nose. The aggressor backed

216

off, dripping blood. It sat up on its hind legs in the middle of its cage, running its paws over its snout, then darting them into its mouth, licking the blood away. In the space of thirty seconds, its wounds were visibly healed. It resumed its attack.

Ray watched transfixed as the monster rat worked like a machine to separate the bars, until finally it was able to counterattack and grab its quarry as it had been grabbed. This, however, was no frantic nip. It held on despite the frenzied thrashing of its fellow rodent. It released only for a blurred instant, to gain a better, deeper grip. And then it chomped down. Though faint, the sound was clearly one of breaking bone. The victim rat's squeals transformed into shrieks of mortal agony. When it was released, it scuttled back to the far corner of the cage, barely able to lift its bloodied head. The attacker also backed up, but only to throw itself one final time between the bent bars. And then it was through and, almost faster than the camera could record, upon the other rat, biting and clawing with demonic fury, until its writhing victim could do no more than shudder feebly. As the roiling confusion of fur subsided, Ray could see that the subject rat was attached to the other's savaged neck, drinking the welling blood.

Ray had seen enough. He stopped the tape and ejected it from the machine. The words on the cartridge's spine came into view. The tale from Dorena Durazo's crypt had Ray shaking with rage and fear. Taking the tape with him, he grabbed his coat, badge, wallet, and revolver and headed to the front door. He shouted up the stairs to his wife that he needed to go to work early and immediately slammed the door, wanting no reply.

Despite his sense of acute urgency, Ray walked carefully to his car, giving the snow and ice the respect his still-aching back demanded. Once inside the car, he metamorphosed into a drag racer, gunning backward into the street, shifting hard and flooring the pedal. At the first traffic light, he pulled the portable "bubble gum machine" from under his seat and set its red lights whirling.

Occam's razor, Ray thought. Dorena Durazo's Dallas record proved that she was an individual willing to break the law for her own ends. She was a pharmaceutical chemist specializing in human blood. She had taken a real risk to look at the corpse of Vincent DeVilbiss. Now Ray knew why. She had hardly known the man. He had come to her for her professional skills, bringing a powder for analyzing and duplicating.

Dorazo had probably assumed DeVilbiss worked for some company hoping to violate patent laws and manufacture illegal quantities of a new and sophisticated medicine. Perhaps she had started experimenting with the rats in her basement, to see if she could figure out precisely what the formula did and sell it to other criminals. Perhaps not. But then DeVilbiss had died, and his killer was trumpeting that the man had been a vampire. All she had to do was pick up a newspaper. If the sensational story was even partially true, it meant that DeVilbiss was being supplied with a powder that made him both incredibly strong and capable of healing almost instantaneously. And if the rat was any indication, the powder also gave him an overwhelming thirst for blood. Not the classic legendary creature, but a very adequate definition of a vampire.

If the news reports about the vampire's invulnerability and strength were true, why not also Penn's published claim that DeVilbiss was centuries old? A woman who, as a student, had formulated hallucinogenic drugs for money beyond what she needed would definitely be tempted by the elixir of eternal youth. The identical tapes proved that she planned to peddle her miraculous knowledge to more than one potential buyer. Struggling to envision all the terrible possibilities of such a powder entering world or even underworld marketplaces, Ray's Roman Catholic mind boggled. Given the prospect of holding off death indefinitely, fear of God could dwindle to virtual nonexistence. Likewise, fear of eternal punishment, even for something as wicked as murder. If human blood was a necessary catalyst for the powder, civilization might collapse under the diabolical irony of wholesale life-taking for life-saving.

Ray was so intent on racing to Dr. Durazo's house that he forgot to call for backup until he turned onto The Great Road. He took the microphone in his hand and pressed the Send button.

218

"Dispatch, this is Unit Six. I'm on The Great Road. I have a code 20."

"Copy, Unit Six. What is the nature of your 20?"

Ray paused with his mouth open. What in hell was the Ten Code for this situation? Certainly his department and probably most others across the country had no shorthand for drug raids, which was what this would be. Raids were the consequence of tips or surveillances, planned out at the station, not over the airwaves in moving police cars. Even if there were such a code, it would not remotely correspond to the type of drug Durazo had replicated. And if the claims in Simon Penn's typed letter had spread like wildfire from just six witnesses trusted to be closemouthed, how much faster would word spread of a powder for eternal life? Ray couldn't trust anyone else with the knowledge. He was also again prepared to go beyond legal police procedures, this time to ensure that the formula and the amber powder in Durazo's possession vanished from the face of the earth.

"Uh . . . sorry, Nicky. False alarm."

"You okay, Ray?" the concerned voice came back.

An Assist Officer, Urgent was not something to brush off. "Yeah, fine. I spotted a 10-35 out here, but it's just some clown feeding more juice to his Christmas lights." Ten-35 meant Open Window.

"Copy. See you at midnight."

"Roger." Ray renested the microphone. The driveway to Durazo's house came into his headlights. He turned in and parked where trees crowded the rutted drive on both sides, preventing the woman from escaping by car. As he shut off the engine he suddenly remembered a reference to "some yellow dust like pollen on the kitchen counter" in Andy Sutton's report on the house DeVilbiss rented. Ray never felt more sure about the meaning behind a collection of clues. What he was unsure of was how he would handle Dr. Durazo.

Ray rounded the dense gathering of trees, shrubbery, and undergrowth that masked the little house from the road. He came to a halt as if he had struck a huge pane of plate glass. An instant after absorbing the unexpected machinery in front of him, he leaped out of the driveway and hid himself against the nearest large tree.

A commercial helicopter sat in the clearing between the trees and the house, nose facing to his right, rotors silent but lamps burning downward onto the patchy snow and ice. Dorena had high-powered company.

Ray rushed back to the unmarked police car. The equation had changed drastically. He grabbed the microphone.

"Dispatch, this is Unit Six again. Real trouble on The Great Road. About a half mile south of the Pike, on the left. All available units. Code 30."

"Copy, Unit Six."

"My car's parked in the driveway. Out." As he spoke, he felt blindly under the driver's seat. The situation demanded all the fire-power he could assemble. Andy Sutton had confided some time back that a "hot piece" was hidden among the seat springs. Ray had never bothered to check it out, never thought he'd have need of such a weapon. His fingertips found a strap, then a snap. He tugged hard and came out with a Beretta, fully loaded.

Ray shoved the little pistol between his ankle and the tight elastic of his sock, replaced the microphone, then headed back through the trees, working his way in a crouch through the tangle of underbrush. As he moved, he drew his service revolver from its hip holster. He kept circling until he could approach the copter from its tail. Before he stepped into the clearing, he cracked open the cylinder and looked at the chambers. He always kept the first one empty against accidental discharge, leaving him five bullets. He snapped the cylinder shut and walked gingerly across the glazed snow to the copter. Keeping his left hand near the machine's underbelly for support, he duckwalked as silently as possible to the passenger door. He reached up, got his free hand around the handle, yanked it open and stood, shoving the revolver forward as he did.

The helicopter stood empty, except for a cardboard box crammed with notebooks, folders, and a three-quarters-filled jar of amber powder.

"*¡Cuidado!*" a gruff voice commanded, from behind Ray.

Ray turned slowly and found himself staring at the muzzle hole of an M10 submachine gun. Its owner was a small man in a two-piece suit and brilliantly red silk necktie, but the outfit made him look no more respectable than a jackass would wearing a Kentucky Derby blanket. Added to diminutive stature, his straight, black hair, dark skin, and prominent cheekbones betrayed the thug as Central or South American.

"*¡Baja la pistola!*" the Latino ordered.

Even if Ray had not taken enough Spanish to understand the man, the motion of the submachine gun spoke clearly. Slowly, he set his revolver down on the frozen snow and backed away. Never taking his eyes from Ray, the South American collected the revolver. He jerked his weapon upward.

"*¡Manos arriba!*"

Ray lifted his hands and walked around the helicopter toward the house.

Coming down the tiny cottage hallway, Ray found Dorena Durazo standing in her dining area, close by a man of Latin extraction but who was taller and lighter-skinned than the thug with the machine gun, as well as more elegantly dressed. Both blinked in surprise at Ray's unexpected presence, as did the man just emerging from the basement, holding another box of materials in his hands. The third character looked more like the thug holding the gun, but he appeared to be weaponless and wore a fur-lined bomber jacket and a New York Yankees baseball cap.

"Hello, Officer," Durazo said to Ray. She wore a paint-spattered Johns Hopkins sweatshirt two sizes too large for her, atop stretch pants. Her hair looked like she had just emerged from the shower. She looked even less at ease than she had in the morgue. It was unlikely that she had expected her company. "He's a policeman," she told the man beside her.

The elegantly dressed man, who was clearly the leader, issued a set of commands to his henchmen, both too rapidly spoken and too colloquial for Ray to understand. Baseball Cap went out the front door. Silk Tie delivered Ray's service revolver to the boss.

"Why is he here?" the boss asked Durazo.

The scientist was clearly flustered by Ray's unexpected appearance. As her mouth worked soundlessly, Ray noted four items on the dining room table: an open attaché case filled with stacks of U.S. paper currency; a suitcase; a makeup case; a sturdy steel cage containing a familiar-looking, large, high-strung rat.

"He's . . . a narcotics detective," Durazo said. "He's visited me before."

"Then why did you resist coming with us?" the boss asked. "You can't stay in this country." In Spanish, he ordered Silk Tie to take the luggage to the helicopter and bring the rope back with him.

"This isn't like selling LSD to kids in Dallas," Ray told Durazo. "You're in way over your head. If you go with them, you'll be a slave in their drug factory until they're sure your powder works. Then it's bye-bye, Doctor."

"Shut up, cop," the boss ordered, "or you'll be the one going bye-bye!" He pointed the service revolver at Ray's face.

"I don't think so," Ray answered, summoning every ounce of his actor's bravado. "Remember all the heat after that U.S. narc, Camarena, was iced in Mexico? You're too smart for that. That's why your goon is bringing a rope back: to tie me up." Ray swung his gaze from the boss and read the scientist's face. His words had acted like kerosene on the flame of her doubt. "Isn't it convenient they had a rope with them?" he asked her. "Maybe in case you weren't cooperative? If I were you, I'd take that money and—"

"I said shut up!" the boss ordered, marching across the small room and delivering a swift kick between Ray's legs.

Grunting from the excruciating pain, Ray sank to his knees. When he lifted his head, however, what he saw made the agony worthwhile. Dorena Durazo had opened the rat's cage, which faced precisely where the boss stood. As he turned toward Durazo, the rat leaped out of the cage, bounded off the table and flew at the man's neck.

Screaming, the boss fell backward into the partially opened cellar door, causing it to slam shut. His free hand clawed at the rat's hold, but the rodent transferred its attack to his thumb. The man cocked his arm and threw the frenzied creature across the room.

In the meantime, Dr. Durazo had grabbed the attaché case, snapped it closed, and ran for the sliding glass door. She had it opened and was halfway out when the bullet from the service revolver caught her in the base of the skull and ripped through her brain, blowing the spectacles off her face as it exited.

An instant later, the first of three bullets from the Beretta caught the boss in the stomach. The man pivoted to aim his weapon at Ray and took the second slug in the arm. The third hit him squarely in the heart, sending him backward onto the floor.

Outside, the helicopter blades began to whirr. Ray looked toward the open front door. Silk Tie was charging up the outside steps, M10 raised. Ray swung the Beretta around and fired until it was empty. He heard the thug grunt as he disappeared from view, but he could not tell if he had hit the man. Mastering the pain in his groin, Ray rolled out of the line of fire, toward the dining room table. A moment later the machine gun chattered, and the chair behind where he had knelt became kindling.

The helicopter noise grew thunderous outside. Ray rolled across the dead man and clawed the revolver out of his grasp, wondering why his damned backup hadn't arrived. A single slug sang into the house and then, a few seconds later, another. The second caught both panes of the sliding glass door, shattering them.

Ray understood that the bullets were meant to pin him down. He took a few fortifying breaths, got to his feet and staggered through the ruined glass door. Another bullet thudded into a wall behind him. Keeping low, Ray circled the house. The vibration of the helicopter was thrumming off the rooftop and the nearby trees. He looked up and saw that it was already twenty feet in the air and rising rapidly. He raised his revolver, aimed, and got off a shot. It was impossible with all the noise to tell if he had hit anything. Then the copter hove left, so that the chimney was between it and Ray's line of fire. Ray waited in vain for another shot. The helicopter flew low over the treetops and was quickly hidden by the bulk of the house.

Ray returned to the back of the house, to see the extent of Dr. Durazo's wound. She lay facedown, half in and half out of the doorway. Her wet hair hid the bullet's entry wound, so that he saw nothing. When he rolled her over, he grimaced at the cavity where her right eyeball had been. And at the rat that had been lapping the blood from the hole. The rat reared back on its hind legs and bared its teeth. Instinctively, Ray's leg swung out, but the rat reacted with unbelievable speed, dashing across the icy back yard and into the darkness.

Intent on getting to the police car and radioing an APB on the helicopter, Ray went straight through the house and out the front door. He was down the first step before he realized the M10 was pointing directly at him. Where the helicopter had sat with its lamps ablaze was now a rough lawn of blue-black shadows, lit feebly by the light pouring out the cottage windows. Among the shadows, Silk Tie lay on his back, holding his weapon aloft. A smooth depression like the track of a toboggan ran from the house under his feet, formed as he had crawled toward the copter. The white track was liberally stained with the man's blood.

Silk Tie coughed, and Ray heard the blood pooled in the man's lungs. The man struggled to keep the weapon from wavering and squeezed the trigger.

Nothing happened. Silk Tie let his head drop back onto the snow. His gun arm collapsed.

Revolver cocked, Ray advanced cautiously on the man. As his eyes accustomed to the outside darkness, he saw a stain filling the shirt behind the tie, a darker shade of red. Ray shook his head. At the academy, he had never hit bull's-eyes in any two sequential practice targets. Either luck or God was on his side tonight.

Silk Tie's chest quivered briefly. Then he seemed to stop breathing. Ray kicked the M10 out of the thug's grasp and bent, to feel at his neck for a pulse.

The cottage erupted with noise, light, and jarring vibration. Ray dove for the ground. Splinters of window glass skittered across the lawn, mixing indistinguishably with jagged spikes of ice, created by the helicopter's landing and by the feet of the participants in the brief, deadly drama. When he realized he was beyond the reach of the explosion, Ray lifted his head and stared at its aftermath. For all the violence, the house looked fairly intact. Through the open front door, however, Ray could see flames licking up through the open floor. If their purpose was to destroy any information left behind, they had done a thorough job of it.

Ray moved with haste to the unmarked police car. As he threw open the driver's door and grabbed for the microphone, he saw flashing red lights speeding toward him from far up The Great Road.

"Dispatch, this is Unit Six. Call in a one-alarm to the fire department for the previous 20. Over."

"What's happened, Unit Six?"

"A 10-80, among other things. When you're done, Nicky, patch me in to the Air National Guard in Lakehurst, just as fast as you can."

CHAPTER SEVEN

December 30

ᕙᕗ

What humanity needs is not the promise of scientific immortality,

but compassionate pity in this life and infinite mercy on the

Day of Judgment.

—Joseph Conrad, *The Life Beyond*

B enedetto Castelli rubbed his hands together with delighted anticipation as the balance of his meal arrived. No mere Continental breakfast for the head curator of L'Archivo di Stato di Firenze, Florence's ancient archive. To be sure, the traditional coffee and crescent rolls with butter and marmalade were already on the table in front of him. But now arrived orange juice, a sticky bun, a three-egg omelet with Swiss cheese, an order of ham, and three pieces of buttered toast.

Father Ferro looked into the dimly lighted depths of the Ristorante John Bull. He might have been able to absorb the unrepentant display of gluttony, but the added weight of Signor Castelli's porcine proportions was too much to watch. Dante sipped his decaffeinated tea and pretended to admire a pretty female customer who dined alone.

"Shame on you, Father," Castelli teased, his mouth half filled with egg. "Remember your holy vows."

Dante forced a smile and nodded his head slightly, still avoiding the display of overindulgence on the opposite side of the table. The attempt at humor would have been easier to ignore had Castelli not been a self-proclaimed atheist and Communist. The huge curator definitely considered his need for food great and the Church's ability to underwrite it unquestioned. Dante's sister, who was fairly high up in city government, had been unable to tell Dante just how Castelli had latched on to such an important sinecure. As far as Dante knew, the man's name in scholarly publishing was nonexistent. He was clearly not a stupid man, but despite his position as head curator of one of Europe's most important specialty libraries he could not be drawn into a dialectic on the classical antiquities. Every time Dante focused the conversation on an esoteric discussion of ancient writing, Castelli steered it resolutely back toward food. Dante wondered if he was being rebuffed not out of Castelli's ignorance but rather because of the man's dislike for the Church.

As a policeman, Dante had long ago resigned himself to the fact that Italy was a country of petty larcenists. Business pilferage was accepted with a shrug. The more expensive the restaurant, the greater the likelihood the check would be mistotaled. And civil servants would not serve without a little greasing. Apparently, Castelli's greasing came through eggs and ham. If you wanted ingress to or information from his library, you took the boss to breakfast. Dante wanted nothing from the library, but he did need to know about a man who was currently doing voluntary work there. Incredibly, despite all his connections in Florence and his one-time employment in the police force, no one had been able to tell him where Professor Mustafa Elmasri was staying. More incredibly, despite his having telephoned a minute description of Frederika Vanderveen to every Florentine who might see her, she also had kept herself completely out of sight. The only apparent scheme to close in on the scrolls was to get to Elmasri through Castelli and see if the professor would cooperate. Now that Castelli was happily stuffing his maw, Father Ferro could finally broach the purpose of their meeting.

"What time does Dr. Elmasri usually arrive at the library?" Dante asked.

Castelli shrugged and glanced at his watch. "Half an hour maybe. Sometimes not until ten-thirty. This is his holiday, after all, and I hear he likes the night spots."

Dante drummed his fingernails impatiently on the table. "Perhaps I should visit him where he's staying instead of coming with you."

"If you know where that might be, you're more informed than I am," Castelli revealed, through a beefy grin. "You see, he's helping us dig out from the blast through the courtesy of the Greek government. They're paying all his expenses while he's here, so he made his own arrangements for housing. He comes and goes as he pleases, and we're grateful for whatever time he gives us."

"I see."

Castelli paused with the loaded fork halfway to his mouth. "You're not trying to steal him away, are you?"

"I'm here to ask him several questions about a manuscript," Ferro evaded. "How's the omelet?"

"Excellent." Fork tines disappeared between tiny teeth (no doubt worn down from all the eating, Dante thought). "You should order one for yourself, since you've got time, Dante. You're all skin and bone."

"No, thank you. But you enjoy it." Ferro rose from the table, taking his briefcase with him. "Order another if you wish. I need to make a phone call."

"By all means. Please. Send the waiter over if you see him."

Dante threaded through the tables toward the public telephone. He dialed a number, which was answered immediately, and identified himself. Then he asked, "Are you keeping an eye on Mr. Penn?"

"He went into the library the moment it opened, Father," the voice on the other end replied.

"No sighting of Miss Vanderveen, I assume?"

"Unfortunately."

"I'll call again at about eleven."

"I'll be here."

Father Ferro hung up slowly, thinking about the right words to use with Professor Elmasri, the phrases that would appeal to an enormous ego without appearing mere blandishments. He returned to the table with his billfold out.

"Something extremely urgent has come up, depriving me of your continued company, Signor Castelli. I shall see you at your library in about an hour."

"But you haven't eaten anything!" Castelli proclaimed, as if the priest had committed a cardinal sin.

"Tea's enough," Dante answered, dropping twice as much as the bill would require on the table, knowing Castelli would pocket the difference. "I apologize for leaving. You have a good meal."

"I shall," the curator affirmed, crooking his finger at a nearby waiter.

Another minute rolled by, literally, on Ray Pental's office clock. He had brought the instrument from home when Karen had bought a new bedroom alarm clock. It had neither hands nor LEDs but rather little black and white plastic rectangles of sequential numbers, fitted together as if on Rolodex axles. Every time a minute elapsed, a number flipped with the click of a wheel of fortune. At the turn of the hour the clatter was jarring. At 3:38 A.M., however, its periodic tripping was a welcome aid to wakefulness. Ray had been told thirty minutes ago to wait at his desk until Chief Littlefield digested Ray's videotape and report. It was like doing solitary time on Devil's Island.

Finally, Francis Littlefield's expensive shoes sounded in the hall. He appeared, holding Ray's report.

"This is bullshit, Pental. Full of holes."

"Only from where you sit, Chief," Ray replied. He was not in the slightest surprised by Littlefield's comments.

"What's that supposed to mean?"

"You're talking about how I got the tape?"

"That, and the phony 10-35 you called in to bring reinforcements to the woman's house . . . except you reconsidered because this had to do with the vampire business. Right?"

Littlefield looked more curious than angry, which gave Ray courage. "The tape was anonymously dropped into my car. That's my story. And the 10-35 was a mistaken window entry. If you buy it, everybody buys it."

"Goddammit, I'm the police chief of a quiet, affluent town. This shit isn't supposed to happen to me!" The chief dropped the report on Ray's desk, crossed the room and pulled over a chair. He eased himself into it and offered Ray a collegial smile. "Go ahead; you have my permission. Talk to me about vampires."

"Have you ever wanted to live forever, Francis?" Ray asked.

"Would I drink so much if I did?"

"Seriously."

"Forever? Nah. Too boring."

"How about an extra hundred years, every year of it at the equivalent of a really healthy thirty?"

"But the catch is I'd be as ferocious and bloodthirsty as that little bastard rat, right?"

"Check Sutton's report on the rented house. DeVilbiss was taking that same yellow powder. Durazo made some of the stuff for him. I'm positive she didn't know what it was for until DeVilbiss made the newspapers as a vampire. That's why she came to the morgue, to compare the face she'd met with the dead vampire in the newspaper stories."

"And the old lady who visited the morgue the night before?"

"Another person taking the powder, making sure DeVilbiss was on ice. Protecting the Society of the Undead or whatever."

Littlefield's cheeks puffed out as he expelled his dismay. "So vampires exist, technically."

Ray was happy enough for this concession on Littlefield's part; the buy-in about the supernatural elements was not necessary to secure his chief's aid. He nodded vigorously.

"Somebody's invented a drug that keeps you young and makes you incredibly strong and hard to kill. Except you also have to drink human blood if you want the drug to work."

"Something like that."

"Fact mimics fiction." A pair of lines suddenly pinched in between Littlefield's eyebrows. "Wait a minute. Wait a minute! What about the scrolls . . . the twenty-five-hundred-year-old scrolls this vampire was killing people left and right to get to? And what about this contract killing he was doing?"

Ray shrugged. "Maybe the original formula's in the scrolls. And he killed to pay for his habit."

The chief dug into his suit jacket and pulled out a cigarette. He waved it in front of Ray. "Here's another clue I don't plan on living forever. But your exculpated buddy, Simon Penn, thinks DeVilbiss was five hundred years old. And then there are all those ancient vampire legends. Who could make such a drug five hundred years ago, much less twenty-five hundred?"

Ray studied the tips of his interlaced fingertips.

"You think this thing is beyond natural explanation, don't you, Ray?"

"You just said it yourself, Chief: only some thing beyond this world could have created such a potion hundreds of years ago."

"Bullshit. There's got to be a logical explanation. We just don't have all the facts."

"You attend church?"

"Christmas, Easter, weddings, and funerals."

"How much of that is unbelievable?"

"True. But, supernatural or otherwise, the real problem is this formula getting into the natural world," Littlefield said, as softly as if he were passing on a secret. "What were you prepared to do, Ray . . . kill Dr. Durazo?"

"No. But I'd definitely have destroyed every piece of paper, film, and tape in her house. I was just a few hours too late."

The desk sergeant appeared at the office door. "They found the helicopter! It's a lease, to some offshore island holding company. It landed on the pad at AT&T headquarters, in Bedminster. By the time their security found it, the engine was cold. And clean as a fire engine."

As Littlefield excused the sergeant, Ray stared out the window into the black night. "It's loose, then. By the end of next year, it could be killing more people than AIDS."

The chief touched flame to the cigarette and drew in deeply. "I don't expect to live forever, but I would like to enjoy my pension. If people believe that drug and human blood can keep them alive forever, I can kiss not only the pension goodbye but law and order as we know it. I'll be working till I'm eighty guarding a blood-bank . . . if somebody doesn't get to my jugular before then."

"So, do we stick to the illegal drug story in my report?" Ray asked.

"Yeah. Until I'm forced to give it up." Littlefield exhaled a great puff of blue-white smoke. He stood. "In the meantime pray, Detective Pental. I'll do the same. The dragnet's up for the man with the baseball cap. Maybe he'll die in a hail of lead, and the lab folks assigned to look at the powder will take the easy way out and mark it as angel dust."

"Angel dust," Ray repeated. "Wouldn't that be ironic?"

Dante found Simon in the Periodicals Room of Florence's main library, head bent low over DeVilbiss's diary, pencil poised above a sheet of paper, decoder wheel in the other hand. When Dante pulled out the chair beside him, its screak across the marble floor made Simon jump. Outside, clouds parted. Intense light poured through the library windows.

"Sorry," Dante said, setting his briefcase on the table. "Any luck?"

"I've got good news and bad news," Simon replied.

"Give me the good news first."

"They're both the same. Beyond the point Frederika had translated, there are only five entries. Here are the headlines." He pushed a scrap of paper toward Dante. "He wrote on December 19th of having slipped powder into Frederika's wine. In the December 21st entry, the bastard records that he hypnotized her and put her on a daily dosage of the stuff. But it's not what he got from the Devil."

"Then what was it?"

"A synthesized version. I checked back to where Frederika started translating, and if you know what you're looking for, he makes cryptic allusions to it every so often. For example, in early December he's pissed that he has to leave Seattle and come cross-country, but he's glad it will bring him to the same state as a 'Dr. DD,' who he writes has claimed to have 'solved the final elements

234

of my riddle.' The entry on December 11th has him paying some unspecified amount for 'a pound of life and the enigmas revealed.' There's an entry on the last two pages of the book, with no date. Frederika apparently didn't try to decipher it. I did . . . at least a few lines of it, guessing it was this 'enigma revealed.' I used the headline from December 11th, and I got chains of Cs, Os, Hs, attached to other chemical elements. The letters are dispersed across the pages, connected by Vs as valence lines. You're staring at the coded formula for supernatural power and unending life."

"Did you not find the doctor's name spelled out anywhere?"

"No. DeVilbiss has a habit of giving full names and details of people he is commanded to kill, but those of his private life he refers to in the French Romantic manner, with initials only. See here . . . Frederika is always 'Miss V.' "

In spite of the coolness of the chamber, Dante felt himself begin to perspire. "DeVilbiss gave Dr. DD some of the Devil's powder to be analyzed?"

"I'd bet my life on it. And he tested it on Frederika. It makes sense. If the lords of the underworld doled out the powder to vampires to maintain control, why would DeVilbiss suddenly have enough to feed Frederika every day also? I know from personal experience that the man thought he was a lot brighter than he really was. He could never have analyzed such a complicated formula himself. He must have entrusted the job to Dr. DD."

"No reference to a pharmaceutical laboratory or the town where he works?"

" 'He' could be a she," Simon pointed out. "All he tells us is that Dr. DD is in New Jersey."

"I told the cardinals I did not believe this plague could be loosed without the free help of men . . . or women." Dante dabbed his handkerchief over his sweaty forehead. "It appears I was correct. So this is how it begins."

"I don't understand why it had to be this way," Simon said, tucking the decoder into the diary. "Why didn't the Devil just deliver the formula to mankind fifty years ago and outrace the scrolls' prophecy?"

"He couldn't. Not without revealing his involvement. A certain state of scientific advancement had to occur, so that the powder's creation could be explained by natural means."

Simon stood and grabbed his coat. "Then it's doubly important that we use the scrolls to prove its supernatural origins to the world." He looked at the ring on his finger. "Any word on Frederika?"

"None." Dante pushed back his chair and stood. "I wonder if she has not reached a wall she cannot climb. Elmasri has proved impossible to track down outside of the archives. If she conquers the pain of daylight and tries to find him there, she will probably spot the men we have placed around the building. Yet a woman as stubborn and determined as you say she is will try to find another opportunity."

Simon smiled slightly as he tucked the diary and papers into his coat pocket. "She'll do more than try; she'll eventually get to Elmasri."

"Then it is vital that we make him cooperate with us."

"Did you arrange a meeting?"

Father Ferro closed the top button of his overcoat, concealing his clerical collar. "No. We will have to wait for him at the archives, like petitioners for a king."

Simon read in Dante's face as well as his words how distasteful the just-stated course of action was.

"Let us walk there now," Dante said, picking up his briefcase. "On the way, I can show you some of Florence's many treasures."

As he entered the Piazza Madonna, Simon's pace slowed. His gaze rose gradually, taking in first the bicolored marble magnificence of the eight-sided Baptistery and then the twin splendors of the Cathedral of Santa Maria del Fiore and Giotto's 82-meter-high campanile beyond it.

"The sacred heart of Firenze," Dante said, in a reverent tone of voice, "and, I believe, one of the most sacred places on the earth. Let us follow this group of tourists around the Baptistery; there is something there you must not miss."

236

They rounded the octagonal building and insinuated themselves among the sizable crowd gathered before one wall. Set into the wall was a pair of huge doors. Each door held five enormous panels; each panel was gilt and uniquely depicted a biblical scene, using various degrees of relief. It was one of the most exquisite works of art Simon had ever seen.

"Ghiberti's Doors of Paradise," Dante told Simon. "Each panel tells a complete story. They go in order, left to right, from top to bottom. There is the Creation of Adam and Eve and the Original Sin. Then the story of Cain and Abel."

"Fantastic," Simon replied, to the priest's obvious expectation for response.

Dante pointed a bit above eye level, at the center of the doors. "There is the head of Lorenzo Ghiberti, the designer. The bald one on the left. Some say you will be forgiven a hundred years in purgatory for viewing these doors. And another ten for rubbing Lorenzo's head. That's why he shines so. If he wasn't bald already, people would have rubbed off the hair by now. How they get over this fence I don't know." A group of German tourists moved on, and the priest stepped forward, to run his hand across the iron fence's contrapposto-shaped, gold-coated spikes. "If this is not impressive enough for you, then wait until we go inside."

The floor of the Baptistery was open, with only a few wooden benches arrayed in front of the simple altar. The first two levels of the interior were striking enough, with rows of gilt-topped columns, Romanesque portals, and multicolored marble designs, but as the structure ascended its beauty became breathtaking. Hovering in a sky of golden tesserae was a Byzantine mosaic Christ, hands and feet pierced, sitting in glory on a stylized rainbow, surrounded by angels above, saints to his flanks, and demons below, judging the dead as they arose from their coffins.

"Do you believe the Day of Judgment is at hand?" Dante asked.

"I don't want to think about it," Simon replied honestly.

"We have more holy sacraments in the Roman Catholic Church than you Protestants have," Dante noted, "but all Christians commemorate two covenants with God. The first is baptism;

the second is Holy Communion. I have been thinking about the blood vampires must drink. I am certain the Devil could have created these creatures without such a need, but he wanted to pervert the Lord's Supper." Dante's words, spoken with force, echoed off the confining walls. "God used the blood of bulls to seal the covenant he made with Moses and His people. Christ made a new covenant in the shedding of His innocent blood. What the Devil has created in vampires is a hideous mockery of the holiest sacrament. Jesus sacrificed his own life, and we drink his blood to gain eternal life after death. The vampire sacrifices the lives of others, to gain unending life before death. As we drink the wine-become-blood in remembrance of Him, so must the vampire drink the innocent blood of his former kind, so that he never forgets who owns his soul."

Simon realized that the upward-gazing Father Ferro had put himself into a semitrance, unmindful of the people around him. Each time he spoke the words "blood" and "vampire" more tourists gaped at him, all with shocked expressions.

"It's time to go, Father," Simon said, touching Ferro lightly on the arm. The priest blinked several times, at last registering those staring at him, and followed Simon out of the Baptistery.

"When we meet Elmasri, I shall speak in English. I want you to be included in the discussion, and his Italian is not very good anyway. The few times I have talked with him, we have used Latin."

"Well, I can handle myself there," Simon said.

"Yes, but I think that is out of place in this situation. He is comfortable with English, and I prefer that you and I be in command of the language nuances rather than this man. *Capisce?*"

Clearly, Ferro was steeling himself for a battle of wits and wills.

"Understood," Simon said.

They walked side by side down the Via de Calzioli, until they reached the Piazza Signoria. It was with difficulty that Simon refrained from dragging his feet in the Loggia of the Lanzi, where stood masterpieces of sculpture by Cellini, Giambologna, and Michelangelo. He followed Father Ferro's quick stride around the corner to the state archives. Several men along the long Square of the Uffizi seemed to be loitering. For all he knew, they were merely tourists, and those watching for Frederika stood behind the numerous sidewalk sales booths. When they walked under the columned cloister, to the doors of the archives, a guard greeted them. As soon as Dante delivered their names, he gestured them inside, giving the priest a set of instructions for reaching one of the inner sanctums. Simon followed Father Ferro through a maze of interconnected rooms. Finally, the priest paused in a doorway.

"Professor Elmasri."

"*Si.* Padre Ferro?" Castelli, the curator, had at least earned his coffee.

"Yes," Dante persisted in English. "And Mr. Simon Penn, from the Rare Manuscripts Division of Princeton University Library." He stood aside, so that Simon could enter the room.

The man enthroned within delicately balanced towers of ancient papers was not quite what Simon had expected. The one photograph in a foreign antiquities journal Reverend Willy Spencer had shown Simon of his former Akkadian mentor and colleague had been a dark one. In the flesh, Elmasri possessed lighter skin, like that of Anwar el-Sadat. He also shared el-Sadat's thin frame. For his age, which Simon estimated to be about fifty, he maintained a Middle Eastern handsomeness. Beyond physicalities, he clearly bore himself as a man of power, import, confidence, and charisma. It was not inconceivable to Simon that many women might find him sexually attractive.

Elmasri rose halfway from his seat and offered each visitor an insincere handshake. "And what is the latest news of the elusive Scrolls of Ahriman?"

"Still missing. But they may have arrived in Firenze within the last day."

"Truly?"

"And they may eventually be presented to you." Elmasri sat staring at him like a wax effigy, offering no response. "After all," Dante went on, "you did work with Reverend Spencer not so long ago, and he was the one doing the translating until his—"

"Death. Would you rather the scrolls came to you?"

"No, not at—"

"I would. They are too controversial for my liking. They've taken on the aspect of a Russian circus. Or should I say a Russian Orthodox circus? For one thing, I avoid translating documents of faith whenever possible. For another, Dr. von Soden rejected them as forgeries in the fifties."

"Are you not Muslim?"

"Once. Long ago. Before I learned to invest my faith in reason."

"May we sit?" Dante asked, looking in vain for vacant chairs.

"Not if you insist on badgering me about changing my mind."

"We have no intention of badgering you. I will, however, appeal to the reason you rely upon." As he had done with the American detective and *il papa* himself, Dante explained his lengthy experience as a policeman and his disdain of the mystically religious. As he spoke, Simon understood at least partly why Elmasri was such a successful scholar; despite his unequivocal antipathy, the man focused full attention on Dante's words.

"As a son of Islam," Dante continued, "you are well aware that Moses stands among the holiest of prophets for Moslems, Jews, and Christians alike." He opened his briefcase and withdrew his Bible. The passage he sought was already marked.

" 'Moses wrote down all the words of the Lord. Early in the morning he built an altar at the foot of the mountain—' "

"And they sacrificed bulls, took the blood and threw it against the altar," Elmasri said. "I am fully conversant with the Book of Exodus."

Dante closed the Bible. "Obviously. But the words I wish to stress are those after Moses read from the Book of the Covenant. He takes the blood and flings it on his people, declaring it to be the blood of the covenant 'which the Lord has made with you on the terms of this book.' "

"And your point?"

The priest reached again into his briefcase. He extracted sharp photocopies of the pages of an early sixteenth-century Venetian book and of a much older Greek scroll. "These should be of interest to you. The Aldus edition we have spoken of by telephone. The scroll is roughly estimated as sixth century."

The professor read the pages slowly. Simon tried not to stare at Elmasri's face for hints of his thoughts. When only the last page remained in the man's hand, Dante said, "The point, Professor, is in the sentence I underlined in red. It refers to the dark angels. Those rebellious creatures put down by God before man walked the earth."

Elmasri sorted through the pages. " 'For their own sake, they cause these supermen to drink the blood of their own kind to survive.' "

"By supermen the scrolls mean vampires. They do walk the earth," Dante affirmed. "They drink blood as Satan's direct perversion of God's covenant with Moses."

Simon realized that Father Ferro's speech in the Baptistery was a rehearsal for this moment. He took a small step backward, giving the priest more physical prominence.

"The scrolls that your friend Reverend Spencer was translating were a gift from God, warning mankind of Satan's minions on earth. As a man of reason, your first reaction would naturally be to reject these words as mythology. But again, as a man of reason, the centuries-long evidence of the suppression of these scrolls and their translations must make you wonder at all the efforts against mere mythology. Five violent deaths in less than a month."

At last, Elmasri's studied mask of impassiveness cracked. His eyebrows rose; his eyes went wide; his lips parted. "And this line of argument is supposed to interest me in adding my name to the list?"

"If what I have stated is indeed true, isn't the service of any godly man, religious or not, to be expected?"

Elmasri sighed. "Is that all you offer?"

Dante turned and reached into his briefcase a third time. Simon noted that the priest did not seem at all surprised by what sounded like a blatant bid for a bribe. The priest took a large photograph out of the briefcase and slid it across the desk toward Elmasri.

"A time exposure of part of the scroll you expressed interest in.

Cardinal Chelli will, I think, look favorably on allowing the scroll's physical review—"

"If I cooperate, of course. *Via mundi et caeli,* eh, Father Ferro?" Elmasri tossed the photograph and all Dante's photocopies aside with theatrical carelessness, then refocused intently on the documents he had been studying when Ferro had entered the room.

"I tell you: if the intent of these scrolls is not made public within the next few weeks, a plague of vampires will be unleashed upon the earth," Dante said deliberately.

"If friendship counts for anything," Simon chimed in at last, "you should know that Willy Spencer wanted you involved in this. One of his last acts was mailing you a copy of all he had translated to the point where he discovered the vampire passages. I'm sure you'll find a package from him waiting for you when you return to Athens."

At last Elmasri moved, circling his cracked lips with his tongue. "You are most kind with your praise." He swept his hand in a large semicircle, taking in the piles of books and papers. "However, as you can see, I have weighty obligations here." His hand rotated palm up, gesturing at the priest. "I am also unnecessary, since you already have the assistance of Father Ferro. He is an authority on Akkadian . . . in fact, the Roman Catholic Church's authority."

"But I am not—"

Elmasri's hand now thrust upward, silencing the priest's protest. "He has published two competent articles on Akkadian texts, in respected journals."

"Nevertheless—"

"Let me end your petitioning, gentlemen. Much of your arguments were presented to me not one hour ago, by a woman whose beauty is far more persuasive than any of your words."

Dante and Simon looked at each other.

'You must know her," Elmasri continued. "Frederika Vanderveen?" He laughed, rolling his eyes upward. "An intelligent, devious, and single-minded woman. We had breakfast together at my apartment . . . unfortunately nothing more. She left me an E-mail message in Athens yesterday, dropping the name of a mutual friend . . . another beautiful young woman, who attended the American School with her and who did extremely well in one of my classes at the University of Athens. I mistakenly thought I was being sought out for my body, not my mind." He shrugged and made a wistful face. "As I say, she was most persistent that I go to the United States and trans—"

"The United States," Simon echoed, dumbfounded.

"Yes. Where the scrolls are. I told her I was much too busy, but I gave her the names of Khalil Al-Hamash at the Jami'at Baghdad, Yuri Vira at Samarkandskij Gosudarstvennyj Universitet, and Osman Baran at Columbia University. If you wish to find her, I expect she will soon be in Baghdad, Uzbekskaya, or New York City."

"It's not about how busy you are . . . refiling papers and chasing women," Dante said coldly, as he collected the documents Elmasri had tossed aside. "You are frightened. Miss Vanderveen also must have made the mistake of telling you how many people have died because Evil cannot allow these scrolls to be translated."

Elmasri pushed himself aggressively up from his chair. "Even if the scrolls are genuine, their very mention of vampires has already turned this affair into a media disaster. If I attached my name to this translating, my hard-earned position as the most respected Akkadian scholar would disappear forever. Use some other scholar to stop your plague. Good day, gentlemen."

Simon came past Dante for the first time and leaned offensively across the desk. "Father Ferro can do the job. Watch the news, buddy. He's about to eclipse you. You'll be lucky to end up a footnote in history."

"Enough, Simon," Dante said, coaxing him backward with a firm grasp.

Simon turned so quickly that one of the precariously balanced paper piles toppled over onto the floor. He stopped, looked down, then stared over his shoulder at Elmasri. "I'd pick them up, except that I have something important to do. Come on, Father." He swept grandly through the door.

Dante took a step, then turned in the doorway. "As a representative of the Roman Catholic Church, I do not appreciate being toyed with, Signor. And I have published three articles," he corrected Elmasri. "They are all more than competent."

"Where's a bar?" Simon asked Father Ferro, stepping from the archive library into the daylight. "I need a drink."

"And I need a telephone." Dante nodded straight across the Piazza della Signoria. "Revoire. On the other side of the fountain."

They found the bar crowded, with acquaintances meeting for a holiday drink and shoppers ducking in from the cold for alcoholic fortitude.

"They make a delicious hot chocolate in the winter," the priest suggested, nodding at a vacant table and rubbing his hands together.

"I need something stronger than chocolate," Simon said, shouldering his way through the tightly packed throng. "I knew Frederika would get to the man, but her efficiency astounds even me."

"Let us speak of her later," Dante said, setting his briefcase on the table and shrugging out of his overcoat. "Order me the hot chocolate, please." He tossed his coat over a chair and strode toward the back of the bar.

Simon hailed a passing waiter and managed to make his order understood. He pulled a pen from his coat and began doodling on a clean napkin that had been left by the previous customers. He sketched a baseball scoreboard, labeling the top team DD for the mysterious doctor and for Devil Demons and GG for Good Guys. The first inning, he decided, had happened before he entered the game. DeVilbiss's act of having the magic powder analyzed and reproduced gave the bad guys a grand-slam home run. He figured he first came to bat on December 21, when he tried to warn DeVilbiss away from Frederika. But the vampire had not been fazed. Then, on December 23, DeVilbiss had killed Willy Spencer. That and the murders of several others in Princeton had to constitute another run for the DD side. On December 24 and 25, the third inning, Simon had killed DeVilbiss, rescued Frederika, sent a demon screaming back to hell, and moved the scrolls. One four-bagger for the GG team. In Switzerland, just staying alive, getting the diaries, and killing the vampiress had to account for one more run for their side in inning four. Simon grimaced and laid down his pen. Obviously, the stress was getting to him. This wasn't a game. Even the metaphor didn't hold up; for one thing, he couldn't see the whole ball field. Who knew how many runs were being scored by the other team at the same time? Even if the contest had a score, he knew their side of it was nothing to be comforted by.

Dante was taking a lot longer than Simon expected. After the drinks arrived, Simon left the table and walked as far into the bar as was necessary to spot the priest, whose back was turned to Simon and whose free hand flew around the telephone mouthpiece as he spoke. Simon returned to the table, knocked back half his whiskey before lowering the glass, then dug into his coat for the diary and decoding wheel. He had another four lines translated into legible English before Dante returned. The man's posture looked like an apostrophe, his expression grim and downtrodden.

"My contacts learned twenty minutes ago where Elmasri is staying," Dante said, sitting heavily. "I wish to scream. Also, they told me about the gun fired last night near the border. A Swiss ski patrolman was killed."

"Do they know who shot him?" Simon asked.

Dante shook his head. "It was *his* gun you heard. He was killed by the hands of someone immensely strong. His two police dogs were destroyed as well . . . by one person."

"A vampire?"

Dante considered sipping his chocolate but pushed it away. "A vampire on skis. Who else could kill a police dog by ripping out its heart? The patrolman was following your trail."

"Then so was the vampire. How could that be?"

"I suspect the cane Wagner gave you. It must have a device like the one inside the bullet."

Simon shook his head. "I gave it everything but a CAT scan right after I crossed the border. You're welcome to check it yourself. But I wasn't the only one who took something from Wagner. What about the statue of St. Cecilia?"

"No. That too is solid."

As he searched for a solution, Simon stared at the sunlight filtering through the bar's windows, tracing interesting patterns across patrons' faces. His face suddenly brightened. "There's a big difference between the cane and the statue. The statue is a human form. So was the Pierrot doll DeVilbiss always kept with him. So was the statue that first spoke to him. A St. Joseph, if I'm not mistaken. Were you sure I planned to walk cross-country before I actually started?"

"Yes. We watched you shopping from a distance."

"Did you speak of it in front of the statue?"

"Yes."

Simon shoved the diary across the table. "Look here. I just translated this. 'Pierrot heard S.P. listening to answering machine.' S.P. is me, Simon Penn. Even if there were enough undead servants of hell to do the kind of triangulating you did, how could they have known to bring skis? They didn't watch me shopping. Amber eyes hate the sunlight, remember? I, on the other hand, had no one to talk with all day . . . except you on the telephone. And I let you believe I was meeting you for dinner." Simon laughed ruefully. "Such diabolical irony. Hell hides inside a saintly statue. The bugger bugged . . . or should I say buggered?"

"Then they know about us following Miss Vanderveen," Dante said.

"And they know that all of us are in Florence." Simon tapped his pen rapidly against the edge of the table. "What they don't know is that we're on to them. A little while ago you asked what we could do to prove to the world that this coming plague won't be manmade."

Dante's back straightened slightly; his eyes took on a glimmer of positive expectation. "Yes. Continue."

"What about capturing a live vampire . . . maybe even his pot of golden powder?"

"Excellent!" Dante pulled the hot chocolate again toward him and lifted the cup. "Tell me your plan."

"The statue's in the car, right?"

"Yes. Safe inside the trunk."

"Great. We put it back on the dashboard." Simon slipped two sheets of blank paper from the back of the diary. "Let's write us a script."

The Vampire was mad as a rabid dog and prepared to savage anything in his path. The drive from Switzerland down to Florence had been a pain in the ass. Not having traveled through northern Italy for nearly thirty years, he was unfamiliar with the highways and had twice gotten himself lost. Even so, he had pulled into Florence before the sun broke the horizon. The problem was that no hotels had empty rooms. Conferences, conventions, holiday weddings, end-of-year-parties, and high tourist season all conspired against him. Several clerks declared that they would have rooms available after noon, but he was damned if he'd endure five hours of daylight, even behind suntan lotion, sunglasses, and tinted glass. He had gotten a good look at his face in the rearview mirror during the night and saw with true alarm that he had never looked so old. He could easily pass for twenty-five. The unavoidable sunlit hours of this interminable chase were killing him, and he was sure that Satan himself had no idea how much longer it would last. The instant he was rebuffed in the fourth hotel, he made up his mind how to survive until check-in time. He took an elevator down one level and began nosing from one shop door to the next.

The lock of the hotel's beauty salon was new but easy to pick. Even better, the door had a note on it, explaining that the business would be closed for vacation from December 25 until January 2. Within two minutes, the Vampire had the door opened. He slipped through, relocked it, and hurried past the booths into a large room at the back which held shelves crammed with wigs and dying supplies, various surplus equipment, a refrigerator, and a desk piled with all sorts and sizes of paper. In the center of the room was a long table surrounded by plastic chairs, evidently the employees' gathering place for breaks and lunch. The Vampire closed the door. A thin shaft of light seeped in under it, more than enough illumination for his amber eyes. He set down the carpetbag that could not be left behind, snatched several cloth bibs from one of the shelves, balled them into a makeshift pillow, and climbed onto the table.

The Vampire was asleep within five minutes. Three hours later, with his brain deep into REM activity, he was awakened by the sound of the front door opening and, a moment later, the outer shop's brilliant lighting flickering on. The cobwebs had gathered thickly in his brain. By the time he had oriented himself and climbed off the table, the inner door opened. Light poured into the room around the figure of a woman, making the Vampire wince.

Without uttering a word, the woman spun halfway around, grabbed an aerosol can from off one of the shelves and rushed at the Vampire. She pointed the can at his face, thumb squeezing downward. A stream of hair spray hit him in the eyes, creating instant pain. No sooner was he warding off the spray with one hand and swiping at his eyes with the other than he suffered an even greater pain, from a kick to his kneecap. He buckled in agony, throwing his hands out for balance as he fell. The spray can came down hard against the back of his skull. He collapsed flat on the floor and lay still.

"And stay down, you ugly little bastard," the woman said, flinging the dented can down at his profile, gouging a deep cut over his eyebrow. "You're the same one who broke in here three months ago and stole all the wigs, aren't you?" She strode to the desk, grabbed the telephone and made use of its long cord to stride back to the doorway light. "The insurance company still hasn't reimbursed me . . . and you also owe me for the self-defense lessons I took. Paid off though, didn't they? This time, I was ready for you, you hideous dwarf." The motionless body on the floor made no reply. The woman, a hard-looking, well-proportioned, taller than average northern Italian of about thirty-five years, dialed the operator and lifted the handset to her multibaubled ear. "Where the hell are you?" she complained into the receiver. "Hello? Get me the police!" She glanced down at the man lying on the floor. He still hadn't moved. In fact, his chest wasn't rising and falling, as it should. The wound she had opened on his forehead, which bled so profusely ten seconds before, had stopped flowing.

248

"Oh, *Gesù e Maria!*" the woman cried out. "Don't tell me I killed you." She squatted, set the telephone down, and took the Vampire's wrist in her hand, feeling for a pulse.

The Vampire shoved with all his might. Even though he had virtually no leverage from his prone position, the woman went flying backward into the doorjamb, the back of her head cracking hard into the wood. The Vampire came up on his uninjured knee and reached for the woman's well-teased, platinum-blond hair. She reacted by clapping both hands simultaneously against his ears. His watering eyes rolled with the intense pain, but he refused to cry out. His left arm came up inside her right arm and slapped it away, but his right hand remained fastened to the woman's hair. He rolled onto his back and at the same time planted both feet into her midsection. Before she could counter his superquick move, she was flipping over his head, down the length of the table, and onto the floor.

The Vampire pulled the door shut and dragged the table against it. White plastic chairs tumbled and rolled against each other, creating an obstacle course. He stood and limped to the wall past the desk, where he had seen an electrical circuit box. He threw it open. Behind him, the woman was pulling the table toward her and stumbling over the chairs, heading toward the strong rectangle of light pouring under the door.

Spreading the fingers of both hands, the Vampire touched all the circuit breakers at once. He thrust his hands outward. The rectangle of light vanished from the floor, replaced by ghostly illumination cast from the hallway beyond the front windows. It was more than enough light for the Vampire, but the woman gasped in dismay. She lunged in the general direction of the closed door and immediately fell over one of the still-rolling chairs.

The Vampire yanked the phone cord out of the wall. He gathered in its length until the phone hung just above his shoe tops. Then he whisked the instrument up over his head and began to whirl it, bololike, in a circle.

The woman scuttled toward the door on her hands and knees. A deep sob escaped from her chest. She paused for an instant to try to make sense of the soft, whirring noise. Failing, she crawled on. She reached the door, grabbed the knob and stood.

The phone sailed across the room in a long arc, which tightened abruptly as its cord met the woman's neck. It described one full circuit before the phone casing, detached from the handset, smacked into her temple. She dropped as if she had been shot.

The Vampire let go of the end of the phone cord and walked casually to the door. His knee had almost stopped throbbing. He shoved the table back against the far wall, bent for the woman, and tossed her onto the table. He looked down on her. Unconscious, she had lost much of her hard-bitten look. He did not like the multiple earrings hanging from each ear. He ripped them all out, tearing through the flesh of her lobes, and dropped the jewelry onto the floor. He also did not like her glossy lipstick. He tugged her skirt down her legs and used it to wipe the lipstick away. On the desk he found a roll of duct tape. He tore off a three-meter length, worried it into a rope, tied her left wrist, ran the tape around the far table legs, and secured her right wrist, so that her arms were drawn back and above her head. She began to moan, so he hurried to one of the shelves for a hand towel. He approached the woman's face. Her eyes popped open wide, straining to pierce the darkness.

"I hope you don't have a head cold," the Vampire told her, as he pinched her nose and methodically stuffed the hand towel through her clenched teeth until she began choking. He secured the towel by running several strips of duct tape across her face.

"So, I'm a hideous dwarf, am I?" the Vampire said. "An ugly little bastard, eh? May I tell you that you are the first woman to speak so honestly to me in centuries? For that you deserve a reward." He put his hand on her knee and slowly ran it up over the top of her stocking to her silk-covered pubic mound, letting her twist and flail as she liked. He began massaging her with sexual pressure, humming an old Italian Christmas melody as he did. He kept at it until she realized the futility of her struggles and let her legs down against the table, squeezing them together as tightly as she could. In answer, the Vampire ripped her panties off.

"The temperature isn't too low in here, is it?" he asked, in a solicitous tone of voice. "I mean, you won't catch that cold if you have a bit less on?" When he got no answer, he violently tore the rest of her clothing away, until she lay naked except for stockings and shoes. He explored her for several minutes, one hand clamped around her throat, threatening to cut off her air if she resisted, the other roaming up and down, pinching, twisting, violating.

"And now for your reward," he said, undoing his belt buckle and unzipping his fly, dropping his trousers, stepping out of them, and pulling her down to the limit of the twisted duct tape, so that her legs hung over the end of the table. The woman began to weep as he spread her legs and pushed between them. "What?" he reacted. "Why do you cry? This is what you tough bitches really want, isn't it?" He shoved himself brutally inside her, thrusting quickly from the first moment, so that he exploded in less than a minute.

"Did I feel like a hideous dwarf . . . or was I a huge Adonis?" the Vampire gasped, as he caught his breath and pulled up his trousers. "You're shaking all over. You must have loved it, even though you'd never admit it. Well, that was your reward. And now for your punishment." The woman tried to scream but only caused herself to gag and cough.

The Vampire ripped the cord out of the telephone. He tied one of the woman's ankles securely with it, jumped up on the table and tossed the cord over an exposed pipe that ran the width of the ceiling. Climbing down, he tugged on the cord until the woman's leg went up, then tied the woman's other ankle high. He grabbed the two far table legs and yanked with all his might. The wooden legs came away with snapping sounds; the tabletop collapsed to the floor. The Vampire dropped the splintered wood and kicked the tabletop away. The woman swung upside down, bringing her weight onto the two ends of the cord. Her curly hair brushed back and forth across the tile floor. The Vampire grabbed the twisted duct tape and tied it to the longer dangling end of the phone cord, so that the woman's hands were up behind her back.

"Now that there is relative silence, open your bag," the voice of hell commanded into the dark room.

251

The Vampire tugged the carpetbag out from under one of the plastic chairs and set it on the desk. He unzipped it and took out the stone hand.

"Better," the voice said, switching to Romanian. "What a wonderful sight. Do you still have the energy for such sport after all this running?"

"I have no lack of energy, but a great lack of patience," the Vampire answered, watching the woman's shocked face turning ever darker from gravity's pull on her vital fluids. "I am glad that you visit me, because I have been giving a great deal of thought to your promise. I may soon, as your Infernal Lordship has promised, experience an apotheosis, but I am not unaware of the irony attached to such an elevation. The evil I have done already to earn demigodhood has taken its toll on mankind."

"It is true. Your contribution to the moral, intellectual, and spiritual decline of your former species has not been inconsequential."

"Which has helped to make me king of the dunghill. A king who, after all these centuries, is still doing all of his own dirty work. Furthermore, if my latest efforts succeed, it will only create a legion of vampires, which will begin a worldwide riot of stake-sharpening beyond anything I knew in the Middle Ages. I could easily be slaughtered along with all the novices."

"Not you. You are too clever."

"I have decided that I do not wish to be free of the need for blood. I like its taste; I would miss pursuing it. What I want instead is to be able to move again in sunlight without—"

"Never!" the voice howled. "If we cannot survive the sun, neither can you. Do not ask this again!"

A shiver ran through the Vampire. Behind him, the woman whimpered. "Shut up, or I'll slit your throat!" he shouted, transferring his fear into anger.

"We are not here to be bargained with. We have at last learned the general location of the scrolls. They are still in the United States."

The Vampire shoved the upended woman, making her spin in a wild circle. "What then do you need of me? I was passed over for this task once already because my English is poor. The little time I spent with Penn and his priest friend hardly improved it. I've paid my dues concerning the scrolls. I'm filthy; I'm tired; my skin is half burned; I look almost my true age. I need my soil and the peace of the crypt. Bedevil another of your servants." The Vampire picked up the hand and went to deposit it in the carpetbag.

"Your English will have to do," the voice said. "There is none other of your kind who speaks it . . . even poorly."

The Vampire paused in amazement.

"We offer you another look into our world," the voice confirmed, "as one of the rewards for your creative, unquestioning service."

"Tell me about the others of my kind."

"In the first centuries of their invention, we created, as you say, a legion. But that proved counterproductive. You understand the reasons. About the time you came to us, we were winnowing down the number. By the year of the Unspeakable One's birth, there were only eighteen. There have never been more than eighteen since. When one is occasionally lost, as you know happens, little time is required to recruit another. Not in this world where throats are slit over harsh words."

"But, in more than twenty-five hundred years, except for those you have made me hunt and kill, I have never stumbled upon another. Even with only eighteen—"

"Your kind are carefully dispersed throughout the earth . . . picked from different backgrounds, different nations, different tongues, so that we may work through you among every people. Six are of the Caucasian race; six of the Mongoloid race; six of the Negroid race."

The Vampire's eyes went wide. " 'Let him who has understanding reckon the number of the beast, for it is a human number. Its number is six-six-six.' "

"We dislike being called 'beast,' even in quotation," the voice said. "Since the two copies of the Scrolls of Ahriman were destroyed and lost, our All-High Adversary saw fit to issue a new, updated warning, albeit through the ears of the madman John. Be grateful the report of your kind was lost in his insane imagery."

"Where in the United States are the scrolls?"

"In the same library where they rested a week ago."

The Vampire grinned. "Yes. That would be the mind of Penn the librarian. I will go for you," he acceded. "Must I travel with haste, or may I at least await the setting of the sun?"

"Wait only that long. The woman librarian has secured the help of Elmasri, the Akkadian scholar. She waits in Florence until he is prepared to leave. The male librarian and the priest fly westward tonight, to reclaim the scrolls. They will be dead the minute after night envelops them. We fear only the possibility of their warning others near the scrolls. But that seems unlikely. And, if they do, you will simply kill those who newly possess them." The voice gave the Vampire instructions on how to dispose of the scrolls, once their exact location had been learned.

"It shall be done," the Vampire promised.

"And when it is, Radu Negru, unending night will have fallen."

The Vampire knew that such poetic pronouncements invariably signaled the disappearance of the voice. He carefully tucked the stone hand back among the soft clothing inside his carpetbag, then turned to face the inverted, still-swinging woman.

"And now to complete my promised punishment. What befits a woman who tortures other women for a living?" he asked his semi-conscious victim. "We could simply leave you there until your brain exploded from the pressure of your juices. No, not good enough." His gaze swept around the room. "Ah, just the thing!" He plucked a professional curling iron off one of the shelves, fitted it to an extension cord, turned the iron to the highest setting, and plugged the cord into the wall outlet. He went to the electrical box and snapped on all of the circuits except the one that fed the outer room's overhead lights. He sat atop the desk for a minute, humming again the old Italian Christmas melody.

The Vampire spat on the iron's tip. "Oh, *Gesù e Maria,*" he echoed mockingly. "I could start a fire if I laid this thing down carelessly. Where can I place it, so that such a disaster is prevented?" He approached the woman.

The Vampire stepped back and admired his handiwork. "I have the feeling not even a superman pleased you. Perhaps this will make you hot." He gave the woman one last spin, snatched up his bag, exited the salon, and locked the door behind him.

"We cannot wait much longer," Dante reminded Simon. "It is already four o'clock."

Simon looked out the glass wall of the room the Florence Airport had appointed as a VIP lounge. The day was indeed slipping away, and every minute of its afternoon had been filled with preparations to transport him back to the United States. Dante, changed into civilian clothes, resumed his pacing across the length of the window.

"One last try," Simon replied, dialing the long telephone number. "Finally!" he exclaimed, when he heard it ring. He had made similar attempts several times in the past two hours, always getting a busy signal. A woman's voice answered.

"Hello," Simon said, simultaneously shooting Dante a thumbs-up sign. "May I please speak with Ray Pental?"

"He's sleeping. He got off work at five this morning."

"I'm sorry, but this has to do with his work," Simon persisted. He thought he heard the woman growl.

"It always has to do with work. I knew I made a mistake putting the phone back on the hook."

"Mrs. Pental, it's Simon Penn, calling from Italy."

Simon listened to a brief silence. "Please hold," Karen Pental told him. He waited for almost a minute, expecting a husky, sleep-filled voice. Instead, Ray sounded very much awake.

"It's good to hear your voice," Ray said, after the initial hellos.

"Thanks. Can you tell me if my message to Rich Chen got through to the police yesterday?"

"Loud and clear. Brother, are you a lucky man. Not only did we find the body in the storm sewer, but they also found that woman out in Seattle. The building was scheduled for dynamiting on January third! They found latent prints on her and sent them to us, since we had originals taken off DeVilbiss's fingers at the medical center.

Perfect match. You still have his diary, I hope."

"Yes, indeed," Simon answered.

"Good. We can corroborate his handwriting. Whoever cleaned up the place he rented did a thorough job, but they missed a piece of mail that had fallen behind his bedroom dresser. He had filled out a warranty card for some soft luggage he had gotten through the L.L. Bean catalogue. It was one of those lifetime guarantees. Could have cost the luggage company a fortune if you hadn't killed him." When Simon failed to laugh, Ray said, "Sorry. All the pressure's bringing out my black humor. Are you calling from a pay phone?"

"Don't worry," Simon said, after switching the handset to his other ear. "This call's on the Vatican's dime. Our mutual friend, Father Ferro, is standing ten feet from me."

"Ah, yes. The cop disguised as a priest. I'm glad you two linked up. Listen, Simon, we've got real trouble on this end. The formula for vampire powder is loose."

Simon knew his distress had registered on his face when Ferro shot him a questioning look. "Yeah, we were afraid of that. Through a doctor with the initials D.D., right?"

"Dorena Durazo. How'd you know?"

"The diary. You're right about real trouble, but there are things we can do to respond. That's the main reason I'm calling. Is the tap still on Rich Chen's line?"

"As far as I know."

"Good. Because two hours ago I left a message on it. I said that he should tell your boss that one or more confederates of Vincent DeVilbiss learned the scrolls were hidden in the library ductwork and don't know the real truth. They're gonna hear specifically about Room B9F within the hour. Anytime after that you can expect they'll arrive to finish the job DeVilbiss botched. I know nobody's buying my supernatural story, so—"

"I am."

"Okay, that's one. What about your boss?"

"Not really."

"I can't blame him. Anyway, for his benefit I said nothing about

256

these confederates having any special powers. But they will. Believe me. I want you to use all your influence to have as many officers in the library as possible. And be sure to put several sets of handcuffs on any creature you catch; they've got the strength of three or four humans. Between the diary, the scrolls, and living proof, I think we can scare the world away from this powder."

"I wish I'd never met you, Simon Penn," Ray replied. "Are you coming home soon?"

"Start counting. In the meantime, be careful, pal."

"Bet on it."

Simon hung up the phone. Father Ferro impatiently held the lounge's outside door open. As Simon grabbed his rucksack and jogged across the room, Ferro let go of the door and started across the tarmac. Simon followed through the chill air at a near run. Ferro's destination soon became evident.

"We're crossing the Atlantic Ocean in that?" Simon doubted, as he caught up with the priest. The airplane in front of them was a white Jet Stream 4100 with no commercial markings. It was a large plane for private business but one of the smallest used by airlines.

"I am as uncomfortable about it as you are," Dante said, "but we cannot wait until your arrest warrant is dropped. Which means that you cannot travel by commercial carrier. We also need privacy in order to complete our little drama. The statue of St. Cecilia is already on board."

Simon took in the panorama of the small Firenze airport. The relatively cloudless bowl of the sky was shifting rapidly toward purple as night rolled in from the east.

"I hate like hell leaving Frederika behind, but I'm at least glad she's not taking this ride."

"Yes. She will be found soon enough," Dante said with confidence. "We are arranging to have all three Akkadian scholars mentioned by Elmasri—and Elmasri as well—closely watched."

"She's fought such a good fight all by herself," Simon said. "I wish I could tell her what I think of her."

"Her fight has not ended; she must stay alive to reveal the scrolls' location," Dante responded, reaching the stairs to the plane. He paused. "You serve her by occupying the attention of the forces of hell. By providence or luck, we have said very little about your beautiful friend in front of the statue. Let us keep her a mystery, eh?"

Simon nodded, already practicing his silence.

"*Ciao,* Giulio." Dante greeted a good-looking young man in a smart navy-blue suit, who had emerged from the plane. Then, to Simon, he said, "Giulio speaks little English, but he is our attendant. If you need anything from him, I will translate."

"Whose plane is this?" Simon asked.

"It belongs to an international construction company with headquarters in Firenze. The owner is a very religious man. He has helped the Church on many occasions."

"That's all well and good, but has this plane ever crossed the Atlantic?"

Dante translated the question for the attendant, who shook his head and delivered a lengthy reply. Dante faced Simon.

"This aircraft has only a fifteen-hundred-mile range. We will need to stop in Shannon and Newfoundland. Its top speed is two hundred ninety miles per hour. As we speak, employees of the Church are seeking a bigger aircraft in Ireland. Otherwise, we shall be in this one for fifteen hours. At least we shall be able to stretch our legs twice," Dante offered, gesturing for Simon to climb the steps. "I think its luxury may compensate."

The inside of the craft was indeed luxuriously appointed. Holding only eight seats, which were dispersed strategically for weight distribution, the narrow cabin did not seem cramped. Thick, dark green carpeting, wide, chianti-colored cloth seats, and stark white Formica tables mimicked the colors of the Italian flag. A dry bar was located toward its nose, with a telephone secured on the counter. Just aft, a fold-down bed was stowed inside a customized closet. The tail had been outfitted with a larger-than-commercial bathroom and a galley. The one limitation that could not be overcome was the cabin's lack of height. Only by walking up the center line could Simon progress without ducking his head, and, at that, he had but an inch to spare.

258

Dante had entered the plane last. He ducked his head into the nose cabin and greeted the pilot and navigator, hung up his overcoat, then took his place in one of the seats nearest the door. From his vantage, he could watch the rest of the plane.

As the engines increased their whine and the wheels began to roll, Dante glanced nervously out one of the portholes. The airport buildings were stained red by the setting sun. He glanced at the golden St. Cecilia, which had been secured in a drink holder on a Formica table between himself and the American. As he had dictated, a gym bag sat on the carpet beside his seat. He made sure it was unzipped. To his right, a magazine rack was secured to the bulkhead. He selected the first journal that came into his fingers, knowing he would only be pretending to read it.

Taking Dante's cue, Simon opened his rucksack and took out DeVilbiss's diary and the decoding wheel. They maintained tandem silence for a quarter hour, as the airplane left land behind and soared over the Gulf of Genoa. The priest watched the daylight slipping away as the sun outraced the jet. Slowly, darkness enveloped the cabin. Overhead lighting winked on. Five minutes later, inky blackness pressed against the portholes.

Dante coughed several times, until Simon's eyes rotated up from the diary. Dante tilted his head slightly at the golden statue.

"The time has come, Mr. Penn," Dante said, no word overloud but each distinctly spoken. "You promised that as soon as I had gotten you out of Italy you would reveal the exact location of the Scrolls of Ahriman."

"When we land," Simon answered, just as they had rehearsed.

"No, now. Otherwise, I will have this airplane turned around."

"Very well. They're hidden inside the library's ductwork, behind a large grill in Room B9F. They're in a pair of airtight containers."

Dante let his arm dangle down, so that it touched the top of the gym bag. "Very well. I shall have the pilot radio the information." Despite his words, he did not move. Simon gave him a quizzical look. "What does B9F mean?"

"B is second level down. The other letter and the number are

259

part of a rank and file grid system," Simon said, squinching up his brows at the priest, who was going off their script for seemingly unnecessary embellishment.

"B9F. That should be simple enough to find. Let us think about the time," Dante said, without consulting his watch. "In Princeton, it is now midnight. We should be at the library—"

The statue erupted in smoke, noise, cold flames, and a thick spray of gold dust. An instant after the initial explosion, a hellish red light shot up from what remained of the statue's base. Dante staggered from his seat, lifting the gym bag as well.

"Ascende, ascende!" he yelled at the cockpit door.

Expanding like a djin out of a lamp, wrapped in a rutilant, translucent bubble, emerged the universal image of evil incarnate. Its legs were spindly, backward-kneed and ending in cloven feet. The upper appendages were thin and tipped with curving claws. Behind the wedge-shaped torso rose what looked to be leathery wings, and below it hung a lancet-tipped tail, which beat against the curve of the scarlet-hued bubble as if it were a solid form. The head was supported by a long, thickly corded neck. Its face thrust forward into a snout, nostrils little more than gaping black holes, teeth triangular and three rows deep. All eight of its eyes shone like backlit rubies. In its left hand it held a pitchforklike instrument. It thrust the pitchfork upward. The cabin lighting died, and the whine of the engines began to falter.

Father Ferro made a swift sign of the cross and flung the gym bag in the direction of the bubble. It vanished in a ball of flame. Remaining in Ferro's hand was a large halogen spotlight with a parabolic reflector and Fresnel lens. He pointed it directly at the demon and thumbed it on.

A burst of light filled the cabin, so intense it seemed to have weight. The beast shrieked, sounding in the small enclosure like the wail of a hundred electric guitars. It pivoted away from the fusillade of photons, shielding itself with its wings. The cabin lighting blinked back on, hardly noticeable in the harsh illumination. Outside, the engines regained their vigor. The plane tilted suddenly upward.

Giulio appeared from the galley, holding an identical spotlight. Before he could flick it on, the demon had raised its pitchfork.

"Hey!" Simon shouted from the floor, simultaneously swinging his rucksack at the bubble. Just as the gym bag had vanished, the bottom half of the rucksack evaporated in flame as it struck the force field. The attack, however, had an effect on the demon inside. The pitchfork's tines wobbled crazily as bolts of lightning shot from their points. The galley wall exploded in a rain of wood paneling. Giulio fell backward, the spotlight popping from his grip.

The engines screamed at full throttle, and the ascent became even steeper. Everything not bolted down rolled, slid, or flew aftward. The creature also reacted, stepping backward on its spindly legs, dragging the bubble with it. Once it had regained a sense of balance it looked down, intent on finding Simon.

The Jet Stream broke through a thick bank of clouds, into the unimpeded light of the swollen red sun. Beams of natural light knifed across the cabin from every starboard window. The demon shrieked again, this time a sound of terror rather than rage. Its wings folded around its snout and eyes. The red bubble rushed inward with a great hissing noise, and the creature vanished.

Dante grabbed the statue, set the still-lit spotlight on the carpeting, and crawled through choking smoke toward the cabin hatch. The plane had begun to level off.

"Help me, Simon!" Dante cried out. "Buckle into the seat behind me, then take my hand!"

Simon made no hesitation in obeying. Dante set the statue down against the hatch, grabbed Simon's hand and gave the door latch a twist.

Much of the light debris that had drifted aft now reversed itself, tumbling or flying toward the partially opened hatch as the falling cabin pressure blew it out. Dante's torso spun around, his legs swinging beyond the doorway. Suspended between the latch handle and Simon's resolute grip, the priest went no farther. A magazine struck the statue, and both went sailing into the icy stratosphere.

"*Giù, giù!*" Dante shouted at the cockpit, his voice trembling from the buffeting of the open hatch.

The plane went into a dive. The outward rush of air lessened. Simon got both hands around the priest's wrist and tugged. Ferro's feet found the carpeting. With a violent heave, Dante slammed the hatch shut. He dropped to his knees and gasped for breath.

Simon unbuckled and rushed forward, to help Dante to his feet. Giulio was using a fire extinguisher to put out the part of the galley wall that still smoldered.

"Christ Almighty, did you know that would happen?" Simon asked.

"When I remembered about the demon who came into the basement after you destroyed the Pierrot doll, I had a great fear of it," Dante admitted. "Fortunately, you also told me of the spotlight you had used against DeVilbiss."

Simon took the handkerchief from his pocket and clapped it over his nose and mouth. "But they aren't invulnerable on earth. And they knew I had already proved it. Why would it risk itself like that? Why not be patient and let their vampires go after us?"

Dante picked up the spotlight and switched it off. "The pride of these creatures got them banished from heaven at the beginning of time. They have not changed. Or possibly they do not have as many vampire minions as we might fear. Whatever the reason, be happy it failed again." He reached up for one of the breathing masks suspended from the ceiling and pulled it to his face.

The navigator emerged from the cockpit, his eyes huge as tea saucers, surveying the damage. Between bouts of coughing, he and Giulio went into a spirited rehashing of the previous minutes.

Simon imitated Dante's action, relieving his lungs with several deep breaths from a dangling oxygen mask. "This was different from my encounter in DeVilbiss's basement," he told Dante. "That time, the demon just beat its wings down and vanished. This time it seemed to evaporate in the sunlight. And the look on what passed for its face seemed panicked to me. Do you think we actually killed it, or am I just wishful thinking?"

"Let us hope the sunlight destroyed it," Dante said, through the mask. "Otherwise, no vampire will come to the library. I only hope it had time to pass along the information we gave. Time is perhaps not the same to them as to us."

"Are you all right, Father?" Simon asked, watching with concern the involuntary twitching of the muscles around the older man's eyes.

"I shall be . . . as soon as I finish my prayers. If film could record true things only, I would have had a camera mounted above that bar. Every church, mosque, temple, and synagogue in the world would have been filled tomorrow. Sancta Maria!"

The navigator approached Dante and exchanged words. Dante turned to Simon. "The pilot says all the instruments are green. The damage appears to be cosmetic. We can reach Shannon Airport in two and a half hours. I think we should go forward rather than back."

Simon snatched DeVilbiss's diary off the carpet and collapsed into one of the seats. " 'Onward, Christian soldiers,' " he said, but with none of the strength he used when he sang it.

CHAPTER EIGHT

December 31

❦

So long as The Blood endures,

I shall know that your good is mine:

ye shall feel that my strength is yours:

In the day of Armageddon, at the last

great fight of all,

That Our House stand together and

the pillars do not fall.

—Rudyard Kipling, *England's Answer*

c✍ɔ

Terry McMullen exited Firestone Library holding the original and two photocopies of his history term paper. Better late than never. Even if he got marked down half a grade for tardiness, he still expected an A. He had really gotten into the subject of the U.S. Cavalry's Buffalo Soldiers and had exhausted every source in the vast library. Thoroughness would be his excuse.

As he came around the reference room's outside wall, Terry saw what he assumed to be another Princeton undergrad, struggling with a cardboard carton. The guy's right arm was in a fresh cast, inside a sling. Bad break during the holiday season, Terry thought. Realizing the unintentional pun, he grinned, then suppressed it for the unfortunate guy's sake.

"Skiing accident, man?" Terry asked, veering toward the hapless fellow.

"No. I haf fall on de walk yesterday," the young man replied.

"Tough luck. Can I help you?" Terry offered.

"Very nice. T'ank you much." With difficulty, the man handed over the box, which was nearly filled with books.

"Whoa, this is heavy. How far you going?"

"To my car. Is in de parking place behind such building." The student nodded.

"We can get you that far for sure." Terry set the box down,

shoved his papers inside it and redistributed the books. He came back up with it on one shoulder and began walking. "I haven't seen you on campus before."

"I am a graduate student," the man replied. "Von East Germany."

"No kidding. I bet you did a dance the day the Berlin Wall came down." The dialogue, stilted as it was on one side, continued to the parking lot and the rented car, which was parked as far from the library as it could be, wedged between the far end of a Dumpster and a row of evergreen hedges.

"In de back seat is goot," the man directed.

"Sure thing." Terry grunted as the full weight of the box came onto his outstretched hands. He grunted again, as the weight of the plaster cast came down with superhuman force on the back of his neck.

The Vampire shoved his victim into the back of the car, grabbed a blanket from the front seat, and threw it over the body. He shrugged out of the sling, smashed his arm against the Dumpster until the cast cracked, peeled off the pieces and threw them into the trash bin.

Climbing into the front seat and starting the car, the Vampire wondered idly if the blow had killed the student. His victim was a considerate fellow, undeserving of such treatment, picked only because he looked about twenty-one, was short and black. In brief, because he looked somewhat like the Vampire. Except, of course, he was not nearly so ugly. In the Vampire's opinion, a wide nasal index and thick lips bestowed nobility to most people of the Negroid race. He believed it was because these were complementary elements to dark skin tone and strong bone structure. This student he had considered average-looking. It would be a risk using his library pass, even duplicating his hair with a curly black wig and his skin shade with the theatrical cosmetic base called "Texas dirt." Undeserving or not, this good Samaritan's life was effectively over. Once they were safe, victims always talked. Much surer to kill them.

The Vampire steered the car into a dead-end lane and drove

down to the end, where the wooded lots had yet to be sold. He parked but left the engine and the heater running. While he waited in the shadows of the university chapel portico, across from the library entrance, he had become chilled to the point of shivering. In view of the facts that this was New Year's Eve and that the university had relatively few black students, he was lucky to have found anyone remotely his size leaving the place. Although the gusting wind had nearly frozen him during his three-hour vigil, the winter sun had breached the barricade of the scentless lotion on his cheeks and forehead, torturing his already supersensitive skin with a sensation of fire. He longed for the blackness and the moderate cold of the crypt.

The clock in the car indicated that the library would close in four hours. Then it would not open again for more than a day. When he had learned of the scrolls' exact location from the voice, he hoped that he had not gravely miscalculated by waiting to take the evening flight out of Florence's airport to Milan and thence a nonstop, red-eye connection to New York. He might have been at the library nonetheless when it first opened had he not instinctively felt the need for extreme guile. If ever a convincing disguise were required, this was the occasion. He could remember no infernal task so taxing as this one. Perhaps, he thought, he was just getting old. Or perhaps it was because he had heard nothing from the stone hand since the voice had abruptly given him the scrolls' location. DeVilbiss had been set up for termination; the white-haired vampiress had been maneuvered to her own slaughter. Was any of what his Infernal Lord had said about eighteen vampires or demigodhood believable? Maybe he should walk away from this suicidal task and henceforth get his powder on the black market, the same way the new breed of undead would.

The Vampire threw off the blanket and reached into the unconscious student's back pocket for his wallet. He found the library card. With luck and skill, he would be able to approximate the photograph. He shoved the wallet into his own pocket, reached down and snapped the student's neck.

Sighing deeply, the Vampire climbed into the driver's seat and

268

put the car in gear. He had not existed for eternity before his creation; he would most likely not exist for eternity after his death. He decided to trust the demons that had supported him for so long. Perhaps he would experience what demigodhood felt like before he discovered oblivion.

The trip home for Simon was longer than expected. Already, it had exceeded Father Ferro's estimate by some five hours and forty minutes. In spite of normal readings on all instruments, the Jet Stream aircraft was deemed no longer safe for the route across the Atlantic. Even if it had been, once the pilot and navigator heard from the flight attendant exactly what had materialized inside the passenger cabin, they elected to remain grounded for several days.

Private aircraft capable of leaping the Atlantic Ocean were rare in Ireland; those that would be lent out merely because "the Lord hath need" were even rarer. Finally, a benefactor was located in Dublin by the ubiquitous *Serafini Segreti*, and the spartan craft was shuttled to Shannon. Only one thing brightened the night-long trip across the vast ocean: when recontacted, Ray Pental had relayed that the police were watching the library.

Resigning himself that he could do nothing to speed their arrival, Simon returned to his minute review of DeVilbiss's diary. He had decoded every entry for which he had a headline key and was now rereading, to glean more clues to the nature of the dead vampire's existence.

"Did I tell you he gave me a little praise in his last entry?" Simon remarked to Dante.

"For your unselfish devotion to Miss Vanderveen?" the priest responded, from the opposite side of the plane.

"No. For my 'nerve and resourcefulness.' "

"Generosity. How unlike our image of the vampire," Dante reflected. "And a few days before that he spared the life of the widower with the two small children. Perhaps the anticipation of his freedom from Satan was guiding him back toward a godly life."

"Perhaps," Simon allowed. "But he substituted the other professor and his wife without batting an eyelid. Whatever good he did, whatever kind thoughts he had, he continued to act like the same monster right to the end."

"A complex creature, to be sure. This is what frightens me," said Dante. "If the average man is offered the chance to become un-aging, stronger, immune to disease by taking some powder and blood, how much of the sleeping monster within him will awaken? I have watched good men become evil simply by being elected to a position of power or attaining sudden wealth. We may lose more than we did by biting the apple."

Simon closed the diary. "I'm tired of looking for answers that aren't here. He was obsessed with helping me conquer his 'land-lords of Hell,' as he called them. Told me where Frederika was; offered me his diaries; gave me warnings. But nothing he did has really given us an advantage."

"Perhaps he will be one of those wretched souls who wander the earth until Judgment Day," Dante speculated. He had just finished a meticulous trimming and buffing of his nails. Prior to that, he had spent half an hour in the plane's bathroom shaving and combing his hair. Simon wondered if his fastidious nature applied to toilet habits as well as eating or whether the ancient literature scholar was merely grooming himself before battle, as the Spartan warriors had.

Simon looked out the window. His eyebrows knitted in per-plexity. "Hey, that's Princeton down there! What's going on?"

"I did not wish to distress you," Dante said. "The authorities learned that we were coming soon after we left Shannon. Our flight plan was changed from Newark Airport to the jurisdiction of the Princeton police 'for the sake of expedience,' as they told the pilot. Buckle your seat belt, please."

The plane touched down at Mercer County Airport at a few minutes past noon. When the door was opened and the ladder low-ered, a man with a perfect haircut and a well-cut suit stood waiting on the runway. The moment the ladder hit the asphalt, he was up it.

"You must be Father Ferro," the man said, offering his hand. "I'm Francis Littlefield, Chief of Police, Princeton Township. Anyone asks, you didn't meet me here. There's a priest from

St. Paul's sitting inside that car over there. Why don't you take a ride back to Princeton with him? I'd like to speak with you a little later in the day."

"I shall be available," Dante said, looking over his shoulder at Simon.

Littlefield reached into his pocket for his pack of cigarettes. "I'll take good care of your friend. Don't worry." He offered the pack to Dante.

"Worrying is part of my profession," Dante said, waving away the offer. He picked up his attaché case and moved out of the plane, pausing only to give Simon a bracing wink.

Littlefield watched the priest's departure for a moment, then pivoted and focused an appraising look on Simon. "Welcome home. Smile; it could be a lot worse."

"Really? How good is it?" Simon asked, having trouble masking his instant antipathy toward the man.

"For one thing, you're off the murder rap. It's now justifiable homicide. You smoke?"

"No, thanks. Neither should you. I'm sure smoking isn't allowed around here."

Littlefield considered Simon's admonition and shoved the pack back into his pocket. "It's about time I gave up this dirty habit anyway. I was seriously considering it as a New Year's resolution, but you and your goddamn vampires have me too stressed out. I've had a long talk with Detective Pental, and I've figured out your strategy with this nonexistent-scrolls-in-the-ductwork business."

"I hope so." Simon reached down for the remains of his rucksack, the bottom of which he had jury-rigged shut with a pillow case and a liberal application of masking tape. He picked the backpack up by the sword cane, which lay undamaged beneath the straps.

Littlefield put his hand under his jacket and behind his back. When it reappeared, he held handcuffs. "You're a cocky S.O.B., Mr. Penn, considering you've got a bunch more charges to answer to. I'll read you your rights on the way to town. If I forget, it doesn't matter; this library stunt of yours'll probably get me fired anyhow. Judge Ditmars has delayed skiing at Killington specifically for you. You're about to be arraigned in record time."

Simon put down his rucksack and held out his hands.

"I'll carry your things," Littlefield said, snapping the cuffs around Simon's wrists. "Maybe you'll stop shooting icicle looks at me if I tell you I'm beginning to believe we've got a real vampire problem here. Whether Satan fits into it remains to be seen. I want you to help pay for this monster hunt you've arranged. As soon as you're arraigned and interrogated, I want you in that library. Duck your head!" He guided Simon not too gently out the hatch and down the stairs. "I imagine with your fear of vampires, you've been staring at strangers all week, right?"

"If you don't look, you don't live," Simon replied.

"Good. Then you can study faces as they pass through the library lobby. Maybe you'll recognize someone who should have been dead when Napoleon was a second lieutenant. Of course, all this is assuming Judge Ditmars doesn't set your bail too high. Do you have ready access to a lot of money, Mr. Penn?" Littlefield asked, as they walked away from the airplane, toward the chief's police car.

"Depends on what you mean by a lot of money. I have seven thousand dollars in lire and Swiss francs hidden in my shoes," Simon said.

Littlefield laughed, as he reached again for his cigarette pack. "You are an *amazingly* cocky S.O.B., Mr. Penn."

Ray spotted Simon Penn's face the moment Ray entered Firestone Library's huge lobby. The librarian stood among other librarians, behind the checkout counter. Directly in front of him lay the pair of turnstiles that admitted readers to and delivered them from the main stacks. Alongside him, a woman was taking care of business; Simon's sole job seemed to be scanning the lobby. He smiled wanly when Ray caught his eye. Ray took the twenty steps necessary to reach the counter, then extended his hand.

"I'm earning a little holiday cash," Simon greeted him. "Bribe money to use in the slammer."

"My dark humor must be infectious. How long have you been here?"

Simon looked up at the wall clock. "About two hours. Not enough time to be much help. The library closes in ten minutes, and then it's not open again until January second."

"Right. My shift is from six to two A.M." Ray noted the walkie-talkie clutched in Simon's left hand. He dipped his head toward the far side of the L-shaped counter. "How about filling me in?"

Away from curious ears, the two men swapped intelligence on their respective experiences regarding the scrolls and the synthetic powder. While they conferred a voice came over the intercom, announcing that the library would be closing for the holiday in five minutes.

"Still no news about the guy in the baseball cap," Ray said, his eyes scanning the exiting patrons as he spoke. "They've linked the two dead men to a drug cartel in Colombia, but we can push the feds just so hard. Basically, they think they're pursuing an illegal designer drug. We have—" Ray did a double take.

Simon followed the detective's eyes. Dante Ferro had emerged from the public-access Reference Room.

"Our mutual friend," Ray said. "I thought he'd be on a plane back to Italy by now . . . chasing Frederika and the scrolls."

Simon watched the priest approach the desk. "He's convinced something big will happen here before New Year's. I can't tell him what to do. If you want him gone, be my guest."

"Father," Ray said, taking the priest's outstretched hand. "Good to see you again."

"However unlikely that seemed," Dante returned. "Who would have thought the chase would bring me back to Princeton . . . and so soon? Tell me, Detective: is your chief a religious man?"

"Not really."

"But he knows all of this story . . . the demons and the vampires?"

"He certainly knows everything I do," Ray said. "That's the only reason he's allowed this operation."

"He sounded to me like he's trying not to believe the supernatural part," Simon contributed.

Ray glanced at the security person turning a peeved female student away from the entry turnstile. "That's what he says. But, deep down, I think he'd love to believe."

"So would anybody," said the priest. "If you were given the opportunity to talk to somebody who had spoken to God—one of the disciples, for example—wouldn't you jump at it? He's as anxious as you or I to interrogate somebody who's talked to the Devil. Otherwise, why should such a politically careful man allow half his men to be used for this?"

"I'm not exactly sure what you're angling for, Father, but you're gonna have to wait to tell me," Ray said, gently turning Dante toward the front doors. "It's closing time."

"But surely you can make an exception for a fellow cop?" Dante cajoled.

Ray laughed. "Former fellow cop. You compromised me enough on your last visit. See you in church."

Dante began buttoning his overcoat. "Then I shall walk around the building all night, watching. You cannot prevent me from this."

Ray shook his head. "Just check in with the guy in the patrol car down near the loading dock. Otherwise, you'll be dragged down to the station on suspicion."

"If you get tired of freezing, Father," Simon said, "I plan to be back at Frederika's house no later than midnight."

"It will have happened by then," Dante said, waggling his finger as he backed toward the doors. "Bless you both." His upraised forefinger traced the sign of the Cross in the air. Then he turned and walked through one of the doors, into the night.

"I wish I could keep him in here," Ray told Simon. "He wants to come up against a vampire a whole lot more than I do." He looked toward the Reference Room entrance, where Detective

Andy Sutton was trading places with Harry Grimes. Both plain-clothesmen were eyeing Simon and Ray, and neither looked happy. "Chief Littlefield may know everything, but it's another matter with the rest of the force. I've done what you said and warned them about the subject being fast and powerful, but even that's got them rolling their eyes. If I were you, I'd think again about hanging around any longer; the other five guys who're spending New Year's Eve here are all plenty pissed at you."

"Five's not enough," Simon said, alarmed.

"Hey, that's a third of the force. All the chief can spare . . . especially tonight. And Father Ferro better be right about something happening soon. Tomorrow, there'll only be two of us here; the next day, zero. The university does not want us here. They've put beaucoup pressure on Littlefield. Tonight, one guy's patrolling outside; one's guarding the loading dock entrance; one the emergency exit; one's hiding behind some stacks next to B9F. I'm roaming the place . . . along with the university's guards. If you're staying, you can keep Andy Sutton company while he watches the main doors."

"You ought to chain the emergency door," Simon suggested, through a grim expression, "and pair up with that officer."

"I don't have the authority to do that," Ray answered. "But I do have the authority to tell you to stay out of any rough stuff that may happen. You're a civilian again, cowboy."

Simon took a step back from the counter and produced Wagner's sword cane. He rotated the golden ring and withdrew the sword far enough for Ray to see what it was. "I'm not a civilian if one of those monsters comes right at me."

"I did not officially see that," Ray said. He glanced at the last of the library users converging on the exit doors. Then he waved his hand lethargically at Simon. Let's face it . . . despite the priest's mystic premonitions, what's the chance some vampire's walking into this trap? I'll bet we could all be somewhere else tonight, partying it up. My wife and I were supposed to be at a celebration in two hours. Third party we missed this season, thanks to those

275

damned scrolls. If she wasn't Catholic, she'd have divorced me by now." Ray tapped the counter firmly. "Stay put!" He moved to the security people at the turnstiles.

"Everything check out?"

The woman who examined all personal materials of patrons leaving the library wore her topcoat, her hat, and a worried expression. "No, sir. My counter says two hundred ninety-seven for the day." She dipped her head toward the uniformed man who had supervised the entrance turnstile. "William's got two hundred ninety-eight."

Ray took a fortifying breath and tried not to look panicked. There was no sense asking if they had noticed that a particular person had entered and not left. Their division of labor made it pointless.

"It's not the first time it's happened, Officer," William volunteered. "Clarice's turnstile has the counter built in." He held up a small, chromed instrument. "I do mine by hand, and every so often I click twice."

"How often?"

William looked at Clarice, then back at Ray. "Two, maybe three times a year."

"Did you check some of the briefcases coming in, William?" Ray asked.

"Most," William affirmed. "But when three or four come in together, I had to let some go by. I checked all the IDs, though, and nobody seemed suspicious. Can we go now?"

William's eyes drifted toward the front doors, where a librarian was impatiently waiting for them with her key ring in her hand. The admission about missing counts was William's patent gambit to release himself and his partner on time for their New Year's parties; the special need to keep an accurate count had been impressed on him when he came on duty.

"Yeah, go ahead."

William accelerated toward the door, trying to catch up with his turnstile counterpart. Ray unsnapped the walkie-talkie from his belt and thumbed it on. "All code 5 officers, this is Ray. Possible

276

suspect still in the building. Be alert." He looked toward the check-out counter. Simon nodded his acknowledgment that he had heard Ray's broadcast.

Ray watched the doors being locked tightly. The librarian rattled them from the outside for good measure, sending a chill up Ray's spine. Beyond the doors, the winter night had smothered the library. Ray took the central staircase down to A level.

If this library were a ship, it would have been an aircraft carrier, Ray thought. Some of the mammoth building's north–south corridors ran two hundred and fifty feet uninterrupted, some east–west ones as much as a hundred and eighty. It had seven floors, stacked like decks, three of them below ground level. Hundreds of rooms and cubicles. Most parallel to the aircraft carrier comparison, there was virtually no way to exit. Certainly not below ground level (except the loading dock), and even where views to the outside world were offered, the tempered-glass windows were sealed, so that books could not be conveniently dropped outside, to be picked up later. Ray had spent four hours walking the place the day before, and still there were areas he had not covered.

Time to take inventory. Ray sat on one of the staircase's cold marble steps and pulled from his outer jacket pocket the greatly reduced blueprints of the building. From his other outer pocket he withdrew a flashlight filled with new C batteries. He reached to his hip, released his revolver, and set it down on the step, beside the flashlight. He dumped six bullets out of his left pants pocket. Every bullet was the Teflon-coated "Rhino" variety. He cracked open the weapon and slid a sixth bullet into the exposed cylinder. No empty safety chamber tonight; not with Number Two Hundred Ninety-Eight missing and unaccounted for.

Reholstering the revolver, Ray thought that he wanted to see the creature that could shake off the savage flowering of a .357 slug. Shivering as he collected his paraphernalia and stood, he quickly revised the notion. The last thing he wanted to see was such a creature . . . and if he did, it might be the very last thing.

B level was where the action would be. Ray descended with a heavy, slow tread. When he eventually got down there, he intended to turn on every light he could find. Ray turned onto the stair landing between levels A and B. He paused, hearing a faint, hollow, metallic noise, like someone popping a tin oil drum lid in and out. A narrow door led off of the landing, labeled A/B9E. He put his ear against it. The noise became perceptibly louder. He tried the knob. The door was locked. He consulted his blueprints, then took his walkie-talkie in hand.

At 4:47, a man vaguely resembling Princeton University undergraduate Terry McMullen had used McMullen's student ID to pass through the library's entrance turnstile. He had carried an attaché case, which had not been inspected. Inside the case were two bottles of Coca-Cola with screw-on caps, a plastic drinking glass, a notepad, two pencils, and a neatly folded white laundry bag. The Vampire had taken an hour reconnoitering, studying wall charts of the building's layout, examining rooms behind doors that would open, visiting each of the seven floors.

At 5:47, the Vampire stood in the deserted southeast corner of C level, removing the first of two flaccid rubber balloons from his pocket. He unscrewed the already broken-sealed cap from one of the Coke bottles and poured half its contents into the plastic glass. He then fitted one of the balloons into the neck of the bottle and poured half the viscous contents of the second bottle into the balloon. He placed the bomb on the lowest shelf of a large bookcase filled with old and very dry books. At 5:53, he repeated the process in a remote cul-de-sac in the opposite corner of C level. By the time he had the second bomb made, the acid component had clouded the inside of the plastic glass. At 6:01, he gained entry to Room B8E and approached the grille to the air ventilation system with his Swiss Army knife open. At 6:05, the acid ate a pinprick hole through the wall of the first balloon. Three seconds later, the bottle exploded in a ball of flame. Ten books caught fire immediately; around the spreading tongues of flame lay thousands more.

Ray retraced his steps and climbed halfway up the staircase, to be well distant from the door when he used his walkie-talkie.

"This is Ray Pental. Which officer is at B9F?"

"Mike Davis, Ray," the answer came back.

"Mike, anybody been near that door?"

"Nobody's touched it since I got here."

"Have a conversation with yourself."

"What?"

"Use two loud voices, one high, one low. Pretend you're a pair of cops. We've got some weird noise in your area, and if it's human, I want them too scared to move."

"Roger."

"Hey, Rasputin," he radioed, using his pet name for Andy Sutton, "what's your 20?"

"Main lobby," Sutton's electronic voice came back.

"I've got noise inside room A/B9E. Take the elevator down to B level and put yourself near the central stairs." From that strategic point, by taking no more than a dozen steps, Sutton commanded views of both banks of elevators, the main north–south and east–west corridors, the main staircase, and the entrances to two auxiliary stairwells.

"Give me half a min', Jonah," Sutton replied.

Ray thumbed the walkie-talkie on one more time. "Security?"

"Here."

"We need you at A/B9E with a key."

"Coming."

Ray approached the door and listened. He no longer heard the noise. He wondered if it had merely been ductwork contracting because the heating had been turned back and if he was about to look like a jumpy jackass. Ray heard a new noise, half a flight down the stairwell. Andy Sutton was approaching, muttering four-letter words.

The second bomb ignited at 6:10, with similar results.

"What's the problem?" the university security guard asked, as he rattled down the stairs. He had been introduced to Ray the day before as Danny. The guard was young and strong-looking. Ray

279

was glad Danny's partner, Rob, had not answered the call. Despite his boyish name, the second guard was a stiff-jointed beanpole not a day under sixty.

"Noise inside the room," Ray said loudly, pointing to the lock. He waited until Danny had turned his attention to inserting the key before setting his blueprints down and reaching to his hip for his revolver.

Danny pushed the door back. The room was not completely dark. Ray caught a pattern of light swinging across one wall in the moment before the guard flipped up the wall switch.

"Nobody in here," Danny said, stepping back for Ray to confirm his words, his eyes going wide at the sight of the drawn gun.

Ray entered. The room was not large. It had a small, round table in its center, surrounded by five plastic chairs. The walls were blank. Solid drywall formed the ceiling, rather than the sound-deadening dropped variety. Only the one door. The room was an apparent dead end. Ray looked in the direction where he had seen the faint pattern of light. Halfway up the right wall was a large air-return grate. Ray approached it. He shone his flashlight through the metal slats. He discerned another grate, of similar size, directly across the duct.

Ray clawed his fingernails under one corner of the grate and tugged. The four screws in its face were securely fastened. "Can we get into that room down there?" he asked the guard.

"Sure." Danny led the way down the half flight onto B level and around the corner, where Andy Sutton stood, still muttering.

"Draw your weapon, Andy," Ray said, as he hurried by the older detective. The pair and Officer Davis followed Danny into the room.

Whatever B9F's original function, it had been turned into a makeshift storage room, with a couple dozen stacked plastic chairs, several cardboard drums of cleaning material, and sealed cartons of paper towels. On the far wall, high up, was the air-return grate. Directly under it, a solitary chair was pushed against the wall, where it had been used by Richard Chen several days earlier and then by Ray himself in setting the trap. Ray hopped onto the chair and ripped at the grille. Its screws had not been replaced; it pulled easily from its moorings. He threw the grille aside and thrust the flashlight into the duct. Just to the left of the grille cutouts, the duct dead-ended. Ray leaned in and shone the flashlight to the right, down the long, shiny tin rectangle. The beam caught a wig of curly, jet-black hair and a white laundry bag. Beyond the bag lay the metal decoy container, opened.

Ray leaned in as far as he could and retrained the light. About thirty feet down, the duct was filled with the form of a small human being, propelling himself backward with astonishing speed. His face was largely obscured by the frantic pushing motions of his hands and arms.

"Halt! Police!" Ray cried out. The echo was painful in his ears.

"You gotta be kiddin'!" Sutton exclaimed.

"Halt, or I'll shoot!" Ray yelled, reaching for his revolver.

"Are you nuts?" Andy Sutton cried out, coming up fast to the chair and grabbing Ray's gun hand.

"Let go!" Ray shouted. He lost his balance on the chair and was forced to jump down.

From the hallway nearby, the fire alarm blared on with a raucous wail.

"What the hell?" Sutton exclaimed.

"It's a diversion," Ray replied, "so he could get away in the confusion. We've got to make it work for us, Andy. Call Central Dispatch! Have the building surrounded, and tell them to stop everybody. I mean everybody. He's small and in dark clothing. And check the ID of every fireman who comes back out of the building. Hurry!"

"Okay, okay," the senior detective said, backing out the door. "Just don't kill anybody!" he shouted, as he dashed for the main stairwell, with the ashen-faced university guard following.

Ray hopped back up onto the chair. He thrust his flashlight again inside the ductwork and leveled his weapon.

The figure had disappeared. Ray's point of perspective made it hard to see, but he thought the duct made a curving turn to the left, some fifty feet ahead. Uttering a short prayer to the Virgin Mary,

Ray boosted himself up and tried to wriggle in. He was too big. Whoever was in the duct had to be very small, very thin, and very strong. He dropped back down to the floor, grabbed a carton of paper towels and jammed it into the duct opening.

"Come with me, Mike," Ray ordered. They left the room and headed in the direction of the ductwork. Ray tried several doors and found every one locked. Glancing overhead, he saw two ducts converging into a larger one. He scaled a nearby metal bookshelf and put his hand to the tin, feeling in vain for vibrations. The noise of the fire alarm made it impossible to hear any movements. He was sure of only one thing: as long as the vampire stayed inside the ductwork, he was confined to B level or the floor below. The previous year, Ray had helped his brother-in-law convert the hot-air ductwork in the Pental home for central air-conditioning, and he had learned that all the joining was done on the outside. The insides were uniformly smooth metal, with no purchase. Perhaps if they were five or six feet across, a superstrong creature might have used the pressure of hands and feet to work his way up to another level like a rock climber negotiating a chimney. But in these narrow ducts, one would be lucky enough just to remain unstuck.

"Follow that duct out, and keep feeling for vibrations," Ray told Davis. As the other officer moved into the dark stacks, scaling bookshelves every few yards to touch the bottom of the duct, Ray worked his way slowly around the central core of B level, keeping his finger on the revolver trigger, flipping on with the head of his flashlight every light switch he passed. Coming around the second turn, he found himself staring at a fire control panel. Two red lights were blazing, both indicating fires on C level. So the vampire would not be sliding downward. If Ray had it figured right, his opponent's plan was to draw everyone below him while he worked his way up. The creature knew now that he was being hunted and that just walking out of the building unchallenged would be unlikely. But neither could he hole up in the ducts; the fires he set would be smoking him out any minute now. He'd emerge from one of the twenty or so doors in the central core area, but which one was impossible to tell.

282

Ray hurried to the main stairwell, snatching up as he went the blueprints that still lay where he had left them. He reached ground level and hopped over the turnstiles, watching the night through the many unopenable windows, willing police car and fire truck lights to come flashing into view. Simon Penn emerged from the shadows of an alcove near the main doors, his sword unsheathed.

"What's happening?" Simon called out.

"Put that thing away if you don't want to be shot," Ray answered. "A diversion. I found one of your creatures in the vent system. A little guy in black clothing. Where's Andy Sutton?"

"I don't know," Simon answered. "I haven't seen anyone since the alarms went off."

"Jesus! Well, stay cool and stay put. Somebody's got to watch this area. Reinforcements and the fire company ought to be here any minute now." Ray caught the first, acrid smell of smoke. He turned toward the center of the enormous building.

Ray used his Stanislavsky training to become a vampire. The solution came with little effort: this creature would probably react as the first one had when he had been surprised by the alarm system. The initial investigation of that break-in had been written up as the university guard kicking on a fire alarm in the final throes of hanging himself from a sprinkler system pipe. Once Simon Penn had blamed the man's death on Vincent DeVilbiss, however, Harry Grimes had found DeVilbiss's fingerprints on every rung of the ladder leading to the library's highest rooftop. One member of the town police also remembered seeing DeVilbiss beside the library that night, and that he "seemed to have fallen from nowhere." The drop from the library's top tower was measured at thirty-two feet, and it was only the first of several drops necessary to reach the ground. Such an improbable avenue of escape for a mortal was likely the most probable choice for a vampire.

Still mentally cloaking himself in the vampire's cape, Ray reasoned that the creature would dare neither the main stairwell nor the confining elevators. That left three auxiliary staircases. Ray headed for the one farthest from where he stood. As he trotted across the foyer, the first set of whirling red lights flashed across the plaza in front of the library. He headed into the Exhibitions Hall, weaving around display cases. Above the wail of the fire alarms, he heard a gunshot from the direction in which he moved. He redoubled his speed, found himself momentarily lost, consulted his blueprints and located the stairwell. He pushed against the heavy fire door and for a moment thought it was locked. Then he realized it had no keyhole. He pushed harder. It gave slightly. He continued pushing until he could shine his flashlight through the opening. He saw Andy Sutton's pants, flecked with blood. He shoved with all his might. The body toppled over, allowing Ray through.

Ray's light found a still life of horror. Sutton's neck had been snapped so violently that parts of the cervical vertebrae had broken through the skin. The smell of gunpowder filled the stairwell, but the detective's weapon was nowhere to be found. The discharged bullet was lodged low in one of the walls. The disbelief that had been his undoing was fixed on Sutton's face.

Ray climbed, two steps at a time. He passed the door to floor 2, intent on moving as high up as he could and then locating the central tower.

The door to floor 3 flew open when Ray was within a step of its landing. Ray flung his weapon up and started to squeeze. Only the gray color of the university uniform prevented him from putting a .357 slug point-blank through Rob the guard's heart. The old man's ticker was not unscathed, however; as he stumbled backward into the hall he clutched at his chest.

"Jesus Christ! Twice in ten seconds!" Rob exclaimed.

"What are you talking about?" Ray demanded, feeling his own heart doing acrobatics against his rib cage.

"Another guy just came outta here."

"A little man, dressed in black?"

"Yeah. He was carrying a gun, and he flew around the corner when he spotted me. Never saw—"

"Which corner?" Ray demanded.

The guard pointed, then pushed himself past Ray into the stairwell, with more power than his skinny frame should have possessed. The door slammed loudly, just as the fire alarms stopped

284

wailing. When their echo died, Ray found himself once more alone, hemmed in on every side by silence.

Ray ripped away all but the bottom two sheets of blueprints. The only entrance to the central tower from floor 3 lay a few feet in front of him. The guard had scared the vampire off, undoubtedly by the element of surprise. Floor 4 had a similar configuration. Both levels had only two stairwells, as they were considerably smaller than the floors below. He could either wait here for reinforcements, controlling this floor's entrance to the tower, or else gamble that the vampire was right now taking the other stairwell up to floor 4. He reentered his stairwell and charged upward like a running back doing stadium step sprints. He burst through the door.

The man didn't look remotely like Ray's image of a vampire. The worst Ray could have thought, glancing at that same face in a crowd, would have been that the diminutive, astonishingly young-looking man was ugly. He still wore dark clothing from head to toe. In his right hand he held Andy Sutton's gun.

In a split second, the vampire's expression changed from surprise to malevolent anger. He was still twenty-five feet from the tower entrance. In a blur of motion, he pivoted the already half-raised revolver and pointed it at Ray. Ray spun around the doorjamb, back into the stairwell. A bullet passed his ear so close he could hear the buzz beneath the supersonic crack of splitting air. Even as he dodged away, his gun hand thrust forward; his trigger finger squeezed off a blind shot.

Another shot rang out. The lone lightbulb that had hung from the ceiling died instantly. Darkness claimed the corridor at once, with only the spill from the slowly closing fire door lighting a portion of the opposite wall. Ray fired again, hoping that the vampire had advanced on the tower door. He heard no outcry of pain. He withdrew his hand as the door slammed shut. Ray flung himself against its hinges, dug into his pocket and clawed out two more bullets. Only a fool would open that door knowing he had just four more shots in his gun. He intended to have six. Hands shaking spasmodically, Ray tapped out the two spent shells and managed to replace them with live ammo. He snapped the cylinder back in place and listened. Nothing. He went down on his knees and crawled across to the opposite edge of the door. Keeping low, he put his left hand on the knob, flung the door back, stuck the revolver through and fired off a fan pattern of three shots. The corridor reverberated with the triple blast. Ray scooped up the flashlight and tossed it onto the linoleum, letting it roll into the open. Its beam caught the tower door, which was still shut.

The vampire obviously wanted darkness. All the lore said they operated at will in the most feeble light. Ray bet his life the creature would not let the flashlight remain shining if he was still in the corridor. No answering shot rang out. Ray closed his eyes for a second, straining to recall the exact layout of floor 4. There were ceiling-to-floor bookshelves on three sides of the stairwell. If he were the vampire, he would have circled around and attempted to surprise his adversary from behind.

Daring all, Ray burst from the stairwell, scooped up the flashlight, took five lunging steps forward and threw himself left, where he expected and found an opening in the bookshelves. His flashlight threw wild patterns of light as he attempted to see everywhere at once. He crouched and flattened himself against one case, whipping his gun left and right. He saw no one. Even though he felt like he was suffocating, he willed his lungs to stop heaving for several seconds, so he could listen. He waited. And waited. And waited. It felt like eternity, but Ray knew less than a minute had passed.

The sound of shattering glass echoed through floor 4, from some distance away. The drop to floor 3's roof would be nothing for the vampire. Ray could not let him escape. He rushed through the dark lines of bookcases, weaving in and out, heading for the source of noise, slowing only to flip on any light switch that came into his flashlight beam. He darted across an aisle and edged warily into the mouth of a narrow corridor. The ruined window lay at the far end. Most of the tempered glass, though cracked and crazed, still held to the frame. Not even a man as small as the vampire could have exited through the opening. Which meant he was still inside.

Ray threw himself onto the corridor floor. The glass of his flashlight shattered on his impact; its beam died. In the same instant, a bullet smacked into the corner of the bookcase behind him. He elbowed his way several feet down the aisle between bookcases, then flipped onto his back, swinging his revolver up.

Another shot rang out, scoring a direct hit on the ceiling light nearest Ray. Ray's ability to see shrank to the length of his arm. He strained to remember just how many shots remained in Sutton's gun. Two? One? As he was thinking, he heard the noise of a motor starting. It was not until several seconds later that he realized the huge metal bookcase to his left was rolling smoothly toward the one to his right. He ran the heel of his shoe along the floor and discovered one track on which the case was moving. He had never heard of such an invention, but its ingenuity came immediately to his mind: for more than 99 percent of the time, the aisles between the library's myriad bookcases were not occupied. To save huge amounts of space, an entire line of cases had been set on tracks and shoved tightly against each other when not in use. A corridor between specific cases was created by a motor whenever a user needed it. The vampire, however, was bent on putting it to a less academic use. Ray winged out his elbows and felt the corridor shrinking. He knew that even if he could make it to the opposite end before he was crushed, the vampire might be calmly waiting to put a bullet into his brain. Fortunately, the shelves were not tightly packed. Acting swiftly, he kicked and toed all the books on the right case's lowest shelf onto the floor beyond where he lay. As the two metal skeletons moved toward each other, he rolled into his makeshift coffin. The bindings of the books on the floor popped and snapped as they were compacted. Ray screamed as if he were in mortal agony, needing to turn one long bloodcurdling sound into the acting job of his life. The motor froze. Ray held his breath. From nearby he heard an answering sound to his scream: the full-throated laughter of evil incarnate.

Soft footsteps faded. Ray lay entombed like a mummy for the count of a hundred heartbeats. Then he began methodically feeding books into the four inches of space not closed, burrowing from his bottom shelf to the bottom shelf just beyond, passing books one by one over his stomach into the space he had left behind. When he reached the third case and his arms felt like they were ready to drop off, claustrophobia set in hard. He started yelling for help from the depths of his lungs.

"Ray? Where are you?" came Simon Penn's voice.

"I'm trapped inside these bookcases. Get me out!" As soon as he heard the motor start, he yelled, "Get to the tower!"

It took only seconds for the opening to form where Ray was trapped. He jumped up and rushed around the cases to the shattered window. Through the rough opening, he saw the figure of a small man running with superhuman speed across one of the library's distant roofs. Ray realized his revolver lay somewhere in all the reshuffled books. The figure disappeared.

Simon came loping back to the place where Ray stood. "The trapdoor's open in the top. I couldn't reach the rungs without a ladder. Maybe they got him outside."

"Think so, huh?" Ray said, reading Simon's dejected face. "You got any other plans?"

The smell of brewing coffee was getting to Officer Wisniewski. Simon could tell that the young man was not keen on continuing their careful sweep of the Vanderveen mansion.

"If you take milk or cream, Officer, you'll have to settle on Coffee-mate," Simon warned. "There's nothing in the refrigerator."

"That's okay with me, sir," the rookie cop said, giving the coffee pot a longing glance. The furnace had been blowing heat since Simon dialed up the temperature, but the huge house had yet to reach the comfort zone. Simon and Dante Ferro had arrived in the back of a patrol car fifteen minutes before, with Wisniewski and his partner in the front seat. All four had come from the township building, after Simon had endured his second set of statements in one day. The people involved, the red tape, and the redundancy had made the futility of the incident in the university library all the more unbearable.

"It'll still be here when we've finished looking through the top floor," Simon said, of the coffee.

"That'll be another ten minutes," Wisniewski grumbled. "This place is huge."

"In my country," Father Ferro chimed in, "they would call it a *palazzo*. Very grand indeed."

"You have your pick of two guest bedrooms, Father. This way, gentlemen," Simon said, pointing down the hallway with the sword cane.

The three men explored each room together, making sure all windows were locked and that there was no possibility of any intruder lurking within. As they came to the last unexplored room, Simon glanced at his watch. It was twelve minutes before midnight; twelve minutes until the New Year.

"It's locked," the officer said.

"It was locked all the while I roomed here," Simon told his companions. "The sanctum sanctorum of Frederika's dead father. I wonder if we should kick it in."

Officer Wisniewski looked dubious. "Not me."

Outside the house, the police car siren bleeped briefly. Wisniewski turned from the door with gratitude and rattled down the staircase. Simon and Dante followed at a slower pace. By the time Wisniewski had the front door opened, his partner was standing just outside.

"They want us to answer a 10-57 over on Stuart Road," the partner said.

"A firearms discharge complaint," Wisniewski told Simon. "They warned me we'd get a few tonight. It's not far from here. We'll either be back within ten minutes or send another car out, okay?"

"We'll have your coffee ready," Simon said, wanting the pair to return. Despite having searched the house from stem to stern, he still felt uneasy.

"Great!" Wisniewski said, bounding toward the cruiser after his partner.

Simon shut the door and moved directly past the remains of his rucksack and Dante's attaché case and luggage to the living room fireplace. "How about a fire?"

"To be sure," Dante replied, leaning his back against the grand piano. "That is another luxury a poor priest cannot afford."

The wood, the firestarter log, and the matches were all handy. Simon had flames licking upward in less than a minute. As he stood and brushed off his hands, the door knocker sounded.

The librarian and the priest stared at each other with uneasy faces. Withdrawing his Walther P38 from his jacket pocket, Dante nodded for Simon to answer the knock. Simon adjusted his grip on the cane and threw the door back.

"I shouldn't have to knock," Frederika said, stepping off the porch. "It is, after all, my ho——"

Simon gathered her into his arms and released all the passion and anxiety he had pent up over an interminable week. As she returned his ardor, the item she held in her right hand fell to the floor, raising a racket when its metallic end struck, then rolled around over marble. Simon was jolted by the noise long enough for Frederika to bend and retrieve the long black tube she had carried through Europe.

"I'm glad to see you, too, Mr. Penn," she said pertly, then turned her gaze on the priest, one eyebrow cocked. "And, I suppose you as well, Father."

Ferro had used the kiss and the dropped tube to reconceal the pistol in his pocket. He made a Continental bow without leaving the area of the piano. "I am Father Dante Ferro, special emissary from the Vatican. My deepest apology for trying to shoot you, Miss Vanderveen." His eyes darted back and forth between the exquisite woman and the black tube.

"Accepted." Frederika closed the front door and walked past Simon, whose astonishment at her unexpected arrival had him rooted to the floor. The fingers of her left hand worked at the seals of the tube. "Did you know that you can rent cars with cellular phones? I'm the reason your two policemen are driving down to Stuart Road. I don't have much time."

"What do you mean?" Simon asked.

"I'm only here to collect the scrolls." She opened the tube and showed Simon that it was empty. "You didn't think I had them with me, did you? Shame on you both." She shot each man an annoyed look. "You'd found out they weren't in the library. Think, Simon! Where's the only place we stopped between stealing them and leaving for Europe?"

Simon found himself yet again staring at Frederika's perfect face. He was elated to see that it was free of sunglasses and suntan lotion. Her eyes were once more their normal blue. She looked tired, but that alone could not have accounted for the difference in her appearance. She seemed to have aged by several years.

"We were here," Simon answered.

"Right. I know you'll want to kill me for this, but I stuck both scrolls under the throw rug in my father's office. Couldn't think of anyplace else on short notice." She dug into her left coat pocket and produced a lone key. Simon noted with pleasure that she still wore the wedding rings he had given her. "Would you be a dear and fetch them for me?"

"Have you found someone to translate them?" Dante asked, arms folded casually, as if they were talking about letters from an aunt in Siberia.

"I'm sorry, Father; I can't linger and chat," Frederika said, heading with steam into the kitchen. "Go, Simon. Go!"

Simon bounded up the steps with the key in one hand and the cane in the other. He had no idea what Father Ferro was thinking, but he himself had not yet decided whether or not to let Frederika go. He hurried to the locked door, fitted and turned the key, and entered the dark room, his hand running up the wall blindly in search of the light switch.

The blunt end of a clothes closet pole shot out of the darkness and struck Simon hard in the temple. The sword cane dropped instantly onto the carpet, but Simon himself did not reach the floor. Instead, he was caught and held up by an immensely powerful hand. Simon's unconscious bulk sank briefly toward the floor as his attacker snatched up the sword cane. Then Simon was dragged one-handed into the hallway light.

The Vampire brought his victim to the top of the long staircase and threw him down, so that Simon fell face first, tumbling head over heels. Only the fact that Simon's unconscious body was limp and unresisting kept the fall from being lethal. He came to a thumping halt two steps before reaching the marble foyer floor.

"Simon!" Frederika called out from far back in the kitchen.

Dante made no outcry but reached the bottom of the steps only a second after Simon came to rest. His right hand, deep in his jacket pocket, was extracting his pistol even before he spotted the Vampire gliding down the staircase.

Recruiting every ounce of speed, strength, and supernatural co-ordination he possessed, the Vampire hurled the clothes pole down the stairs, sharpened end first. It struck the priest squarely in the torso, driving through him and six inches into the wall's plaster and wooden lathing. The pistol fell from Dante's hand. As the Vampire quickly descended, he whipped the cane over the banister, expos-ing the sword within. The wooden sheath sailed through the foyer and across the full length of the living room, shattering the mirror hanging over the fireplace.

Dante wrapped both hands around the makeshift spear and struggled to pull it out. The Vampire leaped over Simon, grabbing the rear of the pole as he vaulted, and used his momentum to drive it another inch into the wall. At last Dante screamed.

Frederika appeared in the living room from the dining room entry, both hands empty. She came to a sudden stop, staring at the carnage twenty-five feet away.

The Vampire advanced slowly on Frederika, whipping the air with the sword.

"The little man from DeVilbiss's chalet," Frederika said, after swallowing some of her fear. "Where's your limp?"

"Gone. Just as de scrolls soon will be gone. I look und look, und dey are under my foots! T'ank you so much für tell me where dey are."

"You're welcome," Frederika said, taking a small step backward, toward the fireplace. "And what do they call you?"

"Pallida Mors," the Vampire replied. "Pale deat'." He grinned widely. His long canines were no longer hidden by dental prostheses. His skin, wiped clean of the Texas Dirt pigment, was scarcely darker than his teeth.

Somewhere in the neighborhood a celebrator was getting an early start on New Year's, setting off a firework that whistled loudly as it rocketed into the night.

"You think you'll kill me, you grotesque little monster?" Frederika said, smiling even though her breaths came in short, clavicular gasps.

"I would rape you until de sun rises except für de police come back soon," the Vampire said.

"Don't let them stop you, superman," Frederika goaded, crooking her fingers in a welcoming gesture, stepping backward again as she did.

A tiny sound of metal sliding up painted plaster caused the Vampire's head to whip around. Using his foot, Dante had worked the fallen pistol halfway up the wall to his hand. Growling his rage at the priest's effrontery, he dashed back to the foot of the stairs and kicked the gun away.

Using the diversion, Frederika noiselessly picked up the fireplace poker, then snuck several steps across the living room. As the Vampire began to turn, she abandoned stealth and rushed full-tilt at him, the poker arching back over her head to deliver a murderous blow.

The Vampire continued to pivot slowly, as if unaware of the woman's attack. Just as she came within striking distance, his motion accelerated. He ducked gracefully under the path of the descending poker and thrust upward with the sword as if his arm were attached to a catapult. His mouth was twisted into a malevolent grin that told her he had sensed her approach for some time and had suckered her into the attack. Twenty inches of tempered steel pierced Frederika's chest before her momentum was halted. She screamed in mortal agony. The poker jerked up violently as she attempted to halt her plunge, striking the Vampire under the chin, ripping his skin open. In retribution, he twisted the sword upward, driving it in to the hilt.

Frederika threw herself backward, ripping the sword's grip out of the Vampire's hand. Her motion was so frenzied that she flew backward into the living room. She struck the piano bench a glancing blow and fell clumsily to one knee. With a tremendous effort, she yanked free the weapon that had pierced her chest. As soon as she did, she began tottering. Her eyes rolled back into her head, and she collapsed sideways onto the thick carpeting, with no effort to break the fall. She lay still, her eyelids open and her mouth frozen into a horrific grimace. The sword lay out from her side, still clutched in her hand.

The Vampire laughed and turned again to Father Ferro. "You see, priest," he said, switching to fluent Italian, "a woman can do what you cannot." He pantomimed the pulling out of the sword and laughed again.

Dante was panting for air. He coughed weakly. Blood dribbled out of his mouth. His eyes, however, were alive.

"Lasciate speranza, padre." The Vampire picked up the Walther P38 and pointed it between Dante's eyes. "No," he decided. "Too quick. You must suffer, as your Lord suffered on the Cross." He dropped the pistol between Dante's legs. "Mr. Penn killed a vampire with a sharpened broomstick. I liked his idea so much that I couldn't help appropriating it. Once you're dead, I'll shove it up his ass. It's what I taught Vlad Tepes so long ago, you know."

The Vampire whisked blood from Dante's chin with his forefinger, put it to his lips, and licked the digit, smiling. " 'This is my blood of the covenant, which is poured out for many.' I wonder if his tasted any different from yours?"

Not expecting an answer, the Vampire bounded up the stairs, taking them two at a time. He returned from Frederik Vanderveen's study seconds later, holding the scrolls. He waved them at the priest as he descended but saw that Ferro's eyes were shut. He moved up close and slapped him across the face. Dante's eyelids fluttered open.

"Look, you impotent bastard!" the Vampire ordered. "I want you to see what you were pursuing before you die. Stay alive long enough to watch them burn." He strode toward the blazing fire, wiping his own blood from his jaw, sticking his fingers into his mouth, and sucking them clean. "Are you saying your prayers inside your head, Padre? Let me help you." He circled around Frederika's still form. *"Pater Noster . . ."*

More fireworks erupted around the neighborhood.

"Addio," the Vampire said, tossing the scrolls onto the fire.

Simon lifted his head and looked at the Vampire. A large, purplish lump had formed at his temple; blood streamed down his cheek; his right eye had swollen shut. But he had recovered himself enough to reach through the spindles of the staircase and push the leaded crystal bowl that sat on the foyer table. It fell to the marble floor and shattered loudly.

The Vampire turned from the fire. "You again?" he sighed. He marched toward Simon, who had begun coughing. "Shall we use the priest's gun to blow away those troublesome hands?" the Vampire asked, over Simon's hacking noises. He laughed and bent to pick up the gun. As he straightened up, his head cocked in surprise, lengthening his neck slightly. He had turned halfway when the sword struck with blinding speed and supernatural force. The blade cut cleanly through, so swiftly that the Vampire's severed head remained balanced on its neck for a long moment. Then it toppled to the floor. His knees buckled, and his body collapsed in the opposite direction. The blood of sacrificed innocents spattered the walls.

Outside the mansion, horns blew; someone shouted with drunken joy at the birth of the new year.

Frederika lifted the Vampire's head by the hair and ran with it to the fireplace, where she kicked the remains of the scrolls out onto the carpet and stomped the flames into extinction. Then she looked at the severed head and spat bloody phlegm at it. The eyelids blinked, and the amber eyes seemed to focus on her.

"Lasciate speranza, monster," she said, in mocking imitation. "Go to hell."

The eyelids descended. Frederika recrossed the room to show

the head to Father Ferro, but he was already gone. She dropped the dripping mass onto the marble floor.

Father Ferro looked peaceful in death, as if he had witnessed the Vampire's beheading and the scrolls' rescue. Frederika stood for several moments mustering her supernatural strength. She opened her coat, unbuttoned her blouse and checked to confirm that the sword wound was closing. Then she tugged the pole from the wall and let the priest down as gently as she could.

"Blue contact lenses . . . right?" Simon's weak voice came from behind her.

"Right," Frederika said, drawing the spear from Father Ferro's torso. "Thanks for the diversion." She moved to Simon, went down on her knees, and put her exquisite face close to his, examining his open eye. "Don't try to get up. Your pupil is dilated; you must have a concussion."

"Okay."

"I'll be right back."

Simon turned his head very slowly, to try to follow Frederika's movement up the stairs. He felt as if someone were tightening and loosening an enormous vise around his temples. When he lost her movement, he refocused on the carnage for a moment, then closed his eyes.

"You moved your head, dammit," Frederika said, coming down the stairs. "Here's a pillow. Just don't fall asleep!"

"Okay, okay." Simon watched Frederika set down a plastic bottle filled with amber powder and a stone hand that looked like it had been broken off a statue. He became aware that she was removing his wallet from his back pocket.

"The vampire's powder," Simon said.

"Yes." Frederika stuffed Simon's wallet into her pants pocket, shoved the plastic bottle into one of her coat pockets, picked up the empty metal tube and the stone hand and carried them to the fireplace. After she had whacked the hand several times against the hearth, she fed the pieces one by one into the hungry flames. Then she gently slid the remains of the scrolls into the metal container.

Over the continued outside noises of celebration, Frederika's supersensitive ears caught the distant wail of a police siren. She rushed back to Simon and brought her head down to his.

"Happy New Year," she whispered, before kissing him.

"Happy New Year," Simon wished in return. And then she was again out of his line of vision. "Where are you going?" he called out, wishing immediately that he hadn't.

"The coffee's burning," Frederika answered, from the kitchen.

The front door knocker sounded. Simon waited for Frederika to answer it. It rapped again, this time with great force. Still, Frederika did not reappear. The hallway felt suddenly colder. In spite of the pain he knew he would suffer, Simon tried to call out.

The front door burst open. Officer Wisniewski and his partner hurtled inside, guns drawn.

"Holy shit!" Wisniewski exclaimed, paralyzed by the grisly scene.

"You okay, sir?" his partner asked Simon.

"I've got a concussion. Please call an ambulance. There's a phone in the kitchen."

Stepping gingerly around the carnage, the partner moved toward the back of the house.

"We came back as soon as we realized it was a phony call," Wisniewski told Simon. He knelt down. "You hang in there, sir; you'll be in Princeton Medical inside ten minutes. Can you tell me what happened?"

"Frederika will tell you," Simon whispered, fighting to keep his eyes open. "Where is she?"

"Who?" Wisniewski asked.

"Frederika Vanderveen. She owns the house. Went in the kitchen."

The officer stood. "Joe! Is there a lady back there?"

The partner strode down the hallway. "Not that I saw. And the back door is open."

CHAPTER NINE

April 19

Greater love hath no man than this,

that he lay down his life for his friends.

—John 15:13

G alloglass?" Bobby Johnson complained. "You can't use proper names in Scrabble."

Simon reached for the score pad, smiling. "I didn't. You think Ernest and Julio also manufacture drinkware?"

Bobby blinked several times through his delicate, wire-rimmed glasses. "I think you made it up. What is it?"

"An armed servant of the old Irish clan chieftains. Challenge me." Simon looked out the recreation room windows, at the barren basketball court. Just beyond was an eight-foot metal fence, topped with barbed wire. Through the fence's weave he could see a ragged line of evergreen trees. The late afternoon sky above them was a hard, cold blue. Except for the barbed wire, there was virtually no clue that Simon sat within New Jersey's minimum security prison for white-collar criminals.

"No, thank you. I've been killed challenging you too often," Bobby declined, as Simon selected five tiles from the draw pile. "How many points is that?"

"Thirty-nine. Triple word score, with one double letter."

"You polecat. I was hoping to win at least one game before you left."

"You'll never beat anyone if you use two S's to make twelve points."

"You also messed up where I was gonna go." Bobby lowered his gaze to restudy his rack of letters. "Librarian."

"Accountant," Simon riposted. Bobby Johnson was a soft-spoken gentleman, originally from Birmingham, Alabama. During his tenure as comptroller of Rutgers University, he had built a reputation as clotheshorse and inveterate bachelor. Five years into his employment it was discovered that he had embezzled over a hundred thousand dollars, spending the bulk of it at local tailor shops and on local prostitutes. His Warholian fifteen minutes of fame had come when he protested the severity of his prison sentence to the press, asserting that consideration should have been given to the fact that he had kept the money circulating in the Greater New Brunswick economy.

"I should know better than to associate with a man who's spent his entire adulthood in the company of the undead," Bobby observed, rearranging his tiles.

"I'm sure you're about to elaborate."

"Everyone who writes a book lives on after death, as long as the book is in some library. Each shelved volume is like a tombstone. But when it's opened, the author comes back to life. You worked in a cemetery filled with undead long before you met Mr. DeVilbiss."

"You have a bizarre mind, Bobby," Simon said, for the dozenth time since he'd met the man.

"I have? I'm not the one who's fought so-called vampires halfway across the world. By the way . . ." Bobby reared back his lips and showed his teeth. "No fangs. I don't want you attacking me just before they spring you."

Bobby had already offered his conviction that Simon had simply stumbled upon a coven of mental cases who believed themselves vampires. No degree of detailed recounting could convince otherwise this man who made a living based on the fact that two plus two always added up to four (except when he was juggling the books). Tired of Johnson's chiding, Simon was glad his true identity had remained a secret at the prison until only six days before.

"And I'll tell you why you and others got caught up believing in these nut cases," Bobby went on. "Times are rife for the vampire legend to rise again from the grave. It feeds the subliminal fears of contaminated blood and of sexual intimacy because of herpes and AIDS. It even capitalizes on growing hopes that science can make us live forever."

"You just keep rationalizing, Bobby," Simon replied. "One dark night not long from now, a 'nut case' is gonna bend the bars of your cell window, climb silently in, and suck you dry. Lay down a word, will you?"

The recreation room door opened on creaking hinges. Detective Ray Pental appeared and gave Simon a subdued wave from the doorway. Simon conceded the game and promised to write to Johnson.

"It's time you left," the clotheshorse judged in farewell. "Gray is not your color."

"Long time no see," Ray said, offering his hand, as Simon approached. "You ready to return to the real world?"

"I don't know. I'm pretty apprehensive," Simon admitted.

"I don't blame you. But you've paid your debt; the Republicans are in office, and the state is not willing to house unofficial guests. Besides, with your cover blown in here, you're a sitting duck."

"I don't suppose the governor would assign you to me as permanent bodyguard."

"No chance. We stretched bureaucracy to the limits stowing you here this long."

Simon shook his head, moving through the doorway. "I can't accept that all this happened and still almost no one believes me."

Ray walked beside Simon toward the prison's front offices, both of them led by a lethargic guard. "They don't believe because the evidence for the supernatural just isn't strong enough."

"And because it didn't happen to them. What about the powder? Has it appeared on the street yet?"

"Not as far as we know. There are some vague rumors coming out of Colombia." Ray let Simon pass first through the final barred gate. "But when they have finally figured out how to duplicate the formula, all they have to do is show the newspaper headlines. You

302

and DeVilbiss created the demand; good old capitalism will do the rest."

"Any other news I should know about?" Simon asked.

Ray looked at Simon's somber face. "Don't think so."

Ray knew Simon craved information about the vanished Frederika Vanderveen. Aside from a reassuring letter to her mother six weeks earlier, delivered with a power of attorney and instructions to sell the Vanderveen mansion, no one had heard from her. Three days into the new year, a rented car with a cellular telephone was traced to Frederika's driver's license. Until that news emerged, were it not for prints matching Frederika's shoe size found in the Vanderveen back yard, Simon's story of her brief return to Princeton would never have been accepted by the police.

"Oh, yeah," Ray said, grasping at anything to make the walk easier. "They finally figured out how Frederika got into the country. At the Florence airport, she picked the purse of a woman named Cindi Hunt. The woman didn't realize it until the day after New Year's, when she tried to cross into France. *We* didn't know it was Frederika who had stolen it until she mailed it back to the woman with an apology. Your clever girlfriend used it to catch a flight out of Italy for Jamaica. She probably never left the Jamaica airport. She used her own passport to fly into Newark, figuring correctly that we were looking for her to try and get straight back from Europe."

They arrived at the release counter. A box with Simon's belongings was waiting. He signed several sets of papers, then rummaged through the box for his keys.

"Does the media know I'm getting out this afternoon?" Simon worried, pulling on his parka.

"If they do, the governor leaked it," Ray said.

Ray let Simon exit the building and take the lead down the narrow pathway to the sally port gate, which opened by remote control. A chill spring breeze blew across the grounds, making Simon's legs and face feel as cold as his heart. He passed into freedom. Just outside the gate sat an unmarked Princeton Township police car.

Suddenly increasing his stride, Ray slapped Simon on the shoulder. "I have a feeling you and I haven't seen the last of each other. Take good care of yourself, pal." He veered off toward the car.

Simon stopped dead in the middle of the road. "Wait a second. I thought I was coming with you."

Ray kept walking. "Sorry. You are no longer police business, and I'm still on duty."

"What do I . . ." Simon scanned the area. The prison had been set in the middle of farmland. The nearest house was a dot on the darkling horizon. Near the line of evergreens, however, sat a long gray limousine.

"See if he'll give you a lift," Ray called out, releasing the smile he had been concealing since he walked into the recreation room. He slid into the police car, slammed the door and started his engine in quick order, denying Simon more conversation.

Simon clutched the box to his chest with both hands and began walking down the road. With each passing yard, the blood pounded harder through his veins.

The back door of the limousine opened. Frederika stepped out, wearing an outfit nearly identical to the one she had changed into after drinking the forger's blood. Her golden hair, pulled up and back, glimmered in the brassy rays of the dying sun. She wore no sunglasses. Simon squinted to make out the color of her eyes. She closed on him with long strides.

Simon set down the box just before she came hard into his arms, kissing his face as a soldier would bless the earth returning home from war. They stood intertwined in the prison driveway, exorcising each other's fears with fierce affirmations of lips and hands. Even when Ray honked his horn, they remained locked in place, like a Rodin masterpiece perversely clothed. The police car steered carefully around them then roared off, the horn blaring again at the bottom of the drive.

After more than a minute, the couple drew back sufficiently from each other for Frederika to offer Simon a wide-eyed stare.

"Take a good look," she offered. "As long and as hard as you like. Dig your fingers around if you want. This blue is all mine."

A plume of white steam, like his despair made visible, escaped from Simon's chest and dissipated in the breeze. She was back from the undead, and all else good could again be hoped for.

"I quit the powder cold turkey on New Year's Day," Frederika announced proudly. "Thought I was gonna die for forty-eight hours. Used up a bottle of Tylenol. And look," she exclaimed, holding up her hand, "I burned myself this morning." The bubble of a second-degree burn showed in white, pink and angry red on her wrist. "It hurts like . . . the dickens, but I wouldn't have it any other way."

Simon took her hand in his and kissed the wound tenderly, but when he turned his face up toward hers, his look was stern.

"Where's my wallet, thief?"

"Right here." Frederika produced Simon's wallet from her coat pocket and handed it to him. "I'm freezing. Don't bother looking for what little money you had; it's gone. Come on." She began walking toward the limousine.

"Gone where?" Simon picked up his box and followed.

"To travel expenses. I couldn't hang around in Princeton, naturally . . . not if I wanted to stay alive." The limousine trunk popped open automatically as they approached it. Simon counted six pieces of luggage in the huge space. "Throw your box and your coat in there," Frederika directed. She opened the back door to the limousine while he obeyed, inviting Simon to step inside. "First of all, I had to deliver the vampire's real powder to the safest possible place." She followed Simon into the limo and slammed the door. The darkly tinted windows turned the late afternoon landscape outside to midnight. Soft, indirect lighting focused the attention on interior opulence. The inside temperature was in the low seventies. On the spacious floor lay Simon's black velvet dinner jacket, concealing some bulk beneath it. Frederika began shedding her coat. To complement the gown, she wore simple gold ball earrings and a tasteful gold necklace. She looked like she was taking him directly from prison to an opera gala.

"After I left the house, I went straight to St. Paul's," Frederika continued explaining. "I told the priest about Father Ferro . . . rest his soul . . . and that I knew he'd been sent by the Vatican. Then I showed what was left of the scrolls. The priest seemed to know exactly what he was looking at. Within an hour, two nuns came and took me to a convent somewhere in North Jersey. Three days later, I was on an official jet, flying to the Vatican. The next day I turned over the scrolls, the genuine powder, and what was left of DeVilbiss's synthetic stuff to the Pope's private secretary." Frederika reached into a coat pocket and withdrew a small golden cross on a delicate chain. "A gift for you from the guy with the big miter. Happy Belated Birthday."

"How do you . . . ?"

"I took your wallet, remember?"

As Simon murmured his thanks, admired the gift, and slipped it over his neck, the limousine started off without direction. The driver, invisible behind a wall of tinted glass, had been well instructed.

"Why don't you put on your jacket?" Frederika suggested. When he lifted it from the floor, he saw a closed picnic basket underneath.

"What about the scrolls?" Simon asked.

Frederika's smile slipped a bit. "They were badly burned. The worst of it was that the passages about the vampires and the seven predictions were on the outside. All gone. They're still debating what to do about publicizing them." She shrugged. "That's up to them now. Of course, they have the Greek translation fragments that Father Ferro first brought to them, but that can't be offered as the genuine thing." She glanced out the window. "The seventh prediction came true last week, you know."

"No, I didn't. But it was inevitable. That means the plague has already begun . . . somewhere."

Frederika folded her coat twice, propped it against her door, and reclined against it. "It might not be as bad as we feared, though. It took several weeks for the Vatican to vet and gather several prominent biochemists who are also devout, discreet Roman Catholics. A couple of them worked with the last doses of Vincent's powder; others analyzed the genuine stuff." Frederika's eyes twinkled. "The two formulas don't match precisely. Dr. Durazo didn't get her replication totally right! It duplicates the factors that enhance strength and senses, and obviously the invulnerability factor as well. But the critical Fountain of Youth element is flawed. When they tested it on baby mice, it only slowed their aging by a couple weeks." Her smile disappeared again. "And they know from me that if the user is exposed to too much sunlight, she ages about fifty times faster than normal."

Simon had already noted that, beneath the carefully applied makeup, years had indeed been added to Frederika's flawless face. The last of her baby fat had disappeared, and the oily sheen of young adulthood was no longer there. Her hair had also lost a touch of its luster.

"You're thirty," Frederika stated.

"Yes."

"I'm twenty-four. At least that's what my birth certificate says. But I'm pretty sure, biologically, we're now about the same age. Ironic, isn't it? DeVilbiss wanted that powder to keep him young forever, but it actually accelerates aging unless you stay hidden down a coal mine. It provided all the other advantages: speed, strength, heightened senses, but too much sun and you're suddenly Methuselah."

"You must have realized it long before you stopped using the powder," Simon said. "What a price you paid."

Frederika pretended to look out the dark window. "The greater sacrifice would have been losing you if I hadn't."

Simon resisted reaching out to Frederika; physical touch would have been redundant. "There's another irony," he told her. "DeVilbiss offered me everything he could think of to help defeat the Dark Forces, but he never realized he had already created a super weapon: you."

"Well, that's done," Frederika said, again daring Simon's stare. "I'm just a regular woman again."

"Hardly."

Simon had noted with joy other changes in Frederika, invisible to the eye but no less profound. Her icy steel bearing seemed to have softened, as had the defensive wall she kept around her true emotions.

Frederika opened the picnic basket. She reached beyond the bowls of strawberries and brownies and extracted a bottle of Châteauneuf-du-Pape. "Pardon me if I don't salute him. A toast instead to Father Dante Ferro." She pulled out the partially extracted cork and handed Simon the bottle, reaching again into the basket for two wineglasses. Simon filled them nearly to the brim.

"A toast to Father Ferro," he repeated.

Frederika carefully clinked her glass against his. "You realize that if this plague can be stopped, he will eventually become a saint?"

"Imagine all the intercession we can pray for," Simon said, before sampling the wine.

"And need to. I have caviar somewhere on the bottom. Do you like caviar?"

"No."

Frederika sat back and scowled at Simon. "It's painful to admit I know so little about you. Do you at least like strawberries?"

"Especially in the off season."

"Then that's a start. The dress-up and the picnic are hokey, I know. But they represent what I wanted for us from the moment I began to truly know you: an old-fashioned courtship. It's stupid, really, considering my reputation."

"No, it isn't," Simon protested. "That also is over. I think this is wonderful."

Frederika lowered her gaze. She seemed on the verge of tears. "It's just that I found this young man who watched me shyly from afar, month after month. An intelligent gentleman, who did everything he could to be my friend, in spite of the horrible rumors he had heard. The last true knight." While she spoke, she worried the pair of rings around the fourth finger of her left hand.

"You never took them off," Simon noted softly.

"Neither did you," Frederika observed.

"I took you at your word: 'Till death do us part.'" The final element of Simon's fantasy had come true. He knew as little about her as she did about him. But the bedrock of willingness was there for building upon. The mutual sacrifices each had already made for the other spoke more eloquently than the rings around their fingers.

Simon bent slowly and planted a pristine kiss on Frederika's lips. Her hand came gently to his cheek and brushed it with a loving possessiveness.

"By the way . . . where are we going?" Simon asked.

"I thought Europe . . . but it doesn't have to be. It's just that I'm very familiar with a country in the middle of Rome where every man is qualified to perform a wedding." Frederika put her forefinger to Simon's lips. "Before you reject me, I want you to know I'm a very wealthy woman, Mr. Penn."

Simon dug out his keys and held up the one to the Zurich safe deposit box. "I am not without resources myself, Miss Vanderveen. I've got about a million dollars in a bank vault in Zurich."

"That's blood money. Let's give that away," Frederika said, looking suddenly serious. "I have enough to last us years. We can travel with no credit cards, no electronic trail to follow. The seventh prediction's come true; the nightmare is beginning. You and I have fought through enough darkness. We deserve a daydream instead, one of those protracted honeymoons the wealthy Victorians indulged in. Look at this." From the limo's speaker deck, Frederika took a copy of the *Washington Post* and handed it to Simon. "Page three. A sudden increase in mysterious bloodlettings in Caracas. Slit throats mostly. Blood stolen from a hospital. A blood donation center broken into."

"It's a Catholic country. Maybe the Vatican can get the word out that the powder isn't all that it's supposed to be," Simon mused. "Maybe the plague can be stopped right there."

"I doubt it. Despite the shortcomings in the formula, I think the Devil will come out of this a million souls richer. Maybe then he'll be satisfied and leave us alone."

Simon looked into Frederika's perfect face, raised his glass, and drained it.

The limousine pulled up to the departures curb at the international flights terminal. While Frederika paid the driver, Simon busied himself transferring his few belongings into an empty suitcase she had thoughtfully provided. Once the porter had collected all their luggage, the couple strolled hand in hand into the terminal, unaware of virtually everyone else around them.

A dark-haired, dark-skinned man carrying a valise rushed past them toward the limousine. His name was Enrique Staunton. He was a purveyor of sophisticated and expensive security systems for business and industry. Born in Venezuela of a native mother and a North American father, Enrique was at home on both New World continents. He was also at home in both the daylight world and that of the creatures of the night. He traveled to South America at least once a month and never returned without a little white powder hidden in his luggage, enough at least to feed his habit until the next trip.

"Goin' inta the city?" Enrique asked the limousine driver. His trick of exiting airports via departures instead of arrivals and catching emptying cabs and limos never failed.

"Yeah. Hop in," the driver answered.

Enrique squinted at the harsh halogen lights in the drop-off area. He threw his valise into the car and stepped inside. The limo pulled away. Enrique was about to settle back when he noticed a picnic basket on the floor. He leaned down to examine its contents and was disappointed to find only one strawberry and the dregs of the wine in the bottom of an expensive bottle. As he lifted his head, he found himself staring at his own image in the mirror that backed the dry bar. Gone were all telltale signs of his addiction to the white powder, the long-time habit he had successfully kicked with the first dose of the new powder. The magic amber powder. He looked and felt so much healthier. He smiled, thinking of the new, secret strength behind his forty-four-year-old exterior. Even his eyes, which had always been a drab brown, were starting to take on a chestnut tone. If only the damned headache would go away.

About the Author

Brent Monahan has had five fiction works of horror published, including *The Book of Common Dread,* to which *The Blood of the Covenant* is the sequel. He has written screenplays for television and has his doctorate in music from Indiana University, Bloomington. He lives in Yardley, Pennsylvania, with his wife, Bonnie, and children, Caitlin and Ian.